Things were finally beginning to come together—then I got careless...

I was so caught up with thinking of what a life with Christy might have been like that I didn't see the car and the two men right there in the parking lot. They were on me with guns drawn before I could even start for mine. Before we could leave, they realized they hadn't figured on what to do with my car so I waited in cuffs feeling like a perfect fool for the second time in fifteen minutes. They should have brought another guy, they decided. They put me in a Buick as they worked out the logistics of getting us to where they were taking me. The Ford stayed in the lot. Before we left the parking lot, they slipped a black hood over my head. I didn't recognize them, but I figured I was with friends of Lawrence and Sexton. But they acted more like Abbott and Costello than hotshot agents. It was a comedy of errors, but these comedians had guns.

"What's the charge?"

"Shut up." The tall one was annoyed.

"At least he had the last meal that I'd want for the day I was going to die." Costello in the backseat thought he was a wit.

"What's that?"

"Hair pie. What else? If I ever—"

The driver told his partner to be quiet.

"Huh?"

I guess his partner wasn't very clear on what he was talking about. The driver was the more businesslike of the two. The one in the back wanted to talk. He liked what he was doing. The rough stuff. The threats and especially the power. He was not much different from the small time hoods I had to deal with in the street. I counted off the details in my head. I also tried to pay attention to where we were going, but after the third left turn, I gave up on that. Instead, I tried to figure out how I was going to get out of this. I wondered what was going to happen to Christy. I also wondered if Sexton and Lawrence were in New Canaan wrapping up more loose ends.

Delicious Little Traitor begins quietly in December 1953 when private investigator Varian Pike looks into the disappearance of a war buddy's niece and soon finds himself in the middle of a secret war between federal agencies. How a bright young college student became the target of a leading anti-communist politician is only one of the challenging and dangerous questions that take Varian up and down the Eastern Seaboard and deep into the past in search of answers. Along the way almost everyone he meets has some kind of score to settle and secret to hide. It's a journey that will leave deep scars and many bodies behind—including Varian's if he can't figure it all out in time.

KUDOS for *Delicious Little Traitor*

There are only a few people working in this utterly unadorned, unsung blue-collar vein, and Jack DeWitt is the master of the genre. ~ Stephen Berg, Editor of *American Poetry Review*

DeWitt creates a palpable portrait of America in the 1950s: what people drove and why, what music came from the car radio, what happens when the defroster breaks down, what school children learned, how memories of combat shaped the post-war lives of veterans, how McCarthyism became a pathology. This is not noir-as-atmosphere and local color. It's noir as our shaping history. ~ Peter Stambler, author of *Encounters with Cold Mountain*

I love this book. This is so engaging—the Northeast winter landscape, the brilliant dialog, the jazz track. Good stuff. ~ Bobbie Ann Mason, author of *In Country* and *The Girl in the Blue Beret.*

The plot is well thought out and the characters well developed. The story has an authentic feel that takes you back in time to the fifties, when life was simpler, but no less deadly for people who knew too much. I found the book to be a thoroughly entertaining read. ~ *Taylor Jones, Reviewer*

Delicious Little Traitor takes you back to the post war world of paranoia and old debts, where veterans felt a special allegiance to others who had served in the war, and where politicians would do anything to avoid any hint of scandal. Where young college students searched for causes, wanting to save the world, and ended up getting in over their heads with tragic consequences. The book is riveting. Once you pick it up, you will be hard pressed to put it down. ~ *Regan Murphy, Reviewer*

DELICIOUS LITTLE TRAITOR

A Varian Pike Mystery

Jack DeWitt

A Black Opal Books Publication

GENRE: MYSTERY-DETECTIVE/SUSPENSE/HISTORICAL FICTION

This is a work of fiction. Names, places, characters and incidents are either the product of the author's imagination or are used fictitiously, and any resemblance to any actual persons, living or dead, businesses, organizations, events or locales is entirely coincidental. All trademarks, service marks, registered trademarks, and registered service marks are the property of their respective owners and are used herein for identification purposes only. The publisher does not have any control over or assume any responsibility for author or third-party websites or their contents.

In memory of Steve Berg and Kent Christensen

And there shall the beasts of the desert meet with the jackals, and the wild goat shall cry to his fellow; Lilith also shall settle there, and find for herself a place of rest. ~ *Isaiah 34:14*

CHAPTER 1

Whenever the weather turned bitter cold, when the streets were filled with blaring carols and when I felt like I was being strangled with boughs of holly, I didn't think about winter wonderlands or a manger in Bethlehem. I thought about a young girl I hardly knew as brave and dumb as only a nineteen year-old could be. I thought about a friend as brave and dumb as a man, who thought he knew everything, could be. And I thought about a woman who could have been everything.

It started on a cold Wednesday back in 1953. I was with some friends. The Wednesday Night Fights were on TV. If it had been Friday, it would have been the Friday Night Fights. If it had been Monday, it would have been the Monday Night Fights. Between boxing and wrestling, you couldn't turn on a television set without seeing two muscular men in shorts or tights trying to hurt one another—or at least pretending to.

We were all veterans. Larry was a marine in the Pacific. Billy had done convoy duty in the Atlantic. Freddie and I had been in Europe. We never talked about the war. But it was always there in the background. So once every week or so we would get together to pretend it didn't matter. But we all knew it did. It was the only thing that mattered. Sometimes we played cards, but, mostly, we watched fights on television and ragged on each other.

This Wednesday, it was at Larry Kennedy's house. Larry didn't have a wife anymore so it was easy for him to host the fights. Two months after he got back from Korea with about six ounces of Chinese steel floating around in his left leg, Katie announced she was going to Florida with Ham Hammernick who used to deliver oil to the house. Two wars in less than ten years had been too much for her. She took everything but the big easy chair she said smelled like Larry and the TV that rolled the picture.

Since she had left in April, Larry had bought nothing to replace his living room furniture. We had to sit on a set of wooden fold up chairs that Larry stole from the Elks summer picnic. On the back of each chair were stenciled the large black letters B.P.O.E. It was a pretty grim setting, but it was Larry's turn. Billy had the best set, a big blond DuMont, but his wife told him that she didn't want the smoke, the beer, and, especially, the swearing in her house anymore. And, anyway, she didn't like us. She wanted her husband to finish the bathroom they were putting in place of a hall closet. We were holding up the job.

We weren't too crazy about her either. She covered the living room with placemats and coasters when we came. But we put up with her because Billy had the best set with the best reception. Larry's picture rolled when the set got hot. On baseball nights, we would turn the set off for the fifth, sixth, and seventh innings so it could cool down. If it were a good game, we would watch right through the rolls. You could almost see everything. When we watched the fights, the set made boxing very acrobatic.

When I got to Larry's, Freddie Greenbaum was there. Freddie didn't come to the fights that often anymore, maybe once a month. He had two hardware stores now. So he had started making excuses. Soon we knew it would be, "Anybody seen Freddie around."

As soon as he saw me, he got up. I could see he had more than the fights on his mind.

"Hey, Greenie," I said. "Long time no see."

"Yeah, I know. I miss it, but the second store is…it needs more work than I ever thought. Look, Varian, can I ask you a favor?" He was very serious.

"Sure, Greenie, long as it doesn't cost time or money."

He gave me a hurt look. "That's all right," he said slowly as if to impress me with his sense of purpose.

"I'm kiddin'. Kiddin'." I knew it was serious.

Freddie Greenbaum and I had spent the last month of the

war together, waiting for our orders and then bunking six inches from each other on one of the Liberty ships that brought us all back like candles in a box. In what had to be one of the biggest games of the war, Freddie Greenbaum had won enough shooting craps on the deck to buy his first store as soon as he got back.

Guys would bet three years' pay on a hard four. I remember one big lunk from Oklahoma. He was a big redheaded guy with a face like a twelve-year-old. Like Huck Finn must have looked. He even had the freckles. I saw him on the deck, looking back toward Europe, one day after he had thrown his pay away on nines and fives.

"Tough luck," I said.

Not talking to me in particular, he turned and said, "I can't make any money on this war."

I knew what he meant, even if I didn't agree. It was enough to be going home with two legs and two eyes. There were too many who weren't coming home at all—men who hadn't died to save the world, but who had given their lives for their buddies. We spent a lot of time on those miserably slow boats thinking about them, wondering how long we would remember them when the ships docked and our lives started over again.

There were lots of guys whose money produced only guilt. So somebody like Freddie had fairly easy pickings. He won so much that I had to guard him so that he could get some sleep. In a moment of euphoria, he offered to go partners with me. He had been thinking about the store for years. He knew there would be a building boom when we got back with lots of guys trying to cut costs by doing some of the work themselves. But I turned it down. I just took the money for guarding him. At the time, I had big dreams, too. I couldn't see myself selling lawn seed and ladders for the rest of my life.

I had been to Paris. I had a picture taken in front of Shakespeare & Co. I saw myself, somewhat vaguely, I admit, as part of a larger world—a world of adventure called to me and not Black & Decker. In the eight years since we had walked off the boat, he never mentioned his generous, drunken offer. He and I both knew that the offer had been genuine, but it was a one-time thing. In the grand scheme of things, it had been my mistake. I knew it and he knew it. It never came up and we were still friends.

"What's the problem?" I tried to make my voice sound serious. It's hard when you only had a good time on your mind.

"Let's go outside."

We made our awkward excuses.

"Whatever you need Greenie," Larry said.

We entered the cold air, each of us taking a deep breath.

"You know Manny, my brother?" Freddie asked.

"Yeah, the doctor. I met him at your daughter's party. The one…" I tried to remember what it was for, but I didn't need to.

"He's got a daughter, too. A year older than Annie. It seems she's disappeared. She's up at UConn. She never came back to school after Thanksgiving vacation."

"Do you want me to look into it for you?"

"I want you to find her. I'll pay whatever you get, and more. Whatever it takes. I told Manny you would help. I should have asked, but he was beside himself. I had to tell him something. I had to do something. You were the only one, the first one I thought of. We go back—If you have something else going, if you have to finish whatever, I'll take care of that, too. Get somebody to take over. I'll pay. What do you need?"

"Hold on, hold on. These things are usually a false alarm. They're kids, you know. They'll drive you—"

"I just want you on this, Varian. I have a real bad feeling about this. Real bad."

"Why?"

"You don't know Lara. She's the perfect kid. She'll call home if she hits too many red lights—she's that way. Annie sometimes forgets where she lives. I wouldn't be surprised if Annie didn't come home at all sometimes, and she's only eighteen. But Lara. I don't know. You meet her once. You can't forget her. Do you know her third grade teacher came to her high school graduation? She said that Lara was the smartest, brightest…"

I could see that Freddie was beginning to lose it. I didn't like seeing him this way. I wanted to tell him that it would be all right. I wanted to tell him the things that a friend would say, should say, those meaningless little gestures of reassurance we offered those who are suffering that were really about our own discomfort. I could say those things to Larry when his wife left him. I could tell him that he was better off without her, even though I could tell that he wished that she had stayed. His eyes told me that he was lost without her. I could tell Larry what I couldn't tell Fred. Because losing wives and children were different. I knew that without having either.

As soon as he told me what he wanted, I was working for him. But I had to be a professional. It was all I had. What I did was find things, fix things, and figure things out. I began to question Freddie about Lara. I could tell that he just wanted me to take over. To fix it. To make things right. To get the weight of it off his shoulders.

"I've got to see Manny."

"Can you see him tonight?"

I knew Manny was waiting for me. "Well, why not? Sure."

"Here's two hundred. That's enough right, to start?"

"What do I want with that?"

"Varian, I want you on this because you are a friend. But it's more than that. I want you because you are good. I don't want this to be a favor. Do you know what I mean? It's more important than that. It's family. My family."

"But you said—"

"I know what I said. But this is what I mean. I want you to work on this full time. All the time until…she's back. Take it from me, I know about business. It's better if, from now on, it's business. And money makes it business. It's the only way."

I knew he was right. I went back in to say my good-byes to Larry and Billy. I told them I had something to take care of. They were trying to follow Chico Vejar as he rolled over and over on the screen trying to avoid Kid Gavilan's left hooks. They mumbled something without moving their crooked necks.

Fred had decided that it would be better if I went to Manny's alone. So we said our awkward farewells as we walked next to each other to our cars. Freddie went to his new Caddy and I to my old Chevy. Just before he got into his car, he stopped and looked as if he wanted to say something. I waited. I stopped and listened to the icy wind coming in from the north. He looked at me and then looked at his shoes. I took the hint and got into my car.

There was already frost on the window and my defroster was on the fritz. There was ice on the inside of the window. I used my hand to try to scrape off a little spot so that I could drive. I remembered listening to Freddie talk his way to sleep after shooting dice for twelve straight hours. He was high from the money and the excitement. As I drove north, I could hear his voice that came from somewhere out of that time...

e⁊ɔe⁊ɔ

"There were times when I thought that the war would never end. I couldn't even remember what my wife's voice sounded like. When I thought of her, it was always like a silent movie. The more I thought about it, the harder it was to remember. Toward the end, I was even having trouble remembering what she looked like. Her letters were like from a stranger. No matter what she wrote about, I couldn't feel anything. Even for Annie. I was somewhere beyond the grave. I was a dead man, walking around with a rifle. You know the thing that brought me back was the first time I heard 'White Christmas.' Isn't that crazy. Me a Jew, and what meant the most to me was 'White Christmas.'"

"At least a Jew wrote it," I told him.

"That's right, isn't it? That's right. I never thought about that. But all I could think of was Christmas. Buying presents, singing carols, sitting by a fire. I told myself that no matter what my family said we were going to have a tree."

e⁊ɔe⁊ɔ

I didn't know why I thought of that as I scraped the windshield. Maybe because it was almost Christmas time. But I didn't think Freddie ever did put up that tree, even if he decorated his store like it was the North Pole.

In the car, I tried to find some music on the radio. I didn't want to listen to Fibber McGee or Molly. The only music station I could hold for more than a few seconds was from Chicago. I still didn't understand why it was easier to get a station half way across the country than one just up the road. I could hear through the crackles and the hiss Joni James pleading, "Why don't you believe me?"

The static was too much. I turned the dial off. Over the years, I had begun to envy Freddie a little. He always seemed to make the right decisions. The only decisions I had made were negative ones. Places I didn't go. Women I didn't marry. Jobs I didn't take. Freddie wasn't a rich man. Not when you compared his wealth to that of the truly rich in Stamford who ran giant companies or who just clipped coupons. I could barely comprehend that kind of wealth.

So no matter how successful Freddie became, he would always be a guy who owned the local hardware store. He had a nice home in High Ridge. A nice wife. Two good kids. And one very special one, Annie, whom Freddie obviously didn't understand. Or maybe he did.

He had followed his dream. He knew exactly what he wanted and he got it. That seemed to me one useful measure of a man. To have a dream and then follow through. It didn't matter what it was, as long as you didn't take too much advantage of others.

What had I done with my dream? I spent my time peeking at human misery. The worst kind. It was my job to get the dirt. To find where the husband shacked up with his secretary. To watch the wife do something with a stranger that would disgust her if her husband even suggested it. To figure out how a guy in Florida set fire to his store in Norwalk. To see if Mrs. Flourney really was crippled from that fall in C.O. Millers Department Store. I really didn't fix things. I ruined them and people's lives as well. It didn't matter that what they did was wrong. Even when they killed, a lot of the time, I couldn't help feeling sorry for them. They were not hardened criminals or real gangsters. The cops handled the cold-blooded killers, the armed robbers, and the hit men. They chased the hopped-up boppers who shoved guns into the mouths of their victims and laughed when they pulled the trigger. I found the ones who just couldn't take it anymore. They were so desperate that there was only one way they could see out of their suffering.

I found out that Mr. Honcharik hit his wife on the head with a bowling trophy and pushed her down the cellar stairs. He didn't do it out of greed or because he had a hot one down at the office. He did it because Mrs. Honcharik made him wash his hands before serving him his supper if he had petted the dog. How many thousand such demands had he endured before he picked up his trophy for "Most Improved Bowler" that she made him keep in the cellar because it was "a dust catcher." He would have gotten away with if he hadn't taken out an insurance policy on her years before. The police were willing to write it off as an accident. But not Philadelphia Casualty.

Manny's house was in Long Ridge. Manny was always one up on Freddie. Manny was a dentist. He had spent the war in Clarksville, Tennessee, fixing the molars of raw recruits from the hills of Kentucky and West Virginia who, according to Manny, had never heard of toothpaste. During the whole war, he had never even fired a weapon, not even on the practice range. Manny was even a better candidate for my envy than his brother, but what made him even more annoying was that he was funny. He told funny war stories of trying to understand what his soldier patients were saying. At Annie's graduation he told us about the time that he worked on a general's broken tooth and the general got a hard on. When Manny was finished filling the tooth, the general pulled him by his tie so that their lips were no more than an inch apart. Manny thought General Walker was falling in love with his dentist. Manny tried to make a joke out of it, winking at his wife.

"I know that almost all women fall in love with their dentists, but a general, this presented a new challenge. I was a good soldier and if the General wanted me..." He laughed as he told the story. "Then, he looks at me, his mouth still distorted from the Novocain, and says, 'Son,' even though he was no more than three years older than I was, 'as long as you are in this man's army, you will make no mention to anyone of my current physical condition. Is that understood?'

"'Yes sir, yes sir,' I said. I was just glad that he didn't want to ask me to go steady. Then the general went on in a solemn tone heard mostly at southern funerals, 'Son, and I say this so that you will not misconstrue,' that was the word he used, 'so that you will not misconstrue what has transpired here. I will explain something to you in the strictest confidence since you are a member of the medical profession.' I thought I was listening to Senator Foghorn. 'It seems that I have a rather unique response to physical pain. The more intense the pain, the more pronounced the engorgement of the member. Do I make myself clear?'

"'Absolutely sir. Yes sir. Top secret, sir.'

"'Son, are you mocking me?' he said.

"This guy had a reputation for being the toughest son-of-a-bitch in the whole US Army. He made Patton look like Pearl Buck. Boy, I was glad I wasn't going to tour Europe with him."

Even Freddie laughed.

Manny's house was a perfect imitation of an eighteenth century Yankee gentleman's country house. He even had black iron hitching posts at the entrance to the long circular drive. The house was painted an understated yellow with black shutters. He had built it right after the war. Although Manny never attempted to hide the fact that he was a Jew, he did everything exactly as he imagined the old Yankees did it. But it never came out exactly right. The rich families with the old names wouldn't have been fooled for a minute. I had worked for too many of them. Manny's house was new to begin with. Those Yankees liked old houses with drafty windows and worn rolling floors that creaked. They didn't like new furniture either. In fact, nothing they had seemed to be new. They drove old cars. Their oriental rugs were worn and tattered and the paint was always a little faded. I guessed they liked to sit in cold rooms in worn out chairs, wearing sweaters without any elbows, drinking the cheapest rotgut whiskey and talking about—what?

How bad things were since Roosevelt? I thought they just didn't want any of those in the trades, as they called them, to get any of their money. They didn't want to pay the Italians to fix their floors or the Irish to pave their drives or the Jews to get anything.

I had the clear sense that Manny knew what he was doing. Mocking them without their even knowing. So everything that Manny had was new, perfect imitations of the old, from the rugs to the carved fireplace mantle. It must have given him some kind of perverse pleasure to build such a replica of colonial America. Manny had moxie.

He was already at the door when I pulled up. He tried to play the host, but I could see in his eyes that he was lost in anxiety.

"Varian, thank you for coming especially on such—"

"It's okay. Freddie and I go way back and you're his brother. So...In any case, Freddie has hired me. So don't be grateful."

"But I am. And about the money—"

"It's taken care of. I don't want to hear any more about that. I want to know about Lara."

Manny's wife Sophie stood to the side with my coat. A tall, stately woman who towered over her husband, she had been crying. She tried to smile, but it came out looking exactly like a grimace.

Manny wanted to know if I wanted a drink and then he led me into a formal living room laid out like a museum of Americana. There was a large eagle over the fireplace and portraits of eighteenth-century gentlemen on the wall. The furniture was elegant dark curved wood. I sat on a very uncomfortable chair that blocked my view to the sides.

I began first by trying to reassure them. To tell them what I tried to tell Freddie. Kids sometimes take off, especially around holidays. They usually turn up pretty quick.

Sophie seemed more comforted by my words than her husband, who said only, "It's not like her."

"Let's start from the beginning. I might ask some questions that you might think are a little...inappropriate, but I have to look for anything that might help us find your daughter."

"I understand," Manny said, without really meaning it.

Sophie nodded agreement and then looked out the window. It was starting to flurry.

"When did you first think she was missing?"

Manny did the talking. "She spent Thanksgiving with some friends near Hartford. She called on the Friday after Thanksgiving to say that her plans had changed and she wouldn't be home on Saturday after all. We didn't think much of it. We were disappointed, of course, but Lara came home regularly."

"Where was she going instead of coming home?"

"She didn't really say. We, I, assumed that she was with her friends. Maybe a dance that night. A concert. I want you to understand. We didn't monitor Lara's behavior...I mean we did...but not like that. She's almost twenty, a sophomore, you can't—" Manny broke off, obviously recognizing that he was babbling, feeling guilty and defensive, angry and frightened.

"Who are the friends?

"We don't really know," Sophie answered.

"You don't know their names or you don't know them?"

"Both. She might have mentioned them when she told us she wasn't going to be home for Thanksgiving. If she did, it didn't ring a bell. It was up in Hartford."

"What if you needed to reach her?" It came out as an accusation. I didn't mean it to be.

"We didn't think—that—" Manny sputtered.

"We were a little angry that she wasn't coming home," Sophie interrupted.

"Was there any problem between you and her?"

"No," they both agreed simultaneously.

The looks in their eyes convinced me they were telling the truth. "How do you know she is missing? That's she's not with her friend. It's only a week since Thanksgiving."

"She didn't call on Sunday," Manny said. "When school started again, we called. Then we called again today and I talked to her roommate. She said Lara hadn't come back from vacation. We called the police immediately. They were not much help."

"Who'd you talk to?"

"I don't...Do you remember, Sophie? I think I wrote it down," he reached in his pocket.

"Storrs police?"

"Yes. That's right."

"There can't be too many on the force. It should be easy to find out. What did they say?"

"They said not to worry. Kids meet somebody and maybe they go to Florida. He said that happened last year. But Lara would never just go off. Not like that. Not to Florida. You'd have to know Lara. She just wouldn't."

"I know. You have to understand that a small force like Storrs is used to dealing with drunks at a frat party or, maybe, the theft of a bicycle. Even in a big city, missing persons are very low priority. It doesn't pay to spend the man-hours when most people just turn up anyway. Unless there is some evidence of foul play. There isn't, is there?

I could see Sophie wince and the tears well up.

"No. No. Please" She began to cry, sobbing into her hands.

"So you want me to try to find her. You don't believe she'll just turn up after some collegiate adventure?"

"I don't know. I expected her to call or walk through the door or something. She keeps in touch. She does. She's a good girl. Then this morning, after talking to her roommate, I had this terrible feeling that we'd never..."

He started to cry. At first, he tried to do the manly thing and hold back the tears by talking on and on, but now the tears wouldn't stop. And he bent over as if he was going to be sick. Sophie sat there still looking out the window, tears streaming down her cheeks.

I wanted to lift Manny up, but I couldn't. I tried to get him focused again. It wasn't that I didn't like seeing a man cry. I didn't like feeling helpless and the only thing I could think to do was my job. "Have you been contacted by someone?"

"No, no. Do you think?" Manny said in a panic.

"If she had been kidnapped, you would have heard by now. Does Lara have a boyfriend?"

"Not this year. She seems to have taken a year off from dating."

"Did she have a steady boyfriend last year?"

"She saw a lot of a boy from school. Jason Melrose. From Greenwich." Sophie was clearly the expert here.

"Did they break up? Have a falling out?"

She knew what I wanted. She didn't answer. She just shook her head no.

"Who broke it off?"

"I think it was mutual. You're not suggesting that Jason might..."

"I need to know a lot more about Lara, more than you probably think I have a right to know, but I need to know it. Were they more than just boyfriend and girlfriend, if you get my meaning?"

"I don't see what that has to do with anything." Manny was offended, but I had to push on.

"It does, take my word for it. You are going to have to trust me. If you don't, I know some very good people in Hartford, who probably know the territory much better than I do."

I didn't want off this case but I had to offer them the out.

"So what is it you want to know?" Manny asked, steeling himself.

"Were Jason and Lara intimate? Sexually."

"No, of course not...I don't think so. She was only nineteen. They might have...I don't even want to speculate—"

"They were, Manny. Lara told me," Sophie interrupted softly, her voice deep and raspy as if she suffered from asthma.

"Why didn't you tell me?"

"Because I promised not to. There are some things women have to talk about that men don't understand."

"But something like this?" For a second his eyes said that this information was almost as painful as the disappearance itself.

He slowly recovered as Sophie turned her fear into anger. "What were you going to do? Tell her to save herself for the highest bidder? Isn't that it?"

"Not now, please not now. It doesn't matter. It really doesn't."

I had seen this too many times before. How a crisis unleashed the resentments of a lifetime in a marriage. The fact that Lara told her mother made it clear to me that this was not about the family. Something was happening between Sophie and Manny, but I didn't think it had to do with Lara, at least not in motivating her to take off. This was not good news to me. As I tried to get us back on track, I started discounting some of my first hunches. One of my first ideas was one of those little private hospitals on the upper West Side in New York City where they undo "accidents." She was obviously the star child in the family. Even in his despair, Manny couldn't help bragging about her. About her grades. About her being the valedictorian. Maybe she didn't want to disappoint them. It was still a possibility, but my gut didn't buy it.

"How did she wind up at UConn?"

There was nothing wrong with the University of Connecticut, but in a region with such a long list of prestigious colleges it was hard for me to figure. Especially the daughter of Manny Greenbaum. Annie was going to Vassar.

"She was counting on Smith. I told her not to put all her eggs in one basket. She should try other schools I told her. But she wanted Smith. Do you know that three other girls from Stamford High with much lower grades got in and Lara didn't? She almost didn't go anywhere. I finally convinced her. She didn't apply to UConn until May. They gave her a scholarship. I would have paid three times the tuition at Smith."

I got a list of her friends and told them I would head up to Storrs in the morning. When I opened the door, a blast of cold air, mixed with light snow, numbed my face, but I knew it was much colder inside 233 Rockrimmon Road.

CHAPTER 2

The next morning the air was the color of gunmetal. The frost was so thick the car looked like it had been sprayed with silver suede instead of paint. I was driving a ghost car. It was so cold that I had to turn my head away from the windshield as I scraped the ice away or my breath would have frozen on the windshield.

I didn't look forward to the trip. My car probably wouldn't heat up until I got as far as New Haven. I would have to drive one handed to keep the window from freezing over. I hated the Berlin Turnpike. I could feel snow in the air. My car didn't handle a light rain very well, much less a snowstorm. But I was anxious to get going anyway. I wanted to get started on this case. I tried to conjure up images of Lara, but I kept seeing Freddie's daughter. If Lara had been at Annie's party, I didn't remember her. Yet, I knew her. I knew she was something special. Manny said that he often thought he didn't deserve a daughter like Lara, someone that perfect. She had planned their twenty-fifth wedding anniversary party and had arranged for about a dozen doctors and nurses from Clarksville to be there. All on her own. He couldn't believe that a young girl could do so much.

By the time I got to New Haven, a minor miracle had occurred. The sun broke through the steel gray clouds like a lantern. The dark snow sky had turned suddenly blue. Then the radio began to work.

I got a clear signal from New Haven where a political commentator suggested that Senator McCarthy was going to feel the wrath of the one-worlders for letting America know how communism had infiltrated the corridors of power, "in the very shadow of the Washington Monument." He had some advice for the Senator from Wisconsin. "Watch your back, Joe!"

I was sick of all the accusations and innuendoes. The fear and the hate. I didn't care if there was one world or two or three. Not the way they mapped them out. I got luckier with a small station out of New York that played modern jazz. I caught the middle of "Cherokee" with Charlie Parker and Dizzy Gillespie. Even on my lousy Chevy radio I couldn't believe how wonderful they sounded trading phrases back and forth like a tight tennis match between two great servers. Parker would soar and then twist the chords until they seemed like a delicate lace made out of sheer air. Then just when you thought that Dizzy had been left in the dust, he would come back commenting on Parker's solo like Mel Allen on DiMaggio's swing then ending it all with one clever joke like Groucho Marx. I wished I had been there in Harlem when it began. More than ten years ago and it still seemed so fresh. It was all happening back in New York while we were huddled around army radios in the mud in France, listening to Glenn Miller and Benny Goodman. Despite what Freddie felt, I knew "White Christmas" was a lie the first moment I heard it. It was a wish that the ugly scars of a war-torn world would be covered under some clean, white mantle. Just re-packaged like Lucky Strike Green. I knew that's what everybody else wanted. But not me. I was too good for it. At least that's what I thought in 1944.

I dreaded Christmas now more than I ever feared a German Tiger. When you didn't have a wife and kids, Christmas was just a constant reminder of how empty your life was. I had spent the first few Christmases alone in my apartment with a bottle of Heaven High, a pistol, and a pile of records. The Bird, Diz, Lady Day, Prez got me through the day. In their world, there was always an edge of despair in even the happiest tune. There was always pain in even the most perfect love affair. In a sly way, they could also laugh at the sentiments of a song like "Willow Weep for Me."

I loved that balance. Their response to the world was an angry cry at its stupidity, prejudice, and cruelty. It was also to laugh at anyone taking it too seriously. To me it seemed like the appropriate Christmas attitude. It wasn't so much "Bah humbug!" as it was "Be cool, man." And it kept me alive, for better or worse. Recently, I had needed only the records to weather the Yuletide season.

I reached Storrs at eleven in the morning. Storrs was hardly a town. The campus was stuck in the middle of an old farm. The buildings tried to recall the architecture of the typical old New England college. But on this slightly rolling, bare plain, the buildings looked out of place as if they had settled here after some gentle tornado. Despite the best intentions, the red brick buildings formed no sense of campus. There was no center, just buildings.

I could see students walking to and from classes. There was a strange disparity between the men and the women. The men looked mostly in their late twenties, dressed seriously, while the co-eds were bright, collegiate, and young. The GI. Bill. I wondered what effect this new population had on pep rallies and snake dances around bonfires. I couldn't imagine thousands of vets yelling, "Sis Boom Bah," during the big game with the Massachusetts Redmen.

I stopped one of the older students walking up the hill toward the library and asked him where the security office was. The university provided the town's police force. The state police patrolled the roads. Mansfield Township Police handled the occasional burglary and run away cow.

After several wrong turns, I found the security office tucked away in a small brick building that looked like a power station. In front of the building were two black '46 Fords with the seal of the university on their sides.

"Are you in charge here?"

"Who wants to know?" The man sitting behind the desk was a big blond farmer-looking kid, probably in his mid-twenties. His attitude annoyed me immediately.

"I'm helping the Greenbaum family try to locate their missing daughter."

"And who the hell are you? King Farouk?"

He was trying to be clever and tough, but he was neither. I bit my tongue. I wanted to throw his legs off the desk and straighten him up. What was he doing sitting here, anyway?

Waiting for a crime wave? I counted quickly to five before answering. I didn't want to make enemies. Yet.

"My name is Varian Pike. I am a private investigator. I usually work for Philadelphia Casualty and Fenner, Horsham & Reed, but the Greenbaums are friends of mine." I flipped open my wallet and pointed out my license.

"I didn't ask for your life story." He liked playing tough.

"How about this, Sonny? You tell me your story. You tell me what you have done since you got the report that Lara Greenbaum was missing?"

"That was just yesterday, for chrissakes. We sent off a report to all the local police forces from here to Hartford. Okay, big shot?"

"You sent a letter to them?"

"A report." Now he sounded like a kid who had misunderstood the homework assignment.

"Can I see it?"

"What?"

"I said, can I see the report?"

He got up and walked toward me. He was big. Maybe six three, 210 pounds. He was angry again. I hadn't accepted his answer. I had seen his type before. He liked to use his size to intimidate. He didn't want a real fight. He just wanted to see me back off. Under different circumstances, I wouldn't have. But I wasn't ready to get in a fight ten minutes after arriving in Storrs. There would be time for Junior, if it came to that. So I shifted gears.

"Look, if I find her first, you get the credit. I do the work. I'm just looking for a friend, okay? It's my job. Did you talk to her roommate?"

"I dunno. I didn't. You think she had something to do with it? Is this a private eye thing or what?"

"It's a place to start. Maybe she forgot something Lara told her. Maybe she left something in her room…"

I quickly became frustrated trying to explain the most basic aspects of police work to this hayseed. I realized that these campus cops were no more than glorified night watchmen. The only way that they would find Lara was if she walked into the office, announced who she was, and even then I wasn't so sure they would figure it out. I just had to get the information I needed and let them know that I was around.

After a few minutes of tap dancing with this Roger Tate, I got a copy of the report, which lacked even an exact physical description. I had the name of her roommate and the dorm room. That was all I could expect, I guess.

As I was walking out the door, Roger the campus cop mumbled something.

"What was that?"

"They always want special treatment, don't they?"

"Who?"

"You know. Greenbaums." He practically spit the last syllable.

I didn't say anything. I just checked off another reason to see Roger before I left this center of learning.

Tammy Kaplan was in the dorm when I arrived. They called her down to the desk. I introduced myself to her and asked if I could see the room. The matron on duty shook her head.

"Don't you think that the circumstances warrant a slight change in the rules?" I demanded. "You can chaperone if you want."

She didn't want to move from her comfortable chair more than she wanted to enforce the rules. "Okay, but leave the door open."

Tammy was anxious to help. If you were going to design the perfect co-ed, Tammy could serve as the blueprint. Her voice bounced as she walked in her plaid skirt and blue cardigan sweater over a white blouse. She was very concerned about Lara and couldn't imagine where she had gone. And to not call?

"Lara wrote letters to her parents. Can you imagine? And not just for money."

"When did you last see her?"

"The Wednesday before Thanksgiving. Just before I left for home. I live down in New London. She was packing."

"What was her mood?"

"Fine, I guess. The usual Lara. Maybe a little more serious."

"How?"

"She's just more serious this year, anyway. She was a lot more fun last year. I was her roommate last year, too. Don't get me wrong, I like Lara, but this year, she's like almost...I don't know, a different person."

"How different?"

"Like she doesn't care about having fun. I know school is school. I have a B average, but you have to let off steam, if you know what I mean."

I thought I did.

"Did she tell you who she was spending Thanksgiving with?"

"No. I don't know who it was. Some dreary political types, I guess. What she sees in politics, my father is always—"

"She wasn't going to a friend's house?" I interrupted.

Tammy was so anxious to help that she kept giving me more than I could bear. "No, I don't think so. She was packing to go off to some rally, I think. Nobody wants to die by an atomic bomb, but, really, can you worry about it all the time? Anyway, Lara was very politically involved this year. Last year it was Jason. I guess it's just a phase. Anyway, I hope so. It's all so boring."

I tried to get Tammy back on track. "So tell more about the Thanksgiving weekend."

"She told me she would see me after break. My ride to New London came before Lara left. That was the last I saw of her. I didn't get back until Monday after Thanksgiving, you know. I was surprised that she hadn't come back yet. Then her parents called and I got worried. Really worried."

She smiled as if she wanted me to congratulate her for caring. I asked her about Lara's other friends and she said she couldn't think of anybody specific. "That is the funny thing. Lara was always out at meetings and was always reading, but she never brought any of her friends here. To tell you the truth, I find it all very boring, very, very boring. Maybe she knew. Do you know what I mean? Anyway, I couldn't understand what Lara saw in it. She is so cute. She was ever so much more fun freshman year. We went to Dartmouth for the Winter Carnival. I'm going again this year, but Lara wasn't interested when I mentioned it to her."

"What can you tell me about Jason?"

"Dreamy. I don't know what Lara was thinking when she gave him the brush."

"She broke it off?"

"O, yes. It was terrible. She was so cold to him."

"I understand that they were more than just friends."

"You know?" Tammy asked with a sly grin.

"She told her mother."

"Wow. Amazing! I could not imagine telling my mother anything. Anything like that. Jason is so much fun. You know once last year Jason put on a dress, a wig, make-up, and we got him by the Iron Maiden at the desk. He spent the whole night here. They didn't do anything, really. I was here. But it was so romantic! I even made a play for Jason when Lara dumped him. But he wasn't interested."

"Is he around?"

"Oh, yes. I notice where *he* is."

"How can I find him?"

She told me where Jason's fraternity was and the names of two professors Lara mentioned the most. She might have confided something to them. Tammy seemed to enjoy the attention that Lara's disappearance brought her. But she didn't have much to add. Lara had changed between freshman and sophomore year. She had become much more serious but, ironically, her grades had slipped. She was spending more and more time on political causes. Ban the Bomb. Reds. Desegregation. "Too, too serious," for Tammy.

I asked permission to look through Lara's things. Tammy was eager to help. I asked her to look through Lara's clothes to see if she could tell what was missing, what she might have been wearing when she left school. The challenge of this puzzle seemed to interest her.

I looked at the pile of books on Lara's desk. In addition to textbooks, there were a number of pamphlets published by the Worker's International Press in Passaic, New Jersey. With dull blue and gray covers, they had titles like *Worker's Paradise: The Promise of Communism* by Horace Wenter and *Lenin's Legacy by* Simon DeVega. I flipped through them and saw that Lara had underlined a number of key passages of left wing political rhetoric: *The Marshall Plan is the most insidious example of bolstering decadent colonial powers in order to protect them from the inevitable workers' revolution. Until America experiences something of the devastation that Europe has suffered, the International Revolution will stall. America is too secure, too protected, and too rich. America has used Europe as a buffer for almost fifty years. The only solution, therefore, is to bring the revolution to America first, before wars of liberation in Africa and Asia.*

I had seen this stuff before. Before the war there was even a rally on May Day right in Stamford, red flags and all. They used to hang out at the League for Industrial Democracy on East Main Street. They had a whole bunch of these pamphlets there, along with the cheap beer. There was a certain cache to being a commie in the 'thirties. There even was a Young Communist League in Stamford. Kids quoting Marx and Lenin and debating Trotsky's status as a true revolutionary. Since Yalta, Korea, and the fall of China, it was no longer fashionable to be a communist. It was becoming downright dangerous now that we were so powerful. It was strange. We had let them march up and down the street in the middle of the Depression singing songs and waving red flags when it seemed that the whole system might collapse if just three more people lost their jobs. There were communists everywhere and nothing really happened. No revolution. Hardly any strikes.

Now just one Red in the State Department, or somebody making a movie where working girls chipped in for the rent, threatened the whole country. The workers that I knew were worried about getting enough overtime so that they could buy a second car or put a pool behind the house they had bought through the VA. The only thing that would get them into a revolutionary mood was if the price of gas climbed to twenty-nine cents a gallon. Maybe we already had a worker's paradise and just didn't know it.

Then I saw *The Book of Judith: Life in the Resistance* that was more dog-eared than the others. At first, I thought it was a religious text, but it turned out to be a confessional book about the adventures of a young Jewish girl in the French Resistance. There were a few pictures of the writer in the book. She bore a remarkable resemblance to Lara. On one of the pages was a Bible quote heavily underlined and marked with a large black *YES!* in the margin: *...and man, whom woman cannot subdue by strength, she subdues by guile.*

I put it in my pocket.

There wasn't much else on the desk. I started opening the doors. There were a few school notebooks, some letters post-marked in September from Sophie Greenbaum. I didn't want to read them. In the back of the bottom drawer I found a diary. It was locked. I felt I had to explain myself to Tammy.

"There might be something very important about Lara in here."

"Oh, yes. I understand."

I could tell she wanted me to let her in on what I found. Unfortunately, Lara hadn't written in the diary since the beginning of November. I flipped back to the beginning. She had a strong and clear handwriting. The first entries had to do with the opening of school. She wanted to be a writer. Some of the entries were sketches for stories.

Professor Harris strode into the classroom like Ponce DeLeon announcing the discovery of the Fountain of Youth to the King of Spain...

Helen looked into his eyes and found only her confusion reflected back at her.

Later Jason entered the picture. She had tried to make a short story out of the night he dressed up in women's clothes. Later, she attempted to describe the first time that they had made love. *When he entered me, I could see his pleasure beaming in his warm blue eyes. I hoped that he had found some small light in mine.* It seemed that Lara was always finding her reflection in the eyes of another. Still later the tone changed, there was much more passion. I didn't think she was writing about Jason.

"Did Lara see anyone after Jason? Any one she was seeing seriously?"

"I don't think so." Tammy clearly wanted an answer to this question as if it would make things easier with Jason.

"Are you sure?"

"Why, did you find something?"

She moved toward me and I could smell her youth in her hair. It was sweet like pastry.

The last entries were cryptic, in some sort of code as if Lara felt compelled to record her life, but at the same time felt some necessity to protect herself from ever having the record discovered.

o liofa vt qkt gf lg lig iqkt

Before the coded entries, there was one long paragraph conventionally written on November first.

I was walking back from Hayden Hall after meeting with CA. It was warm. The first warm day in three weeks and I felt like I could fly. Like a little girl I started skipping by the duck pond where the few stragglers who hoped to make it through the winter on the generosity of students shook their feathers. They looked confused. There was some open water on the pond but they hesitated to go out there. Perhaps they thought it was some mirage, conjured out of their deep need. I haven't felt this good in weeks. For the first time I could just be here, watch the ducks, and not think about politics. Then I looked up in the sky that was almost pure blue. There was one spiral of a cloud that just caught my eye off on the horizon and, at that moment, I felt zero to the bone. My first thought was that it was a mushroom cloud. I stood there for an instant, waiting for the blast. It was just an instant but the mood was shattered. It was all a mirage. I knew why the ducks didn't head for the water. They knew the freeze was coming. What difference would a few hours of happiness make?

I wished that Lara were more like Tammy. I wished she were looking forward to the Dartmouth Winter Carnival and not to nuclear destruction. I wished she were still a girl who could skip unselfconsciously. I slipped the diary into my pocket next to *The Book of Judith*. I told Tammy that I was going to look for Jason and the professors she had named.

She smiled and wished me good luck. "I really like Lara. I don't really understand her, but I really like her." She slipped a piece of paper into my hand. I didn't want to look at it afraid to find a telephone number or an invitation. I patted her on the head in my most fatherly manner. When I got outside, I opened it to find: *Items missing: one loden-green wool coat, two crew neck sweaters—one red and one charcoal, two skirts—one gray and one blue, two pairs of shoes—one pair Weejuns and one pair black pumps. I'm sure she took some blouses, but I can't really describe them. Good luck!!!!*

CHAPTER 3

I put Tammy's list in my pocket and began to search for Jason, the most likely lead. I didn't like the fact that Lara had broken off with him. That counted against him. It had been months, but maybe something had triggered his anger.

The first thing that came to mind when I heard she was missing was that she had gone off with some guy. If Jason heard and was jealous, it wouldn't be the first time an ex-boyfriend tried to step in with terrible results. Tammy's genuine interest in Jason made me think I wasn't going to find some psychopath. I was getting the same uneasy feeling that Freddie had. Nothing in what I heard about Lara led me to think she was off on a lark. I found myself hoping that she was pregnant and checked into some private hospital somewhere. The Greenbaums could deal with that. The alternatives were just too disturbing. Girls just didn't run off without a reason. Not girls like Lara, who told their mothers everything.

I checked the frat house and was told that Jason was at The Husky Grille. Here was another tall blond. The campus was full of them. Another, probably a basketball player, told me that Jason was "real short," about five feet, ten inches, and wearing a camel colored coat.

The Husky Grille supplied the kind of food that students craved. The food that was not available in cafeterias where fish cakes, macaroni and cheese, and stewed tomatoes were standards. They wanted hamburgers and hot dogs, French fries, and milk shakes. It was a popular place. A thick cloud of grease hung heavy in the air. There was also the buzz of youth. On the jukebox I could barely hear Tony Bennett going from rags to riches. Two coeds watched me as I walked across the floor, searching for an ordinary-looking, five-foot-ten, twenty-year-old among the fifteen or twenty who fit exactly the same description. I stopped and asked the girl who was watching me most attentively if she knew Jason.

"Is he in trouble?"

"Why?"

"You look like a policeman."

"I'm not a cop." There was a pause, which allowed me to introduce myself. "No. I'm a friend of Lara Greenbaum's family. Do you know her?"

"Not really, but I know who she is."

"Have you seen her since Thanksgiving?"

"No, I haven't." She turned to her previously silent friend who had the look of someone who was about to hear juicy gossip. She shook her head and leaned forward.

I took a card from my wallet and handed it to the talkative one.

"A detective. Like Philip Marlowe?"

"More like the Continental Op."

The name didn't register. I didn't explain.

"That's dreamy."

"Do you know Jason Melrose?"

"Sure. I get it. You want to talk to him about Lara. He dumped her about a year ago though. I don't think he knows anything. He doesn't go out with her anymore."

"I heard that he was here. Could you look around and point him out to me?"

"Easy." She turned and pointed to a young man two tables away.

"I always know where Jason is." She smiled as if we had just shared a professional secret.

I thanked her and walked toward the handsome young man who looked like a model from Brooks Brothers. He was sitting with a couple of not-so-handsome friends who were laughing at his jokes. He looked to me like a spoiled kid who always had his bread buttered for him. Sometimes on both sides. The world was a giant amusement park for him and he had learned to play happily in it. For him, suffering was a sham like fright on a roller coaster, just a way to win a girl's sympathy. Everything else was all for the entertainment of others. Even from a

few feet away I could see the striking blue in his eyes, the kind
I hate. And I could see how the woman at the table couldn't
take her eyes off of them. The poor boy sitting next to Jason
was for all practical purposes invisible or, at most, an example
of how not to look.

Jason's camel coat was draped over the back of his chair.
Around his neck was a gray crew neck sweater tied loosely so
that it looked like a shawl. An impressive, aristocratic look
that should have been out of place in this grease pit, and yet
which drew all eyes to him.

In front of him were a half-eaten BLT and some chips. He
stopped talking when he realized that I was interested in what
he had to say.

"Can I help you?"

"Are you Jason Melrose?"

"Who's asking?"

Since I had the cards handy, I reached in my pocket and
held one in front of those baby blues. He took it without reading it and placed it face down on the table.

"I'm looking for Lara Greenbaum."

"FBI?"

"Why would you think I was FBI?"

"Considering the fact she was thinking of changing her
name to Rosenberg." He looked at his friends. His friends
laughed. Jason was a regular comedian.

"If you read the card, you will see who I am. Why I am
here has to do with Lara. Do you know Lara is missing?"

"Missing what? Her common sense?" This Jason was a real
card. He must have really cracked them up at the frat parties.

"She hasn't been seen since before Thanksgiving. And I
was given the information that you and she—"

"Have you checked the flights to Moscow?" This one
didn't get a laugh, not even from his friends. There was too
much posing.

"Look, son..." I leaned over and spoke in a whisper but
loud enough to be heard by his friends. The wiseacre look on
his face changed. He saw he was being challenged. I continued. "I didn't come here to trade one liners. If you don't mind,
I don't want to be your straight man. All I want is a few an-

swers to a few simple questions. I want to find Lara. I hope you will want to help me."

I put my left hand on his shoulder and applied just enough pressure to let him know that I was serious. He started to resist, but when I applied enough pressure to numb his neck, he relaxed. He looked across the table and then decided to try charm.

"I'm sorry. I didn't know that Lara was missing. Is she—"

I decided to press my advantage. "I think your friends have finished with lunch."

"Look fellows, do you mind? I'll take care of the bill."

Wordlessly, they grabbed for their coats and stood up. They paused for a minute as if waiting for some signal. When neither of us responded, they awkwardly tried to act nonchalantly as they left the restaurant. Jason seemed to relax as if he had just come off stage.

"Good. I understand that you and Lara were pretty close last year?"

"We were. Really close. She used to be fabulous, then she had to go and change."

"Is that why you broke it off?"

"I broke it off?"

"One of you did. I was just told it was you. Or did I get it wrong?"

The facade had crumbled. He looked intently down into the remains of lettuce and pale pink tomato on his plate.

"I never felt anything like I did for Lara. I still do, but not for what she's become. We had some great times together."

"You certainly dressed for them."

"You heard? How did you hear about that?"

"It's the talk of the dorm."

He blushed and flicked a piece of lettuce across the table. Once again, I was surprised at how young twenty is.

"It was just a gag. She was willing to go along with it, that's what made her so great. She wasn't always looking over her shoulder to see what everyone else thought. She was—"

"You keep speaking about her in the past tense."

"She is for me. I tried. Let me tell you, sir."

The "sir" was unexpected. The humility in his voice was even more surprising. I began to think I had misjudged him.

"Do you think she's really missing?"

"She's missing all right. The real question is why and where. And for how long?"

He sat back and sighed. He began to ask me why things had changed, knowing that I didn't have the answers. He wanted me to know about his feelings for Lara. He wasn't trying to avoid suspicion. He was just sharing his pain. The role of the *bon vivant* must have been very draining for him.

"Despite all the conventional differences, you know: money, religion, background, we were so alike. It was like being in love with your twin sister. But not in a…creepy way. It was so…perfect. Even the negative things we shared. We both had a chip on our shoulders in a way. Lara should have been at Smith. It was the only thing she wanted. She worked hard. I don't even know why she wanted to go there. All I know is that there was no reason why she shouldn't have gotten in. She's the smartest girl I ever met. And not just book smart, you know what I mean? She didn't just know the answers. She knew the questions. She never stopped asking questions."

"And your chip?"

"It's not that important. It doesn't have anything to do with Lara."

"It might. Look, I'm at a loss here. Who knows what might trigger something?"

"You don't think Lara's disappearance has got anything to do with me?"

It apparently had just dawned on him that the reason I was talking to him was that I thought he might have done something to her. If he were guilty of anything, he would have known what I was after as soon as I showed up. I was glad that my second impression of Jason was holding up.

"No, I don't. So tell me. I still want to know about you."

"I'm the first one in our family to go to college. It's my father's dream. At least it was. He didn't make it back from Okinawa. My mother never let me forget that he wanted me to go to school more than anything. You know what he did before the war? He delivered milk. He was a milkman. When I was little, sometimes he'd wake me at four in the morning and take me with him through Darien and New Canaan. He used to tell me that someday he would deliver milk to me in one of those big white houses. That was his big dream. And I had to live it."

"I wouldn't have guessed."

"Most don't, but Lara did immediately, in a way. She didn't know my father was a milkman, but she knew I was not what I appeared to be. She didn't care. She kept saying 'be yourself.' She didn't know that's the hard part."

"So what's the problem? You're here. Your father would be proud. I'm sure your mother is.

"You don't get it either, do you? If I live out my father's dream, then I have to deny his life. I have to become one of those people who live in those houses. I really don't care about what kind of house I live in. I loved my father. I loved the fact that he was a milkman. I loved the sound of the bottles rattling in the truck. The smell of the ice. I loved his blue uniform. He wouldn't even go to Parent's Night because he was embarrassed about the way he dressed. Now I get my clothes at Witby & Gallagher. I'll get the house in Darien and I'll have a job in an office. Which I'll hate to the day I die."

It was melodramatic, but it was clearly genuine.

"You don't have to deny your father to get those things. It's not a trade."

"Yeah, right." He sounded like I had just told him to continue believing in Santa Claus or brush his teeth after meals.

"What happened exactly when you broke up?"

"It was funny. Not really funny. I still haven't figured it out. It was sudden and gradual at the same time. It's hard to explain. Just before summer break, she seemed to stop asking questions and to have all the answers, you know. She was worried about the bomb. I think about it sure, who doesn't? But she was obsessed with it. I tried to make her feel better, but what can you do? You can't go around thinking that everyday might be the last day, can you? Well, she started talking about it like it was some sort of conspiracy to keep...I don't know what, us all in fear. Then she started saying she was glad she was at a state university and not a school for the elite. I didn't believe it, but what can you say? And she said a whole bunch of other things about the war in Korea and why we fought it. You know what I think it comes down to?"

"What?"

"My problems got to be too small for her. She had moved on. To the world's problems."

"How upset were you when Lara called it quits?"

"Very. But she never really called it quits. Not like there was a big confrontation. She just wasn't there anymore. Even when we were together. So I just stopped coming around. I got the message. She was the only thing that I had that was real. She understood me. Once, before we broke up, she said she knew me because my life was just like being a Jew."

"How?"

"You know, trying to pretend to be what you're not. Trying to be just like the rest of the crowd. Or better. But all the time knowing that you're not what you pretend to be. We used to joke about fooling them all. When I told her about the house in Darien, she laughed. She said they wouldn't even let her deliver milk much less live there. She told me to read *Gentleman's Agreement*."

"Were you angry when she drifted away?"

"I was beside myself. I spent the whole summer trying to figure out what went wrong. I almost lost my job."

"Were you angry enough that you would want to get even with her?" I had to ask. He was hurt.

"And hurt her? Never. Look, I would throw myself in front of a train for her if I thought it would make her feel just a little better. I was mad, sure, but it's been almost six months. I have not given up hope. And I won't. This isn't just a college fling. Not for me, anyway."

"I can see that."

"She'll always be—" He stopped as if he realized that he had to limit to his confession to a stranger. "I have just reached the point where thinking about her doesn't ruin every day. Do you think she's in danger? Really?"

I could feel the anguish in his voice.

"When a girl with Lara's history disappears without a trace, you have to be concerned. Terrible things happen. Especially to young girls. The thing is that we have nothing really to go on."

"It seemed like school was less and less important to her this year. But she seemed more serious than ever. Her roommate used to tell me about her." He paused. And looked me straight in the eye. I could see they were filling up with tears. "If there is anything I can do? Anything? Look, I can handle myself."

I ignored the offer of muscle and asked him if he knew any names of Lara's political pals.

"If you really want to know about what came over Lara, you should talk to Browder. He'll know. He's probably in back of it anyway." He was angry now.

"He's the professor?"

"Yeah. He's the one who filled her head—I'm sure of it. I wish—"

He stopped mid-sentence and swallowed hard. Instinctively the actor, he looked around the room to see if he was being watched. He shook his head and tried to eat the scraps of food on the table as if that would help him hold back the tears.

I put my arm on his. "If you hear anything, you have my card. I'm going to see Browder now."

"Okay, okay. You find her, okay? I mean it, if I can help, I'll do—"

The words never made it all the way out of his mouth. It didn't matter much. I couldn't have misjudged someone more. I asked him to check around to see if anybody knew where Lara was going over vacation. He shook his head. He'd ask everybody on campus. I believed him.

The campus building-boom could not keep up with the influx of new students. I noticed at least three newly erected classroom buildings across from the football field. The English Department had taken temporary quarters along with History and Political Science right next to the construction. The Quonset hut, looking like it had been salvaged from the military, was dwarfed by the scaffolding of the new buildings behind it. They had painted it a too cheery Husky blue. The grass leading up to the doorway had already been worn away. There was enough mud and ice and gray snow to make sure that wherever you walked your shoes would be dirty. It reminded me of some places in Europe. I wouldn't have been surprised to see a full bird colonel walk out of the hut instead of a coed.

Browder's office was at the end of a long narrow corridor with a water fountain that meant passage was restricted to single file. A young man was waiting in front of the door, looking sullenly at the wall in front of him.

"Is Professor Browder in?"

"Yeah. But I have a two o'clock."

"Fine. I'll wait."

He resumed his sullen stare at the wall. I checked my watch and saw that it was already five after two. I could hear muffled voices inside the office. Then the door opened and a coed stepped out. She looked at her fellow student and rolled her eyes as if to say, "What can you expect?"

The student walked in and closed the door before I could get a glimpse of Browder. I wasn't sure that I could trust my first impressions after my experience with Jason.

I could hear bits and pieces of the conversation between Browder and his student. With no other company in the corridor, I could put my ear close to the door. Browder was unhappy with a paper the student had written about *Moby Dick*. He seemed to think that the student hadn't read the book that he had just written about. The student wanted proof. He wanted to know if Browder was calling him a liar. Browder read a passage from the paper. "If this is the result of your reading Melville, then I am more concerned than if you were simply a liar and a cheat. There is always the possibility of moral redemption for the cheat, but there is nothing in stupidity that can be redeemed."

It was a good line for the student to exit on. I moved away from the door. The student tried to make a decisive move to show Browder what he thought of him, but I was there blocking the way. I tried to move aside, but he was too impatient. I could hear him mutter, "You bastard."

I wasn't sure if he meant me or Browder. But it didn't make that much difference.

"Professor Browder, can I have a moment of your time?"

He checked his watch. "Do you have an appointment?"

"No, I don't. "

"I'm sorry but my office hours are from 1 to 3pm on Monday, Tuesday, and Thursday, You can sign up at the English Department office."

I realized that despite my age and appearance, he had mistaken me for a student. At least it was better than being mistaken for an FBI agent.

"I'm not a student, Professor." I reached into my jacket and pulled out another card. "I've been hired to help locate Lara Greenbaum. I understand that she is one of your students." I tried to sound professional.

"You're a private eye, Mr. Varian?" He looked again." I'm sorry, Mr. Pike."

"A private investigator, yes."

"And you are working for?"

"Her parents. Who else?"

"And you have proof?" He was suspiciously suspicious.

"I have no proof. But who else would hire an investigator to look for a missing girl, for this missing girl?"

He had still not asked me into his office. He stood staring at the card and then at me. I could see into the small office, which was about the size of a medium sized closet. Every surface was covered with books and papers. There were two metal chairs next to the oversized desk that was barely wedged in against the wall near the one small window. There were so many books on the sill that the window was almost totally obscured. There was clearly no room in the office or money in the budget for bookshelves or filing cabinets. Professor Browder's doctorate was the only thing hanging on the walls. It reminded me of a shyster lawyer's office.

"You haven't answered me, Professor. You seem more suspicious than concerned."

"You have to be, Mr. Varian. These are *parlous* times." He made a point of using a word he thought I wouldn't get.

I was already way past beginning to dislike him. "Forgive me. But what is it you have to be so wary of?"

"Well, I guess you don't know much about what's happening to higher education, in this state at least. For all I know, you could be an investigator for HUAC or the FBI. Are you from Lindzey Hall's office?" He was fishing, looking for a reaction, but he *was* scared. And not about Lara.

"Why Lindzey Hall?"

Then he made it clear that he thought he had already revealed too much.

He made a feeble effort to find some papers. He checked his watch. He mentioned a three o'clock class. He tried to make a joke about football strategy. He was obviously not a football fan. The joke fell flat.

"Are you that dangerous, professor?"

He hesitated and decided on irony as a new tactic. "Certainly. As dangerous as Sacco and Vanzetti or Norman Thomas, or Robert Oppenheimer."

"You certainly think a lot of yourself."

"You have no idea—"

Since he didn't seem ready to talk about Lara, I decided to test his fear, just to shake him up. "In the short time I have been on campus I have heard rumors that you are spreading left wing subversion on campus, corrupting vulnerable young minds like Lara Greenbaum's. Some even call you 'the Red Professor.' Did you know that?" I tried to put irony around the words "left wing subversion" and "Red Professor" so that he might see me as a possible ally, but instead I had really hit a nerve.

He looked around at his small office as if he were a fox in a cage. "Where did you hear that? Who said that? Students? You haven't spoken to anyone in the administration, have you?"

I tried to get the conversation back to Lara. I really wasn't interested in the professor's political problems. "The impression I have gotten from talking to Lara's friends is that she underwent some sort of political conversion under your influence. I happened to see a number of left wing tracts in her dorm room. It was hardly more than putting two and two together. It adds up to four, Professor."

"I won't hear of such rumors. You have no right to slander me. I have not indoctrinated anyone."

He was spinning his wheels. He was frightened, so he tried a new tactic: gaining my sympathy, "Is this a crime? Opening young minds to ideas? Do you know how difficult…You see what I have to deal with?"

"Professor, do you mind if we go into your office?"

He acted as if my request was not about courtesy but security. "Of course. Of course." He looked into the empty corridor as I took the hard chair to his right. He let out a breath.

"You were saying."

"Today, there is no real sense of what a college education should be about. There is no longer a disinterested pursuit of knowledge. Most of my students approach their degrees as if they were qualifying for a driver's license. It is their ticket to success. It provides them with, I think the current phrase is, 'upward mobility.' Or they are veterans who just want a security blanket, not the challenge of discovering new ideas. Occasionally a student like Lara Greenbaum comes along. One who has the genuine curiosity, the sheer intellectual ability, and the bravery to test herself and her beliefs. All I did was point her in the direction of knowledge. I take no responsibility for her growth." He paused as if he had just run the hundred-yard dash. It looked as if he had been ready to make his speech for quite some time. I was a convenient audience. "Then you add—" He had gotten his second wind. "—the current political climate where any idea that even remotely challenges America's claims to perfection and you are likely to find yourself in front of a firing squad."

"A firing squad? Aren't you being a little melodramatic?"

He didn't answer, but his expression labeled me as hopelessly naive. It seemed that no matter what the topic was, it always came back to him and his fear of the government.

I wanted to get back to Lara. "Are you always this frightened?"

He looked at me as if I had asked if wishes really came true. "It's more complicated than that," he said with a great deal of condescension in his voice. "When I was at Michigan, I wrote my dissertation on American literature. It was published in 1949 to almost no response. Then last year I heard that members of Congressman Hall's staff had interviewed several of my students. Lara was among them. They wanted to know if I was spreading anti-American ideology in my classes."

"I'm missing something here."

"Ideologies. They are—"

"No, I know what ideologies are. I even know who Marx and Lenin are. A comedy team, right? What was it about your book or classes that caused such concern?"

"I'm sorry. It seems I took an unusual and dangerous view of American literature, at least to politicians. Rather than honoring the old chestnuts of their school days, I argued that the bulk of classic American literature was a critique of American society—that the great American writers: Melville, Thoreau, Whitman and Emerson were deeply, in today's terms, anti-American. They saw that the American Dream was destined to become the American Nightmare. That was the sub-title of my book—*American Nightmares*. A big mistake, it turns out, because that's all they had to read to condemn me."

"That's too bad. How did they get wind of you in the first place?"

"Who knows? A student might have complained about me. I recognize that I will win no popularity contests here and classes are full of little snitches who are offended if you don't follow Superman's code. You know 'truth—'"

"I know. I know. I also read comic books." I was tired of his explaining. I knew exactly how the kid in the hall felt.

"You never know what anyone knows these days."

"Go on."

He switched from his lecture voice to a play for more sympathy. "One of these book committees that have nothing better to do than look for ideas that they think will damage the moral fiber of the country could have come across the book in one of their own raids on the library. It's hard to say. Your name can wind up on a list for practically any reason. It's amazing. We live in a country that dropped the most terrifying weapon ever conceived of on two defenseless cities, and the issue that concerns them is whether Henry David Thoreau and Ralph Waldo Emerson were anti-war protesters. I am convinced that they had someone monitor my classes last semester. I am up for tenure soon."

"Why do you think there was a fink in your class?"

"To get something on me. What else?"

"I didn't mean that 'why,' but *why* do you think so?"

"There was a student, an older student, who took more notes than anyone else in the class, but who never turned in the assignments. He never took any exams, not even the final. What would you make of it?"

"I have no idea. When were the interviews?"

"I know precisely. They were here from May 15-18, 1953. Those are days that will live in infamy."

"You do love melodrama, don't you?"

"You wouldn't call it melodrama if it were *your* life."

"What did Lara tell them?"

"As far as I know nothing. There was nothing to tell. You have to understand, they don't need anything on you. You don't have to be guilty of anything. All they have to do is to begin asking questions and you are covered in guilt as thick as tar."

"Did you discuss her testimony at all with her?"

"No, I didn't think it was prudent to talk to her at all."

"Isn't that about the time that Lara experienced her so called conversion?"

"To tell you the truth, I don't really understand the term 'conversion' in this context."

"Look, professor, before we go any further, let me ask you a blunt question."

"Are you or have you ever been—"

"No, that's not it. I don't give a damn what your politics are. In fact, I don't give a damn about politics period. No, what I want to know is, how were you involved with Lara Greenbaum?"

"Involved?"

"Do you really need a definition? You know what I mean. You wouldn't be the first. It's one of the compensations for being low paid, isn't it?"

He was squirming, but it was hard to tell if it was because he was lying or I presented him with a possible new threat to his career.

"Not for me. I am married."

"So was Julius Caesar when he met Cleopatra."

"You're not suggesting—"

"I'm asking. In her diary she writes very romantically about an unnamed man. From the context, I would guess that he was older than she was. She doesn't mention his name. Just initials. Why wouldn't she mention the name in her own diary unless there was an important reason to hide the identity of the man from even the most prying eyes?"

"Initials, what initials?"

"C.A."

"Ah." He was off defense. "Great detective work. You saw my name, Paul Browder, and you immediately connected them to 'C.A.' Brilliant."

"We'll see how brilliant it is."

"Are you threatening me? You have the right to do that? Or to read her diary? I am sure that there are regulations that govern even your profession."

"I aim to find Lara. I will use any means at my disposal. And I don't give a good goddamn about you or your goddamn career."

There was genuine panic in his eyes now. He clearly had something to hide. He knew I knew. But he couldn't admit anything.

"Are you still suggesting that I might be this unnamed individual despite the initials? Am I the only professor she knew? There are no older students on campus? Out of everyone, you pick me as your candidate. There are legal remedies to this sort of outrage."

I ignored his outrage. It was too obvious. "I'm not convinced, professor. Young girls, particularly intelligent young girls, are particularly susceptible to the charms of a teacher, especially one who promotes controversial ideas. They can rebel and have their fathers at the same time."

"Ah, an amateur Freudian! Stick to missing persons. You are over your head here. Where do you think the thinking for my book came from? *Reader's Digest*? I was not in love with Lara. I am not her father substitute. I have been married for more than three years. If she had any infatuation with me, she did not communicate it to me, and, believe me, I have been teaching long enough to know all the signs."

"Manifest and latent?"

"Very clever, Mr. Varian. So you are not the ordinary gumshoe. But you are way off base here."

"Am I? Okay, back to Lara. If it wasn't romantic, or sexual, then what was it between you two? The signs point to something."

"We met regularly for a while, a short time, to discuss political issues. Even though my field is English, I am very interested in politics. Thoreau and Emerson are my mentors. I don't see literature as divorced from the polis or politics from the academy. This might not be fashionable, especially with the New Critics. But I...well...in any case, I simply told her about books and she read them. Occasionally we met over coffee, *in public,* to discuss them. In the spring, we did talk briefly about my problems with Hall. I probably confided in her more than I should have, but, frankly, I was scared. But once she testified I didn't see her again."

"When she did what she could for you, you didn't need her anymore."

"That's unfair. I never asked her to say anything or do anything for me. I just knew that she would be a sympathetic witness."

"Unlike the student who almost knocked me over on his way out."

"Teaching is not a popularity contest. Whatever you might think of me, I do believe in what I do. But in these times...you don't know the power that these politicians have when they go on a witch-hunt. Look what is happening to Oppenheimer. He is probably more responsible than anybody except Roosevelt for winning the war. They are turning him into a pariah because he merely suggested that incinerating whole countries might be a little inhuman. It might sound cowardly to you, but I want to protect what I have. I don't ask for much, I don't want much."

He was back to lecturing and I wanted to stop him, but he pushed on.

"If I were interested in material gain, do you think I would be sitting here in an office unfit for a prisoner of war? I am not a revolutionary. I am an Americanist. I truly am. I believe in the ideals of this country. But there are times in our history when a kind of collective madness overtakes us—like right now, in this anti-communist hysteria—that it becomes a very dangerous place for an independent thinker. Already the chairman has called me in twice to check my reading lists. His advice was to make no waves. He thought he was supporting me a hundred per cent. What could I say? And I have pulled back. To my shame. You know there is talk about more hearings on campus. This time on television."

"So where is Lara Greenbaum?"

"I haven't really seen her since October. And that was just in passing. I haven't talked to her at all since the spring, as I told you. I have no reason to lie."

"Where did you see her in October?"

"Walking by the lake, I think. I don't really remember much about it. I waved. She smiled. She looked happy. I suppose I would have noticed anything out of the ordinary."

"Was she with anybody?"

"Not that I remember."

"So you don't have any idea where she might be. Or who 'C.A.' is? Or anything about any political rally her friends think she went to? None of that rings a bell?"

"No, not really. I wish I knew. Do you think she is in any danger? Her family has money, I believe."

"I don't know. No one knows. That's what has me worried. A girl like that doesn't usually disappear without a trace, without a better cover story. Can you think of anyone who might know?"

"There's a boy she was involved with, whom she cared about, but I think they had a misunderstanding. I don't remember his name."

"Jason Melrose."

"Yes. And her roommate?"

"Nothing."

"Do you know what is ironic?"

"What?"

"Lara shouldn't have even been here. At this school. If there were any justice in this world, she would have gone to Smith."

That was the one thing, which everybody agreed about Lara.

CHAPTER 4

I spent the rest of the day walking around the campus, talking to friends of Lara's roommate who added nothing to the little I had learned. The other professor that Tammy had mentioned as a possible lead was of no help.

Professor George Rippey said that he remembered Lara. She was an excellent student, eager to learn, but he hadn't seen her on campus lately.

If he learned something, he would get in touch with the authorities. He flicked my card between his fingers to make the point that he didn't care much for me.

Just as I was heading back to my car, a black Ford pulled up next to me.

A large man with curly black hair that spilled out from under his cap motioned for me to stop. He was from central casting—the small town cop who wants to kick the "city feller" out of his town—the town with something to hide. 'You the detective?"

"Yeah. You the town cop?"

"My deputy told me you gave him some lip."

"I didn't give him any lip. I told him I was looking for Lara Greenbaum. He didn't seem to give a shit. I just asked what he had done about Lara Greenbaum's disappearance. He told me you wrote a letter."

"And you didn't like that answer?"

"Not very much. Not from a law-enforcement professional." I made sure he got the tone.

"And what are you? Some lousy two bit peeper who just wants to be a cop?"

"Right, I wanna be just like you."

He reached for the door with a big gesture as if he was going to do something, but it was clearly a bluff. I didn't want a fight so I played nice with him and kept calm.

"I didn't come here looking for trouble. Just a little cooperation. It's in our mutual interest. If you know what I mean?"

"Is there a reward? Is that what you're sayin'?"

"Not exactly. Not officially. Rewards just bring out the crazies, you know. If you help, I'm sure the Greenbaums would be very grateful."

I hated trying to butter him up, but there was the chance he could help. Money was the only thing that would move him off his fat ass, especially if he was being asked to look for "one of them."

I figured the best thing for me to do was just back off and get home quick. Fighting with a Storrs cop wouldn't help me find Lara. I knew I'd have to come back up here. I didn't want to waste time keeping my eyes open for every black Ford that came down the road. I was not happy, but I stepped back and watched the chief drive off.

I heard steps crunch behind me. I hoped it wasn't Deputy Tate. I turned quickly, my hand moving to my gun. I saw Jason Melrose, looking very nervous or excited. "What was that about? I thought I was going to see a real fight."

"Just a hazard of the profession. Some cops, if you can call them that, don't like the competition."

"It wouldn't have bothered me if you had taken a punch at him. He's a real crumb. Always on us. Always looking for a little payoff if he finds beer."

"Yeah. It figures. Have you got something?"

"Look, I asked around. There's not much, nobody's really seen much of Lara—"

"Whatcha got?" I tried to make it friendly, but it came out short.

"It's not much, but it might help. I hope so. You know ever since we talked—"

I knew he wanted to go over his whole history with Lara. I knew the fact that she might be in real trouble had just hit him. I just didn't have time. The Storrs constabulary might be back. I put my finger to my mouth. He understood.

"So?"

"A friend of mine saw Lara in front of The Husky Grille the day before Thanksgiving. She had an overnight bag and looked like she was waiting to be picked up."

"Did he see who picked her up?"

"Not exactly."

"Not exactly?"

"Well, he didn't think anything of it so he kept walking back to campus and this black Buick almost runs him down when he's crossing 195. As he jumps out of the way, he happens to look back and notices Lara's not there anymore and he thinks she might have been picked up by the Buick."

"Where's your friend?"

"At the frat house. Do you think this is something?"

"Could be."

Jason's friend, George Benedetto, didn't add much to Jason's telling of the story. It was a brand new Buick, black sedan, and no license plate that he could remember. A driver in the front. Maybe somebody in the back. There was a medallion on the front bumper, but George had no idea what it stood for. It was a good lead. Not solid. But good. With nothing else to go on, I had to assume that Lara had gone off in this car that sounded official, maybe government. The trip to Storrs hadn't been a total loss.

Jason wanted to know if there was anything else he could do. I told him to continue to ask around. To keep his eyes open for the Buick. And not to give up hope. He tried to smile. I had the feeling he wasn't going to hear any good news. I didn't have the heart to tell him. I squeezed his shoulder and thanked him again.

By the time I got to Hartford, I had calmed down enough to try to figure things out. It was tough checking out a missing nineteen-year-old. Kids didn't have a real history. Wives and husbands were usually a cinch to trace. Follow the wallet or the crotch, usually in the direction of the sun. But a girl like Lara was tougher.

The last thing I had expected to find was some sort of government connection when I came up here. But here it was. Lara had testified before this Lindzey Hall. She was political. Browder was quaking in his boots. So who had picked her up?

Maybe she was just being held for questioning. Had she lied to Hall and his committee about Browder? But they didn't pick up perjurers with their overnight bags and an extra pair of shoes in front of a restaurant.

Where had she stayed in Hartford? Maybe she had never even gone to Hartford. She had lied about everything else. I had dismissed kidnapping almost immediately. It was even less likely now. At least conventional kidnapping for money. If someone who was not interested in money kidnapped her, I didn't want to think about the possibilities.

In Hartford, government officials drove Fords, Mercurys if they were big shots. The governor had a Lincoln. General Motors apparently hadn't given enough to the party. If it was a government car, my guess was it had to be the feds. Or it could have nothing at all to do with the government. Maybe the plaque was for the Lions or the Heart Association. Maybe Lara got on a bus and that Benedetto kid was just trying to help. I was going back and forth all the way past Hartford with it. I was sure they didn't keep a record of the passengers on the busses from Storrs so it made sense to keep thinking about the Buick.

I kept going over Browder's description of his relationship with Lara. A star-struck student. Attractive. Intelligent. It would be easy for him. I knew a guy who cheated with his brand new mother-in-law at his own wedding. His idea was that if a woman offered it, the guy bore no responsibility. Browder didn't seem like a Don Juan or even Denny Butler. But it was possible. Anything was possible. He thought he was smarter than I was. He thought he was pretty much smarter than everybody. That would give him enough confidence to lie. But he *was* nervous. Maybe it was just his career that he was worried about. And maybe there was something else. Could he have seduced her to get her on his side for the hearings? I needed to know what she told the committee. There had to be a record.

Lindzey Hall was at the center of the political turmoil at the university. I wondered if Lara's political involvement had something to do with him. I had seen his pictures plastered all over the *Stamford Advocate*. Hall had found his niche. Hollywood had been investigated. The State Department and the US Army had both been turned upside down looking for communists. Hall targeted schools, particularly colleges. According to him, Yale was nothing more than a training ground for the subversives who wanted to overthrow the whole country.

"There's not just a fifth column, but a sixth and a seventh at Yale," he said memorably.

That hadn't been my impression of Yale. The Yalies that I knew seemed hell bent on taking over the country all right, but only from Wall Street offices. They were more the old-fashioned kind of subversive, the kind of rich guys who just wanted to keep government out of their hair unless they had an advantage. Rather than overthrow it, they just bought it.

Whatever the threat, Hall certainly knew how to get headlines out of it. I hadn't really paid that much attention to Hall and his crusade, but I vaguely recollected that his newest target was state institutions. I was almost sure, as sure as I could be without any evidence at all, that Hall was involved, directly or indirectly, in Lara's disappearance. I just had no idea how. Or why.

As I headed toward Stamford on the Merritt Parkway, the weather began to turn bad again. I was heading right into it. Now the air had the edge of a Gillette blue blade. The wind pushed sharply against the car. The old Chevy fought back.

Margaret Whiting was singing, "I could write a book." I tried to lose myself in the song, conjuring up a fantasy of a woman who could sing such a song about me. Every time I tried to imagine the face that went with the song, all I could see was the picture that Manny Greenbaum had given me of Lara. Her bright smile. Her youth and innocence. The idealism. Now I was beginning to feel sick.

All I could see were the Greenbaums sitting across from each other in their grand home in an ever deepening, deadening silence. Manny dared not utter what was going through his mind. Somehow, he would learn to accept the blame that Sophie showered on him with just a look. He would grow old in no time. There would be no more stories. No more jokes. The world that had been so good to him would soon become his enemy.

Nothing could be worse than to lose a child. I knew that and I had none. I had seen women in Germany whose dead babies had to be pried from their arms. I saw an old man, whose left arm had been ripped from his shoulders by a .30-caliber machine gun. Mustered into the home guards at the end of the war, he cried when we carried him to the medics. He didn't want to live. His son Josef had been killed on the Russian front. His wife and daughters had been killed in an air raid.

"What kind of man am I," he cried, "to outlive my children?" "What have I done," he asked, "to deserve such punishment? To live knowing they are all gone?"

Even George Hackett his translator could offer no words of consolation. The man died two days later of septicemia.

I had thought that once the war was over, if I made it back, things might change for me. I would try out a normal life. I would find the "right girl" and settle down. As long as it was far off in the future, a possibility that I could control in my fantasies, it seemed to work. At times, she would look like Myrna Loy in The *Thin Man*, or Ginger Rogers in *Swingtime*. She never looked like Betty Grable or Rita Hayworth. I don't know why.

But when I got back home, reality kept stepping in. I had to have a stake. A good job. A place where I wanted to settle down. And if I met somebody and we went out for a while and people started to talk about us as a couple, that look would come over her face and I would lie awake at night. I would see how it would have to end if we stayed together. We would sit in silence across the table from each other. She would wonder about why she was there looking at my face on yet another night. She would find fault with something I did. I would ignore her. I would think of places I hadn't been to. And she would think of men she could have had. Or we would have kids who would give us nothing but pain.

For a long time I thought it was the war that had made me think this way. But the more that I thought about it, the more I realized that I had always been that way. When the Great Depression hit in the early thirties, my father took a special satisfaction in the fact that he had lost nothing.

He used to say, "There is only one way to hold on to money, and that is to hold on to it."

And he did, literally. All that he had, outside of his house and car, was on his person. A roll of maybe 500 dollars, maybe more, at all times. He paid all his bills in cash right out of his pocket. I don't think he ever set foot in a bank. When he died at age fifty-two after working seventy hours a week for almost forty years, he thought he had beaten the game.

My mother paid for his funeral with the roll that she found under the pillow of his deathbed. There was nothing else, no insurance, no pension. Just a small house in the Dublin section of Stamford that he had bought for cash. His whole life he had worked on the fringes of the economy. Buying and selling scrap, booking a few numbers, fixing cars, delivering fruit from upstate to small markets, maybe doing a few illegal deals during the Depression. All small time. The cops all knew him, but he never served time. Yet the thing that stood out was not how he made his money. I didn't care about that, but only that he did it totally without joy. I could not remember my mother and father ever laughing together.

My mother never resented his leaving her with so little. She expected it. That was what made me so angry. She had learned from him. She had squirreled money away over the years and, ironies of ironies, had actually made money during the Depression. I never knew exactly how. She was the amazing one. She took in boarders during the war and then died two weeks after VE Day. Her watch was completed. One man dead, the other safe. I wrote her once during the whole war, under orders. She never mentioned it in any of her simple reports of wartime Stamford.

I didn't get a chance to see her on her deathbed. I got a letter from Mrs. Symanski. "Don't worry," she wrote. "She didn't suffer much. And she was glad you are safe."

And here I was their one and only son. A chip off the old block.

I could have used the heater. The freezing rain was sticking on the windshield like wax paper and the wipers were having more and more trouble dislodging themselves from the glass.

The world was smeared with light. Every car going north threatened to blind me.

An announcer from a New Haven station let me know how many shopping days were left before Christmas. Carlyle's was having a sale.

An announcer was mocking world news. "According to *Muvelt Nep*, a Budapest Monthly, 'the waltz and polka are traditionally democratic dances. The tango, fox trot, and English waltz, though reflections of capitalist decline, cannot be classed with American dances. They may be danced with taste. But the samba, swing, boogie-woogie, rumba, conga, and the like are tools of aggression let loose by the bosses of America against human culture and progress.' Yeah." He laughed. "You can always count on a commie to be a great dancer.

"On the real news, authorities have ordered the evacuation of all French women and children from gravely threatened Hanoi and the Red River delta. According to sources in Saigon, it would take something of a miracle to save Indo-China now.

"But neither the French nor their Vietnamese regent, Bao Dai, showed any signs of being able to work miracles. Bao Dai recently flew to Hanoi, supposedly to bolster the people's morale in the face of the expected communist offensive. He arrived in his C-45 along with a Scotty named Bubi, two bottles of King George scotch whiskey, two guitars, three tennis rackets, and an attractive red-headed airline hostess named Esther.

"Finally, The National Foundation for Infantile Paralysis announced that between January first and December first there were 31, 989 cases of polio in the U.S. The foundation noted that this figure represented a drop of almost 10,000 cases from the previous year."

I couldn't take any more of this good news and turned the radio off. I needed to pay more attention to the road. A thin sheet of ice had turned the Merritt Parkway into a skating rink. Cars, stopping just short of disaster, dotted the road from Stratford to Norwalk.

It felt like my tires were making no contact with the road.

As light as the Chevy was, I had the feeling that if I moved the wheel even a little I would float off the road into the trees. I tried to keep a straight line all the way to Stamford.

CHAPTER 5

I kept on the case for another few days, checking into Hall's background, talking to friends in Hartford, and reading Lara's diary. Only the diary held my interest.

On Monday, Jason called. He wanted to know if I had heard anything. He also wanted to know again how he could help. I told him to keep his eyes and ears open. If he heard anything, I told him to let me know. I was beginning to doubt he would find anything or that I would. It had just been too long with no word. I had checked accident reports, hospital records, and travel bureaus. Nothing.

The next day I got a call from Manny Greenbaum.

"Varian?"

"Yeah."

I knew the news was bad.

"They found her. Just outside Philadelphia. She was murdered, Varian."

He stopped as if the word were from some foreign language whose meaning he had just begun to fathom. I could hear the lump in his throat as it began to close off his air.

"I'm sorry. I'm so sorry."

"Thank you. It looks like she was killed right after she disappeared. The police said she had been there more than a week. There was nothing you could have done. Thank you for your help. If you'll send me a bill, I'll see that you are paid."

"I told you that it's been taken care of."

I could feel the emotion sealed up in Manny's voice, buried in some deep vault, accessible only to himself. I didn't want to talk about money and neither did Manny. It was just his way of keeping me at arm's length. So he continued. All I could hear was the choking sorrow on the other end of the line.

There was nothing that I could say. I thought about telling him I would find Lara's killer, but I thought better of it. This was not a man interested in revenge, or even justice. Not yet. He was alone with his loss. Nothing else existed. Not even me on the other end of the line. His voice had shifted to automatic pilot. I stopped paying attention just as he did.

The funeral was worse. When a child died, it was unnatural enough, but when it was murder, particularly a brutal, sexual assault, it was as if the whole universe had suddenly lost its bearings. Night could no longer be distinguished from day. Up from down. The future no longer existed for the Greenbaums. Every memory of the past was colored by unrelenting agony. And the present was just a simple, single, endless horror.

Throughout the ceremony, I looked away from the Greenbaums. I watched a strange winter cloud above a bare tree. It seemed an appropriate symbol. It hung, pure white, in the sky high above us despite the cold, bitter wind. If I had been the sort of man who believed such things, I might have thought it was some kind of heavenly witness or even something else. I thought that Jason Melrose was thinking the same thing as I watched him watch the sky.

Then I sought refuge in my profession. I tried to think about what the Pennsylvania police had told me about Lara's body. She had been found in a park, covered with leaves. A man walking his dog had found her. She was naked from the waist down. She had been brutally raped. Probably some object had been used on her as well. The coroner had estimated her death as occurring sometime around the twenty-seventh or twenty-eighth of November, two or three days after she left Storrs. There were so many questions. I knew I had to get the answers.

The day was bitterly cold. The ice that had formed on my car during the night still clung to the fenders. I pumped the gas and the starter screamed like a man on the rack who realized that every moment of his happiness had been a cruel joke.

I couldn't face the Greenbaums so I skipped the funeral meal. And I couldn't face the silence of my apartment. I decided to head to the office, but, unconsciously, I kept detouring away from town, avoiding traffic here and a red light there as if I were trying to save time, and all the while heading toward the Sound. There was a spot at the end of Shippan Avenue where the road ended at the water—a place where you could see all the way to Long Island, which still looked undiscovered in the middle of the sea. I had gone there after visiting my mother's grave for the first time. On that day I had decided that I wouldn't stay in Stamford. I would seek a new life in California. Two days later Milton Xydias asked me to find out who was robbing him blind. I found that the woman he had been sleeping with, his secretary, was keeping a young Greek man in much luxury in an apartment in Bridgeport.

On that day I tried to believe in a future. I wanted to put the past as far behind me as the day before my birth. My mother and father were both dead. I was no more alive than they were. Here now, years later, I wanted more than anything to turn back the clock. I wanted to see my father again to tell him that I no longer hated him. I wanted to tell him that I just felt sorry that he had known no happiness in is life. I wanted to apologize to my mother for never telling how much I admired her. She knew that I loved her. I also knew that she thought I saw her as a simple woman whom I was obligated to love.

Now as the past came rolling in off the Sound like the cold wind, I saw myself walking down East Meadow Street. It must have been in the early 'thirties. I was wearing my plaid woolen coat, three sizes too big, and I was kicking the two big pieces of coal that had fallen off Rubino's truck along the curb, smelling the cabbage cooking in the Brzoska house, hearing the McCarthys screaming at each other, and feeling indescribably happy. I had no idea why I was so happy. I would have given a year off my life to be able to know that joy again.

When the car behind me honked its horn, I jumped up as if awakened from a deep sleep. As I turned to see who it was, I noticed that my cheeks were as wet as an English winter. The horn beeped again. I didn't recognize the car, a long, dark-blue Buick sedan, not black, but a Buick. Instinctively, I unbuttoned my coat and patted the gun that rested snugly against my chest.

The driver got out of the car. I blotted my cheeks with my

handkerchief, checked myself first, and then my tail in the mirror. He had the walk. It wasn't a swagger or an arrogant walk. I had seen it in Europe. Fighter pilots, rangers, members of elite units had it. Some boxers had it. And a few executives. It seemed to say: "This is my planet. I don't mind if you're here for a while, just don't get in my way."

I could see the shadow of his partner who remained in the car.

"Varian Pike? Mike Sexton, federal agent. Wouldya mind stepping out of the car?" He spoke like he walked.

"Sure." I got out slowly as he stepped away from the door. They had me in a nice cross fire if they were so inclined.

"I understand that you have been investigating the Lara Greenbaum case."

"That's right. How—"

"Our condolences to the family. And—"

"Why tell me? You must have been at the funeral—"

"It would not have been appropriate," he interrupted. "In any case we were—"

"Checking on who showed up and you followed *me*?"

I could see that I was troubling the timing of his little speech that he had probably been rehearsing to himself since they left the cemetery. There was just the slightest curl to his lip that betrayed his frustration, otherwise he continued with his institutional monotone.

"Now that the case is officially a murder it would be best if you stay out of it," he said. "It would be better not to confuse the locals," he continued with a conspiratorial wink, as if we were pals sharing some kind of joke or secret.

This was his way of getting me on his side. I wondered what he had told the cops in Abington about me.

"I had planned to stop by your office," Sexton said. "But there you were at the funeral. It saved us a trip."

He mentioned how much he admired the work I had done for Hartford Indemnity and offered to keep me informed so I would be the one to tell the Greenbaums whatever he found out. Then he paused. He seemed to be waiting for me to agree with him, to promise to back off, and, I guess, to thank him for taking such an interest in me.

"I hear you," I told him. Then just for effect I suggested that it was safe for his nearly invisible partner to put his gun back in his pocket.

His head turned automatically and involuntarily enough to break his cool. That's all I wanted from him at this point. He raised his hand and said, "Just procedure."

As the Buick backed away from the breakwall, I saw what looked like a medallion attached to the grille. It was the seal of the U.S. Congress. I suddenly felt better. Then an old Ford pulled up along side me about ten feet away. The lone man inside had no interest in me. There was a bottle wrapped in a brown paper bag that he raised greedily to his lips as he looked out at the same sound that had brought me back to Dublin. I was sure he wasn't looking into the future.

CHAPTER 6

The Christmas season, which seemed to stretch longer and longer each year, was even more painful than usual that year. Unfortunately for my mood, a perfect light snowfall had made the whole city look like an engraved series of Christmas cards so there was no place to avoid the Christmas spirit. It hung over the city like a bright, penetrating fog, infecting everybody with good cheer.

All along Atlantic Street, lights were strung on lampposts, ridiculously trying to imitate Christmas trees. Santas stood on every corner, confusing, I hoped, the true believers and the four year olds. Carols by Crosby and Sinatra competed with each other as they flooded the street from different stores. The result was some kind of Christmas nightmare where "White Christmas" collided with "What Child is this?"

Every song reminded me of the message of the season. *Peace on Earth* and *Goodwill Toward Men*. It was that message, the lie of that message, which made everyone's frantic search for the right present so intolerable to me. What did C.O. Miller's sale of fine woolen scarves have to do with peace on earth? What did Town Appliance's special on DuMont console TVs have to do with any sort of goodwill besides customer relations?

I had turned into a Scrooge who lacked even his good old Protestant thrift. I didn't even believe in holding on to a dollar. Bah, humbug.

❦

Two weeks before my annual Christmas Eve nightmare, I headed over to the library to continue my research on Lindzey

Hall. It was a way of keeping my mind off Lara Greenbaum. At least her words. I kept telling myself I should turn over the diary to Manny or Freddie, but I couldn't. I told myself it was because I needed to find her killer. I wasn't going to let it drop. But I also knew that there was something in her voice on the page that had gotten inside my head.

It was wrong. So I concentrated on Hall. I could no longer be sure if he was involved or if I was just working out a fantasy. There was something very fishy about Sexton and his mysterious pal in the Buick. Since our little session at the break wall, it was a lot harder getting information from Abington. I already knew that they were writing it off as the work of a psycho who had probably picked Lara up while she was hitch-hiking. He probably was half way to Florida, looking for his next victim, they said. They seemed to contemplate that possibility with the same indifference that a meteorologist charts the path of a storm. You were lucky if it missed you. If it hit somebody else, that was too bad, but there wasn't much you could do about it. It was easy for the cops not to care. She was from out of state. They didn't have to face the Greenbaums. They did not have their grief etched in their memories.

Hall's bio and extensive clips told me a lot and I could fill in the rest from various sources. Lindzey Hall had been born in 1919 in Norwalk, Connecticut. His father owned three clothing stores, the Student Shops, that specialized in the uniforms of the prep school, the tweeds and khakis, crew neck sweaters, and ties that told the rich they were better than the rest of us because they didn't care about fashion, just tradition.

Hall prepped, as they say, at the Biddle School where at least he knew how to dress, I figured, and then on to Princeton and Yale Law School. After only two years of law practice, he ran for congress in 1950. He defeated Donald Garlits by a narrow margin. I began to check the newspaper coverage of the campaign. It was vicious. A sign of the times.

The campaign hinged on a curiously illogical, yet very contemporary, charge from Hall that Garlits was undermining freedom in Vietnam by urging independence for that country. Garlits had labeled Ho Chi Minh an ally in World War II when he served with the OSS in Southeast Asia. Somehow,

Hall had obtained a document in which Garlits had praised Ho Chi Minh in glowing terms as a Vietnamese George Washington. According to Hall's logic, Ho Chi Minh was fighting France, and France was our friend, ergo, Ho Chi Minh was our enemy, despite his admiration for our country. It didn't matter what Ho Chi Minh had done to the Japs. So here was Garlits giving comfort to our enemy.

Hall's most memorable line of the campaign was "First China, then Viet-Nam, what's next, Mr. Garlits, New Haven?"

I guess reality and phrase-making weren't Hall's strong suit, but no matter how absurd it was, it worked.

Once Hall was in office, he caught "red fever." He pursued subversive elements everywhere he could think of from the State Department to the TVA. The newspapers reported extensively on Hall's recent focus on subversive forces in American colleges. He was going after "pinkos and intellectuals" with both barrels. Speaking like some western sheriff, he wanted them to "get out of town."

The chairman of his committee, Fightin' Joe Dolan from Alabama, seemed to have handed its agenda over to Hall. Dolan called him, "the first real patriot from north of the Mason-Dixon Line since Sam Adams."

Senator Joe McCarthy also had strong praise for Hall. The first series of hearings he organized in 1952 concentrated on the anti-war activities of several University of Connecticut professors, one of whom had been an economic advisor in Roosevelt's New Deal. The fact that their pacifism seemed to have ended on September 1, 1939 didn't seem to matter to Hall. It didn't matter to Hall that one professor he accused of "encouraging cowardice" had served in the Pacific and had won a Navy Cross. Nor did it matter to the press that he had forced these professors to admit to what amounted to "thought crimes."

More recently, he had announced that he was pursuing another unspecified issue of "grave importance" that threatened the very survival of this country. He referred to America as "the last and most fervent hope for freedom in the world." He suggested that the generation of American youth that was destined to rule the world was having its brains washed by a dedicated group of left wing professors who couldn't stand the fact that America had won the war and emerged from it without the damage suffered in Europe and Asia.

"Just because they feel guilty that they have a nice house, a good car, and meat on the table, it doesn't mean that we all must give up the fruits of the American Dream. Let them give up their wealth and let them beg in the streets if they want to be like the rest of the world. Would we tolerate as free expression," he asked, "the burning of the American flag on the town green? Of course not!" He always answered himself, always, to thunderous applause.

The Hall strategy didn't depend on an intellectual argument or mounds of evidence. He favored dramatic witnesses. When he tried to show the damage that pacifists could cause, he brought before his committee a young man who testified that on December 8, 1941 he did not rally around the flag, but instead sought to avoid military service by faking a mental illness. He attributed his decision to avoid the war solely to the influence of his political science professor who had spent almost a full semester trying to prove that World War One was completely unnecessary. The young man broke down as he described the loathing he felt for the military. It wasn't until he talked to an army doctor that he realized the mistake he had made. "If Doctor Falcroft hadn't spoken to me that day, I would probably be a communist today." The young man had later fought in the Battle of San Remo, the paper reported.

I went back through Hall's biography and looked for his military record. There was no mention of any service. Just a cryptic, "After war service, Hall attended law school..."

That was it. No branch of service, no outfit. There might be something there. Hall graduated from Princeton in 1941 and from Yale Law in 1948. There was a gap that could be explained by military service, but why would such a self-styled patriot hide the details of his military service? It seemed too easy. I knew Don Garlits. If there had been a skeleton in Hall's closet, he would have found it. I hadn't really expected to unlock Hall's secrets from reading the *Stamford Advocate,* but at least there were a couple of questions.

It was the beginning of a start.

I quickly grew tired of reading Hall's speeches, which seemed to get complete coverage in the *Advocate*. I started making a list of basic information. He lived in Greenwich. He was married. There were no children. He wore clothes that would have made his father proud. He liked to sail on Long Island Sound. His closest advisors were Malcolm Poindexter, Jim Kennedy, Henri Krims, and Frank Harris. I checked my notes and noticed that the Biddle School was in Pennsylvania, in Bryn Athyn, just outside Abington.

I knew I had to go Pennsylvania. Nothing was working for me in Stamford. There was nothing coming from my few contacts in Washington who wanted nothing to do with my investigating Hall. Not while he had power anyway.

They advised me to wait. "These guys always bite off more than they can chew and then they fall like timber." That's what they said.

Chewing trees—that's what I got from them. I wanted to talk to the Abington police anyway. It would be easier face-to-face. Maybe I could find some dirty little secret of Hall's from his days as a student at Biddle. Maybe he tied his tie with the wrong knot.

I left the library and walked down Bedford Street. Despite my resolve, I found myself forced to think about the season. Two young girls walked ahead of me, excitedly pointing to the elaborate window displays that had little if anything to do with the birth of mankind's savior. In the Bedford Shoe Shoppe, Santa in shirtsleeves stood over his workbench while an elf continually handed him the same black pump. In another, a reindeer, with lights blinking in its antlers, stood at the ready as baseball gloves, bikes, and football helmets were scattered at its feet. If I had children, I thought, it might be different. I might be able to enjoy the season, but all I could see was the message, "Buy this, and buy more."

I had to admit, though, that these two girls seemed to be responding to these displays with complete disregard for the commercial message.

"Oooh, look at that reindeer. Isn't he cute?"

I really didn't like feeling like a Scrooge. I got to the office before I was in a deep depression. Freddie was waiting for me.

"I need to talk."

"Sure."

He looked as if someone chased him into my office.

"You okay?"

He ignored my question. "You know it's not over."

"Yeah, I know. I'm working on it."

"You are?" He seemed genuinely surprised.

"What do you think? You know me."

"Lara wasn't blood. She's not your family."

"But you are about as close as I come to blood these days. Which isn't saying much."

He didn't respond to that. Maybe I had stepped over the line. Surprised him, perhaps. It was the wrong thing to say. I must have caught the spirit of the season. Despite my declaration, he began to launch into his prepared speech, because he didn't have anything else to say.

"I want you to find the guy who did this..."

I decided to play along. He needed to get it out. I didn't tell Freddie the things that I usually told all my clients. Revenge wasn't all that satisfying. Nothing would take away the pain of your loss. Whoever it was who died would want you to go on with living, etc. I knew they were lies, but I had gotten used to saying them, anyway. It was like some professional code. I could see that Freddie wasn't about to listen to that so I nodded and he continued with his speech.

"You can't let the son-of-a-bitch get away with this. Find him and then let me know."

I knew what Freddie meant and I couldn't let him do it. "If this was what it looks like, the way the police see it, Lara was just in the wrong place at the wrong time and got picked up by some maniac. It might just be a matter of luck if he's caught. He could be anywhere. When there's no connection between the murderer and the victim, it's almost impossible—all the usual questions go out the window and so do the answers."

I didn't mention the Buick or Lindzey Hall. Not until I had something solid. I was a long way from that. I didn't want Freddie going off half-cocked. In his present state, he was capable of anything. And I knew how much "anything" could mean for him.

"I don't want a lecture. You stay on it. I will pay you for the rest of your life if necessary."

He stopped talking and stared at the calendar. I hadn't yet flipped it over to December even though it was almost the middle of the month. I could tell by his eyes that he wished that it were that easy to turn back time. He sighed.

I could see that there was something else on his mind. But, as he sat there squirming in his seat, I also knew that it was something that was going to be hard to get out. His eyes kept avoiding mine. He looked to the wall as if he expected to see some sign there that would tell him what he needed to get through this moment. I waited for a few seconds, hoping that the answer would come to him. He looked terrible. His eyes had the look of death etched in black around empty white centers.

"What is it, Fred? What's going on?"

"Nothing."

"Come on. You are sitting there as if I had wired your chair with a few thousand volts. You are looking around as if the cops are about to take you away. And you say, 'nothing?'"

"I know, you're right. But I can't. You won't understand."

"What? We're friends, remember? That still means something, doesn't it? Doesn't it?"

"There are some things that even friends can't talk about."

"Like what, my halitosis?" I was doing a terrible job of breaking the ice.

"It's not a joke."

"But I can't judge that unless you open up a little."

"I couldn't tell my wife."

"What could be so bad?"

"You know I had a lot of time all by myself in the war," he said in the same voice I used to hear on that cot in the middle of the Atlantic.

"When I was up in a tree or crawling through the brush, it was just me. Me and my old Springfield. I would sit there for hours, all by myself, waiting for a German patrol. At least after I lost my second spotter, I went it alone after that. No one wanted to go out with me. They said I was too crazy. Took too many chances. What they really meant was that I got my spotters killed. Ted Ewen and Rex Gonzales. A kid who had never been laid and a street-savvy kid from East Los Angeles who stood up to take a leak when he shouldn't have. They thought I killed them. You know how it is, Varian. The superstitions. You sometimes love your buddies more than flesh and blood. That's how it was for me with those kids. But they thought I took too many chances and got my kids killed. They never really said it. I knew how they felt. I could see it in their eyes. So I said I would do my own spotting. I was twice as crazy when I was on my own. It didn't matter what happened to me. I got a tank commander once, a fuckin' tank commander. A tank battalion was coming down a narrow valley near Saarburg and I had him lined up right in the scope. He must have thought he was leading a fucking parade. I was way in front of the lines. Probably thought he was going to be as famous as Rommel when they kicked our ass, so he was practicing his parade pose. I put one right in his throat from six hundred yards. Better than those mountain boys from Kentucky."

I couldn't see where all this was going or what it had to do with Lara's killer, but I knew he had to get it out. I had had nights myself where I re-played some part of the war like it was some crazy quilt where the pattern came together only when it was finished and seen from a distance. I sat back and watched him pour it out into his clenched fists and tightly closed eyes.

"The day Rex Gonzales got it, I got a letter from my brother. He told me about going to see the races at Churchill Downs. Then he said something about my having all the 'fun' in the war. He had to spend the war looking down the craws of hillbillies who thought toothbrushes were for cleaning squirrel rifles. It was then—thinking about Rex Gonzales who never had a chance, any kind of chance, dead in the middle of nowhere—it was that day that I cursed my brother. I asked God to curse my brother. I was sitting on a hill, looking across the border from France into Germany. I think I always hated him, you know. From the time we were kids. When I was fourteen, I was crazy for baseball. I knew every batting average, every line up. I used to throw a tennis ball against the side of the house for hours, even in the rain, and pretend I was Hank

Greenberg's son. One time we wound up in a game against some kids from the Cove and we needed an extra player so we asked my brother. So Manny hits two home runs and I strike out three times and make two errors. It was never the same again."

He caught his breath. There were a lot of years in his voice, a lot of pain. "It was Manny who went to college. I was the oldest. I went to work at Electrolux to bail my old man out of the Depression. And the day my brother graduates, Pop hands him 600 dollars to help pay for dental school. It was like I was just a mule. He was so proud of Manny. And I cursed him. I wanted him to suffer the way I felt I had. And look what happens. Look what I did. She was the greatest kid. You don't know what she was like. She always used to kid me. Such a smile. You know sometimes I think I loved her as much as my own Annie."

"What kind of a God would listen to such a curse?"

"You don't understand. It has nothing to do with God. It was me. I wished for it. And she had to die so we all would suffer. That's how it goes. You wish bad and you get bad."

"That was years ago. You lost a buddy."

"He was no buddy, he was my spotter. I loved him, yeah, but like a soldier. Who the hell was he? If I saw him today on the street, would I know him? I'm talking about my brother. I wasn't just feeling sorry for myself. I was feeling just like what the guys thought about me, a jinx. The mark of Cain. Nothing could touch me. I was protected until the curse came to pass. I just didn't know when the ax would fall. I didn't really care about anybody but me. That's what it was about."

"How old were you then, Freddie?"

"It doesn't matter how old I was. I was old enough. So were you."

Whatever I said, Freddie was convinced that the only way he could deal with the guilt that he felt was to punish himself.

"The first thing I thought about when I heard that Lara was missing was that day in Germany. It was like I was right back there, feeling that hatred. Wanting something bad to happen. I knew that the bill had come due. The crazy thing is that I really love my brother now. He's a good guy. The night that I got back, he took me away from the family and he never mentioned his part in the war. He said nothing about my being a hero or any of the things I hated. He just told me he knew that I had sacrificed for him. That I should have gone to college. He had a check for me to get started. He still wanted me to go. He said, 'It's the six hundred from Dad plus a little interest.' It was a check for five thousand dollars. I put it in the bank for Lara's graduation. You know I didn't need the money, but he didn't know that. He was just getting started then, too. If only I could have taken it all back. But you can't."

"If wishing made it so, I'd have a million bucks right now and my father and mother would still be around to enjoy it," I said.

"But that's the thing. It's only an evil wish that has power in this world. That's the one thing I learned from killing sixteen men who never knew where the bullet came from. We cannot bring good luck, only bad. I've seen it too many times. Everything was setting me up. Winning the money. Starting the business. Everything. I just wish that it wasn't my brother. Or Lara. Anybody else. Me, absolutely, in a heartbeat, if it would bring her back. I'd even give up my wife, can you believe that? What kind of a man am I to think things like that? How can I face them anymore? He's my brother. I can't even talk to him. He needs me and I killed his daughter."

He sobbed and buried his face in his hands. There was nothing I could tell him. Everybody who had been through the war had his own theory on luck, on what protected you and what made you vulnerable. I knew a guy who wouldn't learn the first names of anybody in the platoon. He called everybody, "Hey you, or face."

A whole platoon was convinced that as long as one private received no letters, they were safe. It was Freddie's misfortune that he was trapped by his theory and there was no way out of his private hell. His loss was much more painful than his brother's and his brother would never really know how much more.

Freddie didn't have to tell me but I knew that this would be the last time we would ever talk about it. He would tolerate no further mention of it.

"Just get the bastard."

I promised him I would. I hoped that the discovery of what happened to Lara might make some kind of sense to him, enough that he wouldn't spend the rest of his life reliving that day in May halfway across the world in the middle of his own lonely war.

CHAPTER 7

The night before I left for Pennsylvania, I took out Lara's diary again. I sat in my old chair with a glass of Old Hickory Rye and tried to find out something more about her. I still hadn't told Manny or Freddie about her book. I told myself why. I wanted to keep this to myself. I wasn't sure I believed me. I promised myself I'd give it to them when it was all over.

The Lara who began writing the journal was full of life. Everybody else was more concerned about Smith than she was. She used it to gain sympathy. She admitted it. But she needed the failure. It was a burden being perfect. Her teachers—her parents—her friends—everybody else seemed to expect only perfection from her. She was tired of living up to it. Now she was eighteen, away from home, and loving every moment of it. She was writing a journal that she meant someone to read. At least at the start.

I am glad to be here. It is still summer and I can smell the crops in the fields. The aroma of clover fills the air. Dad says that we live on what used to be an old farm, owned by the Davenports who were farming before the Revolution. But you'd never know it was ever a farm. Even the plow that Dad found in the old barn looks like a modern sculpture more than a tool. Where there used to be fields, there are woods divided by the stone walls that wander through them like streams. Here it's different. It's simple geometry so beautiful and so real. The kids are okay. Tammy never stops talking. But I like her.

When she first met Jason, she saw it like a movie. They were in line at the library. She looked, then he looked, then they walked across campus, pointed to the sky, sat by Mirror Lake, and talked until dawn. Lara told the story of Jason's father. She didn't mind at all that he was a milkman. She thought everything about Jason and his family was wonderful.

We both have our family burdens. But his is so much clearer than mine. I know I have to do something. I just don't know what it is. Mom and Dad want the best for me. They tell me that at least once every time I talk to them. What's the best? Maybe I should take a philosophy course. Jason is so serious. I want to have some fun. But he's terrific. I'll loosen him up.

The whole first year was a perfect year for Lara, at least until April. Up to that time she tried her hand as a writer and as a sexual rebel. She certainly did get Jason to loosen up and rapidly became a female D.H. Lawrence. She loved the discovery of sex, its risks almost more than its pleasures. She told the story of bringing him to her room. She made plans to take Jason to Paris. She would write and he would deliver milk. They would live on the Left Bank, eat croissants, and drink *cafe au lait.* She tried smoking, but she coughed too much.

It was an old story. It was a Hollywood story, but she made me believe in it again. Then things began to change. A darker tone entered the journal. Now serious issues took the place of Jason and her bohemian dreams. There was the Cold War. There was the day the thought of the bomb robbed her of her pleasure at the lake.

We are the generation who need to understand that war more than those who fought it. It was enough that they put their lives on the line against fascism. We have to understand why that was so important. I wish I could make my father understand why I care so much. He thinks I am mocking him. I'm not.

Understand what? It was hard to figure her out from there on. Then she began writing in her code. If she could write so intimately and directly about every feeling she had, about every intimate act, and about every dream she had, what could be left that she felt she had to hide from prying eyes like mine? What could it have to do with? What could be so serious in a young girl's life? Even more serious than love?

I wasn't sure I liked the new Lara anymore than Jason or Tammy did, but I began to feel that this new Lara was no Hollywood cliché. There was something substantial there. She made you think and wonder why you didn't care if the world went up in smoke. Everybody was right about her. You could see it in her picture. You could feel it in her words. She was alive.

But the real surprise was *The Book of Judith*. It was the story of a young girl whose job in the French underground was to seduce German officers in order to get military information. Judith went way beyond being a teenage Mata Hari. She relished the newfound power of her body to disarm the enemy. She recounted the many times she used a glimpse of thigh and a little breast to transform members of the invincible Third Reich into silly teenage boys. She found herself becoming sexually excited as she mastered the skills of seduction. At times, the book was pornographic. But for Judith there had to be more than sex. What was missing was the climax, what was missing was the death of her partners. She needed that for her satisfaction. She learned how to hide knives in surprising places. She learned the art of poison from a pharmacist hiding from the SS—an undetectable poison that took a day to act. According to the book, she killed twelve German officers. After her first kill she wrote: *I am the Black Widow. I am Lilith. I have finally become Judith.*

In the margins, Lara had added, *And I will, too.*

I hid the book and diary in the trunk of my car and headed toward Pennsylvania. I didn't want to think about what I had just read.

The Abington Police Department was set back off the road. I counted two patrol cars in front of the stone building. It didn't look like there was much for them to do. I was not en-

couraged by what I saw. I had learned that the smaller the police department, the less cooperative it was going to be. Small
town cops spent most of their time chasing speeders or looking for the sixteen year old who stole some hubcaps. They felt
they had to act real important around private investigators.
The cops in the big cities never gave me an attitude. They had
a job to do and they recognized that I did, too. As long as I
didn't interfere with their investigations, they didn't mind my
nosing around. They knew I would only bring them glory if I
stumbled onto something. The only exception was when their
own were involved. Then it was clear that I was not a member
of their club. That only happened once. Two cops wound up
doing time in Danbury because I wouldn't go along with their
beating to death a guy who just happened to be standing too
close to a spot where another cop had been shot. I still avoided
spending any time in New Haven. You never knew how long
those grudges lasted.

I parked in the visitor's slot and headed for the desk. Two
patrolmen were sitting along the wall flirting with the woman
who answered calls. They looked like they should be scoring
touchdowns for the Abington Warriors or whatever they were
called. They could have been brothers. Both were tall, stocky,
and Italian looking. They looked me over so that I would
know they were looking me over before they said anything. I
feared a repeat of Storrs.

"Can I help you?" The one who was closer to me spoke.
His voice suggested that the last thing in the world he was offering was help.

"I would like to talk to Captain Ryan. He's in charge of the
Greenbaum killing, right?"

"You federal?"

"No, private. I'm working for her parents."

"Private."

He said the word slowly as if he had just heard it for the
first time. Then he looked at his companion. I assumed that the
word had come down not to tell me anything.

I pushed ahead anyway. "Yeah, you know, like in the movies." I tried to laugh, but it came out like a smirk.

"No shit! Can I ask you a question?"

"Sure."

"Can you really make it as a private? I mean is there any real money?"

"Depends on what you mean by real. Not enough to buy out General Motors, but real enough for me."

"Like how much? Do you mind? I'm real curious. Do you get paid by the day?"

The curious one, who introduced himself as Tony Russo, had obviously seen a lot of movies. A barrage of questions hit me before I could respond to the first. I decided to treat these questions as if I were flattered by the attention and sincerely wanted to give them career guidance. I could see that the life of a fighter of crime in this suburban community just north of Philadelphia was hardly the greatest challenge to a virile young man who had seen too many movies.

"Depends on the case. For just an investigation, it's usually a hundred a day plus expenses. The best thing is working for insurance companies. There you get a percentage."

"Really? Like what?" He was on the edge of his seat. Even his buddy, who said his name was Ralph Newhouse, was interested now. He leaned over his desk.

"Once I found a boat insured for twenty grand. We knew it was a phony theft, but the insurance company needed proof. The guy loved the boat too much to put a torch to it like he should have. You know, take it out on the Sound, pull a fuel line, poof. Dive overboard. Really hard to prove it wasn't an accident, but he loved that boat. He took it to a marina on Long island and was having it refitted with a new bridge and different paint. It took me two days and I got twenty percent."

"Twenty thousand for a boat. Whew! And you got 20 per cent!" Russo was practically delirious.

"Yeah, I've seen yachts worth a couple of hundred thousand dollars in Greenwich. They're like goddamn hotels on the water."

They continued to grill me, growing more excited with each exaggerated tale of my skill and the easy money they imagined I was hauling to the bank in laundry bags. I was growing tired of being their hero. In between details of my finding witnesses, hiding out in exotic places like Rio and Vienna, I tried to steer things back to the Greenbaum case. But it was impossible. The Vienna story was particularly inventive since I had actually chased a witness in a murder case to a place called Vienna, Georgia, but it was pronounced *Vi-eena*. I changed the location to Europe because I knew Vienna, Georgia, wouldn't make too much of an impression on Russo and Newhouse. It hadn't made much of an impression on me and I was there. The case that actually involved nothing more than looking up a sister's address in the local phone book took on the intrigue of an international thriller. I had to admit it was fun for a while.

During the next lull I slipped a real question in. "Why did you think I was a fed when I came in?"

"Right after we found the body—Tony found it actually— two Feds came around and asked some questions. Ryan said that if kidnapping was involved that would make it federal, but I guess there wasn't enough evidence, not for them anyway. But the captain thought there was. He told me anyway that he was sure that the kid was snatched, I mean, he said, how does she get from way up in Connecticut to down here, anyway?"

"What did the feds say?"

"I don't know really. I wasn't there. Ryan would know. He was there. He talked to them. Anyway, you know this was the second murder around here in the last six months. Before that, what was it, Ralph? Before the war, what was it? That guy who killed his daughter, imagine killing your own daughter! But that was the last one, a real murder I mean," he said as he turned to Newhouse for confirmation.

"Anyway, don't count Harry Lyons who got shot to death when they tried to rob his furniture store. That's armed robbery, you know what I mean, not really murder. All Harry had to do was just give them the money. They weren't there to kill him, just rob him, anyway, you know what I mean."

I said I knew. Ryan would be back in a half hour. Again I tried to steer the conversation away from big cases I have known and loved to Lara Greenbaum. "You found Lara's body, Tony?

"Yeah. It was pretty rough. I've seen a few bodies, you know. Cracked up on 611, just accidents, you know, but pretty gruesome. We lose a few every year. But nothing like that. Somebody really wanted to hurt that girl."

"You should have seen it," Ralph chimed in, not wanting to be left out. "I couldn't believe it. She was worked over with something. Like maybe a claw hammer or a crow bar. Put it right inside her, if you know what I mean. That's not all. It looks like they used a knife or screwdriver and carved her up."

"You mean stabbed?"

"No, carved, like she was a piece of wood or metal. The coroner, Doctor Gregory, told me she was alive when they did it, too. I wasn't supposed to talk to him about the case, but it was my first, you know what I mean. And it was so bad. If that was my daughter, you know..."

"I still don't get the carving. What kind—"

"It's hard to tell. The body was like swollen. It was all distorted. Words, I think, I think it was more like words. I didn't really look that close. I looked around for evidence. I figured the body wouldn't be going nowhere."

"Did you find anything?"

"What do you mean?"

"Evidence."

"Not really. I looked for anything. A weapon. You know the routine."

"It was in a park, right. No footprints? Was there snow on the ground?"

"It snowed two days before we found the body. Doc said the body was there already. We looked for footprints. We moved the snow around, but nothing. Whoever it was, he was really cool."

"What do you mean?"

"This body wasn't just dumped there. It was covered with leaves and branches and everything was arranged to look just natural. It looked like a branch was broken off and used as a broom."

"So you did find something, then?"

"Just where a branch that had just been broken off. No branch though. You could see the new wood, know what I mean?

"So the body was dumped in the daylight?"

"What do you mean?"

"You couldn't be that careful at night, right? So there had to be some light."

"Yeah, you'd have to see what you were doing. I never thought about that. What difference does it really make when they dropped the body? Day, night, you know?"

"Tells you something about the killer. It might help you find witnesses. Is the park used much in the winter?"

"It's hardly used in the summer," Tony chimed in. "I mean it's called a park, but there aren't any ball fields or picnic areas. Just woods. Hikers sometimes. But that's mostly in the summer. I hear people go in the woods for the mushrooms. There's some special mushroom around there. But I wouldn't—"

"Do you think whoever did it knew that the park wasn't used much?"

"They might. Or maybe they were just driving by and saw the woods."

"Where would you park to get in there?"

"I don't know. Anywhere. Depends on how far you want to carry the body."

"I mean, wouldn't you have to know about the park? Would you drive around an area hoping you would find some woods to drop the body off?"

"I figure whoever did it was a real crazy. Who knows what somebody like that would do?" Tony had given his final insight into the crime. That was the explanation, which made sense to him.

"Can you give me directions to the park?"

"Sure, we'll even take you," said Ralph.

"Did you check with the people who live next to the park?"

"Ryan did."

At that moment, Captain Ryan walked into the station house. He had the look of a city cop. His deep blue double-breasted suit was a little too flashy and a little too tight for the suburbs. He stopped to re-light a cigar.

"Are you guys off today?"

"No, Cap'n."

"Then why the fuck aren't you out on patrol?"

"This here's Varian. A private eye from up north. He wants to talk about the Greenbaum killing," Tony said, apparently hoping to deflect attention away from them.

"Good for him. Now get the hell out of here."

The two patrolmen stood up and awkwardly ignored me as they left. I knew that they didn't want to make it look like they had been too friendly. I played along.

"So what's your story?"

I knew that Ryan was the real thing. No adventure stories would win him over. He was a veteran cop and that meant I wasn't going to get much out of him if he wasn't in the mood. I explained to him why I was there and with what I knew from Russo and Newhouse I could test Ryan's answers.

"We don't get many private investigators out here. I used to work with a few in Philly. I didn't think much of them."

"I can't say. I don't know any Philly investigators. I guess you heard about me?"

He didn't respond.

"Two feds told me they talked to you."

"They did? You know how feds are. Everybody else is their busboy, and PIs like you...well, you're worse."

"I know. They want me off the case."

"I know. But you're not off, are you?"

"I'd love to cooperate, but I can't. I know the family. They're good friends."

"That's tough. They want me to tell them if you come nosin' around."

"And..."

"I'll tell 'em. I've got my own ass to protect, but I got no love for them either."

"Where'd you serve?"

"Pacific. Marines. You?"

"Infantry. Europe."

We exchanged outfits. I knew he had it rough. He knew that I hadn't been on a country picnic either.

"Officer?" I knew he wouldn't have asked if he had been brass.

"Right! If you count the times I was busted, I had more stripes than Al Capone's prison outfit. But no bars or stars."

"I didn't figure you for an officer."

"You think all the officers are now feds?"

"Either that or lawyers."

I was trying to get Ryan on my side. He was too cagey to be fooled. I had the feeling he wanted to help me just out of sheer orneriness. He lit up another cigar after brushing an ember off his suit. There were dozens of small black holes dotting the fabric.

"It's a tough case." I could tell he was figuring what he could tell me without getting into too much trouble with the Feds.

"Sounds like it."

"What are you supposed to do? Solve it? All by yourself?"

"I won't get in the way. My clients just want to know all there is to know. They have the right. She was their daughter."

"I guess that's right. I wouldn't want to lose my kid that way. I wouldn't leave it to cops."

I tried to cover some of the material that I covered with Newhouse without giving too much away. Ryan was as good as I thought he was.

He had already figured that the killer was familiar with the area.

"The feds seemed relieved to hear that I thought the killing was local. I figured that they just didn't want a tough crime, which probably wouldn't make them look good. They like publicity and nothing gets them more attention than solving a murder. Her father's a dentist, right."

"Yeah."

"Not big enough for them. If they take over the investigation publicly, people will want answers. They like to wait in the background and then come in at the last minute to hog credit from the local cops."

"Sounds like you have had some experience."

"Too much, I guess. But you have to be careful of them. They all think that they're the only law."

"They must have had something other than the theory that the killer or killers were local."

"I think so. But they wouldn't let me in on anything."

"Like what?"

"Well…"

"You don't strike me as the kind of cop who wouldn't look around." Now I was buttering him up.

"So I did a little checking. It seems that somehow these guys came up with some evidence that the Greenbaum girl took the train to Philadelphia. I'm not sure exactly what they had, maybe a conductor who recognized her picture. They wouldn't go into details. But if she was here already, got picked up in Philadelphia, and dumped out here, they are off the hook."

"But if they knew that why did they even bother checking things out with you? And what about me? Why do they care if I poke around a case that isn't theirs?"

"Got me. They had to be sure, I guess. I think they call it 'redundancy' now in the manuals. And you. Maybe they just don't like you."

"Enough to go back to Connecticut to warn me off? There is something that doesn't smell right here"

"I don't know. This guy's a big dentist right? Maybe they don't want you taking advantage."

"I don't think those two guys would go out of their way to warn a busload of nuns about an on-coming train."

He laughed. A good sign.

"Were the agents named Sexton and Lawrence?"

"I think so. I got it written down."

"Did you take them to the scene?"

"Yeah. There was still snow on the ground. They poked around and then told me to send them any reports if anything turned up that changed things. They also told me not to talk to you if you showed up."

"Look, if they knew I was on the case, they were involved before her body was found. See? It doesn't add up."

"The FBI gets missing person reports."

"Are they FBI?"

"I don't think so. They didn't act like the FBI I have dealt with.

"So what do you think?"

"What difference would it make?"

"I don't know. It might make a lot. By the way, why are

you talking to me now?" I made a mental note to look deeper into Sexton and Lawrence.

"I don't like their attitude. You look okay to me. I trust that. If I'm wrong, I won't be the only one to suffer, if you get my drift."

I nodded. I didn't ask for any elaboration. I didn't want to press my luck.

"I want to ask you about the marks on the body."

"How? Oh yeah, Tony and Ralph. It was pretty bad. She was a good looking kid."

"Do you have photos?"

"They're pretty gruesome."

"I would expect them to be."

He went over to the file cabinet, removed a thick file, and placed it in front of me. I looked at the initial reports. Newhouse's was useless. He was trying so hard to be objective that there was nothing left. *The victim was a Caucasian female 5'6'' five-foot-six, etc.*

Ryan's follow-ups were more useful but didn't really add anything to what he had told me. There were brief accounts of the neighbors he had interviewed. No one had seen anything.

It was strange looking at the nude body of a girl like Lara. I kept hearing her voice in the diary. The fact that her pubic hair was so exposed made her death even more obscene—as if the killer wanted to emphasize her sexuality and force whoever found her to think of it as well. The bruises and the wounds made a mockery of the ripeness of her young body. I could see why Newhouse would rather look in the bushes for clues than look at her.

The worst part of the pictures was the expression on her face. Her lips had twisted into a contorted grin as if she were enjoying the pain that she had suffered. Sex and Death. Death and Sex. The two great facts of life. The only two. Here they were conjoined to make you question the meaning of both. Whoever did it had done a very wrong thing. I could feel the urge to retaliate swelling up inside me.

"It looks like who ever did it wanted to carve the word 'Rat' on her body. See?"

I looked more closely at the photographs. The letters "R,"

"A," and "T" were clear if you were looking for them, but there seemed to be fainter letters in front of those three.

"I figured he was one of those guys who hates women, you know, but who can't keep away from them," Ryan said. "But they usually have something a little stronger than "rat" on their sick minds?"

"Could you make those other letters out?"

"Even under a magnifying glass it's hard to tell. I wish we had better photos. It looks like he tried another 'R.' I guess it's not that easy to write with whatever it was he used. Probably a screwdriver. Probably not a knife."

I figured Ryan was right.

"I don't know. Do you mind?" I took a piece of paper, laid it over the photo, and held it up against the light. I briefly saw three other letters as if they were phantoms and quickly tried to trace the image I had seen.

"What have you got?"

"I don't know. 'V,' 'A,' 'R'? Varrat? A name?"

"It looks like your name."

"Right. I came down here to catch myself. After leaving my signature on the corpse."

"Once a cop."

"It is a weird case, isn't it?"

He asked for the photo. I could tell I had piqued his interest. He was a good cop, just a little lazy out here where there was no pressure on him. If it had been a local girl, he would be working on the case twenty-four hours a day. But I knew how he felt. Random killing, strangers passing through, no way of catching the killer. Cops were human. They didn't like failure. They didn't like to waste their time when they could be sitting around counting the days until their pensions. But now I was here and the juices were starting to flow. I was happy to see that I had not embarrassed him by calling attention, however, indirectly to his lack of real effort.

"You know something? I don't think that is an 'A.' Look, look. It's an 'E.' See how it trails off here?"

"You're right." It's like one of those puzzles in the paper."

"So where does that get us?"

Ryan sat back. He took up another White Owl and slowly

removed the cellophane that crackled like a distant fire. He looked at me with a serious glint in his eyes. He didn't really see me. I could see him mulling over the same question that occupied me. What word ends with "ver" that goes with "rat?"

"River Rat?"

"Could be. But what the hell does that mean?"

"Who knows? Some private meaning. Maybe he's not describing the girl at all. I've heard that guys who kill this way have some grudge they're working out from their childhood. Maybe it's a signature. A nickname."

"Great. But even if that's true, how the hell do you find out who's the river rat?" I wondered.

"It's something to work on anyway. I still have some friends in Philly who can let me go through their files. If the feds are right and the killer is from the area, maybe he's got a record. There's probably not that many killings that involve this kind of mutilation. These guys seldom do it just once."

"We're better off than we were a few minutes ago."

"Even if the killer isn't local, there should be some record somewhere of crimes like this. There was a case, I read about just recently. A traveling salesman would pick up hitchhikers all over the country. They say he killed more than thirty young men. Some fag thing. Some cop in Oklahoma or Texas figured it out by tracing the killings on a map. It could work here if we are right."

Suddenly we were partners. I couldn't say that I liked Ryan. I'm sure that he didn't "like" me, which is not to say that he disliked me. I had simply served to reawaken his interest in his job. I was like a catalyst in a chemical experiment. When it was over, I could be removed without changing the result. Whatever the true nature of our attachment, I was just grateful that I hadn't been given the expected brush-off.

The one thing that united men was work. I had seen it a hundred times. Whether it was fixing a house or a car, building a boat, or solving a murder, if you could get a couple of guys who cared about the work, you would soon have a team. The only thing they had to think about and talk about was "The Work." It made life very simple and very pleasurable. It was how you won wars.

"What do you know about the Biddle School?"

"Why?" he asked. I could see that our alliance was still in its formative stage. Ryan was being the cop again.

"It turns out that I have another client. Two birds, you know."

"Swanky school for not so swanky kids."

"What do you mean?"

"You know, rich kids who don't act it. They try to straighten them out. In my day, it was military academies. Sometimes the kids are troublemakers. Sometime they're just goof balls. Sometimes we see them when they don't 'adjust,' that's the word they use. But they seem to do a good job. We usually don't run into them more than once. Drinking, wildness, you know. Not real bad kids. How can they be when their fathers own the fuckin' country?"

I knew about Cardinal Farley Military Academy myself. One of my best friends graduated from there and he fit the profile that Ryan outlined. A prep school that sounded like a prep school but was really a kind of posh reform school.

"Do you know anybody over there?"

"I do, but I don't have anything to do with what you're working on there and I don't have any desire. The murder is different. It is *my* case."

"I wasn't asking for help. Just some advice. I talked to a Mr. Ryckman on the phone. Is he the best one to talk to about a student from the thirties?"

"I wouldn't know."

So much for our budding friendship. What did he think I was asking? I thanked him for his time and, as I was leaving, he warned me about Sexton and Lawrence. It was more personal than just a general dislike of feds. I asked him why.

"They rubbed me the wrong way."

"How?"

"They overdid it. You know, what a great job we were doing. Like they thought I was stupid. I can take that. But it was something else, too. Like they were making sure that whoever killed that girl would never be caught."

"How?"

"You know. Trying out little scenarios, like she fell out of the sky. You know how there was no way to tell how she got there, who she was with."

"Like they were trying to protect somebody's ass?"

"You got it. That's the feeling I had. At least they weren't unhappy to see how little we had. And another thing. Be careful of those two guys. I think they could do you some real harm. The more I think about it, the more dangerous I think they are."

"What are they up to?"

"You got me. But it doesn't seem they care so much about me anymore."

"Thanks for the advice."

"I think you're a straight guy. You don't want me to be wrong about that."

I tried to smile. "Gotcha."

CHAPTER 8

The Biddle School didn't match my imagined picture of it. I saw no grand gate or winding road leading to ivy-covered Gothic buildings. There was no heavy atmosphere of privilege or wealth. Instead, there were just three bleak, red brick buildings, which reminded me more of small town post offices than a training ground for the rich. Around these plain buildings were patches of dirt, a beaten, barren brown against the blank gray December sky.

There were only three cars in front of what seemed to be the main building. The rest of the buildings looked empty. The students were probably already on Christmas break. The exception was one lone boy I could see walking across a playing field marked by two spindly white goal posts. I couldn't take my eyes off of him. Dressed in a bright red wool jacket that looked like a blanket, he walked slowly with his head down to protect himself from the cold wind. I wondered how he could be alone at this time of the year. The aching loneliness of his gait, which clearly said he had no interest in getting anywhere except out of the cold, made my heart break. I sat in the car, until the boy slipped behind a building, and watched him long after he disappeared.

Inside what was called the administration building, the cold inside offered little relief from the cold outside. Old wooden chairs with red velvet seats and worn oriental carpets on the floors, intended to create the aura of privilege, felt more like a badly decorated funeral home. A woman who introduced herself as Mrs. Coopersmith apologized for not getting up from the floor. She was trying to bleed the radiators at the same time she answered the phone and handled Dean Ryckman's appointments. It was an old heating system, she explained. Then in a puff of steam, she stood up behind the desk, holding a small pan in one hand and reaching for the phone with the other. She smiled and motioned for me to sit down. Her light brown hair was tied in a pile on top of her head. She was beautiful.

"Don't forget which hand is which," I said, trying to break the ice.

She looked puzzled for a brief moment and then laughed as she put the pan down on the desk, making sure I saw she didn't tip the pan into her ear. She took a message for Dean Ryckman and then hung up. "I must look like Lucy."

Now it was my turn to look confused. She held up her hand as she answered the phone again. She told the caller that Dean Ryckman was presently unavailable. With the phone cradled between her shoulder and ear, she quickly wrote a note. It was a very attractive shoulder. In fact, everything about Mrs. Coopersmith was attractive. She looked to be in her early thirties. Her beige dress hung loosely over what appeared to be an exceptional figure, but what was most striking about her was her smile. I instantly felt every cliché from every smile song I had ever heard. I wanted her smile to be my umbrella. The whole world was smiling with me. How could the curve of a mouth be so devastating? She reminded me of Carole Lombard.

"Lucille Ball. You know *I Love Lucy?*"

I still didn't get the reference although I knew who Lucille Ball was. Another actress. A redhead. Mrs. Coopersmith was a brunette.

"On television. Lucy and Ricky. The *I Love Lucy Show.*"

"Right." I pretended to know. I had heard of the show. "I don't watch much television. Mostly the fights. Is she a middle weight?"

"Right now, I think they would call her a heavy weight." She laughed and her smile became a kind of blessing. I hadn't had such an instant response to a woman in years. Here I was 200 miles from home and here she was a married woman. I was not very good at this. And not at all lucky.

It was my turn to smile. I must have been sitting there, grinning like a schoolboy for quite some time, at least past the point where a response was called for from me.

"And you are?"

"I'm sorry. My name is Varian Pike. I talked to Dean Ryckman the end of last week. I have an appointment."

"You're the reporter?"

"Sort of."

"Sort of?"

"I'm a writer. I don't work for a newspaper. I'm freelance."

"I'll let Dean Ryckman know you are here."

I had the distinct feeling that she was as attracted to me as I was to her. I was out of practice, but I was sure the atmosphere in the room had changed. Either that or the heating system had suddenly kicked into gear. It was her turn again to make the awkward pause. Although she had said that she would announce me to Dean Ryckman, she stood there looking at me like I was a piece of jewelry and she was an appraiser. She must have realized what she was doing and a pink color began to spread across her face. I decided not to call her attention to it.

"Dean Ryckman?"

She backed up as the pink turned to bright red. She turned as she reached the door and entered his office. Despite her obvious embarrassment, the turn was charming. It was as if she had calculated to the inch the sweep of her dress, which swirled to reveal long and lovely legs. When she returned to usher me into the office, I was less interested in any information I might get on Lindzey Hall than I was in Mrs. Coopersmith. I was sorry that she wouldn't be staying through my "interview."

If Mrs. Coopersmith was a dream, then Dean Ryckman was another sort of unreality entirely. Here was a man who fancied himself an English gentleman, but without the style. His limp handshake, an obvious attempt to be sophisticated, came off as just being weak. When he sat back down, he was careful to let me see the gold chain, which ran across his pinstriped vest and from which dangled his Phi Beta Kappa key.

"So you are a reporter? And refresh my memory. I know we must have gone over this before."

"As I told your secretary I'm not exactly a reporter. I'm a

freelance writer. I am working on a profile of Congressman Hall."

"And where will this 'profile' appear?"

"I haven't sold it yet. It depends on whether I can come up with something different. Most of what has been written about the Congressman has to do with his fight against communism. His role in the various investigations he has conducted. There have been a few articles about his family. But nothing about his childhood. I thought there might be something in his background. You know 'the child is father to the man.'"

I thought I might impress him with a literary reference and I was right. I had used the writer angle before. It always seemed to work. People loved seeing their names in print.

"I see. The Biddle School, frankly, could use some positive publicity. I won't try to delude you, Mr. Varian."

"It's Pike. Varian Pike. But I usually go by Varian."

"I'm sorry."

"It happens all the time."

"I see. Well, the Biddle School is undergoing a kind of crisis of identity. It seems that the mission that has sustained the school for almost seventy-five years no longer seems to be relevant to modern families. The irony is that we were never more successful than we were in the years of the Depression when our tuition was a genuine hardship for many of our families. And now, during this period of supposed prosperity, it has become increasingly difficult to make the case that our reasonable cost is really an investment in their sons."

He then went on a long dissertation about the wonderful education that students at Biddle received. He described the range of courses from Latin to Physics, as well as the system of tutors in the English sense. I took a few notes to keep up the charade as he criticized public education and praised the individual attention "his boys" received. He seemed sincere. I began to notice how much of his façade matched the buildings of the school. There was a definite fraying at the edges. He was scared.

"About Lindzey Hall?"

"Yes, I'm sorry. But you can see that The Biddle School is very important to me. I have devoted my life—"

"I can see how important the school is to you. Were you here when Lindzey Hall was a student?"

"I was. I was on the faculty at the time. I remember him well."

"How would you describe his stay at Biddle?"

"Let me be frank with you, he was not the happiest of students. Anything to the contrary would not be an accurate account. But the real issue, I think, and I hope you'll agree, is how he turned out. A successful lawyer. A U.S. Congressman. Of course, we can't claim complete responsibility for his success. Yet, we must have done something right. Do you agree?"

"Of course. Why wasn't Hall happy here?"

"Many of our boys, especially at that time, you see the Depression caused a lot of hardship and a lot of anxiety even for those who had means. Many boys came to us under, how shall I say, tense circumstances."

"They were in trouble."

"So to speak. Not serious trouble—in the legal sense in any case."

"And after he got here."

"Boys, all boys, at that age, can be cruel. They test and they try one another continually to see what they are made of. Sometimes they can be unmerciful. In the end, I think it makes them stronger. I really do."

"How specifically was Hall tested?"

"You know." He hesitated.

I knew we were getting in to an area that Ryckman was uneasy about. I hoped I was finally getting something. "Yes?"

"Well, and this is a delicate matter, I want to be sure that it presents—"

"Biddle in a favorable light. I have nothing against this school, but I need to know about Hall if am going to have something new to write about."

"Yes, of course. Hall's father was very successful in the haberdashery business. Well, there are certain...how shall I say?...ethnic connotations to that field of enterprise." He seemed to examine each word that he uttered to see how it would look in print.

"You mean most are Jews?"

"That seems to be the general perception, accurate or not. Of course, Lindzey was—is not Jewish, but that didn't prevent the boys from making fun of him. This is off the record, as they say."

"Of course. I don't think ethnic issues like that should be highlighted. But it helps me to understand him, so I can provide some focus to the piece. You know this might be useful."

"How?"

"Frankly, Dean Ryckman, Hall sometimes comes off as a spoiled rich kid. Overcoming obstacles, you know, that's the real American Dream."

"I see."

I'm not sure he did, but he was hooked." "So what form did this *treatment* take?"

"The usual, nicknames and ridicule and pranks. This was, of course, typical of young men, especially in the 'thirties when we were...how shall I say?...less conscious of these issues. I don't want to give you the impression that there was a Jewish problem at Biddle. All nationalities were subject to the same sort of abuse. You know, the largest increase in our student body since the war has been from families of Jewish backgrounds. And there have been no problems. None at all. I want to stress that. There have been no problems. One thing I would like to mention to clarify this matter and this is all off the record—" He paused for my agreement.

"Sure, of course. I will write only what you authorize. So what were you saying?"

"It occurs to me that Lindzey might have contributed to his own problems at Biddle."

"How so?"

"When he arrived here, he had something of a chip on his shoulder. It was apparent even to the faculty."

"A chip?"

"Even more than most he seemed to feel that coming here was more punishment than opportunity."

"Meaning?"

"Like many of the boys who came to us during the Depression, Lindzey had problems at home. It was a time of great turmoil in the American—"

"What kind of problems did *he* have?'

"I'm afraid that sort of information must remain confidential. And it really has little or nothing to do with his stay at Biddle."

I made a note to look into Hall's background before Biddle.

"Tell me more about the treatment he received from his classmates. Is there something more specific that stands out? Some incidents, situations, whatever?"

I could see him trying to figure out how he could tell me something I could use in the article without showing the school in a bad light.

"There was the name calling I mentioned and a few boys, of the bullying sort, generally tried to make his life miserable. Once they took some of his clothes, and they were fine clothes as you might imagine, and had them altered at a local tailor so that they didn't fit him. The strange thing was that Hall wore them that way for almost a full year. He was quite a sight what with one leg of his trousers about two inches shorter than the other and the jacket slightly a kilter. Even after the rest of the boys wanted to let it go, he continued to wear those clothes. The strange thing was that despite his ridiculous appearance no one laughed. There was a certain fierceness about him that frightened them, I think. In many ways, he won, but he took it too far. He could have triumphed, but he lost the advantage. In the end, he was even more alienated from the student body than he was before. But as a student he was top drawer. One of our best, ever. He certainly took advantage of the academic opportunities here. We have had boys go to Princeton since, but Lindzey was the first. Frankly, and this is off the record, too, I am surprised that Lindzey has turned out so well. There were times that I wondered what would become of him. He was a deeply troubled boy. There was so much anger and he kept in all inside. No matter what they said or did, he just took it. I think by his senior year he could have earned the respect of almost all of his fellow students, but he threw it all away."

"Why did he stay here?"

"I don't think he had any choice."

"His father?"

"I don't know for sure, but my guess is that his father had issued some sort of ultimatum. I think that made it much more difficult for him. That there was no escape, I mean."

"Did he have any friends here at all?"

He seemed not to hear me. It was all too negative so far, he seemed to be saying to himself. He needed one of those new public relations people to handle the school.

"He was the top student academically although the class did not elect him valedictorian. We changed the rules after that, as a matter of fact. It really was not fair. He was brilliant in fact. Troubled but brilliant."

"How about friends? Did he have any at Biddle?"

"None come to mind immediately, but let me check on that."

"So he is one of your success stories?"

"Absolutely. Despite his difficulties here, I don't think that Lindzey sufficiently realizes how instrumental we were to his success. Academically, certainly. One could even argue—this might be pushing it, but I don't think so—that socially it toughened him to be here. Would he be such a fighter in Congress if he hadn't weathered the storms at Biddle? Not every boy who went to Harrow or Eton had a wonderful time, yet who would deny the greatness of those schools? If you could emphasize this—I'm not trying to influence your article, I want you to tell the truth—but if he and others could see how even under less than optimum conditions, most of our alumni have strong feelings, positive feelings about their time at Biddle. You know that he has never returned here or even responded to any of our requests for aid. We even planned to give him an award. In fact, he was here just recently—"

"At Biddle?"

"Oh, no. In Philadelphia. It was in all the papers. He was giving a speech at the Union League. He didn't even return the messages I left at his hotel. We were going to give him a plaque."

"When was this?"

"Just recently. I invited him to address our students when they returned from Thanksgiving break."

"So he was in Philadelphia over Thanksgiving?"

"I know exactly. He spoke on the Saturday following Thanksgiving. He spoke about—what else?—communism. I think he is running the risk of becoming a Johnny One Note, but don't quote me on that. Please—"

"On another topic, do you happen to know what Lindzey did during the war? In looking up his record, I couldn't find any mention of his service."

"Hmm. I believe one of Lindzey's classmates mentioned seeing him in Europe during the war. I'm sure that he was there on government business."

"Do you remember the name of that student?"

"I should. It was at the tenth reunion of his class. Of course, Lindzey wasn't there. But he was the major topic of conversation. He had just been elected to the House of Representatives. His name? O, yes, William Bell. Bell is still in the area, as a matter of fact. He lives in Media. He is on the faculty at West Chester State Teachers College. He's written a book on the life of Stephen Douglas. He's another Biddle success. You might—"

"Do you have an address?"

"I'm sure that Mrs. Coopersmith does. He is very active with the alumni association."

"So a lot of your students have somewhat troubled backgrounds before they come to Biddle."

"Certainly our reputation was made in the area of...how shall I say?...redemption. But that is changing. It seems today that the general feeling is that the problems that young men have are better addressed by the legal system than the educational system. Biddle is not Boy's Town. I want to stress that. Often times the sons of successful fathers have problems forging their own identity. Their fathers are so successful that there is no way that their sons feel they can compete. So they find their identities as 'bad' boys. That's the easy way. Some of them drink. They get in trouble with the wrong sort of girl. They fight. They drive like demons. But they are not criminals. What they desperately need is an atmosphere of discipline and care. But discipline first. Many of these boys need masculine models. Some of them seldom or never see their fathers who are so busy being successful. Biddle provides a structure to their lives. We demand a certain level of performance but, even more important, we provide them the opportunity to find themselves among a group of boys who are quite like themselves. They come to realize that their problems are not quite so unique or overwhelming."

"How did it work out for Lindzey Hall?"

"I'm not sure I follow."

"What you have told me so far makes Biddle a very important component in Hall's life. But if I am to get that story across, I have to have a clearer understanding of the actual transformation that took place. If I knew more of what he had to overcome—I don't want to violate any confidences, but you have to realize that a story like this has to have some kind of a hook. Americans love stories like this. Look at *Captains Courageous,* remember that one? The worse the kid is, the more miraculous the transformation."

"You have to understand that often we don't have all the details about our students. In many ways they come here as *tabula rasas* or blank slates."

We talked for a while longer, but it was clear that Ryckman had told me all he wanted to about Lindzey Hall. After some pleasantries in which he again encouraged me to feature the Biddle School positively in my article, I agreed, feeling a little guilty that I would have to betray his trust in me. He then directed me to his secretary. This was the best news I had had in more than an hour.

"Dean Ryckman said that you could give me the address and telephone number of William Bell."

"That should be easy. He's one of the active ones."

"Do you remember a Lindzey Hall?"

"I know the name. Dean Ryckman's not very happy with him. I tried to reach him when he was in town over Thanksgiving. He wouldn't even come to the phone. I knew he was there. You can tell. I felt like a relative who was trying to borrow money, if you know what I mean?"

"I run into that all the time."

"I guess reporters do." She smiled. She held the smile just long enough for me to feel uncomfortable. There were times when women know they are attractive and this was one of them. It gave them a kind of glow.

She flipped through a pile of index cards and then began copying a name and address. "I hope this helps."

"I hope so, too."

When I got to the car, the lonely boy was long gone. The campus was completely quiet. Before I started the car, I looked at the card Mrs. Coopersmith gave me. In addition to William Bell's address and telephone number, there written in a charming hand: *I think I can help you. Call me tonight at Prescott 4212.*

CHAPTER 9

While there was still a glimmer of light I decided to take a look at the place where Lara's body had been dropped. Newhouse was right. It was not really a park. The woods were thick even without leaves on the trees. Although there were lit windows in the houses next to the park, I could see how easy it would have been to conceal yourself behind the trunks of oak and the heavy pine branches. Instead of looking for clues, I stood for what seemed a long time trying to conjure up Lara's spirit.

This was about as close as I would get to her. I imagined her laughing voice, but there was only silence and sadness in the air. Then a car door slammed off in the distance. When I got back to the hotel not far from the airfield in Willow Grove, Sexton and Lawrence were waiting for me in the lobby. They were trying to look official and intimidating.

Sexton wore a dark blue overcoat and a brown fedora. Lawrence was hatless. He was just lighting a Pall Mall when we made eye contact. He sneered. "I'm disappointed, Varian."

"Don't give up hope. Santa might still bring you a pony."

He didn't get it.

"What are you talking about?" Lawrence looked at Sexton as if he had missed something. Sexton shrugged his shoulders.

"Never mind. It was kind of a joke. They didn't issue you a sense of humor with the hat?" I had hit some kind of nerve and he wanted to hit me. I was hoping he would. This wasn't a dumb country cop. These were the guys I really hated. "How's the Greenbaum case going? Got any leads? Have you checked out the Abington Police?" I looked Lawrence straight in the eye.

Sexton stepped in front of his partner. "I thought I made it clear to you. Maybe you're the sort who needs a little visual aid." He made a move toward his coat. I didn't think he would go for a gun in the lobby of a hotel, but it was a sudden move and instinctively I was ready. "Do you know what these mean?" Out of the pocket came what looked like an identity card. New and nicely laminated.

"You belong to the Triple A and need a tow?"

"I thought we had an understanding." He wasn't about to give me the satisfaction of responding to any insult. I didn't care. It was sort of a challenge, getting a rise out of these guys.

"Exactly. I understood what you were saying. So what? You were warning me off, I don't know why, especially when you didn't even bother to ask me what I found out. That's usual procedure, isn't it? Maybe you two are new at this, I don't know. If you thought that flashing your little card in my face was going to get me off this case, it's more about your delusions of grandeur than my understanding. I am simply serving my clients. I will continue to serve them. Maybe the best way I can serve them is to watch how you junior G-men handle the case of the brutal murder of their daughter. Try to stop me from doing that. Whatever those cards stand for, it's not going to be good for the two of you if you stand in my way."

Maybe they weren't used to hearing any lip. "Do you know who—"

"Let me see that card again. What the hell agency are you with? It sure as hell ain't the FBI."

"Fuck you, you fuckin' little ant." At least Sexton wasn't trying to sound like a diction teacher anymore.

Then Lawrence stepped in. "Maybe if we go over things, you'll have a better understanding. Someplace more private? Where we can get detailed, if you know what I mean?"

"What? So you're a tough guy now? Please, just don't talk me to death."

Sexton tried a sucker punch. Still wearing his big coat, he was slow. I could see it coming so he went down easily. But before I could congratulate myself, Lawrence decked me with something hard, the gun probably. It knocked me off my feet, but it didn't knock me out.

"We've had about enough of you."

"Just answer me this—who the hell are you?"

"Do we really have to go through this again? Maybe we knocked it out of your head. So I'll repeat for the last time— my name is Lawrence and this is my partner Sexton. We're CDA."

"RCA? MGM? TVA? I don't know what the hell that means. What's Lara's death to you anyway? If you are not FBI, what do you care about Lara Greenbaum?"

"Do you know what top secret means?"

"Look, fella, I don't know you from Adam and I don't know him from Eve. You flash a card that could entitle you to a free car wash, for all I know, and expect me to sit up and beg. You have to do a little better than that."

Sexton stepped in and slapped me, just to get my attention. "We can do this easy or hard, tough guy. I hope you choose 'hard.' That's just me. We have rules to follow so you can come down town with us or we can have a nice little chat over a cup of coffee. Otherwise it's our rules. Which is it going to be, tough guy?"

"Coffee, but only because I don't feel like driving."

The coffee shop was almost deserted. A bored waitress who clearly resented the fact that she might make a little more money at the end of the day approached the table with a sneer. She was even more unhappy when all that we ordered was coffee.

I told her my friends were big tippers. She made an enormous effort to smile. It never got past a frown.

Sexton and Lawrence ignored her while I rubbed the back of my head. "What were you doing at the Biddle School today?"

"I know you wouldn't believe that I was looking to enroll, so I'll tell you the truth. I was following a lead. I have information that leads me to suspect that Lara's killer has some connection to the school."

"What lead? What information?"

"It's still very sketchy, but there's a couple of things."

"I don't think there's any connection there. I think you are looking for dirt."

"The only dirt I am interested in is the dirt I found where

Lara's body was dumped. Like the dirt under those fingernails."

I was expecting another shot. They had clearly heard more than they were prepared to deal with. I am sure they would have been happy to beat more out of me or just to kill me, but they had to have orders. They were told to scare me off and I hadn't scared. Now they were told to find out what I knew and I seemed to know more than they could handle. They had lost their cool. They were amateurs. Very dangerous but still amateurs. I had to get them back to familiar territory before they concluded they had to do something with me.

"So this CDA, what the hell's that? I can't keep track these days."

Lawrence took out his card again and held it in front of my eyes and repeated the name very slowly. "Congressional Defense Agency."

"Defense? Congressional Defense. That's a new one on me."

"So what? Who cares what you know or don't?"

"So? I still don't get it. Does Congress mean Lindzey Hall?"

I couldn't resist. They didn't answer, but it had been a direct hit. Whatever they thought about my going to Biddle, they had to know now that I was getting to close to something they didn't want me near, although I had no idea what it could be and I didn't want to encourage them to try to beat it out of me.

Sexton didn't answer my question. "You are here poking into the murder of a Lara Greenbaum. Is that correct?"

"I wouldn't call it 'poking.' But yes."

"And you were hired by?"

"I think you know already. Her parents. The ones who are suffering. The ones who have a right to some answers, some peace of mind. Is that so hard for you to understand? You think that there was some kind of foreign conspiracy here? The Greenbaums are spies? That I am? That Lara had the secret to some new bomb?"

"It doesn't concern you what we think. So no one else is behind this, helping the Greenbaums with their bills? Helping you out by offering information?"

He lit up another cigarette. Sexton kept looking for me to bolt for the door at any moment. He had a big blond cowlick that made him look like a Nazi Alfalfa. All the cops in the world seemed to be blonds this year. I wanted to offer him some Vaseline. But like most feds he cultivated humorlessness the way that Dorothy Parker cultivated wit.

I tried sincerity. "They don't need help. I don't need help. Their daughter was killed. Their very precious daughter. Two hundred miles from home. They want to know why. And they want to know who. This is not that complicated a situation, is it?"

"What do you know about Miss Greenbaum?"

"What do you mean what do I know?"

"I mean what do you know about her? Is English a new language to you?"

"You got me."

"Stop the jokes. They're not funny. You are not funny. What do you know about Lara Greenbaum period." I liked how impatient Lawrence was becoming.

"I know that she was five-feet, six-inches. She was a sophomore in college. She was a bright as a whip and as nice as apple pie. But the thing I know best of all about her is that she didn't deserve to die, not like that, and the son-of-a-bitch who did it is going to pay for it, one way or another. You see the Greenbaums are not just clients. They are friends."

"We know. And please no threats and no fuckin' jokes—" He stopped in mid-sentence. "You're just a joke yourself." Sexton had just about had it with me.

"You don't know me."

"And we don't want to know you. Just don't think about getting more involved in this case. Go back to peeking in windows. This is not about some butcher porking his next-door neighbor. You weren't hard to find this time and you'll be even easier the next."

I had to admit to myself these guys were real good at some things. The butcher's name was Channing and the neighbor's was Kavanaugh. It was a year ago. What else did they know about me? How did they get here so fast? Were they following me?

"I know what it's about. It's real simple: a young woman was brutally murdered and you're more concerned with keeping me out of it than in finding the killer. Is that about it?"

"This is an open criminal investigation. You are out of bounds if you continue to poke your nose into the matter. And we will push your nose right into your face. Do you understand?"

"Right."

"Don't be stupid all your life. You will get hurt big time if you continue—you're in over your head. This is your last warning on this matter." Lawrence liked the word "matter."

"Is that a threat?"

"You're goddamn right. And we're the ones to will carry it out. One other thing—" Lawrence paused dramatically and took a long drag from his cigarette. He looked past me towards the waitress who was sitting behind me at the counter reading a newspaper. "Okay, Varian. Just remember this. No matter how smart you think you are, we are smarter. So for the first time in your sorry life be smart."

The last bit was a little redundant. It told me I had them a little rattled, but also eager for my exit from the scene, one way or another.

"Thanks for the advice. But you still haven't told me what this has to do with national defense. That's your bailiwick, isn't it?"

They didn't answer. They left four bits as a tip. I added a buck. Just to show them up.

I left the hotel as soon as I had freshened up in my room. They had already been there. I was sure that they had somebody on my phone. They were good at checking rooms. But I could tell. You can never put everything back exactly. I was sure when I got back to the office that I would find that they had already been there, too. They probably picked the butcher's story because the pictures were among my best. Mrs. Kavanaugh could have been a champion gymnast given the positions she was able to get her body into.

I drove to a restaurant on Easton Road. I wanted to find a place that kept their phones near the front. I knew I would be followed.

I was afraid to check to see if the diary was still in the trunk. I was afraid they'd see me looking for it.

"Mrs. Coopersmith?"

"Yes."

"This is Varian."

"I know. I was hoping you'd call."

"You said in your note that you might be able to help me."

"Yes."

"I am on a tight schedule. I have to be back to Connecticut tomorrow. Is it possible for me to see you tonight?"

"Yes."

"At your place?"

"Why not?"

She gave me directions to 130 Montier in Glenside. I went into one of the booths in the lounge with my map. I had to figure a very indirect way of getting there. I could lose anybody in Stamford, but in a strange area, it was a lot more of a challenge.

I spotted the Buick across the road when I left the restaurant. It took me a while to lose them, but I did, behind the Willow Grove Air Station in a maze of streets. Before I got to Montier, I backed into a random driveway and waited ten minutes to see if they had caught up to me. When they didn't show up, I found a railroad station parking lot near Montier and parked.

೧ಎ೧

"Hi," I said when I got to the house.

"You caught me by surprise. I didn't hear you drive up."

"I missed the number on the house. I parked a few doors up."

The house was a very nice little stone cottage. You didn't see much stone in Connecticut, at least not in small houses like this, but here in Pennsylvania stone seemed as common as onion on hamburgers. The living room was done in various shades of beige and yellow. A big chair covered with yellow flowers sat next to the fireplace. It gave the room a warm feeling, even on a cold night.

There was even a fire in the fireplace.

"My first name is Christy."

"Just call me Varian. Is that Mr. Coopersmith?" I pointed to picture on the mantle.

"No, that's my father. My husband Joe, that's Mr. Coopersmith. He was killed at Anzio."

"I'm sorry." But I was glad, not that he was dead, but that she was single.

"That's okay. It seems a long time ago. Were you in the war?"

"Yeah, wasn't everybody?"

"Was it bad?"

"Like anything else. There was good and bad."

She hesitated. I wasn't sure if she wanted to hear more of my war experiences. She asked me if I wanted a drink. As she turned to the cabinet in the dining room, I noticed again how attractive she was.

"I have a confession to make." I figured I would have to be straight with her to get her to talk, but she had other things on her mind.

"A confession?" She turned with the bottle in her hand. She was trying to be a flirt.

"I am not really a reporter."

She seemed disappointed rather than surprised. She poured the bourbon slowly into the glass. "I tried some of that new vodka. But I didn't like it. They say it has no taste, but it tasted rotten to me."

"You don't seem surprised."

"I'm not, really. You didn't seem like a reporter. Not that I know many reporters. There was just something about you. What are you? A cop?"

"A private investigator."

"Trying to get something on Lindzey Hall?"

"Yes. If I can."

"Good."

"Why good?"

She handed me my drink and sat across from me in a chair that showed off her legs when she crossed them.

Her dress was a soft clinging green that hugged her hips

without being really tight. "Because he's trying to shut the school down."

"How? Why?"

"He has some kind of grudge against Biddle. Dean Ryckman is so upset. He was hoping that your story might help change Lindzey Hall's mind. I think he's hoping that he would reconsider what he's doing if he saw how much good the school did for him. The dean was so excited when he heard you were coming. He said that you were the answer to his prayers."

"I'm sorry that I had to lie. Sometimes it's necessary."

"Oh, I don't mind. I think it's a little exciting. Frankly, I like the school, but there's not a lot of excitement there. But Dean Ryckman is going to be devastated. The school is everything to him. He wanted to be dean for so long, and now it looks like the school will close while he's in charge."

"What's Hall trying to do?"

"About two years ago Ryckman did talk to Hall. He asked him to speak at commencement and Hall laughed at him. And then he told him that Biddle's days were numbered. The state audited us, not that unusual, but you would have thought we were AT&T, the number of people they sent in. And it appeared in the paper. They didn't find anything, but the way they put it in the paper, it looked like there was something wrong. Since that time, students have withdrawn, contributions have dried up, and the State Education Department has reviewed us twice. If it weren't for William Bell and Frank Broadhurst, who is in the State Legislature, they probably would have closed us down already. Dean Ryckman is sick about it."

"Why is Hall so against the school?"

"I wasn't here when he was a student but I have heard the stories about him. It was awful. It seems that he went out of his way to antagonize the other students and if they did something to him, he got back at them"

"Do you know anything about him that could be used to get him to back off?"

"I'm not really sure."

"But you said in your note that you could help me."

"You're not the only one who bends the truth."

"What do you mean?"

"I saw the way you looked at me. I wanted...I needed some company this evening. I was sure that you would get my drift. I'm not very good at seduction."

She was wrong about that or bending the truth in other ways. She uncrossed her legs and brought her glass to her lips. She wanted me to fill in the blanks. It always surprised me when a woman made the first move. I was from the school that still figured that sex was a man's thing. No matter how many times I had witnessed the power of a woman's desire I was always shocked. Not because I thought it was wrong, but because I held on to the view that women indulged in sex only because they wanted to please a man or keep a man. This despite the myriad Mrs. Kavanaughs of the world who risked everything for passion, even with a butcher next door.

We sat for a while in that awkward stage of beginning desire. She wanted to know how I had responded to her.

"I have to admit that the first time I saw you I was very taken."

She smiled that perfect smile again. "'Taken?' A strange word."

"It's the way I felt."

"And what is it like to be taken?"

"Well—" I had the feeling I was taking a kind of exam. "—I couldn't stop thinking about how luscious you looked. You have very attractive legs. They could be a dancer's. But there is something in your smile that is really special. Smiles are very underrated."

"Go on."

"It's sweet, but there is a touch of wickedness behind the curl of your lips."

"You don't think I was too obvious?"

"Obvious? No, it is just a wonderful smile. Like a Dizzy Gillespie solo, it made me feel happy."

We talked for a while as drinks were poured and re-poured. We wandered through a number of meaningless topics—her chairs, my hands, the shape of her calf, men's shoes, stone houses, the weather, steaks, songs on the radio, the way people knew they were attracted to each other and how it felt different from just wanting someone. I was realizing how long it had been since I had been with a woman I was really attracted to.

Strangely, Lara's words came to me. "There is in that first moment of recognition that there is suddenly an infinite number of possibilities. Nothing is ever as intense."

I was learning about love from a nineteen year old.

"You just know when it's mutual, even if nothing is said. You can feel it. It is so…different isn't it?"

She smiled at my bad editing job. She stood up and I assumed she was getting me a fresh drink. As she reached for my glass, she brought her face to mine. I kissed her with a certain curiosity. Her hunger made my paltry desire insignificant. I was spectator more than participant. She took her hand, slid it inside my jacket and over my shirt, and rubbed my nipple between her fingers. She wasn't waiting for me to make a move, because she probably sensed that we would have been in those chairs till dawn before I did anything. She put her hand in mine and brought me to my feet. She continued to kiss me as her hands roamed over my body and eventually settled between my legs. "You do seem interested! Very interested."

I could feel the sticky spot of moisture widening on my pants as she gently slid her fingers along my fly. Each time she reached the top she would tug a little on the zipper so that it slowly inched its way down.

"I do love the sound of a zipper," she moaned in a voice that seemed to come from a movie screen. 'Sometimes when I am alone undressing myself, and I unzip my dress, I feel sad that there is no one with me to hear that sound. I could be alone all day and it won't bother me, but when something like that reminds me I'm alone, I could scream."

By the time we reached the bedroom she was almost completely naked. I was not sure how she removed all her clothes so quickly and so gracefully. There was a trail that led to the bedroom, but she never had to stop and step out of anything. There was never that stuck clasp or ridiculous hopping when your feet get stuck in pant leg.

I started to undress myself and she stopped me. "Let me."

There was a low light in the bedroom that gave everything

a pink glow. From the large radio on a table across the room, Claude Thornhill's "Snowfall" curled itself around the bed.

As she ran her lips across my chest, around my waist, between my thighs she said softly but definitively, "Just one thing, okay? We can do anything you want. Anything. But please don't try to put it in me, okay? That's the only thing."

"That's okay. We can use protection."

"That's not it. Just don't. Please. I'll do everything I can to make you happy."

We were a duet of tongues and fingers for almost an hour making a frantic kind of music with our lips, hands and thighs. She seemed to know exactly when she had to stop touching or licking to keep me going. She smelled like some deep, fresh moss on a cool mountain rock. I had never been with anyone like her. She choreographed our lovemaking like Agnes DeMille. Always in control, completely athletic, always knowing what would happen next and how each movement of her body would lead to the next peak, yet, somehow she made it all seem completely improvised.

Her body was even more exciting than I had pictured in my fantasies. Younger, tauter, more voluptuous. Her breasts, her hips and thighs were rounder and harder than they appeared under cloth. This was a woman's body. There was nothing girlish about it. As she kneeled over my face I could see the outlines of her tilted breasts in the rose light. If I changed the rhythm of my tongue, I could change the rhythm of her breathing and the movement of her hips. Words that couldn't be understood, but which could be felt, hung in the air just beyond my hearing. Then her body started to throb and the indecipherable words became moans. She rolled to the side of the bed and let out a little, satisfied laugh that made me feel like a man who just reached the top of a mountain.

She tangled and untangled the hairs on my chest in her soft fingers. She reached between her legs and took the moistness there and rubbed it on my nipples. She glazed my lips with her fingers. Her hand moved down my belly and tangled itself in the thicker hair between my legs. She slid down the bed. I could hear her smooth body rustling against the warm sheets and then her mouth was on me and it was my turn to moan.

Her mouth was as skilled as the rest of her body. In a few seconds the darkened room seemed to be filled with floodlights and pleasure went through my body like an electric current.

She got up and got us both a drink. She turned and smiled. She walked like she had just found a million dollars in the kitchen cupboard. I lit a cigarette. She sat down and handed me my drink.

"He is not as interested now, is he? He looks like a little kitten, taking a nap."

"I would prefer a larger feline."

"My ferocious tiger," she laughed.

"Give him some time."

"He has all night."

"You know, I do carry a Trojan, for the protection from disease. It says right on it. They are illegal in Connecticut. If you like a little danger. I think—"

"That's not it."

"If you want to talk about it, I'm a good listener."

"It's just…It doesn't matter. It's my…I just don't…"

She hesitated and then turned over so that she was looking at the ceiling. I had the feeling that I was following her script. I was supposed to ask. She was supposed to hesitate. She took a deep puff on her cigarette and slowly let the smoke out. I could hear it more than I could see it in the dark. Her voice was low and thick with the nicotine.

"You know how old I was when I got married. I was eighteen. I was a kid. I liked to dance the jitterbug and do my nails. That's what I knew about life. I didn't know anything about marriage and I never got a chance to learn. I graduated in June. And I was married in August. And the war started in December. I had three months to learn how to be married. How to be a wife. Joe's father bought this place for us. Brand new. $9,000. That's a lot of money. It was then, anyway. I didn't even get my couch delivered until after Joe was gone. I was still a kid. At first I was the good little war bride. I kept house. Ate at my in-laws. So they could talk about Joe. They loved Joe. I never saw anybody so nuts about their kid. Not like my parents. My father gave us a hundred dollar bill. Joe's father even paid for the wedding when he found out my father wanted to have the wedding at the Elks. It wasn't good enough for his Joe. We got married at the Abington Country Club where my father got in an argument about Mussolini. Can you believe it? They knew Joe better than I ever could. I met him at a baseball game. In May. He loved baseball. He pitched for the Jenkintown Cardinals. Semi-pro. He played right field when he wasn't pitching. I spent weeks studying baseball.

"My best friend's brother played for the Abington team. Joe was twenty. I was eighteen. The one thing that Joe liked more than baseball was to do it. He was like a kid at an amusement park. He wasn't like anyone else. For him it was just pure fun, a game, like baseball. We did it the first night after the game, in his car. After that we did it in the woods, at the shore, against a tree, in his mother's bed, in my garage. He loved it. I loved it. That's all we did. After a year that's all I could remember about him. He wrote to his mother every coupla days. He wrote to me once. He had no idea who I was either. So I took a job at the air base, answering phones and one of the pilots took a fancy to me. At first I told him to get lost, but he kept after me. Sending me flowers. Leaving records on my desk. Glenn Miller and Benny Goodman and my favorite, Artie Shaw. He was so romantic. I know he studied movies, you know what I mean? But I didn't care, in fact, I was flattered."

She turned toward me. I wondered if she expected me to be asleep. I wasn't. I rubbed my hand against her cheek. It was wet.

"So I went out with him once. He was great, funny as hell. He had that way that pilots have, you know the whole world is their oyster. And I wanted him, or, it, so bad. So he takes me to his apartment and we do it. God do we do it! It was just pure lust, not like with Joe. With Joe it was like he was up at bat, you know what I mean? Always trying for a home run. But with this pilot, he knew what making love was all about. I didn't even feel guilty. I came home, god, at four in the morning and I wanted to do it again. The only thing I was sorry about was that I had left him at all. Then about two weeks later I get the telegram. I figured it out. Joe died right when I was out with Jerry, the pilot. Probably right when we were doing it. I couldn't get that out of my mind. What made it worse was that I had loved it so much. Then all of Joe's relatives started treating me like I'm some kind of saint. The gold star wife. Bringing me Irish stew. The neighborhood kids cutting the lawn. I felt like a rat. I couldn't even think about going out for three years. Everybody thought it was because I loved Joe so much. God, I could hardly remember anything about him. And what I did remember was pornographic.

"Then I got the job at Biddle. And then I started looking at men again. That way. I knew it was getting dangerous when I started thinking about the older boys. I know that they were interested in me, cooped up the way they were, right at the time when they're like rams in the spring. Some would make excuses to come to see the dean, I knew that they just wanted to look at me. Sometimes I would give them a show of leg. But that's all.

"Then there was a salesman, a book salesman, who used to come around a couple of times a year. I finally took him up on his offer to go out. I knew he was married, but I figured it was better than robbing the cradle. That night when he was about to...you know. I just froze up. I thought about Joe, maybe for the first time in a year. And I knew that in some crazy way I had killed Joe. I had betrayed him. I didn't really love him. I know how crazy that is now, but I should have been able to keep the pledge anyway. All I could see was his silly, young face, hardly older than the seniors at Biddle, smiling like the happy pig that he was. So I made an excuse. My time of the month. And I made sure he was happy, you know. I haven't been able to do it that way ever since. Most men don't really care. They usually never get anything but the usual at home anyway. And it's not like I do it every night, you know. You are the first in a long, long time. It just gets to be overwhelming sometimes, you know? You need to feel something, to touch somebody . You need to let go."

"I know. You know what you did had nothing to do with your husband's death."

"In the real world, sure. But that doesn't make a difference to what goes on in here." She pointed to her head. "Whatever, it was the wrong thing to do. I was his wife. You know about that. You were there."

"It's not that simple. I saw things over there. I knew guys who loved their wives more than they could stand who wound up with French girls, Moroccan girls, German girls. It had nothing to do with their marriages. It had to do with being alive in the midst of all that death. War suspends the rules. To tell you the truth, the guys who thought about their wives that way, wondering what they might be doing and with whom, always were angry at the other guy, because he didn't have his ass on the line. That's what made the difference. They were home and safe. That's all."

"You are the first one I ever told this to."

I wasn't sure I believed her, but it didn't matter because I believed the story. And I felt close to her. She could tell me anything. "I hope it helped."

"I think I knew you were the right one the minute I saw you. You're not married, are you?"

"No. I was surprised you didn't ask before."

"I kinda knew, but it wouldn't have made a difference, would it?"

"Not much I guess."

"I can tell now that you're not married. As soon as the married ones are finished, they start feeling guilty and I see them looking at the clock. Checking the windows. Fidgeting in the bed. Even if their wives are a hundred miles away. You're comfortable here."

"I just have the feds after me."

"What?"

"It's nothing. Do you want to try?"

"No, no," She laughed as she mocked my naiveté. "The magic talking cure, huh? It's not that easy. I've read some books. I've heard of Sigmund Freud. Don't feel you have to help. Make me a real woman. You listened. That's enough. You're okay. My, my, look at you now."

She slid down the bed until her head was on my hip.

"You know, I wish we had something like this so we would know immediately what we wanted. Do you know I spent a year eating Breyer's ice cream before I realized that all I really had was one of these, what do you call it? A hard on?"

Telling her story seemed to relax Christy and at the same time to energize her. She wanted to know about me and what it was like being a private detective. "I think there might be somebody who could help you. He would know more than Bell. Ryckman wouldn't send you to him because he is one of Biddle's black sheep. But he knows Hall. I heard a lot about them at the reunion."

"Who is it?"

"Jack Veasey.

"The Jack Veasey?"

"You know him?"

"I've heard of him. Who hasn't?"

Veasey was a New York lawyer who had handled a lot of famous cases. There were periodic stories linking him with everything from the Mob to Satan himself. His most notorious case involved a man who was accused of murdering his wife and kids. Veasey had convinced the jury that the man was the victim of the mob. They wanted to frame him. The scenario he had painted was wildly improbable. He even used an actual Hollywood film in court to outline the plot against his client. It was all over the papers for weeks.

"Veasey's in New York," she said. "Maybe he could tell you some of Hall's secrets. There were stories that he and Hall weren't on the best terms. Veasey was Hall's chief tormentor."

I made a mental note, but I wasn't as interested in the case anymore. Later, at three o'clock in the morning, while Christy slept and I stared at the pink ceiling my mind began drifting back to Lara and Hall and Biddle. Why would Hall go after the school?

Because they called him a kike and hemmed his trousers? If there were something else, why would he risk exposing himself? Why wouldn't he let sleeping dogs lie? What had happened to make him so angry? And what had all of this to do with Lara Greenbaum? Could she have found out what went on at Biddle more than twenty years ago? Was it in her journal?

Christy's body was warm and soft. I realized what I was missing by living alone. There was no more comforting feeling in the world than the body of a woman against a man's as she slept next to him.

In the morning it was all business, from her and from me. It didn't surprise me that she felt guilty. Not for what we did to each other, but because of what she told me. She had been much more naked than she had planned. Clothes were easy and fun to remove. Now in the light of day she was clearly having second thoughts. But there was no way to undo the confession. I understood why priests were anonymous in the confessionals and why psychiatrists stayed in the dim light, saying very little. If confession was good for the soul, it was not always so good for the one who hears it.

She wanted me out of the house as soon as possible. I was sure that she regretted having me stay the night in the first place. She wasn't angry, she just wanted me gone. Anything that I could say would have sounded foolish. She knew that in a few minutes she would be answering Dean Ryckman's phone and I would be off to New York. I was just one more soldier she would not wait for. As I walked out the door, all she said was, "Good luck."

CHAPTER 10

When I got back to my room, I couldn't think too much about Christy Coopersmith and the burden of her guilt. Sexton and Lawrence had been in my room again. This time they wanted me to know they had been there. My clothes were scattered under my overturned suitcase. The drawers were on the floor. They wanted me to know how unhappy they were that I had given them the slip. They had gotten tired of waiting for me. But somebody was out there watching. I was sure of it. I didn't have much time. If Sexton and Lawrence met up with me again, I wouldn't get away with just a lump on my head.

I debated with myself whether to try William Bell or head immediately for New York. I thought I could easily lose my tail again. I checked out of the Willow Grove Motor Hotel, still undecided. There was a black Pontiac across the street, its engine running. The exhaust was thick and white like cumulus clouds. It was bitter cold. It had to be Sexton and Lawrence's relief on duty as I didn't recognize the car.

Then I checked my car to make sure the two books were where I'd hidden them and was on the road before they could get out of the car. I decided to lose them before I got to the Pennsylvania Turnpike so I headed west toward Media and William Bell. This time I couldn't shake them. They knew I'd spotted them. There was no pretense involved. They were right on my back. I figured that I could call Bell when I got back to Stamford. They followed me right into New York City.

At a restaurant on Fifty-Seventh Street, I called Veasey's office. I told them I wanted to talk about Lindzey Hall.

"Varian Pike? And you are with?"

"Yes, I am not with anybody. I'm a private detective. But it's important that I talk to Mr. Veasey."

"Mr. Veasey is unavailable."

"It has to do with Mr. Veasey's school days, Lindzey Hall, and The Biddle School."

"I'm sorry."

"Tell Mr. Veasey that there are a couple of very nervous federal agents who have a strong interest in my investigation. I am sure that I could easily convince them that Mr. Veasey is already very much involved."

"Who the hell are you?" Suddenly there was a male voice on the line. Veasey had cut in. Or he had been listening all the time. He sounded more frightened than angry.

"A private investigator. I have been hired to find out about Lindzey Hall's past."

"What does that have to do with me?"

"He was your buddy, remember?"

"You're going to fuck everything up!" He was practically screaming.

"Perhaps. But you can prevent that by talking to me."

"You can't come here." He asked me for a brief resume. A few names to check. He was nervous.

"Where do we meet?"

"Call me back in 20 minutes from a pay phone. If you're not kosher, you better find a place to hide. Some place where they don't speak English."

Twenty minutes later the secretary gave me an address: 124 East 9th Street. Apartment 4D at 8 p.m. She reminded me to make sure that I was unaccompanied.

I had the day to kill. The Pontiac was still with me. I didn't want to waste the day. I had the feeling that Veasey could open a window on Hall. I had no idea what he could tell me, but the tone of his voice told me he had something. I got a roll of dimes from the cashier. I called William Bell in Media.

"Mr. Bell?"

"Dean Ryckman suggested that I contact you about a story I am doing on Lindzey Hall, the congressman."

"Yes, Dean Ryckman?" The voice sounded wary. "What do you want from me? I really didn't know him very well."

"It's not really just about Biddle. I am trying to fill in some gaps in Hall's biography."

"Why not ask him?"

"I've tried, believe me. It seems Congressman Hall wants only the authorized version to be published. I'm trying to find another angle."

"So what do you want from me?"

"Dean Ryckman said that you told him you had seen Hall during the war. Is that right?"

"Yes, but it was just an accident. We met briefly in Paris right after VE-Day."

He was really being careful, but he didn't hang up. He wanted to tell me something. I just had to be careful not to scare him off.

"Do you recall what outfit he was in?"

"He wasn't in uniform."

"But he was in the service, wasn't he?"

"I believe so. At least that's the impression—I mean he was with a full bird colonel who seemed to be taking orders from him."

"What kind of orders?"

"Let me explain. I was a translator during the war. Mostly what I read were enemy newspapers and magazines, reading between the lines, trying to gauge the mood of the people, that sort of thing. Occasionally I was given something a little juicier, like a military document or something like that. This one day I was told to translate some newspaper columns by a Belgian collaborator. It was all hush-hush. I was not to show the articles to anyone and I was to hand deliver the translations to the COS."

"COS?"

"It was a new on me, too. They never even told me what it meant. But they had real juice. My major acted like a waiter at a Hollywood wedding when they showed up."

"Hall was with them?"

"He was running the show. At least in Paris. The same old Hall."

"What do you mean?"

"He wasn't that happy to see me there. He had the same chip on his shoulder he always did."

"About what?"

"About everything. From his first day at Biddle. I tried to be his friend, you know. He acted like I was his valet. He did in Paris, too. When I gave him the translations, I thought he was going to tip me. But he didn't. He just had that look. My father owned a store, too. It wasn't such a disgrace."

I wanted to keep him on track. "What kind of translations?"

"Oh, yeah. He told me that it was just a routine background check. But they don't send two guys in suits and a full bird colonel for a routine background check."

"What was in the articles?"

"Nothing really. Propaganda. The sort you'd expect from a collaborator. We're not talking military secrets here, just the usual anti-Semitic drivel that they all wrote. Some swipes at Americans. What barbarians we are. That sort of thing."

"Do you remember the name of the man who wrote the articles?"

"Sure."

"Yeah?"

"Jacques de Paul. Look, my name isn't going to appear anywhere, is it? I just realized that this could still be classified. I want this off the record."

"Don't worry. Your name won't—"

"Look, I hope you find something that hurts him. What with what he's trying to do to Biddle and everything? And all for no reason. It's breaking Ryckman's heart. That school is his life. He had nothing to do with Hall. It makes no sense. I just can't afford—"

"I know."

"I hope you can bring him down a peg."

"Maybe."

"Don't forget about my name. You got this from official records, if you're asked. Understand? If he ever finds out, I'll never teach again."

"No one will know we talked unless you tell them."

I left the restaurant and headed for the movie theater a

block down the street. I didn't even check the marquee to see what was playing. I knew that my companions would know I was trying to lose them, but there would be exits on two sides to the street. One would have to cover the front. I had a fifty-fifty chance of losing them. If I failed, I had time to try another. Eventually I had to win. I was lucky on the first try. I got a cab as soon as I was out the back exit. Then I took a subway. Randomly, I took the third stop and then another cab. Then another subway and the second stop. It was kind of fun. I really didn't have to lose them until I was close to my appointment with Veasey. But I didn't like the thought that they were watching me. When I finally emerged from the cab, I was in front of the New York Public Library. I went in. I patted my chest to make sure the diary and the *Book of Judith* were still there.

I'd always liked libraries. They reminded me of churches. They had the reverence and the silence without all the sadness. They were great places to think. When I sat down at the long wooden table with the row of green-shaded lamps, all I could hear were the footsteps of the man who pushed the returned books on a nearly silent cart. Across from me about five places down was an old bearded man hunched over a stack of books. Occasionally he would sneak a bite of something from his coat. I was sure that the staff knew that he brought food into the library. But they ignored him. A regular.

I was thinking about ways I could use this time as I removed my coat. I could try to find out what C.O.S. meant. Or C.D.A. I could get some more information on Veasey. As I tried to figure out what my best course of action would be, I felt Lara's journal in my coat. It was like finding your favorite book again. The fact that it was probably my best lead mattered less than it was a chance to read Lara's words again. I wanted it to be like church. I wanted her to make me feel clean again. I wanted to feel her life and not see her death. So I began to read. I skipped through quotes from favorite poets and selections from stories she admired. And sections that sounded Biblical

And she put on her garments of gladness and her

rings, and her earrings, and all her ornaments, and decked herself bravely to allure the eyes of all men that should see her.

I checked the *Book of Judith* and found the same quote right at the beginning. It appeared that Lara was using that book as a how-to book for transforming herself into what?

Then I began to notice something I hadn't seen before. Just before the point she began to write in code the entries were more forced. There wasn't the same honesty. Or the same naturalness. At first, I thought she was being caught up with being a writer, but then I began to suspect that they were phony entries. What I did know of her led me to think that she would not waste her time on entries like: *September is beautiful this year. It has always been my favorite month. I will try to meet each day as if it were the first day of September.*

There were some little snippets of nature essays and brief encounters with fellow students. It was more diary now. Then one caught my eye: *Saw Jack D. and Paul B. at Gully Hall. Didn't see me. I'll see them again at Stag River.*

This was code. Or was I beginning to read into it? Jack D. Paul B. = Jacques de Paul (B?)—Belgian. Too much for a coincidence. This was the clever Lara. But why the code? Was this de Paul still around? I began to understand Lara's first code. It was fairly simple, almost girlish—based on puns, homonyms, rhyming slang, and skipping words. Something, I knew, happened on the first of September. Hall and de Paul were involved. The other code was more code like. I couldn't crack it.

I spent the rest of the afternoon trying to translate Lara's journal. She did see herself as some sort of spy. She had made two trips to Greenwich—*chartreuse witch on Halloween.* She had discovered something about the C.O.S. *Candy O'Sullivan?* There were times when I thought *I* had made the whole code up. But I couldn't stop. Most of what I found simply verified what I already knew. It was clear that she thought she was on to something big and that her new secret lover would be just as excited about it. I needed to crack that other code. I needed to know why she had switched codes. I needed to find out who the new lover was. I needed to go back to UCONN.

By the time I began to think that Lara was on to the Lindbergh kidnapper I knew that I had spent too much time with the books. I got up, walked around the reading room, and looked out the window. There I could see a man in a dark brown coat leaning over a blue Pontiac that contained two familiar shapes. They looked they were pretending to talk about the weather. I knew I had to make better plans to shake them. I had to get to Veasey's undetected.

ာထာ

By six thirty, I was sitting in a small bar about two blocks from Veasey's building after a journey that had taken me from Manhattan to Brooklyn and the edges of Queens. The 236 Bar had the feel of the neighborhood. Dark wood and red imitation leather. There were Christmas decorations hung haphazardly over the mirror behind the bar. But there was nothing festive about them. Perhaps they never came down. The bartender watched over the whiskey in your glass without feeling he had to get involved in your life. On the television over the bar was a show about the aftermath of Stalin's death that nobody was paying attention to, but the reception was good. More than two million Russians had passed in front of Stalin's bier before the funeral. And about ten thousand tanks. The Kremlin looked like Frankenstein's castle. That was what I got from the show.

Overall, it was a good bar with a great jukebox. I listened to scratchy recordings of Ella Fitzgerald with Chick Webb's Orchestra. Even though the "real" jazz buffs preferred Billy Holiday, I still always loved Ella's voice. "You Showed Me the Way," took me back a long, long time. A time when you still could believe that there was some brown haired woman somewhere in a red silk dress who could bring magic to your life. I thought of Christy. Maybe you still could.

I kept my eye on the window and watched everyone who came in. I wanted to be the only stranger in this bar. I had been lazy before. I should have known that there would be more than two guys after me.

There had to be at least four guys, or maybe six?

I felt like a fool, thinking I was leading two guys on a merry wild goose chase through the streets of Old New York. Luckily, it was so cold that the streets were almost deserted. It was easy to keep an eye out for any of my escorts. I seemed to be alone. But I had to be a little more careful. It had been a real shock when I saw them all outside the library. Most of my work involved local cops. They were not a real challenge. Easy to read, their motivations were virtually identical. They wanted to make it home for dinner and not do anything they would have to write up.

Lawrence was right. I was in a different league. I was the rookie out of the triple A who still didn't know how to hit a curve ball. It didn't matter how many fastballs I had knocked out of the park in Denver or Rochester. This was the big leagues. I had to show Sexton and Lawrence that I belonged up here. So far, I was 0 for three.

I tried to figure out what Lara thought she was doing. She certainly had the sense that she was on a mission. But what could she know or find out? She was in the middle of something big. Big enough for feds to follow me up and down the East Coast. To scare a tough mob lawyer. To murder a girl. There just were too many pieces missing from the puzzle to see any kind of picture. Then I thought of Lara. She was willing to risk her life for something. Something. I patted my breast pocket in the hope that what was contained in her journal would immediately make itself known to me.

I left the bar and walked a few blocks in the wrong direction, keeping an eye out for a tail. I figured that I wouldn't see the Pontiac anymore. They had already sent their message with it in front of the library. I checked windows in the buildings on Eighth Street and crossed the street several times. When I was sure, as sure as I could be, that I was free of the watchful eyes of the federal government, I turned toward Ninth Street. Before I got to the building, I saw the police cars. There were four of them, surrounding an ambulance. A small crowd had formed a circle in the cold, rubbing their hands together as the police accompanied the stretcher to the street. The crowd looked like it was applauding.

Even without seeing the body, I knew it was Veasey. It had to be.

⌀⌀⌀

I made it back to Stamford. I no longer cared whether I was being followed. I tried to think of whatever it could have been that Veasey knew. Did it go back to Biddle? Who was Jacques de Paul? Was Hall tied to the mob? To Josef Stalin? What had Veasey done to Hall or vice versa? Had they been lovers? Had they robbed a bank?

At that point, it seemed that anything could be possible or relevant.

The one thing I did know was that I had stumbled into something big. Whatever Lara had discovered, it threatened more than just a congressman's reputation. No matter how much juice Hall had, he couldn't get the C.D.A., whatever that was, to cover it up unless it was tied to something political.

"Controversial Lawyer Slain," read the headline in the *New York Daily News* the next day. The story suggested that Veasey had been the victim of a mob hit. A .22-caliber bullet to the back of the head, the mob signature. Nothing was missing from the apartment, leased in the name of Sylvia Hunt, a secretary with Veasey's law firm. She had been visiting a relative in New Jersey. Very neat and all wrong I was sure. The question that kept eating at me was how they knew I was on to him. Was I that bad? I went to the cigar store around the corner. They had three pay phones.

"Christy?"

"Varian? I'm surprised to hear from you. Really surprised."

"Why?"

"After last night and—were you on the level with me?"

"Sure. About everything? Were you?"

"I mean it. This is serious. You caught me by surprise."

"What happened?"

"Two federal agents showed up at school this morning. They wanted to know about you. I thought Ryckman would have a heart attack. They made it seem like you were some sort of spy, trying to get the goods on an important American.

They said you wanted to smear Hall. They made it seem like you were working for the—

"Communists? Why not? You don't believe that do you?"

"If you just listened to what they said, it made a lot of sense."

"Did you tell them about Veasey?"

"They made a lot of sense. They can be very frightening. You did lie to Ryckman. I just couldn't be sure. I still don't know. This is all over my head. I thought I could trust you. I still do in a way. I was scared. They were very frightening. And they are the government. The dean begged them to keep the school out of it. He's suffering so much. They promised if we would cooperate. That was the only way. You didn't kill him, did you?"

"No, I never even got to see him. But there were feds all over me. They knew exactly what I was doing in New York before I knew."

"I'm sorry."

"It's okay. I have the feeling they knew without your telling them. It was probably a good thing you told them. Did you tell them about last night?"

"Of course not. I'm not about to tell them I took a stranger to bed. Even if you are not a spy. How does that make me look? I told them you asked for a list of the class of '37. I said you circled Veasey's name and asked for his number. Then as far as they were concerned, I just let you into Ryckman's office. You are on the level, aren't you?"

"Yes. That was quick thinking. Whatever you do, don't tell anybody, understand, anybody. Not for my sake, but for yours. Understand? All you know is I said I was a writer and you took me into Ryckman's office."

"What do you mean? What can they do?"

"Who knows? But you'll be okay, if they don't know anything. Veasey is dead. That's warning enough as far as I'm concerned. You didn't mention Bell. He's scared already."

"I forgot all about him."

"Did Ryckman?"

"He was too stunned to say anything except, 'How can things get any worse?'"

used to make jokes about how awful he looked in navy blue and that was it. Before Pearl Harbor, he was going to teach philosophy. Now he lived it. From what I could tell, his philosophy was an equal mixture of pragmatism and paranoia. Louis's independent situation allowed him to indulge his twin passions for modern art and political intrigue. He seemed to know everything that was going to happen in Washington at least two weeks before it did.

With a subtle hand signal, Louis let Amor and Psyche know that I was welcome. Their ears relaxed, but they didn't move from their statuesque poses.

"Varian, what a welcome surprise. Let me show you my new Malevich." Louis was always happiest when he had a new piece of art to show off, especially one he expected would make me look foolish.

"Sure. I can't wait."

He ushered me through the open door. Leaning against the otherwise bare white wall was a small canvas about two feet across painted with a red square and a black square that abutted each other. The red one looked like it was trying to push the black one out of the picture.

"What do you think?"

"The red square is smaller than the black square. And it's winning."

"Yes, yes, you are so perceptive when it comes to art. Why do you think Stalin hated it so much when it was on his side?"

"I have no idea. Louis, they're two squares. Nice squares, I can't imagine better squares, but I think they're wasted on me. What's next? Triangles? Trapezoids? I think art loses something when there is no pubic hair or big breasts."

"A true connoisseur. But what makes you think there is no pubic hair in this Malevich?"

"Just a guess. But I could be wrong."

"It's good to see you, my friend. I've missed our stimulating discussions about art."

"Yeah, me too."

The one area of art we did agree on was music, which was the real basis for our friendship. It was the one place where we didn't play these little games. On a little black metal table

Louis had one of the latest hi-fidelity systems. He was as proud of that as he was of his art collection. Unlike my record player, which had weathered the Depression and World War II in somebody's house before it made its way to Gilley's Used Furniture Store, this really was a "system," as Louis described it. With wires going everywhere, it had "woofers" and "tweeters" which to me sounded like a kid's terms for intestinal gas. But to Louis these words seemed like the language of high poetry. Two large speakers about six feet from each other connected to two separate and enormous glowing amplifiers. The whole set up looked more like lab equipment than a music maker, but I had to admit that it made my "system" sound like soup cans tied to a piece of string.

"Here's the new Miles Davis. I just got it." He lifted the needle to the "turntable," no mere record player for him, with the concentration of a man about to de-fuse a bomb. I could see him holding his breath. He was a big man who never seemed to be very big until he stood right next to you. He had to lean way over to reach the system. He adjusted a few of the many knobs on the front of his "amplifiers."

Then I heard the plaintive cry of a trumpet filling the room as it searched through the whole vocabulary of pain in some musical thesaurus. At times, it seemed that I could literally feel the air on my cheek as it swirled from the mouth of the trumpet. For the first time I could feel what the jazz critics meant when they described Miles Davis's trumpet style in terms of Billie Holiday's phrasing. Just when you thought that Miles had figured out the melody, he would suddenly become aware of the triteness of the song he was playing and brief spurts of harsh and ugly sounds would emerge, economically sabotaging the very emotion he struggled to express. It was a remarkable performance.

Louis played "Yesterdays" again. "Everything is as good as this."

He brought me a bottle of English beer and sat across from me in a chair made of chrome and leather. I sat on a simple metal bench, which showed the marks of the grinder that had shaped its surface.

"What brings you here?"

"A case. Actually, it's a couple of cases with some major complications."

I started at the beginning and recounted the stories of Lara Greenbaum and Lindzey Hall as accurately as I could remember. As usual, Louis did not interrupt. At these times, I always thought that Louis would have made a very successful psychoanalyst, particularly now that it was fashionable to be neurotic. There was just the right mixture of the intellectual snob and detective in that profession. Louis could use his paintings instead of inkblots. I finished my summary.

"I have a few questions. Do you have Lara Greenbaum's diary and the other book?"

"Yes."

"Can I take a look at them?"

"Sure. It's the only real evidence I've got. Just—"

"Be careful? Really? Thanks for telling me, otherwise I would have probably given it to Amor to play with."

"I mean it could be dangerous. I told you I thought I had lost my tail and they followed me anyway. And I am not an easy mark."

"My boy, if these men do work for our esteemed government, I am sure that that vehicle you drive has a small box attached somewhere in the undercarriage that allows them to monitor your movements from quite a distance. If I am correct, they know you are here already. You have implicated me just by being here. So you might as well share everything. I am not concerned. I also have a few electrical tricks of my own I would love to try out. In any case, I will decide on the level of risk to assume."

"Another adventure for the super-spy?"

"Oh, really? Are you prepared to be my Doctor Watson?"

"Yeah, right. I have a hard time writing my signature."

"Okay, enough fantasy. Have you heard Clifford Brown's 'Cherokee'? No other trumpet player has his exquisite taste."

While Louis sorted through his records I looked again at the new painting. I still didn't get it.

"I think you're right about this Veasey character. I knew nothing about this Hall fellow, but Veasey's death seemed phony to me just from the newspaper account. A textbook mob killing. Except for where it took place. A ride to Jersey. An Italian restaurant. Not likely in an apartment, even a mistress's." Louis went back and forth between Clifford Brown's careful phrasing. "He's not like Davis—more Mozart than Chopin," and Lara's case.

"It was a little too much of a coincidence for me," I said. "And a little too close. I was around the corner. And he *was* scared as soon as he heard Hall's name."

Louis looked at me for what seemed like a long time. "You are very lucky that they were impatient. I think what was planned was a double homicide. They were waiting for you. Maybe something happened. Perhaps Veasey got nervous waiting for you and spotted them. My guess is they wanted it to look like you shoot him and then he shoots you. This Sexton and Lawrence know you carry a gun. You're in Pennsylvania. Poking around. They warn you. You're targeted. They were setting you up."

"That's what it feels like. What do you think they know about Veasey?"

"Maybe they didn't know anything. They didn't have to. You put him on the list. And you were good enough to lead them to him and give them the setup."

"They didn't look that smart."

"They aren't. Or you would be dead already. You have to worry about the ones they are working for. I think you are involved in some very big deal here, Varian. Highest levels, as they say. Listen."

We sat in silence for a while, listening to Clifford Brown and sipping a brew the color of root beer.

"Why would they want to cover up the murder of a young girl?"

"You *are* an innocent, Varian. Not just about art, but the world. You assume that order, justice, and law itself are the normal state of things. And that evil or disorder pops up here and there to disrupt the normal flow of events like a thunderstorm in the middle of a lazy summer day. There is no normal state, as you would have it, except among the innocent like yourself. You think you are an outsider. But despite what you think, you're exactly like the ones who work by the clock and sacrifice their lives for their kid's education. You're just like the ones who buy a house on the bet they don't get cancer before it's paid off. The only difference is you don't even have a house or kids. Like them, you don't have the slightest understanding of how the world works."

He looked up at the ceiling as if he were waiting for applause. All of his pronouncements had the same oratorical style—a political rally á la Huey Long or a lecture in Political Philosophy 101—even if he was talking to just one person. I knew I was stepping into it, but I couldn't let what he said go by, even if it had nothing to do with Lara's death. I had to answer him, like throwing a punch at a guy you know is going to beat the shit out of you, but whom you can't let keep insulting you.

"Come on. Everybody down here among the 'common people' knows how rich and powerful the rich and powerful are. And frankly we don't give a shit until they step on our toes. We have ours. There is more money than dirt in this country. Even the poor people are rich, at least compared to almost every other place. What could be worth all these games—find the red under the rug, where's the radical in the basement? It's just stupid."

"Of course, it's stupid. But think about this—when I was in Europe there were days when I considered a pair of dry socks the only item worth using my energy or wits to obtain. I would lie in that dirt and think about a night's sleep in a warm bed with a bright woolen blanket. Dry socks and a warm bed. As the song says, 'who could ask for anything more?'"

"Wait a minute! I thought you were in the Navy?"

"What gave you that idea? In any case, you interrupt. So the war ended and I had a few memorable nights' sleep, extremely satisfying simple meals, and an ample supply of socks. And you know what? It wasn't enough. I would venture to say that most days when you wake you are not as grateful for your warm bed as you thought you would be. Now you throw away food that would have brought you to the heights of ecstasy just a few years ago. So after all the rhetoric about world peace, should we be surprised when snakes go back to acting like snakes? There are men so devoted to their own sense of power that they will sacrifice anyone and anything to maintain it—a young girl, a prep school, a brilliant scientist, even a private investigator."

He didn't expect a response.

"Louis, you really want to look like the world weary cynic, but—"

"But what! And what do you know of the cynics?"

"Only what you're probably gonna to tell me."

"Very good answer. You have spared yourself a lecture. The cynics are worth paying attention to. However, you are wrong about me. I am anything but world-weary. I love this world. It's always exactly and only as awful as I expect it to be. I just understand better than you how it works, that's all. I know that, when you come right down to it, nothing makes sense. You can count on that. You can't trust anyone because we all are completely predictable."

"A paradox!"

"Correct. A plus. Now, you know, we must find out more about Lara Greenbaum's political conversion. Something happened to turn her into Mata Hari. From what you told me I have no doubt that she was a remarkable young lady, but it still strains credibility that she could have discovered something so damaging to Hall that it was worth her life, and that she did it completely on her own."

"Browder?"

"At least. Perhaps a catalyst. Find out more about her work at school. Students are notorious for revealing their enthusiasms. I think this other little book also offers some clues. Do you know the story of Judith?"

"Not really."

"An army led by a general named Holofernes is about to destroy Israel and a beautiful young widow, Judith, uses her wiles to get into the general's tent, presumably with the promise of sensual delight. Instead of the expected carnal pleasure, Holofernes loses his head, literally, thanks to Judith's skillful knife play. Judith then uses the head to rally the troops and defeat the invaders. Sound like something that might inspire a beautiful young Jewess in occupied France?"

"The girl in the book liked to use a knife."

"I am not surprised."

"Do you think Lara was inspired by the book?" I asked.

"Obviously. I haven't read it, but just check out the marginalia. Lara is an enthusiast."

"But America isn't occupied by a foreign army."

"Don't be so literal. I am sure when we look closely enough we will figure it out. There is something here. Maybe more than is in the diary. You know the French have always understood, better than we have, the power of a woman's sexuality. If you ever get a chance, take a look at Courbet's *L'Origine du monde*. You'll like it. No squares, just the voluptuous triangle between a woman's legs. Courbet understood Judith and Lara."

Louis flipped through the *Book of Judith* while I tried to put the pieces that were as confusing as Louis's art together.

"What about C.O.S. and this C.D.A.?"

"We are being buried by abbreviations. It's the modern disease. Remember the good old days when there were only two—the FBI and IRS?"

"And AT&T? And RCA. And—"

"Okay. Point taken."

"C.O.S & C.D.A.?"

"Everybody wants to be in on the intelligence game. Each of the services has its own little spy wing and the Defense Department has one big one. The CIA is brand new, of course, with its myriad little alphabetized arms. There are agencies within agencies like Chinese boxes. If these guys are working for Hall, my guess is that the legislative branch feels left out from all the cloak and dagger stuff. There's probably some obscure provision in some bill for the erection of a bridge in Tucson that also authorizes some kind of congressional agency to protect us from alien ideas. That won't be hard to check out. Hall's war operation might be a little tougher. There were a lot of operations, especially at the end of the war, which were very hidden in the name of security. Hardly anybody knows about them. Most of them had to do with Nazi scientists, rockets, and A-bombs, that sort of thing. This sounds different. I'll see what I can do. Pete McClellen has a contact in Naval History. They hate army operations. Maybe he'll spill the proverbial beans, especially if there is a little dirt. Excuse the mixed metaphors."

"So you think Hall is involved?"

"I would hope so. I would love to put a few dents in his armor. I certainly don't mind anyone looking into the sorry state of college education. It's been a scandal for years. But I don't think his not-so-subtle attempts to create a modern version of the Inquisition are the answer, do you?"

"To tell you the truth I haven't thought much about it."

"My point exactly," he said.

"Why didn't you take advantage of the GI Bill after the war, when you still had the blush of youth on your cheeks?" One of the continuing themes of Louis's conversation was my lack of formal education. It amused him so I tolerated it.

"I thought about it. I just couldn't see myself wearing one of those sweaters with the letters on them. Or a beanie." I couldn't tell him the real reasons even if they made no more sense than the fear of beanies. They were just too personal.

"Excellent reasons for remaining essentially uneducated. Despite all the problems with higher education, it remains one of the few areas in human life where you are allowed the privilege of diverting time from practical concerns while thinking about the meaning of things. Life interrupts soon enough with all of its worries about mortgages, transmissions, and kids' teeth. When you are in college, you can spend a week thinking about what Williams might have meant when he said that 'so much depends upon a red wheelbarrow.' You start to wonder why time goes in just one direction. And no one thinks you are a lazy lout. In fact, you might even be judged 'deep' or 'profound.' It's an experience not to be missed."

I thought about Lara and how excited she was listening to poetry being read aloud in class. "I had a lot of time to think about the meaning of things in Europe."

"Yes, but you see questions raised when there are mortar shells whizzing through the air can hardly be disinterested. Once when a mortar landed uncomfortably near me, a man named Silverman convinced himself he had become a Roman Catholic. It made perfect sense to him. See? The ideal can never be attained when the real is too much with us. That's why campuses are so delightfully artificial. They are playgrounds—the Coney Islands of the Mind."

"You make it sound so...fun."

"But it is."

"If I spent too much time thinking about things, I might become interested in paintings of little black & red squares."

"As well you might. By the way, why are you sitting on my favorite table?" He laughed as I got up and looked for another place to sit.

"You see things aren't always what they appear to be. Let me get you another beer."

I watched Louis leave the large open room that was the center of the house. All of the other rooms were much smaller. The kitchen had been designed with the efficiency of a small boat, the bedrooms looked like dorm rooms, but this room did have a kind of grandeur, despite its emptiness. Through the wall of windows you could see down a thickly forested hill into a small ravine. I was suddenly reminded of the countryside near the German border.

CHAPTER 12

The next day I decided to check out a couple of Louis's hunches and to look further into Lindzey Hall. He would look into the C.O.S. and try to figure out how this Jacques de Paul might be involved in this mess. I wasn't convinced that Louis was right about how the government was always the answer when it came to conspiracies, but I had nothing better to work on. I couldn't stay in my office because I was sure that my line had been tapped. When I checked my car for the device Louis had alluded to all that I found was a little smudge under the rear fender that could have been something or nothing. It was easy to become as suspicious as Louis. He saw something meaningful in the fact that TUMS spelled backwards was SMUT. "Of course they knew!"

I stopped the car near Myrtle Street and ran into "my second office" at Baker's Tickets. It was a lot easier than having a real office with a secretary. Binny was a bookie with four phone lines so I always got my messages as well as a few useful tips on sure things at Roosevelt or Yonkers. And all I had to do for this fine service, he told me, was to collect now and then on delinquent accounts. It's funny how fast the word got around. After the first two collections, Binny never bothered me again to make a collection. He was happy. He continued to take my messages. And I was happy I didn't have to do that kind of work anymore.

Binny said there was a message to call Dave Fenner. I decided to head for Fenner, Hershey & Reed in person. Fenner had contacts in Washington. Like Louis he often knew what was happening behind the scenes. Anyway, I had nothing better to do.

The law offices of Fenner, Hershey & Reed were thick

with the leathery smell of money. The secretaries talked in the hushed whispers of ushers seating dignitaries at a state funeral. They pronounced everything as if you were hard of hearing or spoke Hungarian. The partners had done studies to determine everything from the style of their hair to the length of their skirts, from the width of their ties to the color of their suits. It was all calculated to convey a sense of confidence in the firm. They were going to be the new law firm for the new age. To watch the traffic in the office you couldn't prove them wrong.

Each time an office door opened, I was still surprised to see a man in his thirties behind the desk rather than a gray-haired scion of the sort of family that referred to John D. Rockefeller as "Little Johnny." It was ironic that, despite appearances, so much of their work involved the seedier aspects of Stamford business. This was a "new money" firm. There was no old money nervousness about "The Business," as David called it. "We don't *practice* law."

They had a reputation of approaching negotiations with the subtlety of a ten-wheeler switching lanes without brakes. Despite their reputation, I had found them to be basically honest. They never asked me to go over the line. They wanted everything I could find, as long as it was legal. They played hard, but they didn't want anything to come back to haunt them.

David Fenner, looking snappy in his dark blue suit and bright red-striped tie, was sitting behind a large modern glass and steel desk, the kind that made it impossible to hide one's mess. I never understood why you would want a desk that had one little drawer, large enough to hold your pen and cigarette lighter and, possibly, a small .22. Louis would have loved it. Fenner seemed surprised to see me.

"Varian?"

"You called me."

"I heard you were in Philadelphia."

"Who told you?"

"That's what I want to talk to you about. I had a call from Washington. They want to know what you're up to."

I had the feeling that David already knew most of my story, but I told him as much of it as I could without revealing everything about Lara Greenbaum's murder. I went through the visit to Abington. Sexton and Lawrence played a prominent part. Since I didn't know much about de Paul I left him out until I found out what David knew. Before I could bring him completely up to date, he stopped me.

"You have really gotten yourself into a mess, haven't you?"

"If having high mucky mucks interested in your every move is a mess, I guess so. But I didn't start the mess. I didn't kill a little girl."

He nodded. "When I got the call a couple of days ago, I guessed you were still in Pennsylvania. I didn't know anything, so I couldn't tell them anything. They made it clear they want you to go away. If you don't go away, they will do their best to send you away. They were trying to put pressure on me to put pressure on you. I told them I would talk to you. I made no promises."

"Do you know who *they* really are?"

"Not really. Who knows anymore?"

"I'm sure Hall is involved somehow."

Fenner nodded. He dropped his soft voice down to the point where he was almost inaudible. "I had another call. I have a friend who is an FBI agent. He called out of the blue, yesterday, not so long after this other guy. They are nervous about Hall, too."

"Why? He seems to be doing their work for them."

"That's not how they see it. He talked in so many circles, 'scenarios' he called them that I couldn't really tell what he wanted. He was trying to feel me out. As best as I could tell, he thought that this other guy thought that I had hired you to look into Hall and he wanted to know if that was true. They think in very complicated ways. I asked him point blank what his call had to do with you. He said your name had come up in discussions. You know what I think? Whatever is going on I think you have gotten yourself right in the middle of a Washington war."

"Hall's making the FBI nervous? Why would a super patriot make the FBI nervous?"

"McCarthy is going after the State Department and the UN. Who lost China? And the big question—how did we find ourselves in a virtual stalemate with Russia when they had only about twenty rubles and eight loaves of bread when the war ended? Nobody is safe when they start looking for answers."

"I still don't see what's to be gained."

"McCarthy has changed what used to be a gentleman's game, at least in public. All these guys have always hated each other, but their wars always took place behind closed doors. McCarthy started throwing hand grenades in the hallowed halls. And he made hay, just by picking big targets. You can now make a career out of just asking a few ugly questions. You don't even have to have any answers. It's gets you in the papers. It puts you on the television. Just wonder out loud in front of twenty reporters, 'How did all these commies get so entrenched in high places? Who is undermining the American way of life?' You get headlines."

"But that still doesn't explain why they would care."

"Look, McCarthy is heading for a fall. The Senate is just waiting for him to make the big mistake. You can't hold up a phony picture of a US Senator standing next to a communist and expect everybody to buy it. Especially senators. Even in this climate, he has thrown too many grenades. He's stupid. I don't think Hall is."

"I guess I am missing something."

"They just might be looking out for their own asses. There is certainly dirt there. Maybe Hall has some. I don't know. But I do know they are very nervous. They don't necessarily like rising stars."

"But these guys seem like small potatoes next to the FBI."

"But nobody likes Hoover. He only has fear, no love, no loyalty. Have you ever heard of Hoover's files?"

"Rumors about them. I always thought it was a myth."

"They are more than rumors. And, even if they don't really exist with all the dirt that people imagine is there, the threat of a file's existence is enough. Hoover is supposed to have thick files on every congressman, senator, supreme court justice, even presidents, down to crossing guards, and janitors since he took over the Bureau. They are supposed to contain records from every little crime from padding the postal machine totals to getting spanked by the chambermaid. It's all supposed to be there. Most of it is just bluff, I'm sure. But if someone waved a six-inch thick file in front of your nose, you'd have to wonder what was in it, right? They're the most powerful pieces of paper in Washington. And that's saying something. Just the slightest threat of exposure is enough to make the most outspoken defender of democracy run for cover. This makes Hoover the most feared man in Washington and the most hated. They keep Hoover right where he wants to be." He paused and stared right past me. "What if the files were vulnerable? Who would support Hoover then?"

"Wouldn't it have to be someone with no file who could take him on?"

"Or a missing one?"

"Missing?"

"It seems to be the case with a certain file. The one thing that Hoover has going for him is the protection of those files. If someone has figured out how to get to those files, everything in Washington changes. In a weird way, Hoover's having files on everybody makes for stability and security. Everyone's equally vulnerable. That's why everybody is nervous and you seem to be in the middle of it."

"I wish I knew what I was in the middle of. So Hall has spies in the FBI?"

"Apparently. At least one. That was my friend's tip-off. A few months ago an agent was adding some information to Hall's file when he couldn't locate it. He reported it to his superior and all hell broke loose. That means they have lost their leverage on Hall and they have no idea what he is up to. They don't care what it is, they want it stopped and order restored. They are interested in you because Hall's men are interested in you."

"So are they going to step in and investigate Lara's murder? I'll turn it over to the FBI in a minute."

"That's not the way it works. To tell you the truth they are interested in Lara's killer only if it helps them understand Hall. So far, they are willing to follow you from a distance, but that's all. If they come down on Hall before they know what he's up to, they might force his hand. You know, he launches an attack and then blames the FBI for retaliating against him by trying to link him to Lara's death. But if you do their work for them, they don't have to worry. The sense I got was that if you found something you should contact them. Then maybe they'd do something."

"Then, maybe, huh."

"If Hall has something planned, they don't want to antagonize him until they are protected. It's just the way things are in the nineteen fifties. The glorious Atomic Age. And they say our profession is sleazy."

"It is."

"I know. But we don't wrap ourselves in the flag."

There was a lot to take in. What started out as a search for a missing girl was leading me into...I had no idea. I was still a little confused. "Is Hall really that much of a threat to them?"

"The FBI wouldn't have let my friend give me this much if they weren't convinced that the threat was real. They aren't very fond of sharing."

"I don't know anything about any of this. And I don't care. What's the difference between them? I just want to find Lara's killer. This government stuff is—"

"Crazy. I know."

"No, just beyond me."

He sat back in his chair. It felt like I had stepped in my bathtub for a nice soak and suddenly found that I couldn't touch bottom. I could find a killer. I wasn't about to bring down a government. "This is a little overwhelming. What do they really want from me?"

"Who?"

"Anybody."

"Basically you're the man in the middle. You could always just choose not to play their game. That would be my advice. No offense, but, as good as you are, are you really equipped for something like this?"

"I don't think so, but I don't really have a choice. Do I go to the Greenbaums and say, 'I think I know who had something to do with your daughter's murder, but it's a little out of my league.'"

"But that might just be the truth."

"I know."

"Is it worth your life?"

"I'm not sure it will go that far." I didn't believe that. I knew about Jack Veasey. I was sure Fenner didn't believe it either.

"If you want my advice as a friend and as a lawyer—stay out of it. If I'm right and Hall and Hoover do go after each other, one of them will lose and lose badly. There will be other casualties as well—somebody in the middle like you. In the end it will probably not even be noticed. There'll be a story explaining how a faulty exhaust pipe or food poisoning or something took the life of an insurance investigator who was also a veteran. Take off and...I don't know...at least you will be all right. You could check out somebody for me in Mexico City. It should take you a week or two. But if you're smart you could make it last a little longer. No one would blame you. It's the smart thing to do."

"I appreciate the offer. I do." I knew he was right. "It's just one of those things. I gotta keep at it."

"Why?"

"To tell you the truth, it's just not fair. Maybe I'm acting like a boy scout, but this girl deserved something better. The Greenbaums deserve better."

I knew that Fenner wanted to scare me away from the case, but I felt like the man who had to choose between the lady and the tiger except in my case there was no lady, just two tigers. I didn't trust the FBI much more than I trusted Hall and his boys. If I found something really damaging, I would just be another threat. I knew they might feel tempted to clean the whole slate. I had a whole list of questions about Hall and de Paul. One thing about this mess made me feel a lot better. I was on the right track.

Fenner said he would tell the FBI that I thought Hall was somehow involved in Lara's murder. That might make them protective of me. He didn't want to know anymore. He had to protect himself. I understood that he would tell them what I told him. That was the deal. It was his way of saying, "Only tell me what you want them all to know."

So in the end I didn't tell him very much.

CHAPTER 13

As I left Fenner's office, I knew I had to clear my head. I was right near City Hall in the center of town. Suddenly, Stamford looked very small and quaint like a movie set. There was the town hall right in the middle of the square and the Stamford Department Store facing it, covered in lights, its windows dusted with fake snow. There were fake evergreens wrapped around the light poles topped by fake snowmen with flashing red noses. Through the speakers that blared continuously into the street, I heard the sentiments of the season. "Joy to the World." and "Peace on Earth." But I didn't feel like Scrooge anymore.

I looked at the crowds of people finishing their shopping and I wanted to believe, just as they wanted to believe. Rather I wanted to see in their faces that they believed. I didn't care about the fake holly. I wanted to believe that the real wish, the simple wish that one small gift could bring pleasure to another human being. That it was enough to sustain their humanity for another year. I didn't need a critique of materialism in a world where men like Hall and Hoover played their games of power. Sick games that took the lives of a wonderful girl like Lara or even a skunk like Jack Veasey. I would rather fret over Uncle Charlie's new pipe. Louis was wrong. I wasn't like all the rest. They were content to take what the season offered. I had no Uncle Charlie.

I really had no place to go. And I didn't know what to do next. I did know someone was probably watching me. I eyed the street and saw suspicious cars everywhere, driven by suspicious men, monitoring my every move. So I just headed out of town with my eyes glued to the rear view mirror. I was so distracted that I almost hit two pedestrians and a Sheffield

Farms milk truck. I wound up at the end of Shippan Avenue again, looking out at the Sound.

I was willing to go after Hall, even if he were a congressman, when I saw it as just a personal thing. A man helping a friend. It didn't matter how big the opponent was. But this was not the schoolyard and there was more than a bloody nose at stake. I knew it was going to be hard to walk away from this fight, even if there was some chance I could sort things out for the Greenbaums. I guess I hadn't learned anything since I was twelve.

Lara's words were still in my head. They wouldn't let me quit anyway. I remembered what Sergeant Polk used to say. "Sometimes you wake up and you know as sure as hell that you're gonna die and there's not one goddamn thing you can do about it."

He lived anyway. I hoped I would be as lucky.

The day was uniformly gray. It seemed that all the days since Lara's murder had been colored with that same shade of despair. I couldn't look at the featureless water anymore. I looked up and saw two gray seabirds hovering above, looking lost.

I started the engine and listened to the tappets clacking like a typewriter. It was just a car. Then without a clear destination in mind, I headed away from the Sound. I felt better recognizing the danger and the real possibility of my death. Things hadn't really changed all that much in ten years in the middle of peace.

It felt better just to be moving even without knowing where I was going.

On the radio I heard Charlie Barnet's "Skyliner" and I was back in 1943, on leave in New York, about to ship out. I walked from Greenwich Village to East Twenty-Third Street where I met with some buddies. I couldn't remember much about them. What I remembered was the smell of the city— clean, metallic like a bright, shiny new penny. On the corner of Fifteenth Street, a woman in a dark red dress saw me in my uniform. She was as beautiful as Merle Oberon. I convinced myself that it *was* Merle Oberon. She looked at me in my uniform and said, "Good luck, soldier."

I smiled and kept walking. Because of the gas rationing it seemed like the only cars on the road were bright yellow taxis. I loved the look of those lines of cabs heading uptown and downtown. It looked like a circus or a cartoon. It was my last day in the States for more than two years. I had no wife or girlfriend to remember. Just a thousand yellow cabs. And Merle Oberon.

When the song and my time travel ended, I realized that I was heading back up the Ridges, in the direction of Louis's house. I figured that it was too soon for him to have gotten any information for me, but, at least, I could talk to him. He knew what was going on. And if he didn't, he made it seem like he did.

As I drove up his long driveway, I knew something was wrong. Amor and Psyche did not rise to their accustomed positions instead they looked like there were sleeping. They never slept. Not at their posts. It didn't take me long to find out what had happened. They were utterly dead. Shot, probably from a distance. No one could have gotten that close to them. From the size of the entry wounds, I guessed a small caliber, high-powered rifle, one a sniper might use. Maybe with a silencer. Not much noise with a bullet just large enough to do real damage if delivered with the precision of a marksman. They'd had no chance. I didn't really know those dogs.

Louis refused to let anyone else get close. "These dogs are useful only if they have one master and no friends," he said.

I tried the door. It was open. It was bad enough to feel partly responsible for the death of a man like Veasey whom I hardly knew. But Louis? Why would they want to kill him? The lawyer might have had some damaging information about Hall, but what could Louis know? Frantically, I checked through the house. Because of the open design there were few places to hide. They had ransacked the place. I saw his precious paintings on the floor, books scattered everywhere, and records dotting the floor like black polka dots. I checked the bedroom, which had been completely overturned. My foot crunched on a broken ceramic head that looked like a Hudson Hornet when it was whole.

I called out in the vain hope that Louis had been spared. I

hoped that they had taken him to wherever they would be questioning him. At least then he might still be alive and I might find him. Although Louis always had several operations going, I knew that Amor and Psyche had to do with Lara, Hall, and the diary. What else could they be looking for? With several hundred thousand dollars' worth of art and rare books littering the house, it was clearly not a burglary.

Then I heard a noise from the kitchen. As I moved slowly toward the noise, I pulled out my gun. The noise continued. A large freestanding stove jerked slightly.

"Louis! Is that you?"

The stove moved again.

"Christ! Help me! The goddamn mechanism is stuck."

I ran over to the stove and put all my weight against it. It seemed to be stuck, but I couldn't figure out what it was stuck on.

"Stop! Stop! Oh, shit. My shirt's stuck in the drive. Hold on."

I stepped back and smoothly the stove moved out of the way. Out came Louis.

"What the hell!"

"Varian. I thought I recognized your voice." He put the sleek European automatic that he had been aiming vaguely in my direction on the stove and stood up. "Your friends are not very polite."

He turned and moved the stove back into position. I could see the sweat that stained the back of his shirt. He walked over to the liquor cabinet, took out a bottle of cognac, and offered the bottle to me.

I shook my head. "What happened?"

"As I suspected, you were followed or tracked. They probably knew you gave this to me. Did you tell anybody?"

"No!" I said.

He took the diary from his waistband.

"You saved it?"

"Of course, I saved it. If it weren't for Amor, they might have gotten it, and me. A few minutes after you left, I was putting on a Charlie Parker side when I noticed that Amor was sitting up, with his snout pointed toward that piece of woods over there. The perfect spot for a shot at the house. I was the proverbial sitting moose. It couldn't have been more than a few seconds before I heard that ominous little *plink*. And then another. I didn't even have to look. It was a good thing that I hadn't put the record on. If Bird had soloed for just a few seconds more or less, you would be considering the pathetic remains of my lifeless frame."

"Who were they? How many?" I didn't think my traveling companions from Philadelphia to New York were snipers, but the way things had been going I was ready to accept almost anything.

"I couldn't tell how many there were so I took Falstaff's advice and hid in my little spot."

"I didn't know about this."

"No reason to. I took the idea from a history of Catholicism in England. The nobles who remained loyal to the Pope all had several hiding places and escape routes built into their castles and manor houses. It seemed like a good idea. It's actually quite a commodious space. I could stay in there for days."

"They were after the diary."

"Ssh," he whispered. He pointed to his ear. He made it clear after my initial confusion that he was worried that they might have planted some listening device. Then he whispered, "I would think so. But it could be something else. Who knows what you have? It could be anything. They had to check." He downed his drink quickly without his customary examination of color and bouquet.

"Let's walk outside. Keep an eye out."

We found a spot near the side of the house where we had a good view of the woods. We weren't too exposed. The house protected our backs.

'I wish I had my rifle."

"I know what you mean."

We breathed silently together in a kind of rhythm as we continued to watch for movement in the trees. It was lucky for us that it was winter. We could see almost to the road.

"They were very efficient from the looks of it. The little fish eye I put in the floor is the only shortcoming of my little hiding place. It looks like you are looking through maple syrup. My guess is that there were only two in the house. That means maybe two more were watching the house from outside, if they were pros, and I think they were."

"How do you think they knew about the diary?"

"The roommate. Or, more than likely, somebody like you. They have been watching everything you do and know everyone you talk to. Does it really matter?"

"It might."

"Let's keep the speculations to ourselves for the time being. We have to be careful. I must attend to Amor and Psyche. Will you give me a hand?"

"Sure."

Louis went to the freestanding carport—Corbusier didn't design garages, I guessed. It looked like a miniature factory with metal sides and a roof. He quickly found a pick and shovel and walked to the hill overlooking the small valley down below. I had the strange sense again that I was back in Germany when I was on another kind of burial crew. The air was just as brittle, the trees just as barren. The feelings were the same—the numbness, the confusion, and the anger.

Louis said no prayer. He recited some lines from a poem. I remember only one "Safe quit of wars, I speed you on your way."

He raised his fist in an odd salute. Then he worked silently in the hard ground after laying the bodies of his dogs alongside each other so that their open sightless eyes seemed to be looking over the valley with an eerie kind of pleasure. Like most bodies, they seemed heavier dead than when they were alive. We tried to move as gracefully as possible to preserve their dignity, but I couldn't help grunting when I handed Amor to Louis waiting in one of the single military graves we had dug. I felt like I had violated some trust. Louis left no marker on the grave. When we had finished the task and were walking back to the house, he finally spoke.

"They made a big mistake. They do not know wrath—"

"I don't know about that, Louis. Who are you going after? The FBI? Congress? And don't forget this is my fight?"

"Not anymore."

I knew it was useless to counsel him at this point. I had my own feelings to deal with. I thought of how different I felt over the death of Lara Greenbaum. When a child was killed, you felt sad and helpless. I just wanted to find her killers. I took some pleasure imagining their suffering. But there was no rage. Even though I didn't know, and certainly didn't love, these two intimidating dogs, I could understand Louis' response. I just thought that it might be suicide to seek revenge. For both of us.

I followed Louis into the house. He motioned for me to be quiet. Like a soldier on point, he gave me hand signals as he moved through the rooms. Along the way he picked up a .45, a submachine gun, and his automatic pistol. He slipped a couple of boxes of cartridges into his pocket with the smoothness of a pickpocket.

When we finally exited the rear door, he had a small bag over his shoulder that contained some clothes and a frightening looking knife that had an edge like a toothy grin. "Your car is hot. I have another one down the road."

"What are we going to do?"

"Find out what's going on."

"I know you're pissed, but you have to think about this. You got into this because of me. It has nothing to do with you. Give me the diary and you can walk away from all this. I know there are places you could go until this blows over."

"Until you're dead, you mean?"

I tried to ignore his comment. "Amor and Psyche were dogs, Louis. Wonderful, loyal, intelligent, but just dogs. You don't have to do anything."

"True. Sometimes, my friend, you are more the fool than I had imagined. Amor and Psyche were good dogs. I had an obligation to them. But they were, as you so eloquently put it, just dogs. You seem to forget that I also was in the house. What designs do you think they had on me? Do you think if I meekly handed over the diary, they would have thanked me and wished me a long and prosperous life? Whatever is going on, the death of some eccentric art collector with questionable associations would present them with no problems as far as a cover story is concerned. I do not like to have my life threatened. Look what I did to Nazi Germany. Why should I be intimidated by a mere democracy?"

He paused. He knew I was waiting for him to indicate that he was joking. He didn't give me the satisfaction. He just said, "We have to find out what's in this diary. It has the answers. I'm sure of it."

About a half mile down the road was a detached white garage near the side of the road. The equally white colonial that it matched stood back off the road about 600 feet from the garage.

"I rent this from an interesting widow. I'm sure, like most conservatives, she is a tax dodger and an all-around cheat. She wouldn't tell anyone about her $20 a month gold mine. Let's check it anyway."

He unlocked the large padlock and swung the doors open. Inside I could see a gleaming old black Cadillac.

"It was my father's. The only thing he ever gave me. He didn't want to. He just happened to die. It was really his gift to himself for surviving the war in Brockton, Massachusetts."

I had never heard Louis talk about his family. I was surprised at the bitterness in his voice. The Caddy, a '47 fastback, started immediately even in the cold. Louis pointed to the dash.

"Check the glove box." Inside was a small, snub-nosed .38. "It'll work close up at least."

We were becoming a well-armed militia of two. On the road, I told Louis about Fenner's belief that Hall might be going after the FBI. I told him about the file. Suddenly Louis changed. No longer chatty, he seemed to grip the big steering wheel as if it were someone's throat. He turned the radio off and stared out into the bleak December landscape.

"What's the matter?"

"What you have told me is very interesting. Almost too interesting. It puts one in a kind of dilemma. To stop Hall might be to protect Hoover. I don't think it is possible to get both. The question is which one do you want to help?"

"If Hall had something to do with Lara's death, I know whose side I'll be on."

"As usual you ignore the big picture."

"Big picture? What—"

"Okay, here's a history lesson: do you know who won the war—don't answer, it's a rhetorical question. It wasn't Eisenhower, Bradley, Patton, or even MacArthur. It wasn't the army, navy, or marines. It was the intellectuals—this war was fought with brainpower and we had better, just slightly better, brains. And guess what? We hate that the big war was won by these guys so we pretend that it was the marines on Guadalcanal or the GIs who fought the Battle of the Bulge who made the difference."

"Wait a minute—"

"It has nothing to do with your bravery. It has to do with what made the real difference. Let me tell you three stories—from just a year ago. There was a man, Alan Turing, a brilliant man who took on breaking the German U-Boat codes. Enigma machines. They thought they were unbreakable. He broke them, with a bunch of other intellectuals and various oddballs. The war at sea—where, by the way, we were getting our collective asses handed to us—got turned around. And we could get enough men and material to Churchill to make D-Day possible. Then he started making 'thinking machines.' And this isn't H.G. Wells, it's real. And then what? It turns out he likes boys—young men actually—the English vice. He gets arrested and sentenced to a year in jail. So instead of saying to him, 'You like young men, great, we'll send you a new one every fortnight like it's the Book of the Month Club because without you there wouldn't be any young men left in England.' But no. Never would they—Instead, they offer him treatment for his condition. There should be statues to him in every village square and hardly anyone even knows who he is. Then there is good old Robert Oppenheimer who takes on the impossible task of creating the atomic bomb. He also turns a science fiction idea into a reality in record time. He wonders about the wisdom of creating the H-bomb, a weapon that makes about as much sense as creating a pistol that puts a bullet in your enemy and yourself at the same time. So they reward him by declaring him a security risk and destroying his reputation. How many years did he take off the war with his two bombs? How many Americans are alive today because of his work? And finally there is Liev Aronson who nobody knows, nobody, the one who developed what he called 'decision matrices' that provided a very sophisticated way of predicting what decisions people would make. He laid out long before we hit the beaches at Normandy what the Germans would do in response. He told Ike that the Germans would never buy an invasion at Normandy. Their decision matrix wouldn't allow it. In fact, he encouraged Ike to allow a leak of the actual invasion plans. The Germans reacted exactly as Liev predicted. They laughed at a Normandy Invasion. He was the most brilliant man, the most...brilliant I ever met. Combined with Turing machines, his system will allow capitalism to remain on top of the world because it will tell big business what people will buy. There is no more valuable theory than that. And his reward? The FBI decides to hound him because he had the audacity to join the Mattachine Society in 1950, a group that simply wanted some rights for those who chose to love members of their own sex. The FBI hounded him so much that on June 6, 1952, Liev took a pistol, put it in his mouth, and pulled the trigger. They had the nerve to go to Columbia University to warn them that Liev Aronson belonged to an organization of sexual deviants and was a danger to the students. They had the nerve—He was such a good man and—"

He stopped in mid-sentence. Louis was in state unlike any I had seen before. I was almost afraid. Suddenly he seemed to have a stake in the matter, but I didn't know exactly how or why.

"Did you know him? Was he a friend?"

"Yes, I knew him. Yes, he was a friend. The only friend. The only..."

He looked away from me. I knew from the crack in his voice that he didn't want to go any farther. I tried to get Louis back to the case.

"Do you think Hall has a spy in the FBI?"

"Did you hear what I just said?"

"Yes, but it doesn't help me find Lara's killer."

"Okay, I see where we are. I see where we are going. So to answer your question, it wouldn't surprise me if Hall had someone on the inside. Hoover has many enemies, present company not excluded. And any big intelligence operation assumes that they have been penetrated. They plan accordingly. No one is allowed to know too much, even at the top. They are constantly running little trap operations to catch their moles. A little false information to you, a little different false information to me. Then see what shows up in Moscow or London."

"London?"

"Our allies are the most effective spies against us. It's one thing to spy for the enemy. But what harm can there be in sending advance notice to our best friends, especially if you are receiving regular installments of sterling every month for your little tips. Most of it is meaningless anyway. All you have to do to find out what is happening is to know how to read the *Wall Street Journal*."

"Meaning?"

"Follow the money. Watch which stocks spike a few months before a big contract is announced. Check suppliers. You can tell a lot. The dealers and the generals are always the first ones at the trough. But there are some things we will probably never know. There are layers and layers of combatants out there. Each one only partly visible to the enemy. There are casualties all over the place, but we never hear about them. They'll destroy somebody just to see who gets pissed. It's a good way to uncover allies. Look what it's done for McCarthy. Because he's so venal, they will turn their backs on him but, now, who doesn't know the junior senator from Wisconsin. The whole system operates on Heisenberg's Uncertainty Principle with a little Kafka thrown in. Paranoia and betrayal are SOP now. It's all so murky, nobody, not even those at the top, really know what's going on. It's so complex that small changes produce enormous effects. The only thing you have to remember is somebody is always out to get you. And that they are all evil."

We drove for a while, testing out theories to explain the events of the last few months. We concentrated on the role that Lara Greenbaum might have played. I was less interested in the geo-political themes that so interested Louis than I was in Lara.

"I still think that she was put up to it," I said. "She was somebody's pawn."

"I am not so sure. She is more complicated than that. She went way beyond being some star struck teenager under the influence of some Svengali. I think she saw herself on some kind of mission. She saw herself as standing for her whole generation. Look at her response to the French Judith. We'll know more when we crack her code. She had influences. That's for sure. I am sure we will find out. The rest should follow."

"It sounds like Lara has gotten to you, too."

"She is remarkable. But you are also smitten. Or you wouldn't be risking your life just out of friendship to a man you are hardly friends with."

"It is not like that. I'm just impressed. When I think of what I was like at that age. The war started and I went. I wasn't *for* anything. I don't think I thought one serious thought in seventeen years"

"That doesn't surprise me."

"Lara was always thinking, feeling, looking. I just wish she wasn't so serious."

"It's funny how we complain that the young don't amount to a hill of beans until they get serious about something and then we want them to just enjoy being young."

"I guess so."

One thing that bothers me is how she got to Hall. She wasn't grabbed off the street. She had an appointment."

"Yeah, I noticed that too." I was anxious to get started. Like Louis, I didn't like being a target. Even more, I didn't like being the Judas goat, putting others in jeopardy. I kept wondering who would be next. Christy? The Greenbaums? Jason Melrose? I knew I was being used. For what, I didn't know exactly. It was hard to believe anyone or anything. I thought I trusted Louis, completely, but the thought even crossed my mind that his escape might have been too easy.

"Do you trust anybody?"

Louis took a drag from his Benson & Hedges and smiled. He didn't answer right away. Then he deliberately avoided turning his head toward me. "You know, it has occurred to me that you might be setting me up."

"Me? Why?"

"When it comes to being killed, why is the last of the W's?"

"The what?"

"That's the second."

I had the feeling we were slipping into an Abbott and Costello routine. Or maybe I was playing George Burns to his Gracie Allen.

"You know, the journalistic W's—who, what, where, when and why? When I saw how careless you were in coming to see me, knowing that government men were following you, I did consider the history of our friendship. You know that I have been involved in various...how shall I say?...enterprises. There might have been pressure."

"What was your conclusion?"

"That I trusted you. At least I had no reason to doubt you. I could be disappointed in your ineptness, that's all."

"But why believe me?"

"Occam's Razor."

"Whose razor?"

"Occam was a minor philosopher who came up with a major principle. Assumptions used to explain anything must not be multiplied beyond necessity. It was much easier to assume you were telling the truth, no matter how implausible your story, because the alternative was too complicated. In short, if they wanted to get me, they didn't need you. Or your fantastic story, complete with coded diary."

"Thanks for the vote of confidence."

"Oh, my dear, tell me you haven't gone over my story looking for some inconsistency which would put me on the side of your enemies."

My hesitation convicted me. Louis laughed over my stammered attempt at an explanation.

"I would have been very disappointed in you as a professional if you hadn't considered me as at least a little untrustworthy. You have been relying on old Occam without even knowing it. I rest my case about the value of philosophy."

"Where are we heading?"

"I have a secret place as unknown to others as the garage."

The Cadillac hummed over the Connecticut countryside. It was a helluva car. Louis sat silently, staring ahead at the black road rapidly disappearing beneath us. I half listened to the radio and thought about what we would do next. The early winter night had forced us to turn inward. There was nothing out there to take our minds off anything.

"QWERTY!"

"What? Not more philosophers!"

"QWERTY. That's the code. I knew it had to be just a letter substitution code. I tried reverse alphabet, skipped letters, and a few other basic ones. I knew it had to be a standard one. A smart little girl, this Greenbaum. One of the problems with a code is where do you keep the key to it. The whole code obviously loses its value if someone finds the key. So then you have two things to protect, the key and the coded document. That just increases the problems of security. Amateurs make their codes so complicated that they have to carry the key everywhere making the code much more vulnerable. The key is as important as the messages. Her key was everywhere. She didn't even have to memorize it. All she had to do was look at it."

"I still don't get it."

"That's because you didn't go to college and have to type term papers. Qwerty. The way a typewriter is set up. It's already a code. Think about it. All you have to do is think of the keyboard as alphabetical. It's a high school code. Perfect. Look, I remembered one phrase 'O DCL VOLI.' At first I thought it might be something like Latin with missing letters. It looks foreign. Take out a piece of paper. I used to know this by heart—QWERTY" He continued to recite the letters of the keyboard. I put the appropriate letters beneath them.

"What have we got?"

"*I met with.*"

"Perfect."

Louis stepped on the gas and the Caddy responded with enthusiasm. We were heading north into the night. But it didn't seem quite so dark anymore.

CHAPTER 14

We drove for a few more hours as the old Caddy shook off the carbon and cobwebs it had collected in the barn and began emitting the typical Cadillac deep-throated rumble. Louis seemed to enjoy the responsiveness of the fastback, but he didn't relax as we passed through sleepy towns north of Stamford. He would double back along roads if he spotted a car that looked like a possible tail behind us. He pulled into half a dozen driveways and a few old two-pump gas stations. He lost me a number of times. And I knew the general area and was sitting right next to him. We crossed over Route 107 about six or seven times. Even though Louis was driving with one eye on the rear view mirror and another watching straight ahead, he talked excitedly about breaking Lara's code. He was sure that the diary would provide the information that he needed to find Amor and Psyche's killers.

"Amor and Psyche?"

"Yeah, the sonsabitches killed my dogs."

"I thought you didn't care about them."

"And who else do I care about?"

After heading north for a time, we passed through Bethel.

"Where are we heading?"

"You'll know when we get there."

"Do you think the car is wired?"

"I want it to be a surprise."

An hour later, after skirting Danbury, I saw the signs for Candlewood Lake.

"The Lake?"

"You guessed. Now there's no surprise. I guess now I don't have to carry you across the threshold."

"A honeymoon cottage?"

"To tell you the truth, I don't even know. It could be a shack. About a year ago, I was playing seven-card stud with a few guys I met in Miami. One of them was this guy from New Haven. He needed some money to call what looked like a flush. It turned out that the two queens and the six that Jake Darling had in the hole matched his queen-six on the board so this guy's little boat was no good. Instead of paying me back, he gave me his little cabin on the lake. I'm just holding the deed until he comes up with the dollars. There's no way that anybody could know about it. I've never even been here."

"You sure you're not holding a piece of toilet paper."

"I doubt it. The guy's very big in New Haven. Even a worthless piece of paper with his name on it would be too much of an embarrassment if it came out."

"Then why hasn't he paid you back?"

"To tell you the truth, I never thought about it. After all it was only six grand."

"If he owed me six grand, I would be at his place for breakfast, I'd ride with him to work, and I'd tuck him in at night just so he wouldn't forget. What's his name?"

"Why?"

"I have some connections in New Haven. At least I used to."

"I guess it doesn't matter. Wayne Keyes."

"You're kidding, right?"

"Sometimes. But not about this. What do you know?"

"Keyes was a good guy."

"You know him? What do you mean *was?*

"Don't you read the local papers? You know how many Bulgarians buy Florsheim shoes on the black market, but you don't know that the Chief of Detectives of the New Haven Police Department, the man whose paper you're holding, washed up on the beach last August."

"Really?"

"They said it was a swimming accident. But I think his water wings were filled with lead. He was involved in a case I was working on. Bad cops. Big money. It's one reason why I don't spend too much time in New Haven anymore."

"Who *doesn't want* to kill you?"

"To tell you the truth, I'm not sure anymore. Let's hope Keyes was on the level. About the house, at least."

He was. He certainly was. How he got such a house was another story. As we drove up the long rocky drive, we could see the lake spread out behind the trees. It looked like molten lead. The same color as everything else this year. The air felt like snow. Only the evergreens added any color to the gray landscape. And they were almost black. Instead of a little cabin by the lake, we found a large log structure set on the hill that overlooked the water. Far below the house were a dock and a boathouse. Louis went to the back of the house where he found the old wagon wheel mounted on the stairs that led to the water. Inside the hub was the key.

It took us a little time to get the heat up and to find where to turn on the water.

"This is not half bad."

"I'm not so sure that your friend was just your run of the mill policeman. This stuff is first rate. I'm not a big fan of American folk art, but this is first rate. That's a Rufus Hollins over there."

On the wall were paintings that looked like demonic children had painted them. They were full of flat figures, wildly colored, like lipstick on the mouth of a nearsighted woman. A strangely done landscape of farmland that tilted toward the viewer had purple, red, and yellow crops. In the center, there was the figure of Christ, looking twelve feet tall, with an angry scowl on his face aglow in the center of an orange cornfield. Fire shot out from his fingers like chicken feathers.

There was also a portrait of a sour faced woman in a weird crown whose nose looked more like a mediocre middleweight's than an aristocrat's. Around her head in a kind of halo were the angry words of some prophet. Whoever painted the picture thought this old woman might be the Whore of Babylon or a hated school librarian. Another had two young girls running in front of a farmhouse that appeared to have been built by a carpenter with severe astigmatism.

All the furniture in Louis's house was made of simple woods, some of it out of twigs.

Just as I was ready to comment, Louis exclaimed, "A cop

with taste. I don't believe it. Maybe there's hope for you yet, Varian. And look! Good scotch and a Scott amplifier. Be still my heart."

In the corner was a sound system that looked just like Louis's, except it had just one massive speaker. The house was beginning to feel warm enough to relax in. Louis looked around like a kid whose mother and father finally got it right on Christmas morning.

"You know, if I had known what I had here, I wouldn't have waited so long. I really thought it was a shack. I could get used to this. Look at the view. It's like being out West, in the Rockies. It doesn't look like New England at all. You can almost imagine a world empty of people here."

"That appeals to you?"

"Immensely."

I didn't want to argue. I was tired from the ride, but I wanted to get started on the diary.

"We can wait a little. This is such an interesting surprise. I never would have guessed I would have found this from playing cards with the dour Wayne Keyes. You just never know, do you?"

"I guess you don't. This doesn't look like the Wayne Keyes I knew either. Let's get to work."

It took us a long time to translate the thirty pages or so of encoded messages. We took turns. I kept getting confused having to go back constantly between the diary and the sheet Louis prepared with the typewriter keyboard written in big red letters. I kept translating things from QWERTY into QWERTY or from English into something in between. Louis was much smoother and quicker. While I was translating, Louis explored the house. I could hear him oohing and aahing in other rooms, but I was determined not to be distracted.

Then we both were hungry. We needed a break. Besides the scotch, there were only a few cans of beans and vegetables in the house. We didn't want to leave the house until we had something solid on paper so we quenched our thirst with Chivas Regal and cured our hunger with pork and beans and creamed corn.

The large window overlooking the lake had gone black.

There was no moon to reflect off the water. No lights from the houses across the empty expanse to give any sense of depth. No stars. It was like someone had painted the windows on the walls. I didn't like feeling so closed in. I couldn't help jumping a little every time the house creaked or the wind blew against the windows. Louis was convinced we hadn't been followed. I wasn't sure of anything.

He found a recording of Louie Armstrong's big band. We sat back and finished the scotch.

"Let's see what we have."

I began to read. "'April 2nd. I'm so flattered that CA has taken me into his confidence. He is so brilliant and his work is so important. I am hoping that he will ask me to do more than research. He knows so much about the way things work. Just today, we looked through the records of the Belgian underground. For the first time I have a sense of the sacrifice they made. To tell the truth I didn't even think Belgium was part of the war. I thought they were like the Swiss or something. And anyway I always thought we won the war just by ourselves. I never thought at all about the people who paved the way for us. He also gave me a book written by a girl in the French Resistance.'"

My suspicions that a professor had influenced Lara were confirmed. Who was CA? I hadn't found anyone with those initials yet. Whoever CA was, he was clearly her mentor, taking advantage of her admiration although Lara didn't seem to mind. I told myself she was simply star struck, not responsible for anything she did in the name of truth, justice, or the New American Way. That's what I wanted to believe, anyway. Who was he? Why didn't I know about him? Why didn't Jason?

"'Last night I met with CA again. He is so reluctant to get involved in anything but a professional way. He is so devoted to his work. That's one of the things I find so attractive about him. I wish my father were as devoted to his profession. Sometimes I think he is embarrassed about being a dentist. CA called me a little girl. I pouted. I told him that I was twenty— A big lie, I know! but men lie all the time don't they?—Then I tried something I learned from Judith. I could see him weakening. I undid my blouse and asked him if he thought that he was looking at a schoolgirl or a woman. I lifted my skirt up to my panties and let him see I was a woman. His face turned red and for the first time he had nothing to say. I liked feeling that power over him. It's so amazing how quickly the tables get turned. Older men are so much more innocent and hesitant than boys. Jason practically attacked me when he saw me undressed the first time. I had to use my knee to slow him down. Now CA is mine and it is so easy and exciting. Judith was right.'"

This was not the innocence of first love, but the calculations of a clever woman engineering a conquest. I had the same queasy feeling I had when I first saw the photos of Lara's body. I had violated her again. Now I also felt violated. The image I tried to keep in my mind was of a twelve-year-old Lara. I guess it was a sign of my age that I had a hard time thinking of her as anything but a little girl. But the woman in the diary kept intruding. I could see her undoing her blouse, offering her young breasts, but the words that came out of her mouth were in a little girl's voice, not a woman's, not a movie star's. It was grotesque. I started to skip things that Lara had written, especially her lessons in seduction. Louis objected.

"Read it all. You're a Peeping Tom, for chrissake. That's what you do. I'm sure you have seen much worse than a schoolgirl's puppy love. After Freud, there is no more innocence. In any case, she might let something slip about this CA so that we can identify him. Maybe his dick has a big bend in it or a tattoo of Woody Woodpecker or something like that and we can find him that way."

"For chrissakes, cut it out. It's not funny now. I saw the pictures of her body. I saw the initials carved in her flesh. And I can remember her alive. I didn't have to be close to her. She was so alive, a bright, beautiful kid. I didn't really know her, but she was...I—"

"Initials?"

"I told you."

"No. You didn't tell me. You told me she was mutilated. Nothing about initials, I wouldn't forget a detail like that. What initials?"

"Something like *rat*. Maybe *river rat,* but I doubt it. The *rat* was clear, but there were three more letters, much fainter, *v, e,* or *a, and r.* Something could be missing. Carved right into her skin."

"Jesus!"

"What?"

"If you were only better educated. Didn't you learn any German on your romp through the Rhineland?"

"G.I. German."

"It's German for *Betrayal.*"

"Yeah. Of course. How stupid of me."

"When the Germans caught members of the underground, they often put them on public display. They were labeled *ver-raters*—traitors. Sometimes they just hung a sign around their necks, but when the signs were stolen, they would carve it right on their bodies. I think your hunch about this having to do with Hall's war record is right on the money. Read. Read."

Lara did make her conquests. From what I could tell it wasn't the sort of experience that would make the pages of *Modern Romance,* but that didn't make any difference to Lara. Whoever he was, or whatever he did, he certainly made her forget about Jason Melrose and the rest of her friends. The rest of the diary was devoted to Lara's work for this CA person, who had asked her to go through transcripts of a trial of several Nazi collaborators after the war. The man she was trying to track down *was* Jacques de Paul. From the brief summaries that Lara put in the diary, he had been instrumental in supporting the Nazis against the resistance forces in Belgium and France in the war.

According to the testimony, he had also been a leading Belgian intellectual who supported the Nazi ideology. He wrote numerous articles for the leading Brussels paper attacking the decadence of Western culture, which had come under the debilitating influence of the Jews and other "degenerate" races.

Louis knew more than I did what Lara's description of de Paul meant. But I knew enough to recognize the absurdity of his attacks on George Gershwin and Louis Armstrong whose trumpet serenaded us at that very moment.

"You know I've been thinking? Remember that professor's name? It was Browder, David Browder."

"Okay."

"Yes, think about it. A double code. Qwerty gets us CA. A single letter shift brings us to DB. See?"

"Maybe. That doesn't make sense to me yet. Browder is interested in Emerson and Thoreau. Not war crimes trials. These guys don't leave their specialties."

"He might have a cover story."

"No, that's what he is."

"We'll see."

Then Lara's work took a different turn. From what we could tell from the diary, Lara had begun her research for CA in late April or early May. In May, Hall's investigating committee was on campus. After a month of swooning over this CA, he practically disappears from her journal. She now seems tired of him and his careerism. She had bigger fish to fry. She writes in her journal about the necessity of offering a sacrificial victim. It is a difficult decision.

Sometimes I just stared at the letters on the page—igsgytkytl ol doft—and couldn't bring myself to decode them. There was something pushing her beyond her quest for justice. Something almost scary and very cold about the way she plotted to get Hall and de Paul. She liked it. This wasn't a girl whose biggest problem was not getting into Smith because she was a Jew.

"'I have thought long and hard about this. CA's way will take a long time and there is no guarantee that it will work. I've learned enough about their methods that I know I can convince them. I'm sorry that I can see no other way. But he is becoming too powerful.'"

She decided to volunteer to testify for the committee.

"How'd she know to do that? How'd she know that the best way to infiltrate a group is to betray somebody else? It's classic. But it's not CA."

"Who'd she nail?" he asked.

"She doesn't say. But it has to be that Browder. Who else?"

"If you're right, then I'm wrong about CA."

"After her testimony she was contacted by one of Hall's advisers. He says his name is Henri Krims. He wants to thank her personally for her cooperation. And he wants to caution her. He tells her she is obviously talented as well as beautiful. These are dangerous times, and there are many dangerous men who would try to take advantage of her. Lara smiles coyly and says she wants to make sure that he isn't among them. Krims protests, but Lara thinks that is exactly what he is suggesting. She smiles. 'I moistened my lips. Innocently but provocatively. I have to be very careful with this man.'"

I was furious. I felt helpless. It was like a movie where you hope against hope that the woman won't enter the locked room at the top of the stairs, but you are powerless to change things. I wanted to shake her to her senses.

"She was really in over her head. Did she think she could control a snake just by wiggling her ass like—"

"Shut up." There were no more quips.

"Krims offered to help in her education. Lara knew who this man was. It was de Paul. She was ecstatic that the man she had been researching wanted to get to know her. When she finally got up enough nerve to tell CA what she had done, he encouraged her to meet with de Paul. She did meet with him several times. There are several accounts of the sex between them. She was still experimenting with her power when she seduced CA. Now she saw herself as an expert, a true *femme fatale*. She found her ability to work her wiles on de Paul intoxicating. 'He doesn't recognize that when he gets hard, I win. I want to see his face when I spring the trap on them. When I am Judith.'

"She was right in the middle of it. 'I am getting closer and closer. There is something in the works, and lots of phone calls. Very hush- hush. I almost got the name. They asked me to leave the room twice when there were calls for Hall. HK apologized. He wants me to come to hear Hall's speech in Philadelphia. I think this is what I have been waiting for. I hope so. I need to take a long, hot bath to get rid of their smell.'

"Then she begins to lay out her plan for the final conquest—Hall himself. And that was the last entry."

Dated, as best as we could tell a day or so before she disappeared.

"She really did think she was a spy, didn't she?" Louis demanded. "What did she think? What was she? Eighteen for God's sake?"

"Nineteen."

"Big difference! She loses her virginity one month and the next she is Mata Hari. So she was going to infiltrate Hall's organization and bring him down? And make a big impression on this CA. He ought to be shot. Just because she could seduce some leftist professor, who was probably as easy to seduce as a bull moose in heat..."

"It bothers me, too."

"It just makes me mad. These amateurs." Louis continued to fume about Lara's fate.

It wasn't easy for him to indulge his rage. He tried to make it about the profession, whatever that was. I couldn't find any words to express my shame, guilt, anger, and hate. I tried to forget that it was Lara. I tried to hide in my own profession. I mulled over what we knew. But her words kept getting in the way. It wasn't so much the sex. That did bother me, but I was afraid, for the wrong reasons. Images of her naked body—a mixture of ripe young breasts and horrible wounds. How much different was I from de Paul? I tried to keep on track: a girl, a pretty girl, worms her way into Hall's camp, maybe finds something. She gets caught and they eliminate her. It didn't fit together. It just didn't. Not yet. Then I thought of the Greenbaums and realized that I could not tell them what I had found out about their daughter. I remembered Manny's reaction to learning about Jason. How would, how could he handle this?

"It's more than just Lara being discovered as a traitor," I said. "It's got to be."

"How?"

"Let's assume we're right about Veasey. That it wasn't the mob hit the papers said it was. What does he have to do with Lara's death? Nothing. But he did have something on Hall. I could tell he did. Why would he agree to see me? He was scared. Real scared. And this guy dealt with the mob on a daily basis. I'm sure he'd had to protect himself before. Whatever this is, it's bigger than Lara's discovering that Hall hangs out with an ex-Nazi. We have to look into Veasey. And the FBI? What about them? Where do they come in? They want to know about Hall, too. And the Biddle School? What the hell does Lara have to do with that school? How many things can there be?"

"I'm not troubled by the complexity. Think about this. If Hall has his file, then what is the FBI going to do? They're going to look again. Find something. Maybe something more than they had before. Maybe Lara found out what it was. It's not all that disconnected. It can't be."

"But you're the one who always talking about things never making sense," I said. "Isn't that my...whatever you called it...my tragic flaw?"

"Tragic, yes. But not here. Look at what we know already. The pieces are here. We only see part of the pattern. You don't have to have all the pieces to know what picture is on the puzzle."

"Yeah, just look on the box."

"Now who's the quipster?"

"What about me? Why am I still walking? I'm not that lucky." My head was beginning to fog up.

"No, you're not. Or that good. How can they be sure you are working for the Greenbaums? Maybe it's just a cover. Isn't that what the FBI wanted to know? How can they be sure when your dumb hunch takes you to the Biddle School then to Jack Veasey. Maybe they think Moscow's behind it. Who knows? But they certainly aren't gonna take the chance that it's just some private eye working for a friend. What it comes down to is that they can't figure you out anymore than you can figure them out. And that's your insurance policy for the time being."

"At least we know that Hall and de Paul were responsible—"

"We do?"

"Who else?"

"Look again. I'm not saying you're wrong. You are probably right. They probably even know, or think, you know. But you have nothing to use against them. You have nothing and you are nothing. A hired hand, a gofer, as far as they're concerned. Not a threat to them. Not yet anyway. But you might lead them to the real threat. That's the way they think. They don't believe in blind luck or hunches. They scheme, lie, and plot so they think everybody else does too. A one-man operation that could get something on them? They wouldn't buy it."

"They just have to check me out."

"They have. And they know you know me. They know you work for Fenner. That's why they don't believe it's just you. Even though you have been bouncing around like a pinball in a haystack, they see something different, somebody flying in a straight line right to them, like you know what you're doing. Like you have inside information."

"Like a what?"

"A mixed metaphor. Clever, at that."

"They would think you might be behind this? Why?"

"I have my grievances."

"Like?"

"Like it doesn't matter."

"What about what Fenner said about the FBI?" I asked.

"In short you're alive because they all need more information. For them it's like blood to a vampire. In the meantime, they can afford to let you turn up rocks so that they can squash whatever crawls out. Like me."

"Christy Coopersmith?"

"Who?"

"The woman who put me on to Veasey."

"She's vulnerable. Everybody is."

"I have to warn her."

"Be careful. One more contact could be enough to convince them she knows something. You're the poisoned pill. You have to know how they think."

For the next few hours, we sat looking at the depth of black in the lake, the sound of the Goldberg Variations behind us. I still wasn't convinced about Louis's theories. We had to start with CA.

"Look, Louis, if it's not Browder, we should be able to track whoever it was, easy enough."

"You're right and that's the reason it would be a big help if we knew exactly who this guy is. The question is how to do it without alerting our homicidal friends. We don't want to go stumbling around the campus leaving bodies in our wake. Once we know for sure, we can surgically remove this fellow from the campus and get some answers. Frankly, I don't care what happens to him after that."

We went back to the diary. We looked more closely at the research she was doing on de Paul. According to the one article, she could find in the *New York Times*, he had disappeared after the war. Although there were no formal charges pending against him, they considered him an important witness in the trial of Gerhard Hubler, the German who was in charge of anti-underground activities in Belgium. Hubler was charged with the torture of several dozen Belgians, and de Paul had written a newspaper account of Hubler's "heroic" fight against "terrorism." Supposedly, he had been present during some of the "interrogations" that produced the confessions. This *Times article*, published in 1946, about Nazi war criminals still on the loose, mentioned de Paul only in passing as a Nazi sympathizer. Rather than calling him a criminal, the article only mentioned that he wrote a strong defense of the Nazi invasion of Belgium entitled, "Welcome, Brothers."

Louis got up from the chair and stood looking out across the water. I was still trying to piece things together. He turned to me. He seemed as puzzled as I was but about different things. I was worried about Lara using her body to infiltrate Hall's entourage.

He walked to the center of the room, as if he were about to give the key speech in a play. "I still don't get it about this de Paul. There were hundreds of those guys running around Europe, selling out their friends and country for the glories of the Third Reich. Third-rate pseudo-intellectuals who spent their days convincing us that black was white and that evil was not only good, but also wonderful. But they never really mattered. Look at poor old Ezra Pound. How many minds did he change when he tried to make Benito Mussolini seem as benign as Benny Goodman? I don't even think he changed his own mind. He was just pissed that Roosevelt didn't make him poet laureate or secretary of state. This de Paul seems even more craven than an intellectual whore, but a threat to democracy? Hardly. Yet, he seems to be right at the center of this whole mess. I just don't get it. There's something missing there, too."

CHAPTER 15

Night was ending or day was beginning. We couldn't tell, but it was clear we couldn't go on. Words flew out of our mouths randomly like cotton candy in a drum, not making sense, just filling the air with an empty sweetness. Memories collided with theories. Hunches soon became certainty. The more outrageous the plot the more we believed it. My mouth was dry. I no longer cared what J. Edgar Hoover thought about me, or the Swiss, or vanilla pudding. Louis looked at me through red eyes, his voice worn into a whisper. He ran his hand through his slick black hair and raised his eyebrows like Groucho Marx. He had decided that ties were an interesting topic of discussion. We laughed the laughter of the exhausted and confused.

There was nothing left to say or do. We tried to sleep. But there was no way we *could* sleep. We were filled with the crazy energy of the exhausted. Louis rifled through the pile of records sitting next to the turntable. He wanted something to match the mood, he said. I really didn't care what he put on. I just knew that whenever the music stopped the room suddenly became very empty and Louis seemed very far away. I was left with the voices in my head. And a sick feeling in my gut.

He found a recording of a Beethoven symphony. I kept looking at the black windows. Time had stopped. Beethoven hung in the air like a thick curtain, blocking everything from view. It was completely wrong for our mood. I imagined German maidens getting drenched in a beautiful park exploding with flowers on the first day of spring as P-51s flew in perfect formation overhead. Beethoven's storm was just bad stagecraft.

Louis continued looking through the records as the music

swelled to another climax. He offered no commentary. "Why do you think that you have taken this so far?"

"I've a client. And he's a friend."

"It's more than that. You know that. You have to."

"I don't know. Really."

Louis looked at me like an underperforming student. "You must know there's a good chance that you won't get past this one."

"It's crossed my mind. Once or twice."

"So why? There are a number of ways out of this. Not all of them dishonorable."

"I think you're the one who has to answer that question."

I had already spent a lot of time trying to figure out why Louis got so caught up with the case. He had always been pragmatic. Even in cards. He never threw good money after bad. When the cards were running against him, he didn't try to push his luck. He just kept folding until his luck turned. He used to say that if you waited long enough the cards would always reward you. Here he was on the lam, with assassins on his trail.

And he wasn't even getting paid. It wasn't very pragmatic. There was no percentage. I didn't think it was because of the dogs.

"You have easier outs than I do."

"I don't know if you would understand."

"Try me," I said.

"Whenever I travel through a small town, I am always struck by the same thing. Here there are people living lives that go completely undetected, except by each other. They marry. They have children and die without affecting me or the rest of the world at all. There's a history to the place. A rhythm to its life. A kind of beauty in even the humblest town that appears like a young girl in a crisp white gown as you ride over that hill or round that bend into town. My first response is always a sense of pity for so many lives that seem so insignificant. Then it also always occurs to me that I am more invisible than they are. I wonder if all my careful planning and all my interests have resulted only in my erasure. As I look at their modest houses filled with their grandmother's furniture and their grandchildren's pictures, I feel myself slowly beginning to disappear. I think you are a disappearing man just like me. That's why we get along so well."

"You make it sound like you have been thinking a lot about this."

"I have." He stood up and walked toward the light that was beginning to fill the room. "How can I explain what I don't understand either? I know she made a choice. A big choice. Some of it had to do with the excitement of wielding her newly discovered sexual power. But there was more. She wanted the challenge of making a difference. She wanted to be a hero. There is no higher calling. I used to want that myself. I think I have been offered the opportunity to have another try at it."

"You sound like one of those idealists you always make fun of."

"This is not idealism. Like Lara I want to get back…"
"At?"

"At those who destroy what little good is left in the world. The ones who destroy good men and the memory of their good deeds. And what about you? Oh, you pretend you are in control. Asking questions. Looking for answers. Trying to solve your little puzzles. But you know different." He put his hand a few inches in front of his face. "You don't—" he went on, as I knew he would, "—step back. You don't think about anything in terms of ramifications of your life. Now this Lara, no matter how crazy her idea was, she had an idea. A purpose. Even as a young girl. She wanted her life to mean something."

"But what did she gain?"

"That's not the point. Here you are in the middle of something that could change history and you don't consider what your part is. She did."

"Aren't you the one who is always saying—"

"Forget that. The war was too big for any of us to make a difference—"

"Didn't you say you won—"

"Look, this is one of those moments," he said. "You can define your life. You could even be a hero."

"I stopped talking about heroes when I was eleven."

"Absolutely! That's when all we thought about was being

heroes. Remember! There was life right in front of us, with all its blooming, buzzing potential. Who fantasized about selling somebody a washing machine or figuring out what a piece of commercial property was worth? Did you know any eleven-year-olds who imagined spending their lives in an office? We wanted nothing but thrilling, dangerous, ridiculous challenges. We wanted every day to be a matter of life and death. Yes, we were all going to be heroes. Why give that up?"

"And you haven't, I suppose, living an invisible life?"

"I am trying. Always trying. Sometimes trying. Sometimes failing. Mostly waiting."

I had never seen Louis like this. I kept waiting for him to break character. To laugh. To laugh at me for being fooled. But it didn't happen.

"You think you have life under control because you operate according to a code. Do the job for the client. Be loyal to friends. Ask for nothing you would not be prepared to give yourself. And so on and so on. You never examine the code. What does it mean? Where did you get it? Where does it lead? You just go from one meaningless tangle to another."

"Weren't you the one who keeps harping on how meaningless everything is anyway?"

"That's only the first part. It is meaningless until you give it meaning, real meaning. That's the point. Unless you find a meaning in what you do, there is only emptiness and absurdity in life. That's what Lara did. She went from being pissed off that she didn't get into Smith to giving up her life for a cause. She understood that being a hero sometimes requires you to sacrifice others, not just yourself. That is a hard lesson. She took the hero's way. That's why you can't get her out of your mind."

"It was stupid and a waste. What cause? What meaning do you find in all this?"

"The meaning is that there might be an opportunity to get to the heart of the madness that is eating away at the soul of this country. And rip it out. That is a cause worth dying for."

"You're kidding."

"Not at all."

"How is that different from just finding out who killed Lara? Which at least seems like a real question that might have a real answer."

"But it is the wrong question. What if you said that the Nazis had to be stopped because they killed your cousin Raymond?"

"Yeah, at least it's a reason."

"It's a reason, all right. But there is nothing in it but the personal. It makes no distinctions. An eye for an eye. It is just a code. Not a philosophy."

"What difference does it make?"

"All the difference in the world. For you, the chance to put a bullet in the head of the man who killed Lara would end it all."

"That's enough for me."

"I'm sure it is."

CHAPTER 16

When I awoke, it was as if a bulb had been turned on but the light lit only itself. Nothing was any clearer—life, music, Lara's death, or philosophy. It was already the afternoon. We were still too groggy to think straight or to feel much besides the ache in our backs from sitting all night in chairs made out of sticks. I tried to get things back on track.

"Can you get in touch with some of your contacts in Washington? If we just had one part of this nailed down—Hall, this de Paul, Veasey, FBI or even the CDA—we might be able to build something on it."

"It will be a little more difficult now. The word is out. We're in the middle of a dirty little secret war. Whoever talks to us is at risk. But I don't think we have a choice."

"I'll take Storrs." I started to move toward the door.

"Be careful."

I took Louis's car. He thought it might give me a little advantage. He would make other arrangements. I wondered if he might be nervous about my driving his father's last gift.

"If you crack it up, you will have done what I have been unable to do for years and I will be eternally grateful."

I was happy to be in a car by myself so I could think, but I was still reeling after the long night's musings, the scotch, and the restless sleep to really enjoy the drive. As the miles slipped by, I was in a state very close to sleep. Near Hartford I started to come to my senses. The landscape was still painted a dismal gray brown and suited my winter mood perfectly. I felt trapped and stimulated at the same time. In the army, we were constantly driven by unseen hands, somewhere back of the lines in London or Washington or some exotic city with names out of history books, where it was rumored that the liquor flowed like wine and the women were impressively grateful to their liberators.

Generals would make decisions because they wanted to get one up on some other general and men they didn't know would die. Generals would decide that their careers depended on a swift victory and men they knew only as numbers would die. Other generals would wake up in a sweat, afraid to make a decision and men I knew would die. All these generals were known to us. Whenever there was a change in command, the word would move through the ranks in anxious whispers. We prayed for a leader who was neither a coward nor a hero.

After the war, the issues seemed abstract, impossible to locate, but just as deadly. Clouded and secret, everything seemed to be about fear. In the midst of plenty, holding all the cards, we were threatened by an ideology that seemed to want to take our cars and swimming pools away from us. We imagined hordes all over the world ready to raid our brand new supermarkets. Appearance mattered more than reality. The fate of millions of Chinese mattered less than the appearance that one party or the other had "lost" China. As if it had fallen off the map one day and nobody could find it. Now little men followed bigger men around looking for signs of weakness. It was the opposite of the diagram a biology teacher had shown us of fish in the ocean being swallowed by larger and larger fish. Now it was the little fish who seemed to call all the shots. Men like Hall.

I had tried to avoid these forces. Louis was right about that. I had been living in my own little tidal pool, away from the grand currents of history, just trying to avoid pain and garner, occasionally, a little pleasure out of my life. What I did for a living caused some pain, but it amounted to no more than a ripple across my little pool. A couple's defunct marriage that would have ended anyway even if I had done nothing. A man who ran away from his family and his job, and, when I found him, he committed suicide. What was my share of the blame? I was just a man trying to live in the shadow of the rocks next to those who lived under the rocks. Now I could see the open water.

Despite myself, I wanted to see what was out there. Louis would have been proud.

He also would have howled at my little philosophical reverie. He would have reminded me again of my need of an education. He often said, "The price you pay for a lack of an education is not ignorance, but sentimentality." He was probably right.

If I had been smart, I would have sunk back into my little pool among the scavengers. I could have told the Greenbaums something. It was an open case. The police were better equipped. I could have even gotten Freddie to understand why I couldn't go on. He would have understood, but he would have never forgiven me.

Duty was a strange thing. You knew that your loyalty to the principle as outlined in textbooks was absurd, but you went right ahead and honored it anyway. Freddie wasn't really that close a friend, not anymore. Maybe he never was. There were few candidates for that job. Best friends were for sixteen-year-olds. But he was a friend. And, more importantly, he would have done the same for me. That was the real kicker here. It wasn't a high moral principle that I followed. It was a simple case of a deal, an unspoken pact, where each party knew, without ever having to say it, that the other would be willing to follow through for him if the circumstances were reversed. Louis was right about that, too. It was a code. But the code was slipping. I should have gone to the Greenbaums. I should have told Freddie what I knew. But I couldn't. Not yet. Maybe not ever.

Before long, I saw the signs for the University of Connecticut. As I drove by the campus, I saw very few students. The parking lots were almost empty. The students were already on break, I guessed. That meant that I would have to see Browder at his home. I preferred that. I figured it was safer for him and for me if I didn't run into him on campus. I was sure that's where I had been picked up the first time. They knew I was going to Philadelphia before that cop in Abington tipped them off. I was sure of it now. Then I seemed to remember a guy in a blue Plymouth parked near The Husky Grille. I wasn't confident that I was being careful enough about tails.

I thought again about CA. I still wasn't completely sure that I was wrong about Browder. I had been around a number of smooth operators. He didn't strike me as a likely candidate for membership among the suave and sophisticated. As I considered and reconsidered, I kept coming back to the fact that he was the only lead I had up here.

I stopped at a pay phone and found the only Browder in the book in Willington. I asked for directions at a little eatery near campus where I also gassed up. When I got into the car, I looked around for the suspicious car. I didn't see one. Or any other cars. But I felt something. Something hovering over me in the cool air. I hoped it was just my nerves.

I passed the Browder house and drove a mile or so through old farms and cute colonials that looked like they had been built about three years before the Pilgrims arrived. I wasn't sightseeing though. I drove, like Louis, with my eyes on the rear view mirror. When I was reasonably sure that I wasn't being followed, I stopped in a long dirt driveway and headed back toward Browder's.

The same '41 Ford I had seen on my first pass was still in the driveway. It was too old to belong to the government. The house was a modest white Cape Cod set just back from the road. There was a large semi-circle of dirt in front of it, which functioned as a driveway. There was no garage. I knocked on the door.

A woman, older than I expected her to be, looking considerably pregnant, answered the door. She was wearing a heavy woolen coat. Her nose was red.

"Yes?"

"Mrs. Browder? My name is Varian. Varian Pike. I spoke to your husband a while back. I wonder, if he's in, can have a few words with him?"

"Yes. Just a minute. We lost our heat last night. David's trying to fix it."

She ushered me in as she called to her husband. I could hear the sounds of metal against metal. When Browder didn't answer, she went to the cellar door. The house seemed even colder than the frigid air outside the door. Old houses seem to trap cold. I could hear them talking while I stood in the center of the living room. She was explaining to him that I was back to see him again.

They had tried to make the house conform to its New England style. But their budget didn't allow for many authentic touches. In one corner of the living room was a spindle rocker devoid of a spindle and missing most of its paint. The coffee table was a similarly finished bench. A bright afghan served in place of a slipcover on the worn sofa. There were no pictures of Lenin or Marx on the bare walls. No hammer and sickle crossed over the modest fireplace. The place looked like an advertisement for Americanism.

"I'm sorry. Won't you have a seat? I would offer to take your coat, but I am afraid you wouldn't be comfortable in this chill. David will be with you in a few minutes. He almost has the old coal furnace working. I apologize. My name is Kathy by the way."

"No need to apologize. Nice to meet you."

I sat in a plain wooden chair that was across from the sofa.

"This is our first winter in this house. We are still getting used to its idiosyncrasies. This is the third time the heater has failed. Can I offer you a cup of hot tea?"

"Don't bother."

"It's no bother. The water's hot. I've been trying to warm my insides with it. I'm still amazed at how cold it gets around here."

"You're not from here?"

"Is anyone? Storrs is a place you come *to* not *from.* "

"Your husband told me you just got married."

"A little over a year ago. We had known each other in high school. We met again at a party in Chapel Hill. North Carolina."

"You don't sound southern."

"I'm not. I was visiting a friend and David was doing some graduate work at the University. We're both from southern Indiana."

She kept talking while she brewed the tea. The more she talked the more attractive she became. There was something genuine in her manner. It was easy to discount the effect of the cold on her nose. Like many academic wives, she avoided make-up so that the initial impression was one of dowdiness, but after I adjusted to the sheer naturalness of her complexion, a kind of wholesome beauty emerged. Something of the Midwest, of the heartland. In contrast, even the modestly made-up Christy Coopersmith looked like something of a courtesan next to her. Kathy Browder had a way of making it seem that you were one of her old high school buddies, too and she was just filling you in on what had happened since the senior prom.

"When is the baby due?"

"Not until March."

She made it seem as if March wouldn't arrive till the end of the century.

"It's a boy."

"Really!" she asked. "What makes you so sure? Did I turn the spoon a certain way? I have heard so many different things. The shape of the belly. A craving for pickles. I even heard that if you sleep on your right side it will be a boy."

"I just know. I've never been wrong. Some men can pick horses, I pick babies. It's a gift. I'd rather be able to pick horses."

"I guess outside country fairs there's not much of a living in guessing babies. By the way, what do you do?"

"I'm an investigator."

"An investigator? Oh, yes."

"I guess your husband didn't mention talking to me. I'm looking into the murder of Lara Greenbaum. She was a student here. Your husband was one of her professors."

"I remember talking to him about her death. It was terrible. Just terrible. Her parents must be beside themselves. No, I don't think he mentioned talking to you."

For the first time there was a glitch in her voice. I sensed that she knew a lot more about me than she was letting on. Her eyes had suddenly found a spot on the wall to be a source of great fascination.

"We met briefly. About the time she was just missing. It was before—"

Browder emerged from the cellar covered in soot. "It will be awhile before we'll feel it, but I think it's working."

"Good, hon, you sure look—"

"Professor Browder."

"Yes, Mr.?"

"Varian." I knew he knew my name. I was beginning to get the feeling that I was in the middle of a theatrical performance.

"Yes. I remember. I need to freshen up."

As Browder walked up the stairs, he turned toward his wife. There was a brief unnatural silence—and a glance, that conspiratorial glance.

"Kathy, I think we need a few things from the store. There's a list in the kitchen."

She hesitated and then walked to the kitchen without answering him. I saw that it was a ruse, but I assumed that he wanted to be able to talk to me frankly about Lara. Things had changed since I last talked to him.

Lara was dead not just missing. At least that's what I told myself.

When Browder returned to the living room, he was cleaner but not more cooperative.

"What are you doing here?"

"I have a few more questions I want to ask you."

"Really? You know you have no official standing. I don't have to answer any of your questions."

I could hear the old Ford whine to a start. I could hear gears grinding as she tried to find reverse.

"Wait a minute. I'm not here investigating you. I am trying to find out what happened to her. To Lara. Do you know how she was—"

"That she was murdered? Of course. Everyone in Storrs knows. I am sorry about that. But you have no right to implicate me in your so-called investigation. I am sorry that Lara Greenbaum is dead, but I had nothing to do with it. Your presence here puts me in a very difficult position."

"How? You might be able to help. You might know something important without realizing it. All I want to do is to find out."

"You don't understand."

"What don't I understand? Who came to see you?"

"What do you mean?"

He stood up and began to look out of the window. I began to get the picture. He was stalling me. His sweet, pregnant wife had just gone off to get the police, the FBI, or Hall's men. Or all of them.

"Where did your wife go?"

"What? Nowhere."

There was panic in his eyes. He turned from the window and began looking for a way out of the room. He acted like I was some psychotic killer. What had they told him about me? I was sure he wouldn't tell me much, but I needed to find out what he really knew.

"Who did you talk to? What they tell you? Keep me under wraps until they could take me away?"

"I don't know what you're talking about. My wife went to the store."

"I'll leave then."

As soon as I saw the hesitation in his face, I knew I was right. He was figuring which was worse for him, staying in the house alone with a possible crazed criminal, or explaining how I got away. I knew I wouldn't get anything from him about Lara. But now I also knew that he knew more. He might even be CA. He looked frightened so I decided to take advantage of his fear. I knew I didn't have much time. I grabbed him by the front of his shirt. "Look you son-of-a-bitch. I don't have time for games. I asked you who'd your wife go for?"

"Take your hands—"

I slapped him, more to humiliate than to hurt, but the back of my hand caught his lip instead of his cheek. The blood spurted like a pipe leaking water. He could taste the blood. It was all over his face and running down my hand. He was already bleeding so I hit him again. Not so hard, just for effect. He was a real bleeder.

"Stop. Stop. It'll only be worse for you."

I relaxed my grip, but kept the back of my hand up near his eye.

"They said they were federal agents."

"FBI?"

"I don't know. They showed me credentials. They said

they were federal agents. Anyway, you'll know soon enough. You won't get away. You'll pay for this. My wife—"

"What did they say they wanted with me?"

"I don't know. They just wanted to know what I said to you. Where you were going. Anything. Then they said if you tried to contact me, I should call this number immediately."

"Get me the number."

"What?"

"Get me the number?"

"Kathy took it."

"The grocery list?"

"Right. You will really pay for this." He wiped his lip, but the blood kept oozing. He hadn't been in too many fights.

"I am going to ask you again, do the initials CA mean anything to you?"

"No, what are you talking about?"

"Can you think of anyone with those initials who knew Lara?"

"I'm not going to tell you anything."

My time was running out. Mrs. Browder could be using the phone next door. I tried to remember how close the nearest house was. I couldn't.

"Take care of the lip. It looks real bad."

By the time, I reached the car I could see the tops of two cars winding up the narrow road. In the lead was a dark blue Pontiac. A few car lengths behind was Browder's Ford. She was right there. She wanted to see the action. So much for Midwest wholesomeness. I got into the Caddy and headed right for my pursuers. I slowed down as I passed a familiar Pontiac. I couldn't be sure they were my friends Sexton and Lawrence from Pennsylvania. They were at least the same type. I swerved toward Kathy Browder's car. I wasn't really close to her, but she wasn't used to police chases. She cut hard to the right, ran into a leaf covered dirt bank, and came to an abrupt stop only partially blocking the road. I couldn't wait to find out if I had slowed them down. I could see in my rear view mirror that the Pontiac had already stopped and was trying to reverse course. I was lucky the road was barely wide enough for two cars. It gave me the few extra seconds I needed to find a way out. The roads around Storrs were perfect for a getaway. Twisting and turning narrow roads over hilly terrain made it difficult to maintain a line of sight on a car ahead of you. The Caddy handled like a roller coaster on rails. The bad thing was that now they knew about the Caddy. I would have a hard time making it back to Candlewood Lake.

I lost them within a few minutes. I found an old barn near the road. The white farmhouse in the distance looked empty. I pulled into the weeds behind the barn and rolled down the window so that I could hear the road noises. The Pontiac passed by once without slowing down. I waited there until deep into the evening, passing the time counting the tops of tall weeds that grew in the ditch across from the drive and working out my next step. It would be easier to travel in the dark. Even a big Caddy is nearly invisible on a dark winter night. It was cold sitting there, but the Caddy seats were a lot more comfortable than a foxhole.

When it was dark, I started the engine and rolled up the window. This time I wasn't worried about staying awake so I turned the heater up high. The blast of hot air was almost immediate. I tried to retrace my steps to Browder's house. I was pretty sure that those agents were not sharing their pursuit of me with the local police. In all the time I was waiting near the barn, not a single local cop had gone by. They had to figure that I would get the hell out of there as quickly as I could. But I couldn't do that. It was clear to me that I had misjudged Browder. He did know something. I had to go back. It was the only lead I had.

The only car in the driveway was the same sad blue Ford. A few hundred yards past the Browders' house was a little clearing that was probably for hunters. I pulled in so that a car passing would probably miss me. I had to take the chance. I didn't want to go tramping through the woods on a dark, cold night. I looked around. It was as quiet as a church on a Wednesday.

I could see through the window that Browder had fixed the heater. Mrs. Browder was sitting on the afghan, reading a magazine. A fire glowed in the fireplace. On the bench in front of her was a cup of tea. I waited to see where he was. A few minutes later, he joined her. They looked like they could be posing for a seasonal shot in *Life Magazine.* I watched him as he tuned the radio and then joined his wife on the couch. He said something to her and then they sat in silence.

I made my way to the back of the house. The two windows were locked, but the door was open. Somehow that wasn't surprising. The door squeaked as it rubbed along the scarred floor to the kitchen. As soon as the door opened, I knew I was safe. The classical music was loud and distorted. As if they wanted the music to be their excuse for not talking. I crept in, walking softly, using my burglar's shuffle. The kitchen was behind the staircase. In order to get into the living room I had to walk across the dining room. Browder saw me before I got very far into the living room. He knocked over the teacup as he lunged for the phone. I wondered how he expected me to let him make a call. Did he think it was a game where the phone was "safe" so I couldn't touch him? I had the phone out of his hand before he could dial two numbers.

"What do you want from us?"

"I just want some answers from you. You won't have to make another trip to the market, will you?"

She remained silent while I escorted her husband back to the sofa. The open Midwestern innocence had vanished from her face. Now she looked like those bitter German women I had seen ten years before whose husbands had promised them the world, but who had brought them only destruction and widowhood. Mrs. Browder's dark glare was directed at the man next to her more than it was at me. She bent over and began to pick up the cup and saucer.

"The tea will stain the carpet," she tried to explain.

"I'm sorry to hear that. Stay where you are."

"Whatever you say."

"Were you having an affair with Lara Greenbaum?"

"I already told you."

"Tell him, David."

He looked away from the both of us. "I would not characterize what happened as an affair."

"How *would* you characterize it?" Kathy Browder spat her words with venom.

"Lara was very bright, but she was also very complex."

Mrs. Browder looked stunned to hear Lara described that way. It seemed to hurt more than the fact that they had obviously slept together.

"I'm not asking for a psychological profile. Just tell me what happened."

"One time. It was just one time."

"When?"

"Last spring. Around the time of the hearings. As they were going on, to tell the truth. I was in a terrible state. Lara— it was more like she wanted to make me feel—"

"Oh, please." Mrs. Browder looked like she wanted to split his other lip.

"She wanted to make it better for me. She knew that I was going through hell and for no reason. It was an act of—"

"Really, David." Mrs. Browder looked away dramatically as if to say I will hear no more of this like a little girl holding her hands over her ears.

"You're right. She seduced me. But I let her. That was wrong."

"How big of you. So what happened?"

"What are you, some kind of pervert? I won't go into the details. There was nothing much to tell about it. She made it clear that she wanted to be in my bed. I was very vulnerable. I was under a lot of pressure. She was very attractive."

"Why would she refer to you as CA in her diary?"

"You still have her diary?"

"Why would she refer to you as CA?"

"I have no idea."

"Think about it."

"It makes no sense. Are you sure she was referring to me?"

"That's what I'm trying to find out."

"What about her boyfriend?"

"CA is a professor."

"After the hearings were all over I didn't see her. Not at all. She was not in my classes. It was one time. It was a misguided. I told Kathy."

His wife did not acknowledge his honesty.

"Who were these federal agents?"

"I told you."

"What exactly did they tell you about me?"

"They said they were investigating you for possible inter-ference with an ongoing federal investigation."

"You believed them?"

"It's not a question of belief. They told me if I cooperated, they would drop any inquiry into my teaching and issue me a clean bill of health."

"And if you didn't? I'm thinking of the ideals we spoke of in your office."

"You're kidding. Why should I even consider risking my life for you? Our life?" He tried to make his voice sound pow-erful and protective. "People keep talking about black lists in Hollywood and in broadcasting. Don't you think there are black lists in academia? Don't you think they could keep someone out of the classroom if they wanted to? It happens all the time. We have a baby coming. I don't have very much. But everything is about all anyone can lose."

"What about your self respect?"

"Who are you to question my motives? I don't know you. What do you know about me? How do I know they are wrong and you are right? *They* didn't beat me up. *They* didn't break into my house and hold me hostage. I would gladly trade your life to them for mine. I have nothing to be ashamed of. Why are they so interested in you, if you're just a private eye look-ing into Lara's death? What does that have to do with national security?"

"I'm asking the questions."

"See? Are you really any better than we are? The lone wolf. The rugged individualist against the powerful monster of the government. Really! I stopped believing in those myths when I faced the reality of working for a living. What do I gain by not turning you in? As soon as you leave, I will call them and tell them everything you said. Assuming you don't kill us first."

I think he sensed I wasn't going to kill them so he could af-ford to play it a little cocky. He liked his little speech. It was his way of busting my lip. I was tempted to take him down a peg or two. His upper lip was still swollen. There was a hard lump of dried blood, which looked like a leech just under his nose. I was sure it still hurt.

"I don't think the little woman is impressed. So let's get back to business, who would be the best candidate for this other professor?"

"I don't really know. Do you have the diary?"

"Why?

"I just wondered what she said."

"About you? You want to know how you rated?"

"Don't be obscene. I'm not such a cad. I care nothing about you, but Lara was my student."

His wife winced and moved her right foot back and forth over the tea stain as if it were the visible evidence of her husband's sin. She wanted it erased. She let the air out of her pursed lips in a long, slow sigh and rubbed her red hands over her belly.

"Did they ask you about the diary?"

"They asked if she had left anything on paper. I had no reason to lie. The papers made it seem that it was just a random act of violence. That she might have been picked up hitchhiking or something."

"That's the story."

"You don't believe it?" He seemed to have gotten over his outrage at my slap. I had the feeling that he knew something, but wasn't sure he should be telling me.

"Do you?"

"I have no way of knowing."

"Who might be interested in tracing the careers of Nazis after the war?"

"Why?"

"That seems to have been Lara's interest. Inspired by a professor, this CA."

I could tell by his face that he had somebody in mind, but he wasn't about to tell me. He had already let down his guard. He didn't want to give me anymore.

"What about George Rippey?" I tried a shot in the dark.

"I really couldn't say."

It was the only name that I had and it was a direct hit. His eyes scanned the room like two trapped animals looking for a way out of the cage. He moved uneasily, crossing his legs, as if he was trying to form himself into a ball.

"Even if you made love to Lara only once, you must have had some sense of her, besides her complexity. Something that might help."

"I told you. I really have no interest in helping you."

He turned toward his wife, looking for support. Whatever they had worked out before was unraveling. She stared at the empty wall above my head. I could see her in Indiana in the spring with a brand new bouncing baby boy.

"Give me the number."

"The number?"

"The number you were going to call as soon as I leave."

I ripped out the phone and took the distributor from their car before heading to George Rippey's.

CHAPTER 17

When I left the Browders, I could feel the snow hanging above me in the sky, just out of sight. It seemed to say that things were coming to a head, and a storm was coming. What I didn't know was whether I would be alive to see how it turned out. My time as Judas goat was drawing to an end. Now I was being readied for the slaughter. Now I was getting close to what they didn't want me to know. FBI or CDA. I knew enough to get me killed, but not enough to keep me alive.

By the time I was a few miles down the road, the snowflakes had begun to dance in front of the headlights like summer moths. Then it was just pure snow, heavy, wet and obliterating like the future.

I knew that Browder might have been able to contact the agents by now. For the second time, I hadn't checked to see where the nearest neighbor was. That was a big mistake. I had no idea how much time I had. If I were spotted in this weather, I'd have a hard time shaking them. The Caddy was no Jeep. The roads were slick. There were no tire marks on the road so it was hard to see where the road ended and the fields began. I would be a sitting duck. But I had to see Rippey.

I stopped at a nearly empty diner along the main road. There was just one trucker at the counter. The man behind the counter was not happy to see another customer on a night like this. I ordered a hamburger and coffee to go which made him a little happier. I asked for a phone book. He pointed to a phone booth in the corner. I had parked next to the truck so that if Sexton and Lawrence showed up they wouldn't see me easily. But I kept one eye on my car while I tried to find Rippey's name in the book.

My odd position caught the counterman's attention. "Looks bad out there. It's gonna be a big one."

"Yeah."

"Have to travel far?"

"Boston."

"I wouldn't want to be you. Not out there in that. I wouldn't want to ruin a nice car like that. You don't see many Caddys like that these days. Everybody's got to have something brand new. Nothing's better than those old Caddys."

"Yeah."

"Yeah." He nodded to the man at the counter and said something I couldn't hear. Then he turned to flip my burger. I found Rippey's address. Now I faced a dilemma.

"Hey, Buddy, I've got to make a stop before I take off for Boston. Do you know where Watermill Road is?"

"That's up Gurleyville, isn't it?"

The man at the counter mumbled into his coffee. The counterman gave me directions.

"I'm glad I don't have to go up to Boston. Not tonight."

"Gotta earn that dollar."

"Not me."

He gave me the same directions a couple of more times but I didn't pay much attention. I paid for the burger and coffee. There was already an inch of snow covering the car. It was a heavy, wet snow, more like March snow than December's. The air was no longer bitter cold, as if the snow were a warm blanket. The wind had died down so everything was eerily quiet. The only sound was a neon sign that crackled behind me.

There were still no cars on the road. The snow piled itself against the windshield wipers until I was looking through something that resembled a porthole. I was heading into a long dark tunnel.

I found Rippey's house without too much trouble, although the Caddy kept swerving along the back roads. Once I almost slipped off the road into a drainage ditch. I kept looking for the Pontiac, but the only vehicle on the road was a slow moving pick up truck that inched its way toward, what I presumed to be, home. There was a light in Rippey's front window.

There was one car in the drive, not a Pontiac. It looked English. Foreign anyway. It had to be Rippey's.

I parked on the side of the road. The snow continued to come down steadily and a strong white moon made the whole landscape look like an advertisement for Christmas in Vermont. It was so quiet I could almost hear the stars. Even this modest modern ranch house, sitting among brilliant white evergreens, could easily be a model for a Christmas card. My smooth soled shoes were no aid on the slippery walk. I could see Rippey through the large front window. He sat in an old upholstered chair. Here was no cheery fireplace, no country touches that warmed the atmosphere. Instead, there were piles of books and magazines on every surface of the living room. He appeared to be alone. I figured they had warned him about me too, so I decided not to knock. The local custom seemed to be to leave the back door open. This time I wanted to make an entrance that would confirm whatever stories he had heard about how dangerous I was so I used my shoulder to burst through the door as loudly as I could. Unfortunately, the wet slab of concrete that served as a back porch was as slippery as ice because it was ice. My arrival was more comic than menacing but Rippey didn't notice.

Before he could raise himself from the chair, I was in front of him. The book he was holding went flying to the floor and a sound like an injured cat erupted from his mouth.

"What the hell!"

"No need to get up."

I had forgotten what he looked like. I really hadn't done a good job the first time around. He was taller than I remembered, almost six feet. His hair, which looked like it hadn't been combed in days, hung in random ringlets over his ears and one eye. He had covered himself with a blanket to keep warm while he was reading. Underneath he had on a rich red ski sweater. I could see how he might appear handsome to a coed in a bohemian sort of way. He looked a little like Cornel Wilde with about three day's growth.

"What the hell are you doing here? You can't just—"

"I apologize for not setting up an appointment, but right now it wouldn't be convenient. Just sit down."

I wished I had my pistol. I had left it on the seat in case I ran into the Pontiac. It was still there. I was making too many mistakes, but I would lose the effect of my entrance if I had to repeat it. I was after drama. The effect of a gun in somebody's face is usually enough to insure cooperation. It certainly would have made things simpler. Now I had to keep sizing the professor up to make sure he wasn't going to resist. He was a big man. He wouldn't crumble with a little slap across the face like Browder. I looked him in the eye and tried to look menacing while speaking lazily. It was an awful Robert Mitchum, but it was the best I could do at the time. It was harder than it looked.

"I need to talk to you. And you need to give me some answers. You told me you hardly remembered Lara Greenbaum. But I know that you were much closer to her than you let on."

He turned away as if I would go away if he refused to respond. I kicked over a table piled with books.

"Don't fuck with me, Rippey. I need some answers."

"I don't have to talk to you.'

He started to get up. With just a little pressure from my forearm, he gave in right away and melted back into the chair. He looked toward the bookshelf behind me. On the wall next to the bookcase was a framed cover from a comic book. It was a picture of Captain America practically decapitating a muscular Nazi with his whirling red, white, and blue shield. There was an inscription written under Captain America's prodigious groin area. Although I couldn't read it, I knew it was from Lara. I had found CA. Her hero. Some hero.

But he wasn't looking at the poster. On the third shelf, I saw a few pieces of paper that looked as if they really interested Rippey. I got my hand on top of them while not taking my eyes off Rippey. I quickly flipped through the papers and found a telephone number. The same number that Browder had been given no doubt. Under "CDA" was TR-2768. Underneath he had written "Lara." As if he would forget. I really didn't like Captain America.

"No, you don't. Just sit. I know what you're going to say. You'll say I can't compel you to talk to me. That you have these friends in the government. It's just the two of us here right now. No legal mumbo jumbo is going to save your ass. And I'm not in a good mood."

"Get out of my house. I've nothing to say to you." He started to get up. He was going to make his move, but it was slow and obvious so I hit him. I hit him hard. Too hard. He held the side of his face. There was no blood, but his face was beginning to swell. I didn't mind hitting him at all, but I was afraid I had broken his jaw. And I wanted him to be able to talk. There were tears in his eyes, but he didn't try to fight back. He just slumped over rubbing his cheek.

"You won't get away with this."

"Right, Professor. In the meantime you're in pain and I'm in a hurry." When I was sure that his jaw was not broken, I wanted to hit him again, and again. I kept hearing Lara's words. The admiration. The passion. I wanted to hit him again. But I couldn't because I wouldn't stop.

"You will go to jail. I'll see to it." His jaw was swollen and he sounded like a Red Skelton character. I couldn't remember which one, the drunk maybe.

"That's fine. So what you're saying is you want me to keep beating the shit out of you until you tell me what I want to know. You like it, huh. I've heard about guys like you."

"Get out of here." For some reason he began to clutch his belly. So I slapped him to get his attention. He was too absorbed in his pain.

"Tell me about you and Lara. Maybe we can start there."

"And if I don't?"

He was trying to call my bluff. He tried to manufacture the cocky look of a man who had just filled his straight, daring everybody to raise him. I didn't buy his bluff, but I didn't want to waste what little time I had. Browder would send Sexton and Lawrence here. I either had to keep beating him up or find something else.

Then I saw the two neat piles of paper in folders next to the typewriter on the desk. I moved toward them. I knew I was on to something when Rippey sat up.

"What's this?"

"That has nothing to do with you or Lara!"

I picked it up. It was Rippey's book—*America's Nazis:*

The Influence of Fascism on American Foreign Policy 1945-1951. It was all here. I put one copy on top of the other.

"Was Lara helping you do research for this when she made contact with Lindzey Hall?"

"I told you. It has nothing to do—"

I took the title page in one hand and began to crumple it. Rippey leaped from his chair, arms extended as if he was trying to save his child from a fall. It made him an easy target. I dropped the manuscript on the desk and caught him right in the gut, hard enough to cause him to lose his breath, not hard enough to put him out. I pushed him back into his chair before he could straighten up. I took the dedication page, "for my mother," and threw it in his face.

"Look, whoever you are, I don't know anything. I won't cooperate. That's my book. I've worked on it for four years. My tenure—"

"Fuck you. And fuck your tenure. It's the murder of a nineteen-year-old girl. Not your goddamn career that is at stake."

He laughed. "You have no idea what this is about."

"Tell me then."

He was nervous about the book, but he suddenly was more relaxed. He knew I wouldn't kill him. He had taken what he thought were my best shots, and now he thought he was going to be rescued.

"So the Feds are coming back here tonight. To have a look at your book?"

Rippey would be a cinch to read in a poker game. His straight would win him nothing. I had to do some bluffing of my own. I continued. "Cut the crap, Rippey. You think you've uncovered some earth shattering information that's going to make you into a name. What makes you think that they will let you print it?"

"You are so naive. The CDA has been looking into Hall for years. I am going to help them to nail him. They want it out. They needed someone outside the government. It is going to be big."

"So why are they coming here in the middle of the night."

"Right. Meetings are always at night, in the movies, aren't they?" He tried to laugh.

"Okay, Rippey, who's the CDA?"

He was acting as if I asked him who was buried in Grant's tomb. He thought he was dealing with a cretin. I could see why he was a professor. He enjoyed pointing out the obvious to the uninitiated. When I caught him glancing at the clock, I knew I hadn't much time. By sheer accident I had probably bought myself time by showing up at Browder's. They figured Rippey wasn't going anywhere. They could look for me.

"What if I told you that Hall is the CDA?"

"That's crazy. It's a federal agency, part of the CIA."

"Are you sure?"

"You don't know a damn thing about the government. Or anything else for that matter."

"Apparently there are things you don't know either."

"Hall has his own staff. They're not part of—"

"Right. So tell me about Lara."

"There's nothing to tell. She did help me on some research, but that was just library work."

"On Jacques de Paul."

"Uh." I surprised him with that name. The bravado had faded quickly. "Who told you?" His speech was still slurred, but fear seemed to clear his head. He looked like a man whose wife had just discovered matches from a motel she had never been to in his pockets and he had to explain them.

"Lara. How did she wind up with Hall in Philadelphia?"

"That was not my idea."

He seemed almost relieved to be finally telling his story. He wasn't the cold fish I had first thought. Between quick glances at the clock, he started to relax. He stopped rubbing his belly.

"It was all her idea."

"How?"

"When she realized what I was on to, she volunteered to testify before Hall's little investigating staff, the ones who set things up for the hearings. She thought that if it looked like she was cooperating, they might take her in, so to speak."

She had sold out Browder. That's why she slept with him. It was her way of making things better.

"So she testified against Browder and you let her?"

"I had no choice."

"But Browder is no commie."

"Of course not. Don't be naive."

"You let her betray an innocent man."

"Nothing would have come of it."

"That's easy for you to say. Did he know?"

"Not unless Lara told him. Her testimony was secret. She died before the public hearings. They were going to coach her in Philadelphia."

"And it didn't occur to you that Hall might have had something to do with her death."

"I thought she was kidnapped by a rapist. That it was just a weird coincidence."

"Now who's being naïve?"

"You have no proof. Do you?"

I could tell from his question that he was thinking more about a new ending to his book than about Lara. "I want to know more about how you got her involved."

"You don't seem like you're merely a detective in this regard. I mean Lara's dead. It's a police matter. What's your interest here? Are you one of Lara's conquests?"

"Don't be disgusting."

"I see. You were immune to her charms. I am sure a detective would have whetted her appetite for adventure."

"I knew her as a child. I know her—"

"That's even more perverse. Lusting after a dead girl."

I lost it at that point. I lifted him up from the chair and smashed his back into the bookcase behind him. Books came tumbling off the shelves like snowflakes except with a lot more noise.

"Just shut up and tell me how you got Lara involved."

"One didn't control Lara. She's the one who called the plays, I'm telling you. The only mistake I made was to tell her what I was working on. From that point on, I couldn't have stopped her if I tried. It wasn't enough to expose Hall's connections with de Paul. She wanted to find what they were up to. Now, I told her that was not scholarship but journalism. She said she didn't care. She wanted to bring him down, herself. I tried to tell her. Time and time again, I tried. I even warned her about testifying against Browder. She did it all on her own. I can imagine what she said about him."

"You expect me to believe—"

"Oh, believe it. What do you think? That she was some innocent young girl corrupted by the evil professor? Hardly. Lara Greenbaum was a force of nature. She was on a mission and nothing was going to stop her. Certainly not me."

"But you were going to take advantage of what she discovered."

"Of course. Why shouldn't I?"

"Because her life was in danger."

"I didn't know that and I still don't know that."

"So how could a young girl change overnight like that unless you—"

"Put the ideas into her head? I was just the spark. She was determined to find a cause."

"Why? She was only a girl."

"Hardly a girl. It had something to do with her father."

"Her father?"

"Yes. Her father."

"So what are you saying?"

"She felt terrible that her father had all this guilt about the war. He felt he had let his people down, his family down. According to her, her father never served overseas on the front line, he was a doctor or something. The Holocaust really got to him."

"He's a dentist."

"It doesn't matter. In any case, being a Jew, he felt very guilty about it. Especially after the full enormity of Nazism was revealed. He felt guilty that he spent the war in some safe spot while others, especially his brother, were off on the front lines, risking their lives in the good fight, and not coming back. It's a common phenomenon, survivor's guilt."

"But his brother came back and is doing quite well. At least he was until Lara was killed."

"He did? I had the impression that he hadn't. That's puzzling. I guess it's a more complicated family situation than I had imagined. But I know, from what Lara told me, her father felt like a coward, even when there was no reason to. Lara was going to make it right. She was obsessed with it. Then she had her own ax to grind. She was convinced that she hadn't gotten in to Smith because she was a Jew. I guess it was her first real taste of anti-Semitism. She was going to redeem the family honor by bringing a Nazi to justice. I tried to counsel her. We had a parting of the ways just before Thanksgiving, just before she disappeared. To tell you the truth—" He leaned over as if we were buddies. "—I was almost frightened of her. She had gone somewhere way beyond dedication."

"C'mon."

"You never really knew her. You've no idea. I think she slept with Browder just to make sure that he would look like a real creep—you know, using commie ideas to get young co-eds into bed. I tried to dissuade her."

"From what?"

"From everything. Once it had gone past research, once she had done good work for me—she had gone beyond that."

"Because she was in love. Or so she thought."

"With me? At first, perhaps. But I don't think so. She could make you think that, sure. Fundamentally, I think, she was disappointed in me. At first, I might have been a candidate for her knight in shining armor, but I am only a scholar. She wanted me to be her Captain America. The embarrassing thing is that for a short time I wanted to be as well."

"So she took advantage of you?"

"In a way yes. How shall I say it? She used every means at her disposal to inspire me."

"Spare me the details. So her involvement in your work wasn't just a way of playing up to you, like a girl learning about baseball to get a boyfriend?"

"No, no. Not at all. In the end, I realized that it had nothing to do with me. I knew it the first time we were in bed."

"So you feel nothing now that she's gone. You have her research and—"

"I was devastated."

"So devastated you lied about even knowing her?"

"To you."

"And the police and her parents and—"

"What do I know? What good would it have done to say

that she went to Philadelphia to follow a congressman and wound up murdered. If I said that she not only worked for me, but also shared my bed, who would I help? Would her parents feel comforted? I feel no guilt. There's nothing wrong with what I did? She was of age. I am unmarried. It might be embarrassing, but it's certainly not illegal. It happens all the time."

"What's the story on Jacques de Paul?"

"How do *you* know about him?"

"Who tipped you to de Paul? You didn't figure it out on your own."

"I had published a few articles on the Nazi occupation of the low countries. I mentioned de Paul in one of them. About a year ago I received a letter from a man who said he had some information about former Nazis, including de Paul, and wanted to know if I was interested."

"And you were, of course. Who was he?"

"He said he had served in Operation Rodeo and it bothered him ever since."

"Operation Rodeo?"

"A team of Americans who were supposed to round up Nazis, get it?"

"You didn't think it was a little too convenient?"

"I took him at his word."

"You did? It didn't occur to you that somebody might be setting you up?"

"Why? For what purpose?"

"Think about it. So you find de Paul and Hall hooked up together."

"I didn't. Lara did. She identified him. I could only find one picture of de Paul. I attached it to the list. It was from his college days. Somehow, when Hall came through here with his entourage, looking for Reds, she saw a resemblance between the picture and one of Hall's advisors. It was sheer accident."

"But you really needed Lara to verify his identity didn't you. What was your plan? She would seduce him and he would confess? How hard did you try to keep her from going?"

"That's ridiculous. I had no idea what was on her mind."

"You didn't think she was at risk?"

"Her wish will come true and her story will be told. In a short time Hall will be history and she will get the credit she deserves."

I wanted to hit him again. I knew that I had pressed my luck by staying as long as I had. I picked up the manuscript and began to back away from Rippey.

"Where are you going?"

"When your friends arrive, tell them that I was looking for something to read and I borrowed this."

"You can't—"

"You want to try to stop me?"

I knew that I might have signed Rippey's death warrant by taking the manuscript, but I had the strong feeling that he was dead anyway. I found it hard to care one way or another.

It also occurred to me as I contemplated his fate that Rippey might have already stashed a carbon. He wasn't an idiot. The Feds would want to see the carbon. But there was no time to worry about that. I had my copies. It might buy me a little time if I could get back to Stamford. On the road I was vulnerable. If they caught me, they would have the manuscripts and me. There would be no reason to keep me alive, except—

There were still the issues of the Biddle School and Jack Veasey's death. As I turned off the road that led to Rippey's house, I caught sight of headlights coming over the hill. I turned off mine. There was enough moonlight reflected off the snow to allow me to find a driveway. I slipped in and waited. When no car passed, I knew that it was the Pontiac or its kin. I decided to follow the directions given me at the diner. They wouldn't expect me to head toward Boston. I could double back later along the coast.

I should have paid more attention. I had no idea how I eventually got to Providence.

CHAPTER 18

It took me almost nine hours to inch my way back to Candlewood Lake. About ten inches of snow had fallen throughout the night. The only vehicles I saw were snowplows and a few scattered cars abandoned by the side of the road. There were no roadblocks. If there had been an alert, they would have had me easily. I couldn't do more than fifteen miles an hour. On dry roads, the Caddy stuck to the road like a train. In the snow with summer tires, it was a different story.

I became convinced that the CDA didn't want any local law in on my arrest. I was getting more and more dangerous to them the more I knew. My insurance policy was about to lapse unless I could find just the right bit of information. I hoped that Rippey's book would give me what I needed. Louis would know. I wondered if Rippey and the Browders were still alive. On the radio, I heard the news that it was Christmas Eve morning. "Silent Night" followed. Bing Crosby's. It came as something of a shock. It had been a month since Lara was killed.

I replayed Rippey's description of Lara in my mind. I fought it all the way back to Providence. I had read Lara's secret words. I didn't know the real Lara. What she was really like. The more I knew the more she changed. In my mind, she was nothing like Rippey described. The Lara I thought I knew was young and full of life, a little reckless maybe, too full of herself as a woman perhaps, but an idealist who brought light into the world. She was no *femme fatale*. But the diary told a different story. I knew Rippey was just trying to protect himself, but his Lara was closer to what I read. And that bothered me.

For almost everyone else in Connecticut, there was reason

to celebrate. It was going to be a White Christmas. The kids would be able to try out their brand new Christmas sleds. It was a day off so Dad could put off the shoveling. "Peace on Earth." I thought of the Greenbaums. At least I would avoid my annual depression. This year I had to worry about someone else putting a gun to my head. Maybe this was a sign that I was on the road to mental health.

As I pulled up to the lake house, I realized that my neck was as stiff as a cheap pair of pants. My shoulders ached from trying to keep the Caddy on the road. I was so exhausted that I couldn't think about what I had learned at Rippey's. I would let Louis read the book and sort it out while I slept.

Louis was already up and in a bad mood. In my haste to leave, I hadn't thought about provisions. There was no coffee in the house and the only thing left to eat was a can of peaches. He wanted me to go for food. When I told him about my escape from Sexton and Lawrence, he changed his mind. He would have the peaches and a cup of tea.

"Let me see the manuscript."

"Sure. I'm hitting the hay."

Sleep didn't come as easily as I expected. During the night as I struggled to keep my eyelids from closing, the soft bed overlooking the frozen lake seemed as luxurious as a penthouse apartment. Now that I was back, staring at the ceiling, I couldn't even close my eyes without seeing Browder and his wife, the Pontiac, Rippey's house, and Lara all mixed up together. I tried everything, including coming up with a beer for every letter of the alphabet: Anheiser-Busch, Blatz, Chesterfield Ale, Dab, Excelsior, Flagg's, Guinness, Harp, Iron City…until sheer boredom allowed me to drift off into a fitful sleep where all the main players reappeared in my dreams even more grossly distorted. Lara danced like a harem girl in front of the Greenbaums as several Nazis accompanied her on accordions. The Greenbaums were proud of their daughter's performance. They commented on the excellence of her technique. They told her to remove her top so that we all could appreciate the shape of her breasts. She smiled shyly and then slowly slid the orange cloth from her shoulders. Browder crouched in the background like an ogre under a bridge. His wife's stomach was swollen to the point I could see a fetus the size of an adult moving grotesquely under her skin…

∽∽

Louis woke me about two in the afternoon.

"We just have to get some food. I have been sitting here for an hour trying to figure out how to trap a rabbit. Even you looked appetizing. I thought up recipes for Donner stew."

"Spare me your cannibal fantasies. Do you think it's safe to go out? Is a hamburger worth it?"

"They'd be here already. If they followed you, we'd be doing a little gunfight at OK Corral by now. So I guess it's safe. I don't care anyway, I'm too hungry."

"The phone. You used the phone?"

"I'm not that stupid. I have a DSC2."

"I have a Purple Heart."

"Not a Distinguished Service Cross, idiot. It's a little toy that allows me to scramble telephone signals. Makes them impossible to trace. Or at least difficult enough that you would need a room at the Pentagon filled with vacuum tubes to trace the call. I use it a lot."

"For what?"

"Business.""

"It is impossible to trace?"

"It's at least difficult. Nothing is impossible. Whoever invented it probably also invented the device that allows you to trace calls made on a DSC2. So he can sell both ends. It's a little cumbersome. Here it is."

He picked up a little box that had a tray inside that just fit a phone.

"Here listen to the dial tone. Now listen when I hit the switch." There was nothing. "Neat isn't it?"

"Let me wake up."

"Please, Varian. I am very hungry. There's a shopping list on the kitchen table. Hurry, we have a lot of work to do."

"I'm doing the shopping?"

"Of course."

"The drifts are three feet out there."

"Wear your galoshes."

The shopping trip was uneventful except that I almost got stuck three times trying to find a store that was open and, when I did, I discovered that the items, absurdly specific, on Louis's list were impossible to obtain at the small market near the lake, probably the only store open for miles. Instead of Arabica beans, whatever they were, he got Maxwell House, instead of Jewish rye, he got Wonder Bread, instead of Guinness Stout, he got Budweiser, and instead of Hungarian pastrami, he got American bologna. There were also eggs, milk, and butter, things I recognized right off the bat. At least he wasn't hungry for caviar. I don't know what I would have gotten. Sardines maybe. There was no sign of any Pontiacs. There were few cars on the road.

When I entered the house, I could see Louis sitting at the table. He was sitting in an unnatural position. Head slumped over, arms dangling at his side. I looked for the pool of blood. I put down the grocery bag as silently as I could. I took my gun out of my pocket—I would not forget it in the car again—and put my back against the wall. The long corridor that led to the bedrooms was dark. I thought I could make out a figure in the shadows. I raised my gun and was about to fire when Louis jumped up from his seat.

"Jesus, Varian. You were aiming right over my head. What if I stood up?"

"I wasn't expecting a dead man to stand up."

"I just dozed off, for chrissakes. Hunger makes me drowsy."

"Don't sleep on the job."

Louis reached greedily for the packages. He didn't even seem to mind that I had brought back practically nothing that was on his list. He stuck the knife in the jar of yellow mustard like a Turkish assassin. Between lustful bites, he offered me his assessment of Rippey's book.

"It doesn't ring completely true."

"About de Paul?"

"About anything, especially de Paul. He was a Nazi all right, but he was no architect of the New World Order. This is no catch like a Martin Heidigger might have been. He was a second rate literary type, as I told you, kissing up to the Nazis by knocking Jewish modernism and American mongrelism. He pleased his masters by praising the glories of a United Europe under German domination. The only real evidence Rippey has consists of a few quotes from book reviews that make fun of Franz Kafka and Marc Chagall, found, no doubt, by Lara. And it was Lara who tied Hall to de Paul—that he was Henri Krims, trusted advisor. I'm convinced there is no real research here. The portrait of de Paul is all channeled through this Warren Saper, the supposed man of conscience. I don't buy it for a minute. I especially don't buy Saper."

"So what's the point? Why make him out to be so big?"

"There was an Operation Rodeo all right. That fits what I could find out from my friend in Washington. It's the portrait of de Paul that this Rippey swallows that bothers me. If they are going to tar Hall with de Paul's past, they have to make him a bigger fish than he is. The FBI, or whoever this Saper works for, is just spinning fantasies, hoping that if they appeared in an academic book, who knows? It would look legitimate. I mean de Paul was a Nazi. What could Hall say? He was a Nazi all right. There's proof all over the place on that, but he was not a very big Nazi, or a very smart Nazi, or powerful Nazi. It's typical of the FBI to take a little truth and turn it into a big lie."

"If they knew about de Paul, why not just come out with it? Go to the *Times* or something. I'm sure they have ways of getting things in print."

"Oh, you innocent. That's like saying we have the bomb, why don't we just use it on Moscow? Because they have the bomb, too. Maybe the FBI doesn't want this book published. They just want to have the threat of it to make Hall back down. It's the cold war in miniature. Too many questions would arise if the book came out. Are there other Nazis? Where are they? How many other big shots would they take down? We might all love hating communists now, but there are still a lot of people who aren't too fond of the Nazis. Hall would know that much of the stuff about de Paul is bull, but it might be enough to keep him from launching his all-out attack on Hoover. Lara really nailed him though. She had the makings of a good journalist and a halfway decent scholar. I am sure she is responsible for most of the real research. This Rippey didn't do more than copy what this Saper told him. Somehow, she got a hold of the one piece of damming evidence on Hall, a memo about three Yale professors, all Jews who needed to be 'excised.' Where she found it and how she got it to Rippey, I don't know. She couldn't have gotten the actual memo to him, could she? He knows a lot more about what happened to her."

"I think so, too. But I don't think we'll have a chance to talk to him." I explained in more detail why I was convinced they would have to kill Rippey. "Sure, they're going to have to sanitize the whole situation. It's the way these operations always go. Rippey has to go. But he deserves it. The son-of-a-bitch gives Lara almost no credit. 'Thanks to my student, Lara Greenbaum, for her many contributions to my research.' Like she kept his library card up to date, or something. They knew what they wanted for this job, a third rate academic with a hard on for fame and who wouldn't question what he was being given. I hope it costs him his life because that memo might have cost her life. *Verrat*--traitor, remember. She had to get close to de Paul. She must have been so full of herself after her *conquests* of Browder and Rippey. Poor kid, brave kid. I'm impressed."

"Do you think that Lara really came up with the idea to sacrifice Browder?"

"It wouldn't surprise me. She was a remarkable girl."

"But I don't know if I buy it. You read the diary. She was so romantic. How could she—"

"That's why she could. If she weren't tied to such an unthinking asshole who couldn't see anything except his own glory, she might have gotten away with it."

"Rippey."

"He didn't know who was with Hall and who was with the FBI. He had to be the one who fucked it up for her." It had already occurred to me that Rippey might have tipped them off to Lara. "He didn't know that the CDA was Hall's Gestapo. He talked to them. Who knows what he told them to impress them. We'll probably never know if he betrayed Lara directly or indirectly. But if he did, I'd feel a lot better about leaving him to his death."

How had she gotten the memo? How had Rippey gotten it? It was hard to imagine Lara as a functioning spy. She seemed too young. All nineteen year olds did. A young girl just beginning to understand the power of her sexuality and using it for a big cause. It must have been intoxicating. I wanted to feel disgusted by her behavior. That was what was called for. Why did the sex make such a difference? I couldn't see it any other way. She *was* something of a hero. I had to hold on to that. I had to. I still had a hard time with what she did to Browder. I guess I didn't like my heroes using other people like that. I didn't mention my misgivings to Louis. He would have laughed again at my "sentimentality."

I thought about Manny Greenbaum. How could I tell him that his daughter had died to make his world right? That she had used her body to get what she wanted. That she had done it all for him. How could I tell a man who wanted to give Lara the world that he had given her only his guilt. What could I say to Freddie? Ever since I found the diary I had avoided him. There was too much I didn't want them to know. Who was I to decide? Had Lara gotten to me? Louis was right. I was out of my league. I still had a client and I didn't know what to do. I just knew I couldn't quit.

Louis looked at me as I was trying to sort things out. "I found one thing out about de Paul that might be more important to us than his politics. His proclivities."

"His what?"

"His tastes. Like a lot of Nazis, de Paul thought he was beyond good and evil, that Nazism, at least for the elite, had opened the doors to the kind of paradise only imagined by the likes of the Marquis de Sade. A world where the *ubermensch* ruled. One of the ways that the Nazis seduced intellectuals was to offer them the forbidden pleasures of the flesh unattainable in their ivory towers. But instead of a race of giants, instead of the *ubermensch*, we got a piddling little bunch of *untermenschs* running the show. I mean look at Hitler, Eichmann, and Bohrman and they're still with us."

"Spare me."

"Listen to this then. My Navy friend was able to find out only a couple of things about de Paul. He was not that important, as I said. The one thing that stood out was his frequenting a little bordello that the Nazis had established for collaborators like de Paul. Officially called *Le Chateau*, but it was known in Brussels as *Die Dachtraufe,* the gutter. It was there that Jewish boys and girls were "introduced" to the tastes of the master race before they were shipped out to the camps. The more beautiful or cooperative they were, the longer they could stay. The underground had the place bombed in 1944. It was one of the few nights that de Paul wasn't there, apparently. According to my friend, he had a taste for young girls. Some of them might not have survived his attentions. Lara was a little mature for his tastes."

"I don't want to hear any more about it."

"You have to understand how intoxicating it can be for some squirrely intellectual to have all of his fantasies fulfilled. It's more powerful than any drug, than almost anything at all."

I began to describe what I wanted to do to de Paul. Louis ignored my revenge scenarios, letting me vent all the anger that had been building up since I first heard what happened to Lara. I could not erase the pictures of her body from my mind.

Louis began to ramble himself, about a number of things, Nazis, why Paris was spared, why he preferred Armagnac to Cognac, about his stay in Paris and then, in a voice made more frightening because of its lack of feeling, his visit to Dachau. He never talked much about the war, usually dismissing his experience with a wisecrack or two. Even though he hadn't known Lara, I could tell from the sound of his voice that he had some grudge to settle of his own, and it wasn't just about the dogs either.

We were both somehow back in the war. But in a different way. Once again, I was fighting an enemy that seemed remote and faceless. I knew the chances that I would actually face either Hall or de Paul were remote. Like the Nazi leaders, they had their army of faceless men who stood between us. Just like the war, I had no idea what was really going on. Decisions were made, strategies implemented, and tactics employed—all of it impenetrable to me in the field.

The impact, however, as always, was always the same. It cost lives and risked my own.

Louis was tapping his pencil impatiently. Apparently, he had been asking me a question. "Where do we go from here?"

"We could play the game. We could threaten to publish the manuscript?"

"Who would we threaten?"

"Hall? The FBI?"

"And?"

"And? If it was going to work for Rippey, why not for us?"

"What would we get? The best we could hope for would be to embarrass Hall who might or might not have to resign. He could even beat it. We don't have that much. There's nothing to link him to any murders. Nothing. It's not even an issue in the book. What would any lawyer do with a coded diary? And what happens to us once we are exposed, do we receive the gratitude of a grateful nation? Do we appear on the television, point the finger at Hall, and scream 'I *accuse* you'? The reason these people are so successful is that they have all the cards, the chips, the table, and they call the game. Do you think Lara is the first one who was killed because she knew a little too much or got a little too close to something? If it doesn't happen every day, it happens every week. They can keep almost anything a secret. It's only when they have one of these little power struggles that they are vulnerable. This is a game for knights, bishops and rooks, not pawns."

"So what are you saying? There's nothing to be done?"

"No, I'm not saying that. We still have to sort through things. We just haven't found the Rosetta Stone yet. The key here is information. We know only half the story. How Hall is vulnerable. We need to find out what Hall has on the FBI. If our theory is correct. Without it we can be played. With it we call all the shots."

"Or draw fire from two sides."

"That's the risk. But you can be killed only once. Hall is perfectly capable of doing that on his own."

We spent the rest of Christmas Eve in a kind of hallucinatory debate, each of us going over options, occasionally mumbling something to each other and then drifting back into our own thoughts. Louis had as much of an aversion of Christmas Music as I did, so we avoided the radio. There weren't enough good records to sustain us. We had been reduced to "Highlights In Hi-Fi" which were absurdly edited versions of classical chestnuts which emphasized the latest in Hi Fidelity recordings, especially loud cymbals and exploding cannons. We tried it for a while. It brought the only laughs of the day. Finally, in desperation we turned on the radio. We could not endure more silence.

Almost every station devoted itself to "songs of the season." We spun the dial through Bing Crosby's, Frank Sinatra's, Dean Martin's and Ella Fitzgerald's versions of "White Christmas." Versions of "Silent Night" ran a close second. When we could no longer avoid Christmas, we settled back and stared out the big window.

"What do you remember about Christmas? Louis asked.

"My father saw it as a business opportunity. The best time of the year. He would go to New York and pick up real cheap a box of some toy or other that wasn't selling and go door to door with them. It was the Depression. One year it would be a doll, the next year toy trucks made out of cheap metal. One year I would get a doll and the next a toy truck. Whatever he got a deal on. I didn't really 'get' presents. They would just be there, unsold, in a box, for me to use, if I wanted. I always felt that the few toys left over represented only lost revenue to my father, not the spirit of Christmas giving. My mother would knit me a sweater or a scarf. But nobody on our street got much."

"You know what I never understood?"

"What?"

"The 'Twelve Days of Christmas.' Who was that song supposed to appeal to? Is *it* some kind of code? Does it have something to do with the Restoration, you know, 'Twelve Lords a Leaping.' I don't understand its appeal. I don't understand it at all. And it's such a god-awful tune. Livestock for Christmas! What lover gives such things?"

"I never thought about it. All that counting. I guess I just shut it out."

"I get most of the others. 'O Little Town of Bethlehem' is especially fine. But 'Eight Maids a Milking'! Is it sexual?"

"I don't care."

"About sex? Anyway, I thought we were sharing Christmas."

"By ranting on about some stupid song. What was it like for you during Christmas?"

"It was wonderful, as you might imagine. We lived in a Winter Wonderland. A smart little Jewish boy asked to sing carols at Christmas, honoring a religion that branded him a 'Christ killer.' I constructed my own slightly obscene texts to accompany the tunes that I would mouth enthusiastically. My father always distinguished between two Christmases—the pagan one with its northern symbols of wreaths, lights, and trees that produced fascism, the song of the earth, you know. He saw the carolers that patrolled our neighborhood as likely participants in the Nuremburg Rallies. Then there was the Christian holiday celebrating the birth of the Savior, a Jew, in whose honor there were marvelous celebrations like the Spanish Inquisition and the pogroms of Russia. It was always a festive time in our house."

"You know what's been bothering me?"

"Your sciatica?"

"Biddle. I keep coming back to Biddle. There is something back there that we haven't uncovered yet. Lara's body was just up the road. Veasey's death. Hall's vendetta against the school. I don't know if it will help us get either Hall or de Paul, but I have to find out."

Louis was impatient with me. "Maybe it's just one of your professional quirks. I don't care what happened back there. There is a war going on here and now. I am trying to figure out how to save our skins and do a little damage."

"But it might help if we knew what happened."

"It could be a hundred things that have nothing to do with what's happening now. There are such things as coincidences. You are looking for a pattern where there might be none. Hall might have been caught jerking off and was humiliated by the prefect or whatever they called him. Who knows? Human beings are not that consistent. We have all heard the stories of

Nazis who wept at Goethe's grave. You can't always expect to make sense out of this life. The law of the universe is that anything can happen."

He waited for me to agree. I was not in the mood for a joust with Louis. His voice seemed to jump an octave. "My god, man, you were there in the war. Tell me what you saw made sense. The skinny kid afraid to ask a girl for a date storms a machine gun nest, the punk who saves your life and then robs the dead, the captain with the tears still streaming down his face from the news that he is a father, buys a whore on the streets of Paris to celebrate before the tears dry. Those are just the first ones who come to mind. The child isn't father to the man, the past is no prelude. We don't know from one moment to the next how we are going to react to anything. And you are looking for meaning in something that happened, when? Fifteen years ago?"

"You're right. You are right in many ways about a lot of things. I know. But not here. Not here. I can just sense it."

Somehow, we got through the night. We even managed a little Christmas cheer before we went to bed. I opened a couple of Budweisers and Louis made a quite edible omelet out of bologna and eggs. He offered a toast to "a better world." He tried to make it sarcastic. The moonlit landscape might have inspired us to write a new carol if we had been Rogers and Hart.

Christmas Day dragged on and on. We spent the morning listening to Handel's "Messiah" which Louis conducted like Toscanini and then the day began to turn sour. There were church services from St. Patrick's Cathedral and from a Lutheran church in Minneapolis. There were countless expressions of season's cheer and we sank into a mutual silence. The only bright spot was a version of "It's Christmas Time" by a rhythm and blues group called the Five Keys. The artificial cheer that permeated the airwaves only made my situation that much bleaker. It was not only the season of the Birth of the Savior, but of the Slaughter of the Innocents who were never remembered. I was still planning to head back to Philadelphia, despite Louis's cautions.

"Why would they expect me to go back there?"

"Because, if you're right, and there's something there, and it's still covered up, they have to keep it from being uncovered. Start thinking like a detective, goddammit."

"But if there's something there, we might be able to use it to get Hall."

I was whining. Louis accepted the fact that I would go and leave him to avenge Amor and Psyche on his own, if that was what it was about. He began to plan for our departure. We both had had enough of sylvan beauty. We knew that the Caddy was no longer safe. We needed two cars. We had to wait until the next day to get them in Danbury.

"Do you think anybody has been here since Keyes died?"

The few mementos scattered around the house made it clear that no one had assumed ownership after Keyes death—a couple of photographs of Keyes, one signed by his father, a stern police sergeant. A few pictures of the lake. There was a decided absence of a woman's touch in the decor. We could think of no woman who would have hung a picture of a seemingly rabid dog, which uttered biblical quotes, cartoon fashion. With nothing better to do, Louis began opening drawers.

"We have nothing better to do. Let's play detective."

I knew Louis was mocking me, but it was better than sitting around or listening to Louis lecture me on the "Big World Picture" or modern art.

It was amazing how much we turned up in a house that looked devoid of personal objects. There were bills: including a tax bill in the name of Rose Coughlin, a letter from a son, a corporal, stationed on Okinawa that was a singularly uninspired description of the camp and his daily activities and, probably, instigated by his platoon sergeant. What made it especially pathetic was the fact that Keyes had kept it, perhaps the only written communication he had ever received from his son. I thought of the letters that I didn't write.

The two books that we found on a table in the bedroom confirmed our belief that Keyes, far from just being the hard-boiled cop that he was by reputation, was something of an aesthete. One was a collection of photographs of small objects, including vegetables and the other was a collection of nature poems.

"More middle brow than the art. I wonder if these were here when he bought the place. Rose's books."

I found two guns in a closet. One an old flintlock rifle that was so rusted it couldn't possibly fire. The other a nice old western Colt in a fine leather holster complete with bullets. Then in the back of the bottom drawer, Louis discovered a catch that allowed the drawer to open only part way. Louis freed the catch and removed a large black photo album. On top of it were two books: *How to Photograph the Nude,* and *Gypsy Boys.*

"It seems Mr. Keyes had more exotic interests than just sexy rutabagas."

The book was filled with snapshots of young men, boys really, in their teens, done with the latest Land camera, which was also hidden in the drawer. There were hundreds of them. Not pornographic, rather they clearly aspired to a kind of art. A boy emerging from a misty lake; a boy, his body in a sinuous curve, standing in the fading light of day; a young man, languidly lying on a patterned rug; a boy holding a wreath of flowers toward the camera in some sort of gesture of submission. All had the same tough, street-tested expressions that belied the arty poses their bodies assumed awkwardly. In the pictures, Keyes evoked some sense of a past, alien to the shores of Candlewood Lake, more at home on the Mediterranean, two or three thousand years ago. The one thing that was sharply in contrast to the atmosphere of classical serenity, that all the shots strove for, was the fact that in each and every one of the pictures the subject had an erection.

"This camera, an instrument which might provide for the democratization of sexuality, and he uses it to recreate sentimental Victorian classicism. What a waste!"

Louis didn't seem to be as concerned with the subject matter as with the style. I kept thinking of the secret life that Wayne Keyes must have led. In my brief encounter with him, he had been anything but a sensitive type. He had a reputation for dishing out his own version of justice when things did not go his way in the courts. It came as no surprise at all to me that he was on the take. I had seen so many cops who thought they were the law and therefore above it.

Why should criminals be the only ones who profited from crime?

Keyes made perfect sense to me when he was just a cop. Now I wondered what this man who had a belly like Sidney Greenstreet's, who smoked acrid Muniemaker cigars, and wore ill-fitting suits thought when he opened the pages of one of his books and contemplated two curved peppers on a pure white plate. What vision possessed him as he posed his young punks, probably picked up for stealing hubcaps or carrying a switchblade knife, with flowers laced in their greasy hair?

"You see? It makes no sense, does it?"

"We could make sense out of it. If we cared or needed to."

"*A posteriori.* It's like Freud. You can explain everything after the fact. But you can't predict what anyone will do. That's why Freud is not science. It's just a modern form of astrology. Amusing at dinner parties, but not a serious theory of human behavior. You can see latent homosexuality in everything that Keyes touched, but only after you know about his homosexuality."

I didn't know enough about Freud to argue with Louis. I didn't think that sex could explain everything either, but I wasn't about to agree or disagree with Louis who looked like he was itching for another argument. Louis had been cooped up for too long. He had to strike out. It didn't matter what I said. He would find fault. Louis even took my silence as disagreement. He continued to defend his position that human beings were essentially a jumble of contradictions.

I drifted off while Louis spoke, quoting from Plato and Kant and a dozen others who sounded like random residents of a refugee camp. I wanted to be somewhere else, too. The problem that I had was that I had no place like Louis that contained all the things I valued. Or Keyes for that matter. I couldn't conjure up any vision of a perfect place. I just knew that I didn't want to be there, by the lake, with Louis, figuring out things. I was lying there on the sofa, wondering what I was going to find in Pennsylvania. Wondering if I would ever come back. I didn't want to argue with Louis. I didn't care if he was right. I didn't want to prove him wrong. I didn't know what I believed. I just knew where I had to go.

CHAPTER 19

There was nothing picture-perfect about Philadelphia's Christmas. The dreary landscape, heavy with the smell of soot, brought no carols to mind. The colored lights that hung haphazardly on a few houses looked more mournful than festive. In front of a small brick house with a broken down Nash in the driveway, a small snowman, already losing his limbs, looked like a ghost. There had been snow all right, but no more than enough to cover Glenside like a shroud.

Louis had bought two cars in Danbury on the day after Christmas. The salesman was shocked to have such a customer so soon after a holiday and a ten-inch snowstorm. He treated us like we were lawyers who brought news of a rich dead relative.

Louis wanted no sales pitch so he just walked across the lot and pointed to a '50 Ford sedan and a '52 Olds convertible and asked how much for both. I could see the stunned salesman tried to calculate quickly what kind of pigeons he had, but Louis was too fast for him.

He peeled several hundred-dollar bills off his roll and began listing his requirements: the names on the registration, the delivery of the cars, the new tires that he wanted on the sedan. When Louis reached fifteen bills, he folded them neatly and placed them in the hand of the salesman.

"We need them in two hours."

"Two hours? We're a little short staffed. It's the day—" Louis reached for the man's hand and, before he knew it, Louis had placed a C-note between his fingers.

"Two hours."

"Yes, sir."

On the way back from "Ray's Reliable Used Cars," I tried

to get Louis to tell me what he was planning to do. He ignored me.

"He thinks we're the mob 'on the lam' or whatever they say. It's just what I wanted. I hope I didn't over play it. Drop me off at the general store."

We stood in front of the store for a few minutes as if this might be the last time we would see each other.

"I wish I could stay at the lake. It would be a lot safer."

"Why not stay? You know you don't have to risk—and you've got your little device."

"It's too late for that. I need stuff back at my house. There are people I need to see. I'll keep my eyes open. You do the same."

He still hadn't told me *his* plan. Mine required no stroke of genius. I had to start with Christy. I didn't want to drag her any farther into this mess, but I had no other choice. I told myself as soon as I could I would get her out of town to safety somewhere.

On the uneventful trip down to Pennsylvania, I kept mulling over the details of the case. It didn't get me very far, but it made the time pass more quickly. Except for a little miss in one cylinder before it warmed up, the Ford ran smooth. The heater worked fine. I missed the familiar sound of the Chevy six, but the Ford was fine. I parked at the railroad station and walked to Christy's house. Kids were playing war with snowballs in the small park at the end of the street. All I could hear was one kid screaming at his best friend, "You're dead. You're dead. I got you!"

Even at two in the afternoon, there were lights on in her house. It was that kind of day. There was only one car in the driveway. I hoped it was Christy's.

"What are you doing here? Did you hear what happened?"

"What?"

"They came on Christmas Eve and shut down the school. I was off, but Dean Ryckman was there. They chained the doors shut. Can you believe it?"

"Who did it?"

"Somebody from the Department of Education with the sheriff. They said they were investigating financial improprieties at the school. But it's Lindzey Hall. I know it. Dean Ryckman is devastated. What are the kids going to do? Right before Christmas. How are they going to find other schools? What a Christmas present! He doesn't deserve this. There is nothing wrong with the books. I know. I work on them. There is not enough to steal even if you wanted to. There's hardly enough money to buy donuts and coffee."

She was so distraught that she saw me only as a friendly face. She seemed to forget my part in the drama of The Biddle School. There was no suspicion in her eyes.

"It was such a lousy Christmas. I didn't even go to my in-laws. I told them I had a cold. I'm so afraid that Ryckman might do something stupid."

"Like?"

"Like take his life. They're talking jail."

"They won't do that."

"You don't know what this school means to him. He has been there for more than twenty years. Biddle is everything to him. He wanted it to succeed so badly. Where's he going to go with such a cloud over his head? What's he going to do?"

"Maybe we can help."

"How? Hall has everybody scared. Bell wouldn't even talk to Ryckman. He tried a few more prominent alums. The same thing. They'll all desert him like rats on a ship. It's not fair."

"This isn't about fair. Not now. We'll get him."

I was trying to buoy her up. But she wasn't listening anyway. I could have told her that I brought her Post Grape Nuts for Christmas and she would have nodded and thanked me. Christy hadn't mentioned herself in her grief over the closing of the school. I wondered what she planned to do, but I pushed ahead on Hall.

"I need to find out more about Hall's time at Biddle. There is something back there that he's trying to cover up. What happened to make him so angry with the school? It's gotta be more than just name-calling. If we could find out what it is, we might be able to put pressure on Hall to back off. The school might be able to re-open. What other chance is there?"

"I've no idea what it could be."

"I need to talk to Ryckman."

"I don't know about that. You are not exactly number one on his Christmas list."

"Try. Give him a call. Let me talk to him."

It was surprisingly easy. Ryckman seemed anxious to talk to anybody, even someone who had betrayed him. He wanted Christy to come with me.

For all the airs about him, Ryckman lived in a very neat but modest house in Jenkintown, a few miles from the school. Like many houses in the Philadelphia area, it was actually two houses, owned separately, side-by-side, attached by a common wall. Across the street, the twins, as they were called, were imposing. They looked like huge Victorian mansions. Some, however, appeared very odd, reflecting the differences in taste of their respective owners. On one side lived a fan of the color blue: blue shutters, blue trim, and a blue door, attached next to a passionate believer in brown. On some, the siding didn't even match. Ryckman's, at least, maintained the illusion that it was a single house. The only signs that his house was, in fact, two different houses were the two different front doorways, one green and faded and Ryckman's, in polished natural wood.

He had tea ready as we entered the extremely tasteful living room. Each piece of furniture was covered with something—a throw, a doily, an afghan as if everything had to be protected. His wife hovered in the background, fetching napkins, wiping her eyes. She merely nodded when we were introduced.

The house was a museum of Biddle's history. If Ryckman had children or a life outside the school, you couldn't tell by the house. There were pictures of athletic teams and class reunions on the walls and a large painting of the administration building above the mantle.

Ryckman immediately took my hand as if we were old friends. I tried to interrupt him when he began the litany of injuries he had suffered. Like Job, he demanded to know why he, a just man, had to suffer. I had no answer to that question. He ignored Christy's own plight. It was all raining down on his head alone.

"If you are ever going to get your school back, we need to

find something about Hall that will cause him to back off. While there is still time."

"I don't know if that is possible. It was so awful. The only bright spot in this whole wicked affair is that they came on Christmas Eve. There were no students to see my humiliation. Can I ask you this, Mr. Varian, what is your real interest is in this matter? The federal agents I spoke to—"

"They were working for Hall. So take what they said with some grain alcohol, if you know what I mean. There was a young girl from Connecticut murdered not far from here."

"I read about it, awful."

"I was hired by her father's brother, a very good friend of mine, to find her or her killer. I have very good reason to think that Hall is involved somehow."

"How? You don't think that Hall is a...murderer? It's too much to hope for." For the first time, there was a spark of life in his eyes.

"Don't get your hopes up. I don't think he actually did it. He seems to have a number of associates who are not reluctant to kill. Even if he ordered her death, it would be almost impossible to prove. He's very smart."

"How does it help then? To know—"

"He's a public figure. Mud has a way of sticking to them. If we can find enough to damage him or if we have enough to threaten him, he might back off you and I might find out what happened to Lara Greenbaum."

"Why would he have any interest in this co-ed?"

"I don't know exactly, not yet."

"Why was Jack Veasey killed?" Christy chimed in.

"But that was a criminal case. Organized crime. Jack used to associate with a very rough crowd. Even while he was at Biddle he was a handful." Ryckman was trying too hard to help.

"I don't think so. Again, there is no way to prove it. But let's start there. What do you think he knew about Hall that might have caused his death? You know I was on my way to meet Veasey when he was shot."

"Oh, my god!" I wasn't sure if Ryckman's response had to do with Veasey or me.

"Veasey was one of Hall's tormentors, wasn't he?"

"I really have no idea. They certainly weren't friends. Jack was always a ringleader. Veasey was very close to Thomas Thorpe, Raymond Halliburton, and Joseph Castille. They called themselves, the Dead End Kids, after the movies, you know. Isn't that absurd? After slum children, and with their advantages! All of them came from very well to do families, except for Castille, so it was a kind of a joke for them, as if they were deprived. I think it was just their way of thumbing their noses at their families. They did get in a lot of trouble, mischief mostly.

"Where are Thorpe, Castille and..."

"Halliburton. Thorpe and Halliburton were both killed in the war. Castille, I'm not sure about. Did you ever find an address for Joseph Castille, Christy?"

"I don't remember, but I don't think so. I would have to check. But the records are locked up, remember?"

"How could I forget?" Ryckman tried to turn his comment into a joke. Stiff upper lip and all that.

It didn't quite work, but I appreciated the effort.

"It's getting more and more difficult to keep track of people since the war. No one seems to stay in the same place anymore. My parents lived in the same house the whole time they were married. The same for my in-laws."

Ryckman showed a little impatience with Christy's comments by shifting in his chair and placing his teacup noisily in the saucer. So he lost the points he had just gained.

"Do you think this Castille might have stayed in touch with Veasey?" I asked.

"Perhaps. Those four were not the most likely candidates for active alumni. But you never can tell, remember Daniel Ross?"

Now it was my turn to keep the discussion focused.

"Is there anything that they did or might have done to Hall?"

"Like?"

"Boys, at that age, you said that Hall was a target. Do you think that they might have sexually—"

"Accosted him? Hardly? Those four were notorious for

their exploits, but they were decidedly heterosexual. In fact, that was the source of most of our difficulties. They had an affection for...how shall I say?...girls of a certain reputation."

"You mean sluts?"

I couldn't help showing my impatience with Ryckman's attempts at propriety. I felt bad as soon as I said it. Mrs. Ryckman decided that the attic needed reorganization or something. In any case, she headed up the stairs.

"I wouldn't use that word—*sluts*." He said the word as if he had just stepped in something foul. "But they were girls from common backgrounds, easily seduced by Biddle boys."

He seemed proud of the "superiority" of even his bad boys.

"So there was no sexual...whatever between Hall and these boys?"

"Not at Biddle."

"It happens everywhere. Even in the United States Army."

"These were hardly sexually frustrated young men. We even had to restrict them to campus after one incident where all four boys had their way with a gullible young girl from Willow Grove. Fortunately, we were able to make arrangements with the parents of the girl. She was technically underage, although you wouldn't have been able to tell by looking at her."

"What kind of arrangement?"

"The usual."

"You paid her off."

"Her parents, I am sure, saw it as a windfall. We had to protect the reputation of the school. I have often suspected that her parents encouraged her."

"And the boys had to stay after school?"

"It was more severe than that."

"What? They had to write 'I will not gang rape' five hundred times on the blackboard?"

"I resent that."

"I'm sorry."

I wasn't, but I had to let the matter drop if I was going to get something out of Ryckman.

"Well, there has to be something. Let's forget about Veasey for a moment. Tell me more about Hall."

"I told you just about everything. I did. I was honest with *you*."

"I know. I know. What about why he was at Biddle in the first place?"

"I suppose that I don't have to worry about violating Lindzey Hall's privacy any more. You know that Lindzey's father owned a clothing store and that Lindzey was always well dressed. It seems that there was a dance at his old school and Lindzey was looking particularly natty. You have to remember that this was at the height of the Depression. Some of his classmates felt that he was trying to show them up. They began to tease him and a fight broke out. Lindzey was cut up some. A week or so later one of the boys, who had tormented him, walked out of a building and found himself doused with gasoline. Then Lindzey knocked him down and threatened to set him on fire. Someone called the police. Later he said that he was merely trying to frighten the boy. He said he never would kill someone just because he had been teased. I interviewed Lindzey when he first came to the school. He was a very presentable boy, but he did have a real coldness about him. If I were the police, I don't know if I would have believed him."

"They probably didn't. But what could they do? We're just fishing here. Does anything else come to mind? Anything at all that has to do with Hall or Veasey or anything?"

"Once he had to be hospitalized, I think it was for an infection. You can't blame that on the boys."

"Nothing else?"

"The one thing that I didn't mention doesn't seem to lead anywhere. There is certainly no scandal attached. Nothing to be ashamed of."

"Like what?"

"I told you that Lindzey Hall was very much a loner. That he never made any efforts to fit in, to be accepted. There was one exception to that pattern of behavior."

"Which was?"

"We had on the faculty a teacher of German and French to whom Lindzey became very attached."

"How attached?"

"You seem to have a prurient interest in Hall's sexual relationships. Especially if there is some hint of homosexuality about them. As far as I know, his relationship with Mr. Harttmann was purely intellectual. But that doesn't mean that it wasn't intense. Boys can become very attached to their teachers in an environment like Biddle where a close, *intellectual* relationship between teacher and student is encouraged. For many of our boys, being at Biddle is the first time in their lives that anyone considered them seriously as thinkers. This can be very important in their intellectual development. Usually one or two teachers are particularly inspiring on the faculty. They tend to be witty and exciting as teachers, sometimes even a little unconventional. They draw students like flies to honey. What was unusual about Hall's case is that he was inspired by the most unpopular member of the faculty."

"How so?"

"Joseph Harttmann was a native of Belgium. But you would have thought he was from the House of Hapsburg, the way that he carried on. He was the most arrogant, insufferable—I remember the first time he had lunch in the faculty dining room and he asked for wine. Wine in an American school! As if he didn't know! We had milk and apple juice. He took the little bottle of juice and held it up like a fine vintage, took the cap off and pretended he was 'experiencing' the bouquet. Now I know the difference between a Burgundy and Beaujolais, but he just didn't understand the protocol of American schools. That was the attitude he carried into the classroom. He ridiculed the students. He made fun of their pronunciations but, more seriously, he made fun of them, mocking their aspirations. There were many complaints. The main effect of his teaching, as far as I could tell, was to increase enrollment in Mr. Berkson's Spanish classes, which had been under-enrolled until then. But Lindzey Hall seemed to relish Harttmann's affectations. I think he liked the fact that they were both outsiders, you know. They saw themselves as two intellectuals in a world of philistines. Lindzey took both French and German, intermediate and advanced, even though he was required to take only one foreign language. He excelled in both. I used to hear them conversing in German as they walked across campus. Lindzey even began to supply Harttmann with clothes from his father's shop. Harttmann fancied himself a fashion plate. He used to tie his tie in an odd way. I guess it was European."

"So Hall had one teacher he admired and who shared his contempt for his classmates. What was the upshot?"

"Only that Harttmann left in the middle of the school year, right after Thanksgiving. He had been hired on a two-year contract, but he resigned in the middle of the second year and went back to Europe. That was it. Nobody saw him leave. He didn't even clean out his mailbox. He cited a family emergency. With everything that was happening in Europe, this was 1936, remember, everyone in Europe seemed to be having some sort of crisis or another. Frankly, if he said he was going off to join the circus, it wouldn't have made any difference. Everyone was happy to see him go. We had already decided not to renew his contract."

"What was Hall's reaction?"

"Nothing overt, but I remember that he seemed to withdraw even further into himself, if that was possible. He devoted himself to his studies with an even greater intensity. I suppose, now that I think of it, I would have to say that his demeanor changed from a kind of haughty indifference to something more like anger. He had this look on his face. Others kept away even though he was not the largest boy."

"Do you think he blamed the school for Harttmann's departure?"

"No doubt. Harttmann made it clear that he thought Biddle was beneath him."

"Do you think that Hall thought the school had fired him?"

"I assumed that Harttmann told him something. They were very close. They both cared very little for Biddle. If Harttmann told anyone he was leaving, it would probably have been Hall."

"Maybe he didn't tell him. It was between semesters. Maybe he thinks you ran him off?"

"But that was more than fifteen years ago. Do you think he would hold a grudge for that long?"

"Who knows? He seems to go through life with various

chips on his shoulder. He has a lot of scores to settle. I think we are getting somewhere, but I'm not sure it's enough to help you, yet. There are still too many missing pieces. Do you have a picture of Harttmann?"

"Why? Do you think he has some part in this?"

"Just a wild hunch. Do you have one?"

"I don't think so. As you might imagine, we did not socialize. I did not collect snapshots."

Christy remembered that each yearbook had pictures of the faculty. Ryckman called to his wife upstairs to go to his study and take out the yearbooks from 1936-37. Harttmann wasn't in the 1936 edition, but he was in the 1937 yearbook, posed with chubby Mr. Berkson who wore an ill-fitting plaid jacket and an equally ill-fitting grin. Harttmann looked very European in his neatly tailored tweed jacket and floppy black tie. He was tall, towering over Berkson. They made an extremely odd couple. A cigarette was in Harttmann's right hand. His slick black hair gleamed in the picture like fresh paint on a new car. The sneer on his lips seemed to suggest that posing for yearbook pictures, especially with someone who looked like Mr. Berkson, was as distasteful to him as drinking milk at lunch. I asked to borrow the book. Ryckman hesitated, looking as if I had tried to take a book from the school library with an expired card. Reluctantly he agreed. He didn't ask for collateral.

We spent another hour or so going over Hall's experiences at Biddle, trying to dredge up anything, which might provide a clue to his vendetta against the school. Christy and Ryckman were both exhausted with the questions. Even with his own career at stake, he couldn't come up with anything. What was clear was that Ryckman had let Hall go his own way. Hall had intimidated him, even then.

Christy was not much help with Hall stories since she had not arrived at the school until after the war, but it was clear that Ryckman relied on her. Like so many secretaries and gal Fridays I had run into over the years, she seemed to have a better handle on the job than the boss. Because the school offices had been chained, she would have to rely on her memory. But she seemed to know the entire list of Biddle graduates by heart.

Mrs. Ryckman asked us if we would like to stay for dinner. Obviously, she had not cleared the invitation with her husband. He made it clear, even while saying "By all means," that he was tired of our company and that, despite the help we might be able to provide him, he didn't think that it was appropriate for us to break bread together. I understood. There was enough of his kind in Stamford. Even a knight in shining armor was no more than a servant to some.

CHAPTER 20

On the way back from Ryckman's, Christy tried to defend her boss. She recognized that he was a snob, but she wanted me to understand how devastated he was. His whole life was destroyed. The school meant everything to him. He was just reverting to the one thing of value that he could still claim as his own, his snobbism.

"He didn't mention the criminal charges against him if they find something wrong with the books." She wanted me to see that as heroic.

"That's not nobility. That's just embarrassment."

"You don't know him the way I do. He's not all that bad."

"I wonder if Mrs. Ryckman would agree with you?"

After that, we drove in silence. Christy had not brought up anything about the two of us. I expected her to say something. I wouldn't have been surprised if she had pledged eternal devotion or if she said that it had all been a big mistake. She sat in the car, looking straight ahead. There *was* a kind of nobility about her.

I wanted to say something to her about the way that I felt, but whatever came to mind sounded to me like I was feeling sorry for her. I wasn't. But that's how it sounded to me, so it would probably sound that way to her, too. It was one of those moments when you knew you were supposed to say something, but nothing came to mind. The stage was set. The cue had been given. There was even music. I could imagine the lines. I could almost hear them being spoken. But they wouldn't come out of me. Instead, I sat in silence, drinking in the heady aroma of summer flowers that spilled from her hair as we drove through the cold and empty winter night, hoping that she understood.

Christy offered me some supper. I drove past her house. And around the corner. She laughed.

"Is this how it always is?"

"Only when a congressman is trying to kill me."

I pulled my car into a driveway on the next street. I dropped her off and told her that I would park the car away from the house, "just in case." I didn't want to tell her exactly where. What difference did it make other than to let her know I didn't trust her? She said she understood. I wouldn't have blamed her if she had just told me to get lost. Instead, she noticed the bag of clothes I picked up outside of Danbury in the back seat. She reached over and grabbed it.

"Just in case," she said.

On the way to Christy's house, I tried to think about Harttmann. For the first time Hall, Biddle, and the war were possibly connected. I knew who he was. I didn't know how or why. But I knew he was de Paul. As interesting as that was, more interesting was the fact that the closer I got to Christy's house, the less I thought about Hall, Harttmann, and Biddle and the more I thought about her.

She was in the kitchen. She offered me a beer. I took a beer from the refrigerator and watched her move around the kitchen. She had thrown a checkered apron over her maroon dress. Rather than hide her figure, it seemed to accent it. She was browning sliced onions in a pan.

"Do you like steak?"

"Of course. Who doesn't?" I tried to think of something witty to say about beef. Nothing came to mind. I was feeling nervous. I wasn't sure why.

"Why don't you relax in the living room?"

"I like watching you cook."

"You're not watching me cook."

"Okay, I like watching you."

'It makes me uncomfortable."

"That I think you move like a dancer?'

"No, I'm just self conscious when someone watches me cooking. I move around a lot." She made a motion with her hand to scoot, get out of her kitchen. I stood my ground.

"And I don't need a line. You don't have to seduce me."

"You think that it's a line?"

"To tell you the truth with you I don't know what to think."

"What do you mean? I haven't said anything."

"It's not what you say. It's what you don't say when you are saying it. Does that make any sense?"

"No. Does it make sense to you?"

"Yeah, kinda. I know you're different. A lot different from the book salesmen and real estate agents I have been with. I guess I expect you to be different. It's just that I have no idea who you really are."

"I am who I am. I don't hide anything. When I said I was a writer—"

"It's not that. That was just part of your job, like a salesman's spiel...the surface. I mean something much deeper. When we spent that night together, it was just my needs that took over. The next day when I tried to think about it, you were a kind of blank. You were wonderful. I mean that. You seemed to understand what I wanted. And what I needed and why. You didn't make any judgments. Not all men are like that. They have to prove so much. You didn't. You listened to my story. You *are* a good listener. I appreciated that, I really did. Then I looked for you, and I wasn't sure there was anybody there. You have a way of not being there. That next morning it was as if you had already disappeared before you were out the door. Maybe I'm looking for too much. Maybe it's just that I'm not used to being in the middle of so much."

"When your life's in danger it makes everything different." It came out as more warning than an explanation.

She turned off the heat to the pan. Her deep brown eyes were glazed with moisture. She had said too much. I had said too little. What had started as a little fling was beginning to turn into something else. Neither one of us was sure that was okay.

"You like being the tough guy. It keeps you—"

"I'm not that tough."

"You are. And it's not unattractive, take my word for it. It's very...exciting." She turned away as if she had forgotten to stir something.

"Maybe you are trying to make too much of it. It was one night."

"I know. And if you had just been interested in a little fun that would have been fine. It could have been like…how does it go?…like two ships. It wasn't—This is hard for me."

"It's hard for me, too."

"Then help!"

"That's the point, isn't it? I just don't know what you want me to say because I don't know what you really want."

This time turning away wasn't enough to stop the tears. She walked out of the kitchen into the bedroom. I couldn't hear anything. She returned in a few minutes.

"You could have turned the onions."

"I don't care about the onions."

Christy took off her apron. I knew we weren't going to eat for a while. The onions were left in the pan. She poured herself a bourbon over ice. She added just a little ginger ale. I took my beer into the living room.

"Let's just take a break. It's my fault. I am getting a little too caught up in the fantasy. I have no right—"

"Of course you do."

Christy sat back in her chair while I stared ahead.

"What are you going to do now?"

I hesitated. Did I get up to kiss her? Should I say something? "What would you like me to do?"

"I mean about Biddle and Hall and the young girl. I'm a big girl. You don't have to worry about me. I don't think I should have worn the apron. It affected my—"

I laughed and she laughed.

Christy brought me another beer and turned on the radio. June Christy was singing "My One and Only Love" and I tried to lose myself in her voice. The song seemed like some sort of a sign or omen. Had I found my one and only love? I didn't feel in love. I wanted to be near Christy. I wanted to care for her. I wanted her to care for me. But I didn't feel like the song.

Christy went back to cooking. She was singing along with the radio. I had the strange feeling that I had fooled her. And that made me feel very bad.

I didn't taste the food. Christy was acting like the perfect homemaker and the coquette at the same time. She offered me salad and actually winked. She whirled into the kitchen like a wife in a *Good Housekeeping* ad. She was happy and that very happiness annoyed me because I couldn't tell if she were pretending. After dinner, we sat at the table and a silence entered the room drowning out even the radio.

"How much danger is there—for you—for me? "

"Unfortunately a lot. These are serious men playing for serious stakes. I know they feel they can get away with murder."

She didn't say anything more. We sat for a long while listening to songs that all promised a love that was true. And others that offered a winter wonderland. After what seemed a long time, Christy told me she wanted to try to make love the way that she had done it with her husband. "The regular way."

"Why?"

"Because that's what I want. Now. It's time."

The Biddle School and the war were far away for the moment. We would have this night together. Whatever happened after tonight would happen, as it had to happen. Christy wanted me to know that there were no strings attached.

In the dim light, her body was even more flawless than I remembered it. She stood next to me, took my hand, and guided it across her belly, then up to each breast. When she slid into the bed next to me, I could hear her hard breathing. She seemed to be caught between the desire to get it over with, to test her new conviction that she could return to the land of the normal, and the equally strong desire to prolong this evening to make it equal her fantasies. She wanted to build to some kind of peak and she wanted it already over so that she wouldn't be tormented anymore.

I was beside the point. I didn't mind and she didn't notice. I was comfortable again. I could devote myself to her needs. I decided to take over. I began to kiss her lips, her ears, her throat, her breasts, lingering over each kiss, running my tongue along the many different textures of her body.

I moved down in the bed and began to tease her belly and her hips with my tongue and hands. Then with her body arching itself slightly with each flick of my tongue, I moved down between her legs with its thick tangle of moss. She hesitated as my tongue glided over the knot of hard flesh in the midst of moist hair, wondering if this was the time. She started to reach for me. Ignoring her, I continued to run my tongue along the top and against the sides, feeling her hair moisten with my saliva and her juices. I took the whole of her into my mouth and began a gentle sucking motion. She kept her hips in rhythm to the pressure of my lips, moaning, "No, no, no," while grasping the back of my head and pushing it against her and then, pulling it away slightly. After a few minutes, her legs began to tremble and then her whole body went rigid. "Oh. my god, oh, oh!"

She brought me up to her face. Magically, there appeared a prophylactic in her left hand.

"I have to be careful. Do you mind?"

I didn't answer. Feeling powerful, I took the foil and tore it open with my teeth. Just the sound of the tearing wrapper seemed to take her to even further heights. Then it fell out of my mouth. She moved to the side, laughing. It was a good laugh. A laugh that proved she was alive. "Let me."

Her hands were shaking. When she finally put it on me she took moisture from between her legs, rubbed it on me like a lotion, and then brought it back to her.

"I don't like how I look. It looks dead. Like weeds. Not like you."

"It is gorgeous in its bi-valved roundness as plump and delicious as a sweet ripe plum."

She laughed again. "That's ridiculous. You don't mean that." But she seemed to hope I did and was glad. Then she lay back and closed her eyes.

The tears began as soon as I entered her. She began to roll with the rhythms of a small boat on a calm sea, slow and even. Whatever my intentions, she was back in control. After several thrusts, she would stop and pat me on the back like an encouraging coach, and then the rocking would begin again. Slow at first then faster and faster. She was sobbing and moaning at the same time. I watched her face with fascination. She never opened her eyes. I envied her pleasure. I wondered if what made it so memorable was that it was the first time with me or the last time with her husband or maybe the pilot. I didn't have much time for wondering. With the suddenness of a wrestler about to make a pin, hers legs gripped my waist and she let out a cry that seemed to come from another body somewhere deep in her past. So caught up was I in her pleasure, I almost forgot to join her.

During the night, I awoke and watched Christy's face. She was still working on her problems. Relaxed and content, I could feel the heat from her body as it covered us like a blanket as she stared at the ceiling. I wondered what she was thinking and couldn't ask. She had faced down one of her demons, but there were clearly others. Finally, she seemed to fall asleep.

The one thing that bothered me about the whole affair was that I didn't want to say good-bye in the morning, but I had to get away to do what I could to keep her out of the mess we were in. I didn't know what else to say, but I knew I didn't want to say good-bye. I leaned over to kiss her. She woke up startled.

The reality of the morning seemed too much for her. I had the feeling that she had been waiting for that night for too long. She had to be disappointed. We are always disappointed that milestones aren't as satisfying as we imagine. She offered to cook me breakfast. She asked where I was heading. She wanted to know what I thought was going to happen to Ryckman, but I could tell that she had no interest in what my predictions were. When I got out of the shower, she was already dressed. I could smell the coffee. She was polite, pleasant, and impatient. I had coffee. Although nothing was said, we both knew that this parting was different from the last.

ぐつどつど

I was so caught up with thinking of what a life with Christy might have been like that I didn't see the car and the two men right there in the parking lot. They were on me with guns drawn before I could even start for mine.

Before we could leave, they realized they hadn't figured on what to do with my car so I waited in cuffs feeling like a perfect fool for the second time in fifteen minutes. They should have brought another guy, they decided. They argued about whose responsibility it was. This was certainly the second team. They put me in a Buick as they worked out the logistics of getting us to where they were taking me. The Ford stayed in the lot.

Before we left the parking lot, they slipped a black hood over my head. I didn't recognize them, but I figured I was with friends of Lawrence and Sexton. But they acted more like Abbott and Costello than hotshot agents. It was a comedy of errors, but these comedians had guns.

"What's the charge?"

"Shut up." The tall one was annoyed.

"At least he had the last meal that I'd want for the day I was going to die." Costello in the backseat thought he was a wit.

"What's that?"

"Hair pie. What else? If I ever—"

The driver told his partner to be quiet.

"Huh?"

I guess his partner wasn't very clear on what he was talking about.

The driver was the more businesslike of the two. The one in the back wanted to talk. He liked what he was doing. The rough stuff. The threats and especially the power. He was not much different from the small time hoods I had to deal with in the street. The driver saw himself as a professional. I tried to remember their faces as we drove off. I counted off the details in my head. I also tried to pay attention to where we were going, but after the third left turn, I gave up on that. Instead, I tried to figure out how I was going to get out of this. I wondered what was going to happen to Christy. I also wondered if Sexton and Lawrence were in New Canaan wrapping up more loose ends.

CHAPTER 21

We had been driving around for what seemed about an hour. I heard the wind against the car windows, but I had no idea where we were or where we were going. My captors had settled down to small talk and provided no clues to our destination. It was just a job for them now. Like deliverymen, they just wanted to unload the goods.

I figured we'd wind up at some out of the way spot where they could put a bullet in my head without anyone noticing or caring one way or another. Maybe the papers would describe it as a suicide or they might make it look like another mob killing. That would work. They could place me on Veasey's street the night he was killed. I could see the story. I thought the hood was excessive, a little too theatrical.

One of them smoked cheap cigars. The other preferred the aroma of cheap cologne. As the excitement of my capture faded back into the dull routine of waiting to die, I started to get bored. It was taking too long. The cuffs were hurting my wrists. And there was a lump in the seat that bothered my back. It was hot under the cloth hood. At that moment, staying alive was less important than the lump in the seat. If I was going to die, I thought at least I could try to be more comfortable.

Then the car groaned to a stop and the driver helped me out of the car. I braced myself for a bullet. Instead, they escorted me like bouncers in a classy club, hardly paying attention to me, just moving me along efficiently. They didn't take the hood off until I was inside what appeared to be a large stone mansion furnished like a museum. Then they pushed me toward the library. Our shoes made loud clacking sounds on the hard floors. It sounded like a church. I found myself in front of a tall, distinguished-looking man with a pencil-thin gray mustache seated behind a desk. His head was completely shaven. He wore a dark double-breasted, pin-striped suit. He lit a cigarette and held it between two fingers in an exaggerated European fashion. He looked extremely pleased with himself. But to me he looked just like all the oily grade-B movie villains with foreign accents who had names like "The Black Mask." Despite the new hairdo, I recognized him from the picture in the Biddle yearbook. It was Harttmann. Or de Paul. Or Krims. Whatever his real name was.

"So you are this Varian."

"That's correct. I am this Varian and he is that one." I pointed to one of my captors.

He nodded to the two men behind me. "We have an amusing fellow."

"So what am I here for?"

"You are being questioned."

"Kidnapped. A hood over my head. In cuffs. Why not just make an appointment? You know where my office is."

"I simply want to know why you did not follow our advice?"

"Advice? I was told to back off from an investigation of a little girl's murder that you don't seem too anxious—"

He laughed.

"What's so funny? You think Lara's murder is funny?" I tried to twist out of the chair. I wanted to see him gargle his teeth.

I felt a blow to the back of my neck. My interrogator waved off my attacker. I felt a sharp pain travel from my head through my back to my left leg.

"I know everything about you—sewer rat."

"What's to know? I'm an investigator investigating. Why do you care about what happened to this little girl unless you had something to do with it?"

"You are a very stupid man."

"That's probably true. But you didn't answer my question?"

"My questions. Not yours. I want to know what you and David Fenner and the others are up to."

"You are a smart man, at least your accent makes you sound smart, so you know I am up to one thing, and one thing only, finding Lara Greenbaum's killer."

"This can take a long time. And it can be painful. Or it can be pleasant. We have no interest in you because you are nothing. If you tell us what we want to know, you can go back to your sewer."

"You'll let me go home if I talk? Right."

"Of course."

This time the blow came with more force. I saw the proverbial stars and, just like in the movies, the long inky black pools spreading out before my feet. I blinked and barely held on to consciousness.

"I am a very careful man. I can afford to take a little time with you. You seem to invite pain. Perhaps that is your pleasure. Mr. Donch and Mr. Gerhard will be happy to oblige you. They tell me they don't like you very much."

"And that's supposed to scare me?"

"It should."

"I have the feeling you are planning to deal with me as just another Jack Veasey. So why should I help you out?"

"Unless you really do like pain, it's in your interest."

"You don't know anything about my interest."

"You are one of these American tough guys, yes? A war hero, yes? Like James Cagney or Humphrey Bogart?"

"Tougher than a Belgian Nazi, I bet."

"Of course. But not smarter."

"So why did you kill Lara?"

"I said that I will ask the questions."

He motioned with an exaggerated turn of his wrist and this time I got one across my face. My mouth filled with blood. I spat it back across the desk and de Paul flinched. He didn't like being challenged. He signaled again and this time I felt a tooth crack.

Despite his theatrical airs of sophistication, he was just a bully. I just wanted the chance to show him what happened to bullies, but like Louis used to say, that was schoolyard thinking and I wasn't in the schoolyard. I didn't care.

"So tell me about the unfortunate Professor Rippey."

"The last time I saw him he was doing fine."

"You know what I mean—the manuscript." He did really enjoy this. I wondered what Lara had to endure from him. The kind of hate I felt even cured toothaches. I spat again, this time on the floor.

"I'm not much of a reader."

He started to motion for another blow and then stopped.

"If your good friend, this Diamond, has it, you will have cost him his life. Does that make you feel heroic?"

"Do you think Sexton and Lawrence are a match for Louis?"

"A homosexual?" He laughed again. "I certainly do."

I heard the laughter behind me. If wishes came true, I would have a chance at them, too. But more than that, I just hoped Louis was on the alert. He had to be, but the snipers who got Amor and Psyche might just as easily nail Louis from a distance. I did have faith in Louis's abilities. I had seen him in action enough times. He didn't lose his cool, and he had no qualms about taking a life. That was enough to make him dangerous, but as he frequently pointed out, "Anybody can be killed, anybody, even a president."

"What do you care about the book? It's boring. Lots of facts about a war people would just as soon forget. What's the big deal?"

He ignored my question. Tired of reminding me that he was asking the questions, he began to quiz me again about Louis and Fenner, about the Greenbaums, about Rippey, and about the book. He was especially interested in my visit to Fenner's office. That was very important to him. I thought that I might as well tell the truth. It might shake them up.

"The FBI wanted to know what I had on you. They're very interested in the career of your boss."

"They are fools. Sponsoring that silly book."

"That silly book might make your boss look like a fool. Or you."

"There's nothing we have to fear from the FBI. It's the—"

He broke off and I could see he was angry with himself for almost saying too much.

I was encouraged. It was a sign I might be getting to him.

If that were true, there might still be a chance for me. "No, maybe not, but don't you think that the good congressman might be having second thoughts about his favorite adviser. You could easily be seen as a real liability now, with your dirty little secrets. Even if Rippey's book doesn't nail you, how does he know that somebody else might not discover the truth about your little romp in the Nazi playpen? If Hall hasn't realized this, maybe I should talk to him."

"Shut up. What do you call this, whistling in the dark?"

"I think it's more like blowing a bugle."

"Very colorful. Jack Veasey was colorful too."

I had to try a little more offense. The stuff in the book didn't seem to threaten him. I had to reach. "You asked me about everyone and everything, but you left out Lara's diary. Don't you care what she had to say about you in her intimate record of your relationship?"

This was a surprise to him. He took a cigarette from the gleaming cigarette case and began tapping it on the desk.

I sensed there was someone else in the room. But I knew if I turned around to look I would just get whacked again. When de Paul got up from the desk and walked behind me, I could hear whispering, but that's all. It had to be Hall.

"Congressman, I'll only be a few minutes."

This time I was hit with something hard, a gun or a black-jack. When I came to, Hall was standing next to de Paul. "Find out what he knows and get rid of him. I don't like it that he is in the house. The Graftons will be home today. Make it quick. What's that on the rug?"

His voice was cold and distant. I would see what Ryckman meant about his eyes. They were deep blue and ice cold. He was dressed like an *Esquire* model. He never looked at me directly. I was the subject of his conversation not a person. As de Paul stood up and walked him to the door, he appeared a little nervous with Hall. Here was the chink in the armor. The teacher had become the acolyte. I could hear him say that I was not a problem. It was almost over, he said. It was too late to take chances.

He mentioned Lara but not the diary. I was feeling a little light headed. My tooth ached again. My wrists were raw. I had to stay cool myself. Hall left with the curt suggestion that it was time to end it. He still hadn't looked at me directly. But de Paul turned to me, trying to regain control as he walked back toward the desk.

"What could a…whore possibly have to say?"

"You didn't know about it, did you? I thought you knew about it when you had Louis's house trashed. I guess they were just fishin', huh? So you didn't know about it, did you?"

"Even if it exists, it is of no consequence. Amuse me. Tell me about this supposéd diary." He was not very good at pretending.

"It's not *supposéd.* How do you think I wound up at Biddle? You know when I was hired. Do you think an ignorant private dick like me would have gotten on to you and Hall so quickly if I hadn't had it all drawn out in front of me like a map? You know I'm not that smart."

He was struggling to regain his composure. I was hoping I had found the insurance policy I needed to stay alive.

"And what did you find in this diary?"

"Oh, you want me to what? Let me think. You want to tell you how this little girl found out what happened at a second rate prep school in…what year was it? 1936? You want me to tell you where I hid the diary so you can kill me quickly so that the Graftons will not be, what? Upset that someone not of their breeding is sitting in one of their antique chairs and bleeding on their fucking Persian carpet? Right. You're crazier than I thought."

"You will tell me everything."

"Really? What are you going to do, put bamboo under my nails? Oh, that was the Japs, right. How would the Nazis do it? Make me look at Hitler's paintings? I already have a fucking toothache. Nothing could be worse than that. Why would I tell you anything?"

"To save your miserable life, of course. And Mrs. Coopersmith's."

I tried not to react. He *was* open to a deal! And I had my little window. I had to think straight. It was all bluff so I had to be careful.

"Right, I give you the diary and you give me a limousine

ride home and wish me well, I can see that happening. Just like I can see myself hitting sixty-one home runs."

He hesitated and tapped the top of the cigarette case. He wanted to believe I was bluffing. That meant the bluff was working. He wanted to give me over to his henchmen, but, as he said, he was a careful man. I had to push a little to convince him that I knew something that could really damage him.

"She knew all about what happened at Biddle. I don't know how but she did. Did she spend some time with Hall, you know, where they could share little secrets?"

"He doesn't—" He looked at the men behind me and paused in mid drag. He waved the two guards out of the room. They protested. He reminded them I was still cuffed. They would wait outside the room. If he needed them, he would call. Nothing would happen. They had better not wander away.

"What could she, a mere girl, possibly have known?"

"Your ugly little secret. She knew a lot, remember? She knew enough to get one of your little memos to Rippey, didn't she? How does it feel to be outfoxed by a little girl?"

"You kept describing her as a girl. You have no idea. She was a viper. A vampire. A traitor." He paused for effect. "But I do have to say she was a delicious little traitor."

He wanted me to react, to lose it. But I wouldn't. To keep images of Lara away I kept imagining him bleeding from wounds all over his body.

I decided to push it. "Got to you, didn't she?"

"You are an idiot. It will be a pleasure to watch you die."

"I thought you only liked to watch little girls die."

"What did you tell your friends at the FBI?"

"I guess you don't know so much about capitalism."

"This is about money?" He was disgusted at my motives, yet he seemed comforted as I fit the mold he had of degenerate Americans for whom everything had a price.

"What else is there? You know my life. You can dismiss money because you have so much access to it. I can't afford that luxury. I want—"

"What is it you want?"

"Money and the time to spend it. Lots of both."

"You are really in no position to make a bargain. You are hopelessly outclassed here. This is a matter of national security."

"That's a laugh. This has as much to do with national security as the master race had to do with ball room dancing."

"Your pathetic existence could be snuffed out immediately and who would care? You might have some exaggerated sense of your own worth, but it is shared by no one. Who would mourn the death of a son of a rag picker?"

"He was an entrepreneur. Which in my book is better than a traitor."

"Of course."

"So what are you two up to? A new world order? A Fourth Reich?"

"It is beyond your comprehension."

"And it's worth the lives of four, five, six people, what's the count up to now?"

"It's worth the lives of six million and more." He was trying to impress me.

"It's a good round number, isn't it?"

He was still trying to figure out if I was bluffing about the diary and what was in it. He knew enough about Lara not to be surprised that she would have kept a record. I just hoped my leap into the unknown would convince him. As Louis used to say, and I hoped still could say, "A good lie is always mostly truth."

He played with his cigarette and acted as if he were studying my face. I spit again. This time against the side of the desk.

"I'm getting tired of waiting. Either call your boys back in or let's make a deal. As you said, I mean nothing. Without the diary or the manuscript, who is going to believe me that a congressman and a former Nazi are going around the country killing people to protect some cockamamie plan to...what? Keep foreigners out of the National Hockey League? Whether I'm dead or alive, it doesn't matter to you, right? What's one out of six million? But it matters to me. So you give me some money and I give you the diary. I live someplace warm. You can run the country. I'd be a fool to double cross you. What do you say?"

He hesitated. Then he spoke slowly as if to emphasize how serious he was. I wasn't convinced. He still looked like a schoolteacher to me.

"It might be arranged. The money is not a problem. But first you have to convince me that this is not some sort of pathetic charade to save your life. I need some particulars."

I reached back into the bits and pieces that had come from Ryckman, hoping that the guesses I made from what little I knew of what happened at Biddle would make sense. I mentioned Veasey and Thorpe and Castille. I suggested that sex was at the center. I threw in a young girl. Why not, it fit the pattern.

"And then you left, Mr. Harttmann. Leaving poor young Mr. Hall alone in a cruel and hostile world. How could you do that, Mr. Harttmann?"

I had to skirt around the big question since I had no idea what de Paul's secret at Biddle might be. I hoped he would fill in the blanks. It seemed to work.

"I knew she was dangerous," he said as if talking to himself.

"A mere girl?"

"I told you, she was no girl. She was just a whore who…"

It seemed that he wanted to talk about her. I had the funny feeling that, like everybody else, he had been impressed with, maybe even attracted to Lara. It was a disgusting thought. He stopped in mid sentence.

"How will you get this diary to me?"

"I will make the arrangements. Your goons will be with me the whole time."

"I will tolerate no attempted heroism or deceit."

"Look, it makes sense for both of us to deal. You have power. You seem to have commandeered a whole section of the federal government as your personal errand boys. If I double-cross you, I am dead. That's clear to me. But I have something you need. You are a careful man. You wouldn't have survived if you weren't. You need to protect yourself, too. So we make a deal. My life for your reputation. The money will simply allow me to ease a guilty conscience fifty thousand ways. We both win."

Although de Paul clearly didn't like being in a game where he didn't have all the cards, we negotiated the terms back and forth. I think he would have preferred to torture me to get the diary, but his research had probably told him that torture hadn't worked in '44 and it would be a waste of time now. Instead, I could see him calculating the risks of letting me live, looking for a flaw in the arrangements that would give him the opportunity to take my life and the diary at the same time.

When the deal was made I tried to make conversation about Hall. I still wasn't sure what his role was in Lara's murder. I couldn't tell at this point if he even knew about it. And de Paul didn't respond to my queries. But it was clear he wanted to say something. One thing that intellectuals can't resist is the opportunity to hear themselves pontificate. So, instead of information about Hall, I got the lecture on the coming decline of America. He suggested I would understand since I had fought bravely, foolishly, but bravely.

"You Americans are fools. The Communists will exploit your sentimentality by making a victim of every bastard race that you have allowed to crawl into this country to degrade it. Until they have you by the throat. I was brought here to prevent that."

"By who?"

"The United States Government, of course."

When de Paul called out to Donch and Gerhard, they entered quickly, obviously prepared to take care of me right there. They were disappointed when de Paul told them they would drive me back to Connecticut to recover the diary. He gave them instructions for getting the fifty thousand. And that made them angry. But I knew de Paul had no intentions of letting me spend it.

On the way out, I caught a glimpse of Hall sitting in the large living room. He was going over papers spread out on the table in front of him. He looked up. I was surprised at the hate I saw in that handsome face. He stood up and walked toward us, ignoring me again. He pulled Donch aside. They talked for a few minutes, Donch nodding the whole time. When Donch grabbed my arm to lead me out, Hall finally looked at me. There was real venom in his voice. "I don't know who you are, but I have nothing but contempt for a man who would use a girl to do his work for him. Then to conspire with a man like Jack Veasey. All to destroy me."

"We do what we can."

"Whatever arrangements have been made, you will stick to them no matter. Any deviation and there will be consequences."

"That goes for me, too."

"Get him out of here," de Paul said, standing in front of the library door.

I wasn't sure if Hall was being straight or rehearsing the role to see how it fit. It wouldn't have surprised me if de Paul had convinced him somehow that I was the killer, part of some plot to bring Hall down. Whichever was the case, what it told me was that de Paul would make sure that I would not be around to make my case to anyone. I had gone from Judas goat to fall guy.

I had told de Paul that we would make the exchange in Dave Fenner's office. It seemed like a good idea. They knew I had seen Fenner. They knew almost everything. I also knew that somewhere before we ever got to Stamford I would have to act. If I waited until they had the diary, I would have nothing and they could arrange for my death and accompanying story without any worries. I had to look for the right opportunity. Although I had contempt for Donch and Gerhard, I knew they were still professionals who outnumbered and outgunned me.

When we got into the car, I asked that the cuffs be taken off. Donch looked into the rear view mirror for Gerhard's reaction. They had received no instructions about the cuffs.

"Look, what the hell do you think I'm gonna do. Strangle you while you have a gun on me? My mouth is killing me. My arms are killing me. My wrists are raw and your boss and me are good friends now. We have a deal. I'm on your side."

"Real funny and don't try anything funny."

I figured that they would be on the alert for a while so I thanked them profusely and tried to engage them in conversation to lull them into some sense of security. I asked them about Veasey. I wanted to know which one of them had shot him. Donch looked in the rear view mirror.

"See the gratitude we get. He's acting like we're murderers when all we did was save his life."

"Yeah, real gratitude."

"How did you save my life?"

"Do you think Veasey was about to pour his soul out to you. The only thing he was about to pour was lead into your sorry ass. If we hadn't gotten there first—"

"Yeah! He was sitting there with a big ass pistol. He was gonna ventilate you. Right in the middle of winter, too."

They laughed. They were probably right. Veasey was hardly the sort who would spill his guts to a stranger. I had been so concerned about losing the CDA that I never really prepared for Veasey. The fact that they might have saved my life so amused Donch and Gerhard that the ice was broken between us. Gerhard could now focus on what really interested him— Christy Coopersmith. He was a horny bastard. He wanted to know details. He had seen her at Biddle. She looked like a movie star. She was a hot number.

"What was she like?" And suddenly they both became sixteen year olds.

Donch was just as eager. "She's a widow, right?"

"Yeah."

"Widows, I heard that they really like it. They really miss getting it regular, you know. Even the old ones. And she's young. Was she like that?"

I didn't like betraying Christy, but I figured that they wouldn't be telling anybody if I got them first. And if I didn't, I would be dead anyway. Even so, I couldn't tell the truth. So I made up a story that I thought would please them, right out of a blue movie. Gerhard was especially intrigued with the image of Christy kneeling on the stairs and taking it doggy style. Donch preferred the descriptions of Christy's skillful tongue. They wanted more and more details.

"I told ya we shoulda taken him at the house. She probably woulda done us all. If she was that hot."

They debated for a while. Donch was convinced that Gerhard had robbed him of the most exciting evening of his life. This led to other grievances on both sides. They had turned into the Bickersons with an unfunny aura of real violence. Donch sounded like he would kill anyone who crossed him. Their argument gave me the opening I needed. Somewhere on a fairly deserted stretch of road leading to Route 1 I made my move. I swung my left arm up and caught Donch right under his nose hard enough to hear a faint crack of bone. He was stunned enough that he couldn't stop me from reaching his .32. I broke a few teeth with the gun before I pumped two bullets into his gut. There was a look of great surprise on his face like he had just come home to find his wife imitating Christy on the stairs. I then put the gun to the back of Gerhard's head.

"Pull over slowly."

"You're crazy."

He tried to turn his head to see his fallen partner.

"Pull over."

"What are you gonna do?" His foot slammed into the gas pedal. I guess he figured I wouldn't risk my life by shooting him when we were doing fifty on a slick road.

I could see the handle of a revolver coming from inside Gerhard's coat. He was a southpaw. Quickly he was a dead southpaw with a bullet in his head and I had to try to steer the car to a stop from the rear seat. I couldn't really manage it on the thin sheet of ice that covered the road. Fortunately, Gerhard's lifeless leg had slipped off the gas pedal. We swerved and then we hit a tree. My head hurt only a little bit more than it had before. But I could feel my knee swelling like a balloon. I kept Donch's little .32 and scrambled out of the car as best I could. In the impact, Gerhard had hit the windshield and Donch had rolled into me, leaving my left arm drenched in blood. Even if someone in one of the big houses set back off the road hadn't seen me, I would have a hard time looking inconspicuous as I tried to make my way back to Glenside wherever that was from here. Somebody would see me. I was hurting too much to even think of a good story. It had not been a good day.

CHAPTER 22

It was after three o'clock in the afternoon before I finally made it back to Glenside. The winter sun provided light but almost no heat. The cold wind turned my face into a piece of raw meat. My eyes ran. My neck hurt. My tooth ached. The leg that had banged into Donch's head felt like it had grown to something the size of a softball under the knee-cap. I limped. I couldn't focus on anything but the next step. I knew how to do it. Just keep focused on the next goal, that tree up there, that sign in the road, until you got there and picked the next one. I knew how to do it because I had done it too many times. I just was out of practice.

I had walked through strange streets with strange names that seemed written in a foreign language with too many "y"s and "w"s, trying to stay on my feet in smooth soled Florsheims. Thank god, I didn't have to run from anybody. After the maze of exclusive neighborhoods where no one seemed to be home, I happened on a train station. A commuting train took me to central Philadelphia. In the massive railroad station I felt like a fugitive. I tried to keep cool. No one paid much attention to the big blood stain on my arm, but I noticed every cop in the city and Philadelphia seemed to be full of them—all looking like big city cops, overweight and mean.

I walked downtown to the Reading Station and caught the train to Glenside. The ride allowed me the opportunity to think a little. I knew I still had quite a few hours before Donch and Gerhard would be overdue in reporting to de Paul unless the car had already been found. He wouldn't let much time go by before he would send the rest of his dogs after me. They had already gotten me once. There was no reason to think they wouldn't get me again. I wouldn't get the drop on them and de

Paul wouldn't care about the diary. He'd take his chances on that just to get rid of me. I couldn't play that hand again. I wondered if I should have given him the diary. Maybe they didn't know "qwerty." It might have saved my life. I couldn't give him Lara's words. Under any circumstances. Not to him.

I still didn't know exactly what he and Hall were up to. But de Paul let it slip that it did have to do with the FBI. But what was the purpose? I didn't know politics, not like Louis anyway, but it seemed to me that Hoover and Hall were on the same side. They both were making a big stink about commies. They both wanted to clean house. I didn't care about politics except it gave me the creeps when they made it into a moral crusade. If they could just tell the truth, there were only two guys left, them and us. We wanted to win.

I had to think about my next move and Christy. Then there was Louis. I had to get to him. My head was whirling. Pain, fear, and guilt made a lousy cocktail.

The train pulled into the mostly empty station. The sun was bright and even lower in the sky. I held my hand over my eyes as I used the train as a shield to check the parking lot. When it pulled out of the station I felt totally alone and vulnerable. I was really jumpy. A man walking his dog near the tracks was suspicious. A woman looking out her window was watching me. At the used car lot across the station, the two men standing in the showroom must have been talking about me. My car was still there. I wondered if there was a bomb in it. I fingered Donch's gun in my pocket. When I reached Glenside Avenue, I headed for Christy's house. I hoped she was home. I hoped she was still alive.

The street was quiet. I could see lit Christmas trees in a few of the windows. Two young boys were trying out their Christmas sleds on what was left of the meager snow. They had made a little run of packed snow on the sidewalk across the street. As far as they were concerned, they were on the bobsled run at Innsbruck. They paid no attention to me. There was a light in Christy's window.

"Varian? What happened?"

She noticed my sleeve immediately. She ushered me into the house like a nurse at the front. She ignored my sleeve, put her hand softly against my cheek, and let out a low sympathetic, and very sexy, moan. It wasn't meant to be sexy. She brought me coffee and a towel wrapped around ice. She used the damp edge of the towel to wipe away the dried blood from my face.

She knelt down and asked me to take off my pants and I tried to make a joke but my jaw was still numb from the cold wind and it came out like I was drunk. In a way I was.

"I want to see your leg. You're limping."

The knee was swollen, but not as bad as I thought. She took the ice filled towel and placed it on my knee. It was cold. Pain shot up my leg into my gut. I winced.

"You should go to the hospital."

"It's okay."

She held the towel just above my knee. I could see her hair. I could smell the flowers again. Feeling gradually came back to my face. The warm coffee helped warm my hands. She wanted to know what happened.

I told her that two of Hall's men had picked me up and I had escaped. I skipped over the gory details about Donch and Gerhard. I told her that I was concerned about her safety. She ignored the warning and tried a joke of her own.

"If you wanted me to go away with you, all you had to do was ask. You didn't have to get beat up."

"It isn't funny. They know about you."

"I know. I know."

She went to the kitchen for more ice. I kept waiting for the door to swing open and to see Sexton and Lawrence.

"I'm fine. We have to get out of here."

She didn't answer. When she returned, she said that I would need some clothes. She looked at what was in the bag she took from the car and laughed.

"Were you heading for Bermuda? I think there are some things in the closet." The only things she had left from her husband were a baseball jacket and a couple pairs of pants. He never wore suits, she said, as if that admission reminded her again how young he was.

"Where are we going to go?"

"I don't know. We'll figure that out when we're on the road."

"Keep the ice on it. It will help the swelling. You don't think anything's broken?"

"Just my toof."

She left the room and I could hear her in the bedroom, going through closets and opening drawers. I felt bad that her whole life was being turned upside down. I would feel a lot worse if we ran into Hall's men. I called for her to hurry.

As she helped me with my pants, she didn't look scared. I was impressed. She wanted to talk about Hall.

"I was thinking about something Ryckman said about Hall. You remember how he was once in the hospital. You said that you thought something must have happened to him at Biddle to make him so bitter. It had to be something really bad. Maybe bad enough to put him in the hospital."

"More than name calling."

"Yes, that's right. The more I thought about it, the more I thought so, too. Did they beat him up? Biddle would try to hide it if one of its own had been beaten by some of its *boys*. Maybe Ryckman didn't even know what happened. He wasn't dean then. And then I remembered Helen Bishop. She was the school nurse. She's retired. But just before she retired, right at the time Hall started trying to hurt the school, she said something. I can't remember exactly what she said. Something to the effect that Biddle deserved what was happening. I never really liked her or knew her very well. I really didn't want to pursue it with her. In fact, I thought it had more to do with her bitterness than it had to do with Hall. She didn't like to do anything. She was—"

"Do you think she knows something?"

"She might."

"Do you know where she is?"

"Yes. Yes I do. She lives in North Hills. Not far from here and I found her."

Christy was proud of her detective work. She explained how she remembered that Helen Bishop had written to the school about money she thought they owed her. The letter was at school but she remembered that the address was different from the one she had so she had to make a change in the records. She used to update the lists at home. It was there in a big pile of papers. She was proud. I told her she did great. I knew we had to get out of town, but this was something we had to get on right away.

"Let's go see her."

"Shouldn't we call?"

"I want to catch her by surprise. I don't want her thinking about this too much. I don't want her thinking too much about the worth of what she knows. She might go back to Hall for a better offer."

We took Christy's car to North Hills. We didn't talk much. Nothing was said about the night before. She asked me how I had escaped. I still didn't tell her I had shot two men that morning. Christy said she simply wanted to help. She wasn't worried about herself, but she had confidence in me. I said that I appreciated that, but that I wanted to get her to safety. As soon as we saw Bishop, she'd have to get out of town, some place safe.

I could see right away why Helen Bishop was not a favorite of Christy's. A tired and angry woman in her late sixties who spoke through a fog of tobacco and alcohol, she greeted us at the door of her run down frame house in a dirty flowered housecoat. It was after four and she still hadn't really dressed. She kept her foot wedged against the door as she talked to us. She wanted to know if Christy finally had her money.

"Overtime, you have to pay overtime."

Christy tried to act friendly. She reminded her how they worked together. She mentioned Ryckman's plight and Helen Bishop laughed. Before she could slam the door in Christy's face, I pushed two twenty-dollar bills in the opening.

"There might be more."

The house smelled like stale beer and dead cats. On the mantle was a single picture of a man in a World War I uniform. There were no children's pictures, no other pictures of any kind. A smelly yellow cat walked into the room and curled up on a worn chair.

"What do you want to know?"

Christy spoke first. She appeared to really enjoy being a detective.

"Do you remember when Lindzey Hall first started putting pressure on Biddle, you said to me that Biddle deserved the treatment it was getting from him. What did you mean?"

"You know Lindzey is a big congressman. Do you know he sent me a card once? Right when he became a congressman. I remembered him. He asked me to write to him. I didn't. At the time, I was drinking. But I kept the card. For a while anyway."

I stepped in. "Do you remember a time in 1936, I think it was, when Lindzey Hall was injured? When he spent some time in the infirmary? Was he beaten?"

"Not that time."

"That time?"

"Oh, Lindzey had a rough time at Biddle. I treated his cuts and bruises lots of times. That first year at Biddle he musta had a dozen fights. He gave as good as he got, but there were usually more than one of them."

"Why?"

"Who knows? You know boys. He didn't have to do anything to get them going. Maybe they were jealous of the way he looked."

"Was it Veasey and his pals?"

"Yeah, mostly. They were the ones. Tommy Thorpe, Ray Halliburton, Joey…"

Christy chimed in. "Castille?"

"Yeah. Nasty boys. Real nasty. And Jack, the ringleader. They were a bad bunch. Too rich for their own good, if you know what I mean. Always after young girls."

Helen Bishop was warming to our visit. The two extra twenties I put on the table hadn't hurt. She offered us a beer. I drank my Rheingold's out of the bottle.

"Why was Hall in the hospital?

"I really don't know. I came in on a Monday morning and he was there. All it said on the chart was to call this doctor from Chestnut Hill if things took a turn for the worse. Not the way we usually did things. He shoulda been in the hospital. I just brung him his food. He was by himself in a room that wasn't even part of the infirmary. It was an examination room that they put curtains around. To keep him separate, you know."

"So what do you think happened to him?"

"That night when I was getting ready to leave. Lindzey was sleeping. I couldn't see a mark on him. He was such a beautiful boy. He didn't have a fever. So I decided to check him out. I pulled back the covers and I saw what had happened."

"What?"

"His…thing was bandaged. It was a big bandage like his…thing had been cut off and put back on."

"Cut off?"

"It looked that way. I don't know who put the bandage on. I used to hear about boys who would do that to themselves, but not Lindzey, he wasn't the type. Such a waste. He was a handsome boy."

"What do you think happened?" I wondered what Helen was really looking for when she pulled the sheets back.

"It looked like somebody tried to cut it off. He wouldn't talk about it. And I never said anything. I didn't want him to know I knew. You know boys and how they think about their…things."

She looked to Christy for confirmation. Christy nodded more to get her to continue than to agree.

"He was just a young boy and you'd have to call him handsome not just good looking. I was a lot younger then so I paid attention if you know what I mean. Nothing wrong, mind you. I just brought him his food and a couple of aspirin. Some days later the doctor closed the curtains and took off the bandage and he was back in school like nothing had happened. I felt so bad for him. Do you know his mother died when he was four? In a car accident. He wasn't a bad kid. They just kept after him to the point…"

I was getting impatient. "To the point where…"

"Where he got mean himself. He just stopped caring. He was nice to me. He sent me a card. I didn't even think he remembered me. I know they did something to him. I couldn't prove it. But I know they were responsible. They were there that weekend. They got caught with that little whore and they had to stay in their rooms. They would take it out on someone like Lindzey. That's what they would do."

We spent another hour with Helen Bishop. I tried to get more information about Hall and Veasey. The one additional thing that Helen was able to retrieve was the date. I thought it might prove to be useful although I wasn't sure how. It had happened the weekend after Thanksgiving in 1936. By the time we were ready to leave I had decided that she wasn't the hag that she first appeared to be. She was just a sad and lonely old lady who had been robbed of her husband in World War I. She had nothing to offer us for supper, but she wanted us to stay anyway. She tried to engage Christy in talk about Biddle. Christy had softened considerably as well. I was sure that she saw something of herself in Helen Bishop. Helen was feeling so much better about us that she offered the money back. She was bribing us to stay longer. I looked at my watch and agreed to stay, but not to take the money back. She was very happy with that arrangement. Helen was now given to monologues. She didn't like Ryckman. He was a stuffed shirt as far as she was concerned. She repeated that Biddle deserved what it got.

We said our good-byes. Christy gave her an awkward little hug at the same time I was trying to help her with her coat. Then she said, "You know I read somewhere where he had kids. And I was happy. I was happy he could have kids."

As we walked to the car, Christy wanted to know what I thought happened to Hall.

"I'm not really sure. I have an idea. It's pretty gruesome, but it makes a certain sense, if you know guys like Veasey and I did and do."

"How? You think *they* did it?"

"Why? What did you think? "

"First thing I thought was he tried to castrate himself. Lonely, no friends, just tormentors. But, I also thought it might have something to do with de Paul."

"Like what?"

"It's not that hard to imagine. A sophisticated snob and an alienated snob. The love that dare not speak its name."

"I can see that. But why castrate himself."

"I don't know. I'm reaching."

I could see that Christy was enjoying the game. She had a lively mind that was not afraid of dark places. We were hardly aware that we were in the car heading back toward her house. She was so engrossed in each scenario I had to remind her to keep her eye on the road when she almost missed a turn.

"I know. I know. I'm not going that fast. What if it was Hall who made the move toward de Paul? And was rejected?"

"You are getting good at this. If I ever need a partner—"

"I do need a job now, Varian."

"Then answer me this, why would Hall rescue de Paul from what he was facing in Europe?"

"Gimme a minute."

She was serious.

"First, let's figure out how we are going to stay alive."

"Okay, okay. I'm just trying to help."

"You are. I mean it. You're terrific."

As we crossed Limekiln Pike and Christy shifted into second gear, the gears began to grind. She laughed. "I'm usually pretty good with a stick shift."

"Yes, you are." But it was the case that had us excited.

"What if he was afraid de Paul would tell somebody."

"Then he would kill de Paul or leave school or bribe de Paul or make sure that de Paul wound up doing time with Hermann Goering. I've seen Hall. What you say makes sense for a certain kind of boy, but not Lindzey Hall. Remember what Ryckman said about Hall, the time they sewed his clothes all funny. He didn't hide. He didn't run away. He wore the humiliation like a badge of honor. What did Helen say? He went right back to school. I'll give him that. He doesn't strike me as the type to cut off his own pee pee.

"I hate that word."

"Which one do you like?"

"I guess I like 'cock.'"

"Okay, but what word do you like?"

"Funny man! So what's your theory?"

"What your theory leaves out is Veasey. How did Veasey and his buddies get on Hall? They called him 'Jew boy, Hebe, Kike.' But he wasn't a Jew. What would be the most obvious sign that he wasn't a Jew? What if they tried to circumcise him? Helen is wrong about the kids. The Stamford papers said he has no kids. What if they really did cut it off? Wouldn't that make him want to punish the school?"

And suddenly I knew I was right. For the first time I felt just a little sympathy for Hall. Just a little, but that didn't make things right. Lara was still dead. I was glad that Veasey had a little bullet in his brain, not just because he probably was going to kill me. I had the strange sensation that I had solved something. But, in truth, nothing that Helen Bishop had told us would keep Hall and de Paul away from us or get them in trouble.

When we pulled into Christy's driveway I realized that I forgotten my plan. I went to Christy's to make sure she was safe, to help her leave town. That was the optimistic part of the plan. The pessimistic part had to do with Christy disappearing forever with a new identity. In that plan, I would have no place in her life. What I saw in front of Christy's house made all the plans irrelevant anyway. It was Captain Ryan of the Abington Police.

CHAPTER 23

Ryan slowly got out of his car as Christy pulled into her short driveway. I figured he had heard about Donch and Gerhard. There wasn't much I could do. I wasn't about to kill a cop like Ryan. I repeated David Fenner's number to myself.

"Varian, can I talk to you for a minute?"

It didn't sound like he was ready to make an arrest. But he didn't sound like we were long lost friends either. He started walking slowly toward us. We were standing a few feet away from the front door when he stopped. He noticed my lip and my limp.

"What happened to you?"

"Had a little accident."

I hoped he didn't know what happened to Donch and Gerhard. He wouldn't have approached the likely killer of two federal agents so casually if he had. I hoped.

"If you think that's bad." I pointed to my tooth. I asked him how he knew I was there.

"Had a report that somebody was being kidnapped in the railroad parking lot. When we got there the only thing we found out of the ordinary was an old Ford from Connecticut. I just figured what with Mrs. Coopersmith here right around the corner. I figured I'd see you here sooner or later. It's been quiet otherwise. What happened?"

For some reason I decided to trust him, up to a point. "Two Feds wanted to talk to me."

"About the Greenbaum girl?"

"Yeah. Among other things."

We went inside. Christy made a fresh pot of coffee. The rich smell of Eight O'clock Coffee mixed with the sweet smell of pine in her living room. Out of habit, she turned on the lights to the tree. Maybe it was just habit or a way of putting Ryan in a giving mood. She brought me a bottle of Bayer's. Between my tooth and my knee, she figured I needed a handful. I had the feeling something else was on Ryan's mind. He looked around the house like a cop on a case. I saw him eye the pile of men's clothes that Christy had left on the dining room table.

"So what were these other things they wanted to talk to you about?"

He was playing it the right way, waiting for me to bring whatever it was I had to him, all the while trying to make me think he knew something.

"You were right," I finally said. "They don't want to find Lara's killer. They are trying to protect him. There's a man who works for Hall who used to teach at Biddle who killed Lara. I'm positive about that. But I couldn't prove it. Hall is protecting him."

"Why would they want to kill some co-ed from Connecticut?"

"It's a long story."

"As I said, it's not a busy day."

I filled Ryan in as best I could while I tried to protect myself. There were a few things I had to leave out, especially what happened to Donch and Gerhard. I was surprised that Ryan didn't react very much to what I told him. I had been right about him being a good cop.

"How'd you get away?"

"It's another long story."

"I think I know how this one turns out."

"You know? Have you been playing with me?"

"How could I not know? Two federal agents dead. The same ones who were asking about you. And I don't play."

"So why…"

"Aren't you under arrest? You might still be. It depends on how much I believe you."

"Okay, I'm telling you I killed those two men. They kidnapped me. It was no legitimate government investigation. I had no choice. It was self-defense, but I know what my chances are."

He took a sip from the coffee cup and placed it gently back into the saucer, complimented Christy on her coffee, and made a weak joke about his wife's inability to brew a good cup.

I couldn't tell what Ryan was up to. "So where does that leave me?"

"I'm not here to do anything right now except find out what's going on. I've been around long enough to know that things aren't always so clear-cut. I'm usually right about people. I had you pegged for a straight shooter. I figured you were doing your job. But something has been bothering me about this case since the beginning. There was something queer about those guys. Right after I talked to you I got a visit from two guys. Not the ones who were killed. Two other ones. They were a lot more interested in you than they were in finding that girl's killer. I told them you were going to Biddle and they almost—excuse my French—shit a brick. They were trying to hide something. I couldn't figure out what it was. Plus I didn't like their attitude. A girl from Connecticut is found dead in Abington and they are more worried that some private eye is looking into a private school where this congressman went years ago. Then the FBI calls and wants to know what those two guys are doing here and they want me to keep an eye on them. Everybody's watching everybody and nobody except you really seems to care what happened to that little girl."

"You didn't buy my story about Biddle."

"You kidding me? A private eye has two cases in the same small town two hundred miles from home. I knew right away that you had a lead, but that didn't add up either. But from the beginning, nothing has added up in this case. What you just told me makes some sense, but it doesn't answer the questions about Biddle. Why Hall would want to close the school. And what about Jack Veasey? How did he happen to die so conveniently? Another Biddle kid. So I started looking around. I asked myself what could have happened back then?"

"November. 1936?"

"You're not too bad for a private eye. How did you connect Marie Considine to this?"

"Who?"

"Marie Considine. The girl who was murdered by her father or, more accurately, whose father supposedly killed her."

"Tell me more."

"I was just a young patrolman in Philly when the case broke so I didn't know about it first hand. But everybody knew something about it. How could you not pay attention to a story about a father who kills his own daughter? Especially when there's sex involved."

"What does it have to do with Hall?"

"I'm still really not sure, but it was the only thing that stood out when I looked back. I found some interesting information. It seems that Marie was at Biddle the night she was killed. Marie had a bad reputation. A wild kid. Her mother died when she was little. Before she was thirteen she had already been caught with a couple of eighteen year olds. She liked older guys. There was a group of boys at Biddle who had more money than sense."

"Veasey, Thorpe, Halliburton, and Castille."

"Right. Good. They had been restricted to the campus over Thanksgiving break because of what they did to another girl. I guess they got bored. They wanted a little fun. Somehow they got Marie up to the school. Hardly anybody was around."

"Hall was there."

"He was?"

"He was in the infirmary."

"I didn't know that. The only one that I could find who was there was a Mr. Harttmann, a teacher, who had guard duty that weekend.

"He did? He's the adviser to Hall I told you about. Spent the war goose-stepping in Belgium."

"Huh. Maybe there *is* something here. Because he didn't have any family here he was assigned to watch the kids who didn't get to go home for the holidays. His name was on one of the police reports. He didn't have much to say. Why was Hall in the infirmary?"

"He was there because somehow he had gotten part of his...dick cut off. I think it was Veasey and his boys. I think it probably started out as a joke. Circumcise Hall. They were on him about being a Jew."

"Nice boys, but it fits the picture I got from the Considine file."

"But if they were there with this girl, do you think they killed her?" Christy was sitting on the edge of her chair. She wanted to be a part of this.

Ryan was just as excited. The juices were running again. You can spend just so much of your life chasing speeders and catching shoplifters.

"No. I don't think so. It doesn't fit. How would that hurt Hall and this Harttmann? Why would Veasey have to be killed then?"

"Well, when the body was found in Considine's back yard, the next morning, the old man—old man, he was thirty seven—anyway, Joe Considine was grief stricken, but he let it out that his daughter used to give him…used to masturbate him. 'Relieve him' was how he put it. He swore that was all that ever happened between them. He swore he never really had sex with her. You know, all the way, as if that made a difference to anybody. She was his daughter, after all. But that's all the jury had to hear. He had no chance. He swore and swore that he never would kill his daughter. He swore that he loved her. She was only fifteen. I believe now that he was telling the truth. Once they had a suspect like Considine the Abington police never really investigated the case, as if they could have if they wanted to. The DA never brought up in court about what Marie had been doing that night or how she got home. Or whether the sex she had that night was with a bunch of boys and not her father. No one ever really wondered, officially anyway, why Considine would kill her in his backyard and then leave the body there to be seen by everybody the next day. They just wanted him dead and gone. He was a civic embarrassment. Of course, the guy had a bad lawyer, a kid who handled mostly real estate. Considine wouldn't plead, but he offered almost no defense. I guess like everybody else he felt that anybody who would have sex with his daughter deserved to die no matter."

"What do you think happened?"

"Whoever killed her dumped her in the yard. All you had to do was see the pictures of the body to know that. You didn't have to be an expert in forensics. The girl had sex or was raped. That's clear. If the boys did it, how did they get her home? They were more scared about breaking the Biddle rules than they were about any rape or murder charge. They had no car anyway. Would they send her home in a cab? Maybe. But there is no record of one being sent to Biddle that night. Let's assume she's killed by somebody at the school who took her home that night. It wasn't the kids. That leaves this Harttmann. As good as any suspect. Better than the father."

"Why? Why not some guy who picks her up hitchhiking?" Christy offered.

"It's a real possibility, but—" Ryan had already thought about that possibility.

"But then there's no connection to Hall or Harttmann that they would have to keep buried."

"And Harttmann wouldn't suddenly feel like he had to be back in Belgium," I chimed in.

"Right. Right. Veasey said, in his statement, that the girl wouldn't have sex with all four of them. Not at once anyway. So they kicked her out."

"You believe his story?"

"Let's see where it takes us. What if this Harttmann sees her wandering around the campus, angry, maybe in a daze, and he offers her a ride. A pretty young girl. A little tarted up. No underwear."

"No underwear?"

"None on the body. None near the scene. More on the side of the father if anybody thought a minute about it. My guess is that if they had looked at Biddle they might have found them there. It seems that Veasey had her in bed when he invited his buddies to join them. That's when she bolted. So this teacher finds himself in a car with her. He wants a little for himself. He reaches over and finds that under her skirt there is just Marie. Maybe he sees this as a green light no matter what she says."

I stopped Ryan and told him what I knew about Harttmann/de Paul and his taste for young girls.

"Did they interview Harttmann?"

"If you can call it that. He was just noted as being on campus. He reported nothing unusual. And then within days, after Considine is arrested, he's gone. Back to Europe."

"I like it. But there is still a missing connection between Hall and all this. After all, he is the one going after Biddle."

"I still have a lot of questions myself, but I think we're on the right track. What you told me makes me even more convinced."

"So where does that leave us?"

"The only one left who might know what happened that night is Castille. The others are dead. He might be willing to talk. Especially if he hears what really happened to Veasey."

Christy said that she might be able to help. She hadn't realized it until then, but she had become something of a detective herself in her job as alumni coordinator. She had had to track down a number of missing graduates. Look at what she had done with Helen Bishop.

She needed to get back to the school. Could Ryan get us in?

"Just one thing?" I had to ask. "Why aren't you arresting me?"

"Because there is no crime that could involve you."

"I don't get it."

"They don't want you caught. At least by cops like me. They want to take care of you themselves. So they put out a cockamamie story about these guys having a fight and a tragedy results. I'm surprised you came back here. They know where you were. Why weren't they waiting for you?"

"It's not that big an operation. As best as I can figure, there are only four soldiers, maybe six. I guess that the others are back in Connecticut trying to tie up loose ends there. I hope they weren't any luckier than the guys they sent after me."

"You're probably right. But you are still going to have to get out."

He nodded toward the clothes on the table.

"I know. I know." I picked up a jacket and put it in small bag. "We have to find out a coupla things first. After all we have police protection now."

He laughed when he heard that. "This is all unofficial. If they show up I hand you over. Understood?"

"Understood." But I wasn't really sure I believed him.

Ryan offered to drive. They wouldn't be looking for a police car.

The school looked even sadder than before. I noticed peeling paint and clogged drains above the entranceway. Christy still had her keys. The inside of the building had the musty smell of death. Christy said it was because the heat was off. I thought it was something else.

While Christy looked through her files, Ryan and I sat in Ryckman's office, pretending to help. I studied Ryan for a while as he leafed through some of Ryckman's papers.

"Why are you taking a chance on me? You could be a big man with them."

"I'm through worrying about being a big man. Those guys don't know nothing about gratitude. They might just be worried that I know a little too much."

I could see it wasn't self-interest that was motivating him. "It's more than that."

He hesitated. I could see that he was uncomfortable with the question hanging in the air. He had already told me that he had been in the Pacific. That should have been enough his face told me. I pushed anyway. I was bored and he intrigued me. After all, he was trying to save my sorry life.

"The war?"

"What else?"

"So."

"We all have stories."

"I know. What's yours?"

"Mrs. Coopersmith. How ya doin'? Come up with anything."

I heard a lot more of the old neighborhood in his voice this time.

She didn't answer. I peeked through the door and saw that she was on the phone with somebody. I opened the door and pointed to Christy so Ryan would see.

"So. Crack the case?"

"So don't be condescending."

"That was affectionate kidding not condescension."

"Really! Next time warn me."

She was flirting, but I had the feeling that she was enjoying being "one of the boys," even more.

"So?"

"The Castille family moved out west in '49. Someplace in California. They didn't know for sure."

"Who didn't?

"The people who bought the Castille house in Rutledge. And there are no known relatives in the area."

"They told you this, too?"

"Of course. I figured that people always like to see other people get a little money, especially from dead relatives."

"Clever. You really do have the makings."

"It's what I have been trying to tell you."

"But the upshot is that we really don't know anything."

"I wouldn't go that far. "

"Hah. You have been holding back, clever girl."

She smiled. "I do know how to use a phonebook so I tried a few of the neighbors. I figured at least one might have known the Castilles."

"And they did?"

"I found out that Joe Castille, big surprise, was something of a black sheep. 'The kind of son who was born to break a mother's heart,' to quote Mrs. Anzalone."

"And?"

"And he shouldn't get any of the money. His mother should get it all for what she suffered. She should get it down in Florida. Not her rotten son who, to quote, Mrs. Anzalone again, at least had the decency to change his name."

"Change his name?"

"To Joey Castle.'"

Ryan heard the name from the other room and let out a yell. He was standing in the doorway before we knew it.

"Joey Castle? It's too good to be true."

"You know him?"

"Of him. Every cop does. Big dreams, but always just a small time hood. Acts like he's connected, but never is when the boom falls. They like to leave him holding the bag. In fact that's what they call him. 'Joey Bags.' The last I heard of him he got a year for strong-arming some union workers at the shipyard right after the war. You know kickbacks for getting war work. When the war was over, they could afford to look the other way."

"You know where we could find him?"

"If he's still alive, he'll be easy to find. Let me have the phone."

CHAPTER 24

It turned out that Joe Castille a.k.a. Joey Castle a.k.a. Joey "Bags" was safe under lock and key, doing three to five for selling television sets that belonged to Star's Appliances out of a truck on Delaware Avenue.

On the way over to the Fairmount Prison, Christy was like a kid who was going to the circus for the first time. She rattled off theories and speculated about Veasey and Harttmann. At one point, while Christy was spinning a particularly complicated web, Ryan looked at me and winked. He was as taken with her as I was.

I had more questions than theories.

"I thought you said that Veasey and his pals were rich. Rich kids usually don't wind up with monikers like 'Joey Bags.'"

"Joe Castille wasn't poor. He wasn't rich either. His father owned a paint store in Sharon Hill. He was always in trouble. He liked the life of a hood. His folks thought that Biddle would straighten him out. But he met Veasey and his buddies who were the typical spoiled rich kids. It was inevitable that Joey would wind up where he is. He never had the brains that Veasey did. Just look at the difference. Joey selling hot televisions from a truck and Veasey winds up a mouthpiece for big time gangsters."

The prison was stuck right in the middle of a residential neighborhood. It was an ominous presence out of an old movie. It even looked like it was in black and white, but Ryan said that the neighborhood loved it. "It's a great deterrent to crime."

Ryan had arranged for an interview room away from the visitors' room for our meeting with Castille. The guard knew

Ryan. We entered the small room that contained only a wooden table and three chairs. The guard apologized for not having enough chairs. When Ryan made the arrangements, he hadn't thought Christy would be there. She wanted to stay and I didn't want to let her out of my sight. For a couple of reasons.

They brought Castille in cuffs. The guard attached one cuff to the chair and asked us if we needed something before he left. Castille looked exactly like all the punks I knew in Stamford. His black hair was long and greasy with a carefully formed curl that hung loosely over his forehead. He wore the collar of his prison garb turned up like a hood. He immediately asked for a cigarette even though we all could see the pack of Camels in his shirt pocket. Ryan gave him a Lucky, which he looked at the way a wine expert looks at a glass of Muscatel. He put it behind his ear and took out a Camel.

"What's up? Who's she? Hey, baby." He nodded in Christy's direction and then tilted his head as he looked her up and down.

"I'm the school nurse."

"Hey, I'm over here," Ryan said. "I have some questions."

"'Bout what? I have appointments, you know. I have fuckin' people to see and important fuckin' things to do."

I wanted to grab him and throw him to the ground, but I didn't want to step on Ryan's toes on his own turf. Since I was beholden to him for other reasons as well, I let him take the lead.

"About you and Jack Veasey."

"I didn't have anything to do with Jack getting off'd. He was my friend. Anyway, I was right here. You can look it up."

"We know who killed your friend."

He sneered. "You do? Then it's your duty to report it to the police."

"It was another old friend of yours. Lindzey Hall."

The cool and arrogance had slipped from his face like a cheap Halloween mask. He took a deep drag from his Camel.

"You shittin' me?"

"Not really."

"Tell us about you and Veasey and Hall back at good ol' Biddle," I said.

We jockeyed back and forth for a while and then Joey settled down. We got him to focus on their treatment of Hall. According to Castille, they didn't really have that much against Hall. Veasey actually tried to make friends with him when he came to Biddle. Hall wasn't about to make friends. Joey had seen it before. Kids sent to Biddle against their will because they got in trouble back home. Veasey, who was always the leader, waited. Guys Veasey was interested in always came around. Veasey could get cigarettes, booze, even girls. And you wouldn't get beat up if you were his friend. Jack even gave him a nickname, "Hallstein" They didn't mean anything by it. That was the way it was. Castille was the "wop" for a long time. You couldn't let it get to you if you wanted to fit in. But Hall was really pissed. He didn't like it at all. Then he picked a fight with Tommy Thorpe. The smallest one of them. Hall wasn't a bad fighter and got Thorpe good, but Veasey couldn't let that go by. Not one of his boys. Veasey had always wanted a gang and he had one because he stuck up for his boys. He really gave it to Hall. But he gave him another chance and Hall just spit right on Veasey's pants. You can't get blood out easy. After that, they really went after him real good. Beat him up. Fucked with his food. They messed up his clothes. Castille thought Hall was a strange guy. He had no friends, but he wouldn't join up.

Ryan wanted to know how Hall wound up in the infirmary that night in November.

"You know about that?"

"Yeah, we know. We want your version."

"It was a joke. That's all. One time Jack saw that Hall wasn't cut, you know. So he says we should scare him. Veasey had a blade so we grabbed Hall one night in the showers and Jack tells him we are going to make a real Jew outta him, you know. Hall is really pissed. We weren't really going to do it, you know. It was just a joke. Well, Jack nicks him. There wasn't much blood. I guess it got infected or something. Hey. I'm cut. And I'm a goddamn Catholic. It got worse. He fainted one day. So they put him in the school hospital. We knew why he was there. Real hush hush. Nobody else knew. One thing I'll say for him. He never squealed, you know. Jack went to see him, you know, to tell him he was fuckin' all right for not squealing and Hall tells him he will kill him if he ever tells anybody else. You know they had to cut almost the whole thing off?"

He paused and took a long puff on his Camel. "You weren't bullshittin' me? You think Hall off'd Jack? I think the guy's crazy. You gotta protect me. I know things."

"Why? You're in protective custody already. What do you have to be worried about?"

"I figured it out. I was the one who told Veasey. That's right, me, Joey Bags. About that Considine girl."

"What?"

"I told him about Harttmann."

"Told him what?"

"A few weeks ago. Around Thanksgiving there's a picture of Hall in the paper and there's this guy in back of him I recognize. It's Harttmann. His hair is cut off. He's older. He's got a different name, but I recognize him. It's Harttmann. You get a lotta time to think here so I start going over what happened back..."

"In '36?"

"Yeah, yeah, whenever. We had this girl up at school. Jack thought he could get her to do it with all four of us. We had talked about it for a long time. We tried once before and it almost worked. She'd only do us by hand, you know."

He looked self-consciously at Christy. I was always amazed when criminals were embarrassed in front of a lady. He shrugged his shoulders as if to apologize.

"Don't worry about me," she said. "I'm not easily shocked."

"Okay, so Jack anyway hears about this girl. A townie. He hears she'll do anything with anybody. He tells us she's the one. There was nobody at school and she said she'd come, but when she gets there and sees the four of us suddenly she's scared. Jack's real smooth. He tells Tommy to stop laughing and take a hike. Then Jack gets her to take off her pants, you know. Just to give us a show, but she gets scared again and wants to go home. Jack is pissed. He tries to get her to do it with just him. She runs out of the dorms and Jack drags her back in, but we weren't gonna do anything now, you know. We were just pissed. We thought she was a tease. Well, Harttmann comes by, tells us we're scum, and takes the girl with him. The next day we find out she's been murdered. We thought the old man did it, like everybody else, but I got to thinking. Veasey came down one day to see me a coupla weeks before Christmas I guess, right after Thanksgiving anyway, and I tell him that I think Harttmann did the girl. It was just something to think about, you know, how weird things are sometimes. I figured there was no way to do anything, not after all this time. They have limits and stuff. I had no proof. It was just something to think about, man. I went over the whole night. Veasey thought we could use it anyway. A congressman doesn't need no scandal. They always want to avoid scandal, he said. Jack needed somebody to get some of the federal heat off him. There was talk that they were going to call him in for some kind of investigation. He said that Hall might even be able to help me get some time off, you know."

"Do you think Hall knew about the girl?"

"Maybe. She was up there, but it was late. That's not what pissed him off. You know, that we had a girl. He thought that Harttmann got bounced because of what happened. And he blamed us."

"What do you mean?"

"You know, he thought because we had a girl when he was supposed to be watching us they canned him. Maybe they did, but I don't think so. Biddle didn't want any kind of scandal. They didn't even bounce us. They even got a lawyer for us who got the cops to agree not to let anything of what happened that night get into the papers unless it had some bearing on the case. So we told them everything. But Hall blamed us. You know I think he was more pissed when he thought we got Harttmann fired than he was when we cut off part of his dick. He thought he was so much better than we were. Now his great buddy turns out to be a rapist and a murderer! So what are you going to do about me?"

"You'll be protected."

"Here? You gotta be kidding. You can get somebody killed here for two packs of cigarettes. Even Luckies."

There was nothing we could do for Castille so I thought I'd just try to calm him down.

"You don't really know enough to convict Harttmann. You have no real evidence. What would you testify to?"

"Yeah, it's nothing. And Jack's dead."

"Maybe it was just a coincidence."

"Maybe I'm the King of fuckin' Siam?"

It didn't work. So I thought I'd at least get some more information from him. But he was as nervous as a cat in an electrical storm.

"Did Veasey contact Hall?"

"I don't know. Maybe. He *was* really excited when I told him what I came up with. He kept saying that I wasn't as dumb a wop as he always thought. I just thought it was kinda funny. But then he's dead. I thought it was just his bad luck. You know, get involved with one family and another comes along and they want to send a message. Now you come around."

Joey Castle continued to plead for his life. He wanted to be sent out of the state. He said there was no way to protect him in Philly. What if Jack told them who put them on to him? If they could get to Veasey, they could get to him. We knew he was right, but we didn't care. Christy wanted to know why he stole televisions when he had all the advantages.

At first, he ignored her question. Then he looked at her with contempt. "I coulda sold paint cans to rich bitches like you instead. I coulda been just like my old man. I coulda gone through my whole life without ever having a taste of the big time. You don't know the times I've had."

On the way back to Abington Ryan wanted to know what I was going to do. "You know we don't have anything. Still."

"I know."

"You know they still will be coming after you."

"I know."

"You know they will get you."

"Probably."

"She doesn't have to be involved."

"I know."

Christy didn't like the way the conversation was going.

Suddenly she seemed to realize that this was not a movie, I was not Alan Ladd, and she wasn't Veronica Lake. There might be real consequences involved. But she wasn't as afraid as much as she was frustrated.

"There must be something we can do," she insisted.

"The only thing that might keep them away from us is if Louis is still okay."

"We have to find out."

"We?"

"What else? I'm not going to sit around waiting for them to show up."

"I wasn't planning on you sitting around. But you're better off away from me. The more we're together the more you are in danger. It's cold here. Go where it's warm. Go to Florida, California, or Mexico.

"And they won't find me there?"

I couldn't lie. "At least you'll stand a better chance than you would with me."

"How much better?"

"Better."

The only thing that Ryan could do for us was to lie if they came looking for him. The fact that Glenside wasn't crawling with feds meant we were right that Harttmann and Hall would try to handle this themselves. They didn't want anybody else involved. Christy wondered how they could do that.

The *Evening Bulletin* on Christy's porch had it as the cover story. There had been bad blood between Donch and Gerhard. Donch had deeply resented Gerhard's recent promotion. While on a routine assignment, they had continued their fight in the car when Donch must have shot Gerhard. In the scuffle, Gerhard shot Donch and then rammed the tree, dying in the impact. A spokesman for Congressman Hall, to whom the agents were assigned, regretted not separating the two men. With so little money allocated to the Congressman's important investigations into subversion on American campuses, the congressman had no choice but to keep them together. The spokesman, who had to be de Paul, but who was called Henri Krims, rejected any suggestion that subversives might have been responsible for the deaths of the agents. "The evidence is clear," he said. "However, this doesn't mean that communists wouldn't kill government agents if they had the chance."

Christy went into the house to pack a few things for the trip. Ryan and I kept a watch on the house from the street. I still had Donch's gun. I missed my own. Ryan stopped talking about the weather.

"You know when I came back from the war I was ready to live the perfect life. I left Philadelphia, settled in Abington and looked forward to watching my kids have kids. I was coming back to a great country that wasn't like all the rest. That's what I thought anyway. We've got our problems, but it's a good country. We weren't trying to conquer the world and we could have. We had the bomb. I was glad everybody seemed to think like me. Then Korea, McCarthy, and this Hall. Everybody's after everybody. What's wrong with everybody?"

"I wish I knew."

"I'll watch your back from here, but you know it isn't going to make a difference."

"I don't know, maybe with just a little luck."

"I think we both used up all our luck by 1945."

"You would have been a good man to have in the next foxhole."

"You too. I appreciate what you have—"

"Yeah."

Christy came out of the front door with two large suitcases. It looked like she was planning a long trip. I walked up the driveway to help her get them in her car. I heard Ryan's car start behind me. When I turned around, he was gone. I hadn't even shaken his hand.

It was almost eleven. It was very dark and very cold. The longest day of my life and I wouldn't have been able to sleep even if I had the best bed in the Waldorf. We started toward the Pennsylvania Turnpike. It was just as easy to head west as east.

"You still have the chance to change your mind."

"I know and I haven't."

"I could take you to Harrisburg. I could drop you at the station in Newark. You could get a train to anywhere from there."

It was crazy. I shouldn't have asked. She had no business going with me. But I couldn't just let her go. I had more reasons than I could count for sending her on her way, but she was in a bubbly mood setting out for New England and, probably, certain death. It was crazy, because I was just as happy as she was.

"Ever since I saw *Christmas in Connecticut* I wanted to go there."

"You're great. You don't have to be the tough guy. I can't really protect you."

"We've made it so far. I don't want to be alone. Not anymore."

"Look, we have to be realistic."

"Why?"

"Because this is real."

"I know. I'm not a kid. I know what I'm doing, even if you think I don't. Right now it's the only thing I can do. I can't explain why. You can't guarantee they won't find me even if I leave you. And, if we both make it, you won't come looking for me."

"How do you know that?"

"I know. I'm a detective, remember?" She smiled. At least I think she smiled.

CHAPTER 25

hristy's radio seemed to get only one station, a small independent out of Camden. They were doing an end of the year survey of the top songs of the year. I couldn't believe the music that Americans thought was the best of the year. "April in Portugal" reminded me of the kind of music you would hear at an amusement park. "I'm Walking Behind You," made Eddie Fisher sound like someone had him by the throat. When the announcer started to introduce the surprise hit of the year, "Doggie in the Window," by Patti Page, I reached for the dial. Just when I was about to shut it off I found a station from Trenton that was also doing a review of 1953, but instead of "You You You," by the Ames Brothers, there was the group led by trombonist JJ Johnson, featuring "the latest trumpet sensation" Clifford Brown.

"Now that's better," I said.

"You like that better?"

"You don't like jazz?"

"Not that kind of jazz. I still like big bands. Benny Goodman. Artie Shaw. I used to love Artie Shaw. He was my favorite."

"That's not jazz," I insisted.

"It's not?"

"Listen."

On "Capri," Johnson, Jimmy Heath, and Brown came right in strong together like a marching band and then JJ broke away from the group into a remarkable solo while Kenny Clarke danced around the time on the snare and cymbals. Off to the side Percy Heath stood looking over their shoulders while his bass made witty comments about JJ's solo. Then Clifford Brown stepped up to the plate like the Babe following

Lou Gehrig in the lineup. As good as Lou was, this was the Babe.

"It doesn't sound like a song. It keeps changing. The drummer doesn't even sound right. He's like behind the rest. He's not even a good drummer. Not like Gene Krupa. You can't dance to it. Look."

She started to mimic dance movements.

"See. It's slow. It's fast. It's someplace in between. There's no steady beat."

I tried to explain what was happening as best I could. Louis was so much better putting it into words. I tried to tell her that what she heard was intentional. That was the style, to explore rhythm and harmony, not just play catchy tunes. I pointed to this solo and that one. I tried to get her to listen to how the drummer was working both with and against the soloists, intentionally. This was not really dance music. It should be listened to closely. Like classical music. I quoted Louis about how jazz and standup comedy were the only art forms originated by Americans and I had the realization that I was acting exactly like Louis when he was trying to explain to me the joys of modern art, except that I was doing a really bad job of it. I wanted her to like it. It suddenly was very important. I didn't want her to fake it. She had to really like it.

"Just listen. Let yourself flow into it. Think of each instrument like a voice."

"I'll try. Is this what they call modern jazz?"

She tried to listen, I'll give her that. But you can't fake it. Like you can't fake loving escargot. Or paintings of black and red squares. The station faded away long before we got to the George Washington Bridge.

The only thing that would come in was the news. Senator Joe McCarthy continued his attacks on the UN. There was a conspiracy in the UN to disarm America. Joe Stalin loved the Democrats who supported his plans, he charged.

Ford offered "World of Tomorrow" power today with its Y-block V-8. Paul Harvey told the story of the invention of the pneumatic tire.

Christy was as tired of the news as I was. She turned the radio off.

"You said that Lara was really involved in that book about the girl who slept with Nazis and then killed them."

"She was."

"And what if her real target wasn't that de Paul but his boss. What if she tried to get close to Hall and she discovered his secret. What if she reached inside his pants and found out he had a little tiny pee-pee?"

"That's not funny."

"I'm not trying to be funny. Wouldn't that—"

I turned on the radio and found nothing but 101 strings playing a holiday medley. I left it there so that it might wipe out the images in my head. There was an uneasy silence in the car.

"Can I ask you something?"

"Why do I get the feeling that I don't really have a choice?" I tried to make it sound light, but it came off like I was being accused of something.

"You have a choice. You always have a choice."

"What is it?"

"I know it's none of my business, but why haven't you married?"

"I guess I never met the right girl."

"The world is full of right girls. You know that's not the reason."

"But that's the truth. When I think about being married, it's never with anybody in particular. I imagine a woman, just a woman. I could describe her to you, but I have never met her. It's a—"

"Describe her."

"It's—well, she likes jazz." It wasn't even close to being a joke.

"You don't have to be…"

I had hurt her and she didn't deserve it. But she was trying to scale that wall again and I was ready with the boiling oil. I could see how she was all confused about us. She had assumed some things and now she wasn't sure. Here we were with our suitcases filled with her and her husband's clothes, and here I am sitting there in her husband's old baseball jacket, and we are trying to outrun the men who planned to kill us by going right to where they were. The fact that her life might be in danger was much less troublesome to her than the thought she might have misunderstood something between us.

"Maybe she looks like Lara."

"That's not right."

Now she was angry. But she had also been waiting for me to say something. About us. About me. Somehow, it was my turn to say something. She wasn't interested in understanding jazz. It must have seemed too much like learning baseball for her husband. She waited in silence for me to speak with an intensity that was much more painful than any third degree I'd ever gotten from a cop. I tried.

"Remember that night when we were—"

"I remember. It was last night."

"No, I mean the first time."

Now that I had put her life at risk, I couldn't talk about what I felt for her. How could I tell her that I loved the huskiness in her voice and how the words that came from her mouth made my ears smile? I couldn't bring myself to say, how everything she said was smart, funny, and gave me chills. How the little freckles under her left eye looked like the map of Greece? How could I tell her that when I looked at her face I forgot about island dreams? I was as happy as a man could possibly be just watching her sitting in a chair. How could I tell her that no matter what I felt about the whiteness of her thighs, or the shape of her red wide mouth, or the touch of her hand on the small of my back, I was sure we would find ourselves facing the same guns that killed two stupid dogs? And maybe my very good friend, the same friend I lured into the case. How could I tell her that I should have taken her to Newark or Pittsburgh and not to Connecticut, no matter what she thought? How could I say that her life was more important than anything else was and then explain to her why she was still here next to me? All I knew was that I couldn't protect her because I didn't want her out of my sight and for that pleasure I was willing to risk her life. How would that sound? I couldn't tell her any of that. So I stalled.

"I'm sorry. It's just that this doesn't seem like the right time to go over this."

"I don't think there will there be a right time. I have the feeling that there would always be a reason for making it the wrong time. Just as there were probably reasons all those times before." She was right.

"There weren't that many."

"It doesn't matter how many." But it did, it clearly did.

"I didn't mean it that way." I had reached the point where there was nothing I could say that would make things right. I was sorry. The last thing in the world that I wanted was to hurt her. And that's just what I had done. "What I started to say was remember you said that there was some kind of wall around me. You were right."

"I'm sorry. I shouldn't have said that. I had no right. After what you've been through. Look what you're doing now. Risking your life because—" She shifted again. From prosecutor to sympathetic friend. I was getting confused.

"Because I was paid."

"That's not the reason."

"Yes, it is. In a way. As long as I'm getting paid, I can justify what I'm doing. It says that I'm not a total fool. Maybe I got that from my father. But you *were* right. There is a wall."

I was feeling a little exhausted. We were nearing White Plains. I began playing with the dial on the radio again and was able to get WSTC from Stamford. They were playing polkas. I left the dial where it was. The day was ahead of us. There were clouds in the sky. Oom Pa.

"What about me?"

"What do you mean?"

"What do you think of me?"

"I can't. I just can't. You have to know I think you're great. But beyond that, I can't...Can we wait until this over? We're not out of it. Our lives are on the line. How can we know what we really feel? It's too..."

"It's just because we might not make it that I have to know. If something happens to you or me, I need to know the whole story."

"It won't matter."

"I'm not asking you to propose. I'm terrible at darning socks. I haven't really thought about that, about the future.

Maybe you think I have. Not every woman thinks about nothing but marriage. I was married. Not for very long, I'll admit, but I have seen a lot of marriages. It's not my idea of paradise. But I do still think about love. I think that's important. I have really missed that in my life. When you glimpse the possibility of love, it changes things. It changes everything. I think I could love you. It makes me look at you differently, at life differently, at everything differently. This is a big step for me. All I want to know is if you think it is possible."

It was one of those questions you ask when you really want only one answer. I wanted to answer her. I wasn't sure that I could give her the one she wanted, but she deserved the truth. The problem was that I didn't know about that either.

"I can't say right now. I just don't know. You are—"

"Don't list my good qualities. I hate that. Is it because I have been with other men?"

"Are you serious? I'm a grown up. I don't expect women, even widows, to be virgins."

"You're a man. It bothers men. I know it does. I probably told you too much."

"I don't know what that means. I don't know about other men. What does that have to do with me? This was your life before you met me. I had a life before I met you. I wouldn't want to answer for what I have done."

"You see. It's not something to *answer for.* You think you're being very generous. I'll forget if you…But it does bother you that I have been in bed with other men."

"Don't. You don't know what bothers me."

"That's the point. I'm just sorry. I thought you were different."

"Maybe I'm not. I don't make comparisons. I know what I feel. All I'm saying is I haven't thought about it one way or another. That's the truth. That's not what's on my mind."

"And if you thought about it?"

"I don't particularly want to. Is there something wrong with that?"

"It is something, if we get out of this, you'll have to answer. Maybe not right now, here in a car on the way to god knows where. Not for me Varian, but for you. I mean it."

I felt more panic at that moment than I had the whole time I was with de Paul and Donch and Gerhard.

"That's the one thing I don't get about men. You want the impossible—a woman who knows everything about sex, who will do anything, but someone who has never done it with anybody else but you."

"You think that's true?"

"I know it's true. You are all so easily fooled. I have done it myself, many times. 'Oh, you big handsome brute, it's so big!' You just tell them, 'I have never done this before, but you get me so hot, I want you to put it in here' and then you roll over and it's like they just scored the winning run. You can even see their chests swell up."

"I don't think that's me."

"You think you're better than that?"

There was a ton of anger in her voice. She wanted me to see her with other men, to imagine her doing everything. She wanted to implicate me. I hadn't given her the answer she wanted. She wanted to hurt me. I could understand that. I didn't mind being hurt. What I didn't like was just the fact that she was hurt. I could feel the tears in her throat. I didn't like it at all.

I could hear her chest heave, but she wouldn't cry. I had to change the focus. I hoped to change Christy's mood by talking about the case.

"What about this? Hall and de Paul are on different tracks. They're not together on Biddle. Let's say that de Paul did kill that girl. Let's say that he made it appear to Hall that he was fired from Biddle. Let's also say he let Hall take out his anger on Biddle. Now let's assume that, in addition to de Paul's firing, he has his own attempted castration to deal with. Does he want the world to know he has half a dick? So Hall hears from Veasey and it's about the Biddle. Hall doesn't know about the murder. He thinks castration. He thinks Veasey is going public. And maybe he is just in the middle. At the wrong place at the wrong time. What do you think? It might explain a few things."

"I don't know. You're the detective."

CHAPTER 26

By the time we reached New Canaan, the silence Christy had wrapped herself in chilled the inside of the Ford. It was much colder than the winter air that buffeted the old two-door sedan. There was no snow in the air just a chilling to the bone. Inside the car and out.

We drove by the long drive that led to Louis's house a few times. I had Christy look into the woods around the house for any signs of a stakeout. Fortunately, it was easy to see almost all the way to the house through the bare scraggly trees. In the summer, an armored division could have been hiding there and we wouldn't have seen anything.

On our third pass I turned slowly up the driveway. I had the .32 on my lap. Christy was looking to the rear. Louis's Willys Overland was sitting next to the house. There were the Olds and my Chevy looking pathetic with their flat tires and a few bullet holes.

I got out of the car slowly, Donch's pistol in my hand. Immediately, I could see the evidence of a gun battle. Pieces of concrete around the front door were scattered like confetti. There were two gaping holes in the wall. Next to the door and just above it. It looked to me like the work of a shotgun. There were other holes in the walls that had been made by pistols or rifle fire. I counted fifteen without paying much attention. The door was open.

The inside of the house smelled damp, like dirty clothes left in the rain. I expected to see the place trashed. But except for the cool and the damp aroma of the air coming through the shot out windows, the place looked just like Louis was about to step out of the bedroom to play the latest Miles Davis recording. I didn't see the book. I remembered that Louis didn't know Christy's car. If he saw it coming up the drive, he would probably hide in his secret spot. I walked to the stove and began knocking on the floor, calling out, "Louis, Louis, it's okay. It's me."

By this time, Christy was right in back of me. "Do you think he's hiding in the oven?"

"No, he's got a secret place under here. He used it when they killed his dogs."

"There are two fresh graves outside."

"I know. That's Amor and Psyche. The dogs. I helped bury them."

We went to check the graves anyway. I could see what Christy meant. Even in a few days the dogs' graves would have weathered more than this. I reached down and felt the mound of earth that covered the dogs. Something or someone else was buried here.

"I have an idea."

We took another quick look around Louis's house and grounds before heading down the hill. At the garage at the bottom of the hill I stopped and looked in the small windows that ran across the top of the door. The door was padlocked, but it was loose enough to pry apart so that I could check it out. My heart was pounding. The last thing I wanted to see was a fender.

"Young man, young man."

I turned quickly, my hand on the gun. There was an old woman in a heavy coat and a plaid scarf wrapped around her head. She wanted to know what I was doing there. I said that I was looking for the man who had a Cadillac for sale. She believed me, I think, only because Christy was with me.

"Oh, I don't think so. He would never sell that car. It belonged to his father. In any case he is away. I saw him leave yesterday. Or, was it the day before. I never can be sure these days. He must have been in a hurry because he didn't even wave to me. He usually waves to me from the garage when he takes the car out. He knows I spend a lot of time by the window, since my husband died. You came all the way from Pennsylvania to buy a car?"

She was very observant. I wondered if Louis had hired her

to watch who was coming up the road. She seemed like a Hollywood version of the nosy neighbor.

"No, no. I'm from Stamford. This is my cousin from Pittsburgh. She just gave me a ride. I'll just try to call Mr. Diamond.

"Mr. Diamond?"

"The man who owns the car."

"But his name is Gardner."

I must have looked confused because I was. But what could I say. Louis was even more paranoid than I had thought to use an alias with his neighbors. I said my good-byes and got back into the car. Trying to make a graceful exit and not arouse an old woman's suspicion, I reached in my pocket for a random piece of paper. I told her that I had the owners of two cars I was interested in mixed up. It seemed to satisfy her. She said she often called her grandson "Ed" when his name was "Kevin."

"What now?" Christy asked.

"I think I know where he is, if I can remember how to get there."

I could feel the old woman watching us as we drove away. I knew generally how to get to the place on Candlewood Lake. It was the specifics that troubled me. It took us an extraordinarily long time to get there. The trip seemed even longer because Christy was still giving me the silent treatment. I tried to act like a jovial guide, reminding her that she wanted to see what Connecticut looked like. I pointed out the sights along the way, inventing famous people who lived in the big houses set back from the road, but all my attempts at changing her mood failed dismally.

Somehow, I found the dirt drive that led to Louis's secret hideaway. When we got to the top of the rise, where the log house sat like a colonial fort, I caught a glimpse of the Caddy. Things looked calm and peaceful. I couldn't see any evidence of a firefight.

Remembering, this time, that Louis wouldn't recognize the car, I honked the horn and told Christy to wave her arm out the window. I did the same in between honks. With all that noise, I figured that Louis would never mistake our entrance for the arrival of federal troops. By the time we reached the front porch, he was standing near the doorway, smiling, holding a Thompson machine gun.

"Lose your way, strangers?"

"Looks like you had some fun back in New Canaan."

"These things happen when you're famous or infamous. I forget which I am."

I hadn't realized how much I was worried about Louis, but I knew now because it felt like opening day and I was batting third. I was so positively giddy that I forgot to introduce Christy.

Louis was never one to ignore formalities. "You are forgetting your manners, Varian. You bring Merle Oberon to me and don't even have the courtesy to introduce her to me. How rude of you."

He was obviously taken with Christy who looked particularly stunning even in her plain gray coat and blue tam. He had ignored my expressions of glee at finding him alive. He was making the point that his survival was less significant to him than matters of etiquette.

"I'm sorry, Louis. May I present Christy Coopersmith from Glenside, Pennsylvania? She has been a big help to me. She is—"

"I can see that she is remarkable. I am honored to meet you Miss...Mrs.?"

"Mrs. I'm a widow."

"I am so sorry."

"There is no need to be. It's been a long time. My husband was killed in the war."

"You must have been a child bride." Louis asked her to enter his "rustic getaway." Before I could follow her into the house, he pulled me aside. "Have you lost what little sense you might have had?"

"What?"

"Her. This isn't the time for a little romp in the woods. You're risking her life bringing her here. Don't you have one ounce of goddamn sense?"

"I tried. She insisted."

"She…what? Overpowered you? You simply have to get rid of her."

As soon we entered the cabin, Louis almost completely ignored me. He offered Christy "an inferior but drinkable Claret." He pointed out the primitive charms of his log cabin and promised her the moon on the lake. He asked her about her tastes in music. He apologized for not having any Frank Sinatra or Doris Day. He had brought only a few recordings. He had left his home in New Canaan in haste and had time to select only a handful of recordings. He did have an Ella Fitzgerald that she might enjoy. He was flirting with her, acting like we were rivals in a Noel Coward play.

I was feeling ignored. I knew it was intentional. I didn't believe that he could be that angry with me. Just for bringing Christy? For putting his life in jeopardy? For being the cause of him losing his dogs?

"So, Louis, what happened?" I tried to butt in, feeling like an Archie to his Reggie.

"When?"

"You know, back at the house."

He looked to Christy as if he was trying to calculate whether to impress her with a story featuring his heroics or to attempt modesty. I hoped he didn't opt for the Gary Cooper approach. It didn't suit him. I was amazed at how smitten he was with Christy. Louis seldom talked about women and I couldn't remember the last time I saw one at his house. It had been so long that I hardly blinked when de Paul tried to diminish his capabilities by labeling him a "homosexual." It was something that had occurred to me a number of times as we listened to music. Too often I had the feeling that I was "on a date" but there was never any attempt to make things physical. There was so little sex in Louis's talk that it hardly mattered to me whether he liked men or women. He was more likely to get excited over a line of poetry than a glimpse of a curved leg or muscled chest.

"As soon as I saw the paper about Rippey, I knew they'd be coming back to New Canaan."

"What happened to him?"

"A fire. The paper said he fell asleep with a fire going and sparks must have hit the rug. Terrible accident, wasn't it?"

"There was no fire in the fireplace when I was there because there was no fireplace. They must have been in a hurry to come up with that story."

"I don't think it mattered. The house burned to the ground. Did you know he had a wife and two kids?"

"Not in the house!"

"No, no. In New York somewhere. They're divorced."

But I didn't really care about Rippey.

"I found out some other news," he said. "They were going to call Browder to testify at the public hearings, but they withdrew the subpoena before it was served. Guess when?"

"Right after Lara was killed."

"Exactly."

Christy was clearly already engrossed in Louis's story or she was also trying to make me jealous but, in any case, she sat as if she were listening to the "Gettysburg Address" delivered for the first time. She wanted to know who Rippey was. I started to explain, but Louis interrupted. I felt like a sophomore in high school. He told her about his connection to Lara and about the book. She wanted to know what had happened in New Canaan. She had seen the bullet holes.

"As soon as Rippey told them you had the book, they would have to come for us both and fast. This time I was ready, but they were just a couple of cowboys."

I wondered if it was Sexton and Lawrence. I described them.

Louis was annoyed that I had interrupted his story. He gave me a look that made me feel like a heckler in a tough nightclub. From his description, they were too young and too big to be Sexton and Lawrence. Then I remembered New York. I remembered the four who followed me through the city keeping me busy when there had to be somebody watching Veasey's place waiting for him to show up. I wondered if I had missed any others. Now the question was where were Sexton and Lawrence? Louis wanted to continue.

"They wouldn't have lasted a week in a real army. They came up the drive like they were arriving for dinner and they must have thought they saw something or somebody in the door. Maybe the ghosts of Amor and Psyche. I hope so. It would give me a great deal of pleasure to know that they protected me one last time. But whatever it was they saw, they began firing like it was a Sunday turkey shoot. One had a shotgun. The other had a pistol. I had a Thompson. But I was so surprised at their amateur approach to the business of killing me that I almost forgot to open fire myself. I was above them on the ledge that runs around the living room. I had a perfect line of fire. They started walking toward the door, 'guns a blazin' as they say in old Dodge City. I waited until they were real close. I wanted to see their faces. I kept waiting. It was just too easy to kill them that way. They needed to know…"

"What?" Christy leaned forward as if she was about to hear the secret of life.

"Something of what they had done, not just killing my dogs certainly, although I was angry enough about it. The death of that young girl was certainly enough to justify the taking of theirs, but it wasn't even that. Varian will laugh, but I didn't like what they were up to."

"I am surprised, Louis."

I was more than surprised. I was moved. The cynic with the heart of gold.

"Then what did you do?"

"Well, suddenly, they were in the house. I hadn't planned on that. I didn't want to shoot my Malevich or Goncharova and my Marantz was right in my line of fire. I had the drop on them so I wasn't worried about myself. I ordered them to drop their weapons. The tall one looked up at me as if he had just seen Jesus Christ descending on a cloud and immediately dropped his pistol. The one with the shotgun was not as smart. He was dead before he could raise the gun to his shoulder. It's a lot easier to aim down than up. And quicker. Unfortunately, his companion panicked and reached for his pistol. The ground was too hard to dig new graves. I buried them in Amor and Psyche's graves. There was a certain poetic justice to that. I hope my dogs' spirits hound them for eternity. Their car is deep in the woods with my old Olds."

"It must have been awful." Christy leaned forward to catch the emotion she expected to spill from Louis.

"Not really. I missed hitting the hi-fi although I now have a few holes in a very nice Persian. So all in all…"

Louis had opted for "twarn't nothin" modesty. I was disappointed in him and annoyed with Christy. I knew what she was doing and that made me more annoyed. It was as if I were thirteen about to scream at her, "But you told me you liked me best!"

Louis offered Christy another drink and tried to engage her in some conversation. He wanted to know more about her. He said that I had mentioned her, but I had not done justice to either her beauty or her charms. He loved her hair, he said. Her smile was like the sound of a flute.

I saw some small reaction when he mentioned me, but I couldn't tell what it meant. Then Louis asked me to fill him in on what had happened in Pennsylvania. I tried to muster up my story telling skills, but it came out like a police report. I couldn't even make my escape from Gerhard and Donch sound exciting. "So where does all this killing leave us?"

"They have got to stop and think now that we have eliminated four of them," he said. "It's a small operation. Hall doesn't have an army at his disposal. I don't think he's going to arm the lawyers he has working for him."

"There's still Sexton and Lawrence."

"Indeed. But I have some other news for you. Hall is going to be on television tonight. I think it might be interesting."

"Where's the television set?"

"We will have to find one."

"Do you think it's safe?"

"Of course not." Louis suggested politely that Christy might stay back at the house while we went off in search of a television. She would have nothing to do with such a plan. She told Louis that she was not going to let us out of her sight. He looked at me. I said nothing. I just realized that we hadn't had any sleep. I knew that because I was dizzy and my tooth was aching again. Louis pointed us to the bedrooms. Without saying anything, we headed for separate bedrooms. I was asleep before my head hit the pillow.

Louis woke us with a plate of bread and cheese and the
warning that we had to hurry if we were going to catch Hall on
television. He took a European automatic and placed it carefully in his belt. I still had the .32. I wished it were a little bigger. Louis threw me a piece of cheese and we headed off into
the night in the Cadillac. As we drove through the empty roads
that ringed the lake, I told them what Hall had said back at the
mansion about possibly thinking I was Lara's killer. "They
have so many alternative versions of the truth, I don't think
they know what they believe. But it tells us that de Paul and
Hall aren't in lockstep, or should I say 'goose-step?'"

About fifteen minutes before "Newsmakers" was due to be
aired we found a roadhouse, *Jake's Big Lodge* that had a big
sign out front, announcing that it had television.

"Let's hope there're no fights on or we might have one
ourselves."

"But there's always a fight on."

Luckily for us, the bar was almost empty. It was one of
those bars, which tried to look like a hunting lodge but wound
up feeling like an old barn instead. To provide the right atmosphere there was even an old moose head on the wall above
the bar. It looked more startled than majestic, as if it had just
stuck its head through the wall above the bar. A rusty musket
wrapped with equally rusted wire was attached to the ceiling.
It looked like the plan to hang old rifles from the ceiling
hadn't gotten very far. The two guys at the end of the bar were
too wrapped up in whatever misery would bring them to such
a place that they hardly looked up at the screen. The promised
clear picture was nowhere to be seen. Instead, it looked like
two guys were wrestling in the middle of a blizzard. Louis
approached the bartender and handed him a ten spot. He probably didn't have to, but it made him a lot more attentive. He
changed the channel and brought us our drinks. Christy ordered a Johnny Walker Black Label on the rocks. I think she
did it to make an impression. Still in my wounded mode, I reminded myself what Louis thought of blended scotches and
was glad that Christy had probably lost some points. We waited for the show to begin.

Through the swirling dots came a picture of the capitol

dome and then a picture of a college campus. A voice intoned Hall's pledge to restore America's system of higher education to its rightful place as the first and most important bastion against communism.

Then there was Hall sitting in what looked like the same room where de Paul had questioned me. It looked more like a movie set on TV. I resisted the urge to point out the fact that I had been there. Hall was sitting behind the desk, but de Paul was nowhere to be seen.

A reporter, who could not be seen, asked Hall why he had taken on the task of investigating American colleges and universities. Hall repeated what he had said many times before about the vulnerability of young minds to alien ideas. He explained how youth was a time for questioning and the commies knew that. They took advantage of the natural curiosity and idealism of the young. They planted their seeds of doubt about this great country.

I had read versions of this speech before in the *Advocate*. In person, it sounded different. Calm. Concerned. Hardly fanatical. Then the reporter asked him what communist influence he had actually uncovered in any college during his investigations. I was surprised. It was a good question.

Hall shifted the subject. He paused and put his hands together on the desk. He tried to look serious, even sad. "In my investigations into communist influence in American colleges which is so pervasive that any reasonable person would be and should be shocked, I started to ask myself how did this situation come about? I know that the colleges themselves did not set out to become mouthpieces for communist ideology. I know and respect the presidents of too many fine institutions to believe that they have been anything more than the unwitting victims of a widespread communist conspiracy."

He paused again as if what he had to say was almost too painful to say to the American public. But there was that same coldness in those pale, hard eyes that I saw when he dismissed me from his presence.

I could see the boy behind the man, and I saw that he had never really suffered at Biddle. He could not suffer. It just fed the hate. And there was so much of that. He made de Paul look like the quisling he was, a petty criminal in comparison. Yet other than piggybacking on McCarthy and shutting down the Biddle School, I couldn't put my finger on anything he had actually done.

But I knew he could do anything.

"As repugnant as it was, I kept coming to the same conclusion. I couldn't understand how anti-American ideas were being foisted on our children at colleges and universities all over the country. How had so many communist professors come to assume powerful positions in colleges and universities across the country? I came to the reluctant and sorry conclusion that those responsible for protecting us and our children had let us down. I think it is time to get to the root of the problem."

He managed to get just the right quiver in his voice. He was suffering for us. His voice said that he wanted to get to the bottom of it.

Hall refused to be more specific. All he would say was that he would be requesting hearings to investigate who in the government was responsible.

"That was the signal," Louis whispered. "Hall has just alerted Hoover that he is coming after him."

"Why would he do that? What's he doing?"

"I don't know, but I think we have pushed him to act now. Maybe he's ready to deal. Maybe he's rallying the troops. In any case, he has to seize the stage before things become unraveled. It's a preemptive strike."

"Why didn't he name Hoover?"

"It would be too much for the public. This is just a tease. He has to string it out. He can always back off. No one will remember. Those who know, know. He's letting them know that he's ready to act. It was an impressive performance."

'Who could believe such an obvious phony? I mean the hand wringing, the sad look."

"Look." Louis pointed to the two men at the end of the bar. They had abandoned their drinks.

"Damn right," one said.

"Fuckin' commies, sorry ma'am," said the other.

"See what I mean?"

I still didn't believe it. I wondered if de Paul was already out of the picture. Hall had to know what was in Rippey's book.

Christy wanted to be part of things. "So what do we do?" she said eagerly as if she were ready to grab the musket off the wires and march into battle.

As I watched Hall, I thought less about Hoover and the political battle that seemed ready to begin than about the young boy with the chip on his shoulder who came to Biddle those many years ago. The image in my mind was confused with that boy I watched walking across the playing field on that first day I showed up at the school. For the first time I felt a deep pity in my gut for that boy. Then I wondered if I were watching myself in a red plaid jacket walking against a cold wind so long ago. I couldn't tell anymore.

We left the bar with a bottle of Black Label.

"Let's review our options." Louis wanted to take charge.

Christy was anxious to follow. I drove. Louis began to lay out the situation as he saw it. I could see him in a uniform. He was clear and concise. No emotion. He even seemed to sense that Christy was watching him with adoring eyes. Maybe not.

What it came down to was that we had only the book to use for collateral. The diary was useless. We could not pin Lara's murder on de Paul. And Marie Considine, forget about that. And Rippey's killers were dead and buried and so were Veasey's or vice versa. It didn't matter.

Even though it was a weak book, it scared de Paul and Hall enough to kill to get it. However, there were some problems with how to handle it. There was a lot of nervousness about political issues these days. McCarthy had raised duplicity to an art form. Anybody was vulnerable to innuendo. Black lists existed in every profession.

Louis seemed to be thinking along the same lines as me. "A dead professor's story with sketchy documentation, who would take a chance on it? There would be pressure from the government not to publish, regardless of what anybody thinks of Hall. Some of our pet Nazis are working in our rocket and missile programs. They are celebrated. And the government won't jeopardize them for anything. Worst of all any attempt to try to get someone to publish the book would take time. Too

much time. Hall knows that. He isn't about to sit around waiting. We might just be able to walk away from the whole thing,
if we stay quiet, then maybe Hall will consider going after us
as more trouble than it's worth."

"What are the chances of that?" Christy asked.

"Not real good." I answered. "And even if they did lay off
that would mean Hall and de Paul would get away with it,
with it all."

"They'll fall. Eventually. They all do. They will over reach
just like the fabulous senator from Wisconsin who is about to
destroy himself. It's inevitable." Louis was trying to take the
long view.

I didn't like it. Hall had given me the chills. "I don't think
so. McCarthy is a clown. He doesn't care any more about
communism than he does about life on Mars. Hall is different.
Didn't you feel it in the way that he talks? He's really dangerous."

"He's impressive, yes. He's learned from McCarthy. He's
smoother. Joe will say anything just to get a headline. Hall is
very careful. He doesn't yell. He doesn't interrupt. He doesn't
sweat. He's cool. But then look at the men he picked to do his
dirty work. Minor leaguers."

"Even if they catch on to Hall, what's gonna happen?"
Christy asked. "He won't get re-elected? Big deal."

"In this imperfect world one cannot hope for a perfect solution," Louis commented. "We have done a lot and we need to
think about protecting ourselves. There is no telling how they
will react to the loss of their men. They might crawl into a
hole for a while or they might come right after us. The second
time they would get us. I'm sure of it."

Although I knew he had a point, I didn't like it. I looked at
Christy. If she was scared, she was doing a good imitation of
being brave.

"So what do we do?" She had the makings of a good soldier.

"There is one bit of information that might be worth something," I mused. "The FBI doesn't care about the book. If we
are correct, they supplied most of it to Rippey through this

Saper. What they don't know is what Hall's plan of attack is. That's the missing piece."

"Can we trust them?"

"It is not about trust. It is about controlling damage. They have an interest in that. They all do."

We seemed to have run out of options. There was nothing more to say for the time being.

When we reached the house we found that the fire was almost out. Louis and Christy picked me to find some firewood. There was an old pile in the back of the house. When I walked back in, I could hear Louis explaining to Christy how the Epicureans had the right idea. "Live unknown."

He extolled the pleasures of the mind as the essence of life. Then he reached in his pocket and offered her a roll of bills. She refused to take it. He shook his head. I felt like a voyeur. I walked back out on the porch overlooking the lake. I had forgotten how cold it was. The air was crystalline. My breath hung in the air like smoke from the barrel of a gun. I tried to concentrate on the beauty of the inky black lake reflecting a golden moon. I could see lights in the hills in the distance, but my ears strained to hear what was going on in the room behind me.

I was outside for about a half hour when Christy knocked on the window. She waved me inside. The sight of her smiling face made me act like a pouting child who needs to be begged to come to supper. I shook my head even though I was freezing in my light jacket. I tried to rub my bare hands inconspicuously, ignoring her. Then I was crushed when she didn't beg me to come in. I was still acting about fourteen. Maybe eleven.

In another half hour, my cheeks were numb. I couldn't strike a match to light a cigarette. My toes ached. The moon on the lake was no longer even interesting. I walked back into the house. Christy was sitting on the sofa while Louis tried to explain why he loved jazz so much. I almost turned around but my cheeks were burning. I hoped it was because of the sudden heat against the cold flesh. I rubbed my face and headed for the bottle of wine. It was empty. So was the scotch.

Louis continued his lecture as Charlie Parker toodled up

and down the scales of "Steeplechase." Christy still wasn't sure that she "got it," but she had a better sense of how some-one else could.

"It's like the time we had an artist come to Biddle to ex-plain modern art to the boys," she said. "Before I heard him talk I used to laugh at pictures I saw in *Time* magazine that looked like a two-year-old's finger painting. I still wouldn't want to buy one of those pictures, but I was impressed at how passionate he was about his painting. He wasn't joking."

I couldn't help wondering where that artist spent the night.

I wasn't so sure that I wanted to go to the FBI. If we couldn't trust one part of the government, how could we be sure of any other part? To me they all seemed to be the same, playing their secret games of power, destroying enemies, re-warding friends, keeping the country in fear. I was afraid of getting sucked in by them. How did we explain the deaths of four CDA agents? "There are murders all over the place. Lara, Veasey, Rippey. There has to be a way to trace them to Hall and de Paul."

"You're being naive," Louis insisted. "They can insulate themselves from all those murders. And forget the blood on your hands."

"What about the de Paul writing on Lara?"

"You can prove he did it?"

"He practically admitted it."

"Practically, that's good."

Christy thought that we could trust the FBI. "Why would they do anything to us if we help them?"

Louis leaned over and softly whispered loudly enough so I could hear, "I want you to be safe so take the keys to my car and a pile of my money and don't stop until you reach the Pa-cific Ocean."

CHAPTER 27

L ouis spent the next two days negotiating with the FBI. He met them first in Danbury. He told me to wait for him back at the house. If we were together, they could just take us both in and have everything. It was a kind of insurance if I stayed behind with Christy. And I needed, as if I needed reminding, to protect her. He urged me again to see if I could get her to go away. He offered money. I refused. He called me bad names.

When Louis was away, Christy seemed less indifferent to me. We even started talking again. At first, she wanted to talk about Louis. Then she started talking about the house. How much she liked the view. She always loved being on the water, she said.

"I'm sorry about what happened in the car." I felt like I could say some of the things I couldn't in the car.

"Are you? For what? Was it your fault that after two days I began to hope that we would be spending the rest of our lives together? Are you sorry because I started acting just like I promised myself I would never act again? Are you sorry that I became a love struck girl again? And I bet you never even hit .300."

"No, but I could hit the long ball."

"You still can."

"Don't be so hard on yourself. It wasn't just you. What I couldn't say—"

"You said what you had to say very clearly."

"What? I've been going over it ever since we got here. Help me out. What did I say? What did I do wrong?"

"You were right. This isn't a good time to talk. It's like one of those, what do you call them, 'foxhole promises'?"

"It's not—"

She wouldn't let me finish. She smiled. She brought her fingers to my lips and whispered, "It's all right. I don't hate you. I don't hate you at all." Then she gave me a sisterly kiss on the cheek.

"And Louis?"

She laughed. She laughed a full laugh that seemed to give her vertigo. I thought she was going to fall down.

"I don't think I'm equipped for Louis, maybe I should be the one—" She couldn't get the words out before falling to her knees and holding her sides. It was a laugh that had been days in the making.

Louis walked in and wanted to know the joke. Christy waved him away. I shrugged my shoulders. So Louis ignored us and went to get a new bottle of wine. He told us about his meetings with the FBI between sips of ruby hued Bordeaux. "In the beginning, they just wanted to get their hands on any-thing we have without any promises. No deals." Louis de-scribed them as "Your typical bad blue suited, wrong collared, silly tied arrogant bastards. I convinced them they weren't dealing with a novice. We met the second time in a restaurant outside Sherman. I had given them time to talk to Washington. At the Inglenook restaurant, they were more interested in talk-ing, but what they really wanted, as I had suspected, was what Hall had on the FBI. On that, they won't budge. If we can come up with that, we have the makings of a real deal. With-out it, they have no real leverage against Hall. As one agent said to me, 'Hall dumps his Nazi buddy and expresses shock that he had been duped by his old high school teacher.' I pointed out that the fact that de Paul was his teacher made his being a Nazi almost useless even if he had dropped the gas pellets at Belsen. Hall could easily survive the disclosure. Look at the stories they had already constructed. And not a ripple of doubt. Rippey's book just didn't give them enough. 'We know,' the agent said, 'because we gave him just about everything he had.' Without Rippey it is almost useless. They still want the book, but offer no guarantees if we don't come up with Hall's point of attack.

"They don't care who has been killed already or how many

will be killed, meaning us. This is a war of attrition. And the weapon is information. They're all wondering who is out to get them. The FBI is more afraid of this new CIA than they are of Hall. In fact, they probably think Dulles is backing Hall. It goes around and around and around. And the communists, my god, they laugh at communists. God knows who they are afraid of, but whoever they are, it's only good Republicans and Democrats not Bolsheviks. This one thing is clear— Hoover will do anything to stay in power. They'll scapegoat us if they have to. They'll pin the Lindbergh kidnapping on us or Pearl Harbor if it will protect them. Even if we come up with what they want, they still might think they would be better off if we lived only in the memories of our relatives. And I don't have any relatives. That'll show 'em."

Christy listened to Louis's reports in rapt attention. "I know I don't know much about politics. I can't even tell you what the difference is between a Democrat and a Republican, but this is our government. Hall is an American. The FBI. Why do they want to destroy each other? What's going on?"

"What's always gone on since Caligula and Claudius. A struggle for power by insiders. It was the story of Rome for hundreds of years. The difference is that we don't know how to keep score any more. Look, we were fighting in Korea for more than three years. What was it? A war? No, it was a police action. Did we win? No. Did we lose? It depends. And we will have more of these strange little encounters with an enemy we can't even really identify. In Vietnam. Guatemala. In Iran. India."

I was getting impatient with Louis's lecture. I didn't want him on a world politics rant when he had just made it very clear that we had almost no hope of getting out of this with our skins intact. I interrupted one of Christy's questions. I wanted to know how we were going to get the information about Hall's attack on the FBI.

Louis was just as impatient with me. "I don't know. You're the detective."

We took a break to cool down. Christy wrapped herself in the bright red plaid blanket and walked out onto the porch. I could see her light a cigarette. "Can I join you?"

"Of course. This is awkward. I want you to know that I don't...I still care for you. I just need to step back."

"Can we make a deal?"

"Sure. I mean it depends." She didn't want to appear too eager, but I didn't mind.

"When this is over, can we meet here again? I'll ask you for a cigarette."

"Wait a minute. Wasn't that a movie? Bette Davis and the guy with that funny little mustache?"

"You know, I think you're right."

She laughed again. This time it was her full laugh that meant that everything was still possible. This time I could join in the laugh. We went back inside.

"Another joke?" Louis wasn't his usual bubbling self. I figured the best way to get things back on track was to go back to Lara. Somehow, she was at the center of this. Not just a naive star-struck girl who managed to be in the wrong place at the wrong time.

"I keep thinking that Lara knew something more," I said. "Maybe it was their plan? Maybe it was Biddle? She wasn't killed because she found out de Paul was a Nazi. She had to be a bigger threat to Hall, de Paul, or maybe to their whole plan. If the FBI knew in advance what Hall had on them, what could they do. How would it make a difference?"

"It would make all the difference in the world. You don't know the resources they have. You don't know how capable they are of altering history. But it takes time. They can't work their wonderful magic on documents, the memories of witnesses, and the interpretation of events without time. If Hall suddenly makes his charges, the press will be unleashed and they won't be able to control it all. There will be damage. They don't want damage. Not to the sacred, perfect, unsullied FBI."

"Maybe if I have a look at the diary?" Christy asked eagerly.

"Why not?"

Louis was sitting in the big plaid chair staring at the fire. It was his thinking chair. Christy went into the kitchen and washed the dishes. She was very efficient. "The Theme from

Moulin Rouge" played softly on the radio in the background. It felt like camp even though I had never gone to camp. I had to keep reminding myself that our lives were on the line.

I kept going over Lara's murder hoping that something would suddenly throw everything into the clear light. "Remember de Paul carved the word 'traitor' into her body. He was angry. He wouldn't have done that unless she had something on them. They wouldn't have killed her just because she was trying to get dirt on Hall. They must run into that all the time. Journalists, Democrats, Fifth Columnists, Dodger fans. Political campaigns are full of spies. It comes with the territory, doesn't it?"

Christy looked at me and shrugged her shoulders a bit and then told Louis her idea about Lara discovering Hall's secret in his pants."

"You know that's not bad. But our only hope is that she found out something else. Something the FBI would be interested in. The tragedy is that she was killed before she could tell anybody. If she did find out, it was in Philadelphia. She didn't have her diary."

"Do we know she didn't contact anybody for sure?" Christy was back in the game.

"She didn't send anything to her father. Rippey didn't have it. Probably. If he did, Hall has it now. Her boyfriend? Her roommate? It certainly wasn't the FBI."

"Let's assume she did find out something right before she died, it's our only hope so we have nothing to lose making such an assumption," Louis suggested. "Let's also assume that she had a chance to get rid of or hide the information before de Paul got to her. How would she do it? Remember she was bright, dedicated, and in danger. Maybe she even knew that Rippey had exposed her. So she wouldn't give it to him. A phone call. Unlikely. We would have heard. The mails? Maybe. But a letter should have shown up by now. On her body? Your friend Ryan would have found it. In the woods? In the car?"

"What if Ryan found it and didn't know what it was?" she asked. "Or didn't even know he found it?"

I had heard that tone in Christy's voice before. Her mind

was racing. She smiled that old smile which filled me with life for the first time in days.

Even Louis was intrigued. "What do you mean, Christy?"

"Ryan was looking at the murder of a coed, a sex crime, probably committed, he thought, by some stranger who picked her up at the station. The last thing on his mind was a case of political espionage. He wouldn't be looking for the kind of evidence that would interest a US congressman or the FBI. He didn't get suspicious that something more was going on until you, Sexton, and Lawrence showed up. Maybe he looked at the evidence again, but he didn't necessarily know what to look for. We all admit Lara was clever, so she had to hide the information where it wouldn't be easily discovered in case she was searched. She had to figure they might search any new-comer to Hall's inner circle even as a matter of routine. She couldn't have expected to be killed. It might still be there."

"Where?" I wondered.

"I don't know. It could be someplace as obvious as her pocketbook."

Louis was as excited as Christy. "She's right. Whatever she heard might just have been a phrase or a word. She didn't have to hide the *Encyclopedia Britannica.* She could have written it on anything. In any form. She had a code. There's lots of ways. On the back of a picture—"

Now we all were fishing.

"Maybe it wasn't even written. It could have been an object or something. Who knows?"

Louis looked at Christy with the same admiration as Ryan had. I looked at her with a feeling more complicated than mere admiration.

ぐつぐつ

We sat around through breakfast the next day searching for alternatives if we couldn't meet the FBI's demand. Louis, at one point, offered us asylum, as he described it, in Montreal where he had some sort of arrangement with some French-Canadian veterans.

We entertained that idea for a while and then abandoned it

when we reminded ourselves of the climate in Quebec. Tired of fantasy, we tried to get back to reality.

"We have to find out what Lara had with her when she was killed."

I called Ryan in Abington. He was glad, and a little surprised, to find us still alive. I explained that I thought there might have been something in Lara's effects that might explain why she was killed. I held on while he went to get the file. Her clothes, of course, had been kept as evidence. Her father wanted everything that wasn't evidence. Ryan went through everything with the DA and they sent what they didn't need to the family. "I have to tell you, there wasn't much there."

I thanked him and told him it was the only hope we had.

"What are you looking for?"

"Salvation."

"Well, god bless."

I immediately called the Greenbaums. Mrs. Greenbaum answered. Manny was at the office. I asked her if she still had Lara's things. She sounded hurt that I would even suggest that she would get rid of any evidence of her daughter's life. I asked if I could see what she had.

"Do you have a suspect?"

"We have some possibilities. "

In talking to her, I realized how much this was now about saving my tail and not about helping them at all. I had forgotten her pain. I didn't tell her the complete truth.

She would be home. Christy went with me. Louis stayed behind. The trip to Stamford went quickly since Christy was obviously in a better mood.

"Did you mean what you said?"

"When?"

"Outside, last night?"

"Bette Davis?"

"Right."

"I never meant anything more in my life."

"Good. I don't care if it is from a bad movie. I'll be there."

Mrs. Greenbaum met us at the door. Freddie was there. Manny was on his way.

"Did you find something?" she said almost in a panic. "We were starting to give up hope. We hadn't heard anything."

Freddie was even less friendly than Sophie was. "What's been going on, Varian. What are you doing dressed like that? And the limp."

"It's a long story."

"Really! I've got a lot of time myself. Most of it I spend by the phone."

He was anxious and angry and hardly acknowledged Christy's presence. I tried to explain that it was too early to make any judgments. I asked to see Lara's things.

"What are you looking for?"

"Anything."

"What makes you think there might be something here? You know something. We have a right."

"As soon as there is anything to tell you, you will know," I lied.

"I don't like this, Varian"

Sophie Greenbaum emptied out a little cloth bag. She seemed numb. "This is all they sent. Is there anything else? Do you think she might have known—"

"I don't know."

"Why was she in Philadelphia? How did she get there? Who was she with?"

"I don't have all the answers yet."

"What answers do you have, Varian? Can't you see Sophie is almost out of her mind?"

"I know. But speculation isn't going to help right now."

"That's for me to decide."

I wondered how my manhood was stacking up in Christy's eyes now. I started to go through the bag. Manny arrived and raced into the living room.

"Have you got something?"

"He doesn't want to tell us anything," Freddie said.

I explained again how it was too soon to say anything definitive.

"Why would Federal Agents want Lara's diary?"

"What?"

"A couple of days ago two agents came to the house. I tried to call you a dozen times."

"Who were they?"

"They said they were investigating Lara's murder. Because it was out of state, they said. They wanted to know if we had Lara's diary. The only one we had was from high school. It was locked. Why would they want her diary? Do they think she knew who killed her?"

"Perhaps. They have to look into everything. Were they FBI?"

"I don't know. I think so. That's what I assumed. Why? What has her diary have to do with her murder? Do you have it? I called you. I called a hundred times."

"Were their names Sexton and Lawrence?"

"Yes, I think so. Do you know them? Do they know something? Do you have the diary?"

"Did they ask to see Lara's things?"

"No, just the diary. Do you have it? What were they looking for? What are you looking for?"

I knew that Lara's roommate would tell everybody I had taken the diary, but I was afraid to open that whole can of worms. I had the feeling that my friendship with the Greenbaums had already reached the breaking point. So I lied. And continued to look through Lara's things.

"If I find something. Anything. A clue. I'll let you know. I want to find Lara's killer. You have to believe me."

We spread the contents of Lara's pocketbook on the table. There was her driver's license, her lipstick, a make-up case, some bobby pins, about a dollar in change, a sanitary napkin, an eyebrow pencil, an old movie ticket stub, a few snapshots of her mother and father, her cousin Anne, and Jason. I checked the back of the pictures. Nothing. No notes. I looked inside the various compartments. The only find was a wrapper from Beeman's Pepsin Gum. I opened it. Nothing.

"Do you have anything else?"

Manny was beside himself. It was as if we were ransacking his daughter's grave. "You are obviously looking for something. We have a right to know."

Sophie brought the coat down. I pulled the pockets inside

out and a used Kleenex fell to the floor. Sophie seemed embarrassed at such a discovery. I started to unravel it and even Manny slightly recoiled. Maybe he didn't want to be reminded that his daughter was a woman. That gave me an idea.

"Give me the Kotex."

Manny and Freddie both hesitated, waiting for Christy or Sophie to respond, and I knew I was on to something. I took the napkin from Christy and tore up the first layer. Inside was a small scrap of paper. On it three names were written in faint eyebrow pencil: *Claus Fooks, Harry Gold, and Leonard Abbott*, what looked like *a bomb*, and some dates barely legible.

"What is it?"

"I don't know. I don't know."

The names didn't mean anything to me. The Greenbaums didn't recognize them.

Manny was ready to strangle me in frustration. "What's going on? Why would Lara have those names in there? Are those the names of her killers?"

"This could be something. Just hold on. Give me a little time and I'll tell you everything I know."

"Are you going to show those names to the authorities?"

"Manny, just give me a little time. Trust me a little longer. This is very complicated. This is not an ordinary murder. Lara—Lara wasn't kidnapped by a stranger."

"How do you know that?"

"Who would do such a thing to her?" Sophie was almost beyond control. She was reaching for me. I couldn't tell if it was for comfort or to rip my eyes out. Christy tried to comfort her but she pushed her open arms away and slumped on the floor. Manny couldn't decide whether to continue his wife's attack or help her up from the floor. That left Freddie.

"I thought I could count on you, Varian. I thought I could count on you."

"You can, Freddie. Believe me. I have to do it my way."

"Not anymore."

"Please just a day or two. Don't tell anyone we were here."

"Not the FBI?"

"Please. We go back. It's complicated."

"So tell us."

"Not until I know. Just a coupla more days, Manny. Just a couple." I just wanted to get back to Louis who might be able to unlock the secret of the three names. Manny and Freddie continued to remind me how important it was that I find Lara's killer.

They wanted to know again and again what I knew. God knew what Sexton and Lawrence told them. I just appreciated the fact they didn't just call somebody with a badge to take us away. Sophie sat in the corner, looking down. Finally, she said, "I know it won't bring her back. Nothing will." Then she walked out of the room. Manny looked away.

On the way back, Christy said she was impressed at how I had found the names.

"Lara was just so clever. I didn't know her but now I think I know how she thinks. If I had a daughter—No, the truth is it's more like—"

"You're in love with her?"

"Yes, but not like that. Not really. It's just hard to explain. I've gotten to know her, her dreams, everything she did wrong, and she did some terrible things. I know what she thought about the spring, everything she loved and hated, like no one I've ever known, and nothing makes me think the less of her."

"That's love." She gripped my arm. "No wonder the Greenbaums are so devastated. But that doesn't tell me how you figured—"

"She was so smart. And such a...she knew a man wouldn't touch one of those, even a clean one, unless absolutely necessary. There is almost no time when it's absolutely necessary. And as soon as I saw it I knew it. I knew why they wouldn't touch it."

"Why?"

"I guess it's just fear or ignorance, I don't know. But I never knew a man comfortable with those things. That's why all the jokes, I guess. That's all."

Then as we got back at Candlewood and were about to get out of the car, Christy wondered who the names would benefit most, the Greenbaums or us. I had been wondering the same thing.

CHAPTER 28

As we walked back into the cabin, it was as if everything had changed. I still felt bad about the Greenbaums, but I hoped that I could make it up to them when we figured everything out. I wasn't sure I really believed that so I didn't think very hard about exactly how that would work. The important thing was that Christy was next to me and there was a warm glow coming from her. The chill was gone. I began to think about the future, a future with her. In my euphoria, I began to think that her jokes about working together weren't a joke anymore. Well, why not? There were Mr. & Mrs. North, and Nick and Nora Charles, and Christy was good, as good as they were. I was smiling to myself to the point that Christy wanted to know what I was thinking. It was hard to tell her after confronting the Greenbaums.

I said "nothing really." And smiled again.

"They've had a rough time."

"I should have told them more. From the start."

"They'll understand when things clear up."

"I hope so."

I didn't believe it. I didn't want to think about Freddie and I tried not to think about Sexton and Lawrence, but I had to. Would the Greenbaums tell them we had been there? I could understand why they might. Even if they didn't, Sexton and Lawrence would find their way to the lake. Eventually.

"They know a very different Lara than you do."

"I don't know what I know about her."

"I think she found something out that she wasn't ready for."

"How could a nineteen year-old be ready for Nazis and the federal government?"

"No. I don't think that was it. She found out she had power. Even if it was just between her legs, it was real. And if you're not ready for it, like that sad girl who was murdered back in Abington, it can get you in a lot of trouble."

"I just wish she'd told somebody."

"Like her father? Her mother? She had already gotten the better of two professors. She was beyond that."

I still couldn't square the little girl I used to know and the Lara I now knew. I could see Louis watching through the windows as we walked up to the house. I knew he had the Thompson in his arms.

When Louis saw the names, he immediately recognized them, at least two of them. He said he should have known. We filled him in on what had happened at the Greenbaums. But he didn't pay attention. The Greenbaums weren't his concern. He wondered how Lara could have gotten hold of the information. We constructed a few possible scenarios. As long as she didn't hear it in de Paul's bed, it didn't matter to me.

"Lara was bright all right, just not a good speller, he said. "She must have overheard them talking. The first name is 'Klaus Fuchs.' The name doesn't ring a bell?"

"No. Some Nazi?"

"How about the Rosenbergs or Whitaker Chambers or Alger Hiss? Heard of them?"

"Of course."

"Well, Klaus Fuchs was more important than any one of them. Much more. He really did give the atomic bomb to the Russians. He made the Cold War possible. He was a real spy, not like the others. A volunteer who walked right up to the Russians and said, 'Guess what I have for you!' He never took a dime. In fact, he was insulted when he was offered expense money. A dedicated party member to the end. And he worked, guess where? At Los Alamos."

"What happened to him? How do you know all this?"

"It was in all the papers, even *Time* magazine. Fuchs is already in jail. He was tried in England. Do you know how long the trial lasted? No? An hour and a half. An hour and a half! The court had barely enough time to get its wigs on straight. Do you think somebody was a little embarrassed? Do you

think there was something to hide? Of course. They didn't
want to raise any questions with a long trial."

"Whoa! Go back a little," I said. "I don't get it. If it was in
Time magazine, how is it such a big secret? Isn't it just old
news? How can it bring down anybody, much less J. Edgar
Hoover?"

My question stumped Louis for a second. I was kind of
proud, but still confused. I was missing something and so was
Louis. He tried to retrace the Fuchs case, as he knew it, trying
to tease something useful out of his memory. "Fuchs was a
German scientist in 1940. He came from a long line of social-
ists. He didn't like Hitler very much and Hitler didn't like him.
So he got out of Germany when he got the message from the
Nazis that he would be better off in a place like Dachau. A
German scientist who was actively disliked by the SS, it was
easy for him to get clearance to work on the atomic research in
England. Then about 1944 he was transferred to Los Alamos
where he began working on bomb design and assembly, about
as important a job as you can get, and that's where he began
meeting with Harry Gold, the second name. Gold was his contact. I am not sure where he is now, but if he's alive I'm sure
that Hall has to have him in his pocket. He was the courier.
Fuchs gave him the whole bomb down to the Philips-head
screws. He used to drive to Santa Fe all the time to meet Gold
at some crummy diner. No secret radios in the mountains. No
codes. It was hardly complex intelligence work. After the war,
Fuchs went back to England to work on their *secret* bomb.
They caught up with him in 1949 or so. Right after they nomi-
nated him for the Royal Society and other honors, they finally
figured out that he had given the Russians the bomb right under their noses. He got fourteen years. Can you believe it? The
Rosenbergs get the chair and who knows what they actually
did? But Fuchs—he was the real deal and he gets less than a
two-bit armed robbery. The FBI had something to do with
bringing him in. At least they took credit. They count Fuchs
right up there with Dillinger and Pretty Boy Floyd."

"I still don't get it. Hall is going to take out Hoover with
one of his best cases. This is too subtle for me."

"It's all here. You're right, it is subtle," Louis agreed. "But it's probably also very simple. We just have to put two and two—"

"Okay, let's go over it again. So this Fuchs is in jail. The FBI catches him. There is nothing top secret about that. It was in the papers. I still don't see how you bring down Hoover with this. If anything, it might make him look good. I wouldn't be scared, if I was him. So why kill Lara over this?"

We went over it again and again. Louis was frustrated that we were stuck in the middle of nowhere. If he only had access to the court papers, to the newspaper stories, to the summary of the investigation, he could figure it out. Then he stopped. "That's it, it has to be. The investigation. It's there."

"Where?"

"Here."

"Didn't I see this bit in an Abbott and Costello movie?"

Louis ignored me. "Look at it again. It's not so obvious if you think about it from another angle. Who do you think was responsible for keeping the Fuchs case so low profile? Why didn't we want him tried here? Why has such a big deal been made of the Rosenbergs or what's going on with Oppenheimer now? Somebody has to take the blame for the Russians getting the bomb. Why not Fuchs? The man who actually did it? I'll tell you. Because if you look too close, there are too many questions. It's the biggest story of the whole goddamned century. Somebody in the press, somebody with some clout will figure out what it took us an hour and forty-five minutes to figure. There are a lot of questions that nobody has really asked—in public, at least. It's gotta be in the third name. That's the key. He's the one who can pin it on the FBI."

"I'm glad you cleared things up."

"I'm still working on it," Louis snapped. "It could be Gold's contact? Or somebody in the FBI? No matter who it is you still have to wonder about how they handled this case. Why wasn't there any outrage here that he gets off so easy? No hearings. No McCarthys waving secret documents. Fuchs is tried in England in an hour and a half? Who was responsible for security at Los Alamos? Who cleared Fuchs? What did his file look like? How did he manage to go regularly from Los Alamos to Santa Fe to meet with Gold without being detected?

This was the most secret place on the planet. Don't you think they kept track of everybody's movements? Don't you think they knew what he was doing? It has to be that they let him do it. Not because they were in league with the commies, but maybe just because they were too stupid."

"What do you mean?"

"What was atomic power before the war? Science fiction, fantasy. It was Buck Rogers flying through space. It was atomic cannons blowing up moons. It was anti-gravity propulsion and time travel, too. If somebody came to you in 1935 and said that they had an idea for a bomb the size of a sofa that would turn Minneapolis into dust in 30 seconds, you'd give him a strait jacket, not a research grant. I know these guys and how they think. They don't understand baseball much less quantum mechanics. They hate intellectuals. Look at Liev Aronson, my very best friend, who knew what the Nazis were going to do before they did. But he had a funny voice not MacArthur's sexy sunglasses and corny corncob pipe. They got what they needed and were embarrassed. They are stupid and cruel people. When that bomb really exploded in the desert, I'm sure there was a lot of scrambling going on in the agency. Somebody probably just put him in the 'oops' file and said we got to save our asses.

"Oops?"

"Yeah when they really mess up, like kill some innocent people in a shootout or wreck the life of an innocent man, it goes into a file which is very, very hard to find. Hoover doesn't like mistakes, but he won't tolerate embarrassment."

"That's it? Hall is going to embarrass Hoover."

"You don't know how powerful a threat that is. Think of what an aggressive congressional committee might do with this story if they think Hoover is vulnerable. If they think they might finally be free of him. Don't forget this is not a vague innuendo about communist sympathizers in the State Department who might have lost China by having dinner with the wrong sorts or Hollywood directors who try to sneak commie messages into films about Jesse James. This is the goddamn atomic bomb. And everybody knows about it. They just haven't thought about it. It was given away right under our noses. If Hall wants to go after the FBI, this *is* the perfect case. It's right in the public view. It can't be denied. Hoover is ripe for a fall on this one, absolutely. But they still need a smoking gun, some new angle, somebody who knows everything, and this must be it. This third name."

"I'm sure the FBI will know who it is."

"One thing about espionage, my friend, never sell information that you don't understand the value of. You never know what it's really worth. It could be worth your life. We have a little time left to deal with the FBI. I need to find the connection between this Abbott and Fuchs and Gold. I have to admit that you two did a great job."

ぐ/うぐ/う

The next morning Louis went off by himself to Stamford where he was going "to poke around." To be on the "safe side," in case Hall was still on the warpath against me, he suggested again that Christy and I go up to Canada. Things were coming to a head. There was no sense taking chances. Christy refused. She said it was like leaving a mystery movie right before the end. Instead, she suggested that we help Louis "poke around." He said he couldn't let us do that. The people he had to talk to didn't want to be known by anyone else.

"What about your fancy phone?"

"They don't trust anything they can't see. Look, Varian, make sure she's gone before I get back."

I shrugged my shoulders.

"This isn't a game."

"I know."

So Christy and I stayed behind. It wasn't so bad. Things continued to relax between us. She had taken her lumps and I had taken mine. We were like two fighters who had fought hard for fourteen rounds. When the bell rang in the fifteenth, we were a little bloodied, but we had earned each other's respect. Now I began to imagine what she looked like under her clothes. I kept staring.

"What are you looking at?"

"You. I like looking at you. Do you mind?"

"Only when I feel like my clothes are about to catch fire."

"There are other ways to take them off."

She smiled and changed the subject. "Do you think Louis will find what he needs?"

"He usually does."

"How does he know so much?"

"I don't really know. I know he had a hush, hush job in the war. But I have no idea what. I don't even know what service he was in. He had made a lot of friends in Washington, but he decided to sit it out on the sidelines after the war and play his games. Using what he knew just to make a lot of money."

"He is rich, isn't he?"

"Money never seems to be a problem with him. But it's not about being rich, I don't think. Money just gives him, 'leverage,' I think he calls it."

"There's something else. I don't know what it is," she confessed. "He has a something...you know sometimes when he's not looking and doing his charm routine, there's something cold behind his eyes. This might sound crazy, but sometimes he reminds me of Hall."

"Really? I don't see it. Louis likes the game, to play the game." I was interested in another game. I tried nuzzling Christy's neck.

Then suddenly I had the sense that I had misread her again. This was too confusing for me. Even Klaus Fuchs made more sense than she did. I told her that we should get our things together. Just in case. We had gotten a little sloppy.

I watched Christy as she picked up her clothes and moved her things around. She still moved with the grace of a dancer—Ginger Rogers more than Merle Oberon. She hummed a tune while she picked up her things and straightened up the room. There was a big fire in the fireplace so I had nothing to do.

I decided to have another look at Rippey's book to see if there was something there we had missed. It had been on the small table next to Louis's chair. It wasn't there. I checked the rooms.

"Have you seen Rippey's book?"

"I haven't seen it at all. Actually, I was surprised you

didn't have it on display. I thought it was important. I figured it would be in a place of honor."

We both looked through the house.

"Louis didn't take it with him, did he?"

"Not that I noticed."

"What about the diary?"

"I put it back on the table."

I had a sudden feeling of panic. I kept hearing Louis trying to get Christy out of there. It wasn't like him to harp on things like that. Why he was so anxious to get rid of Christy. He couldn't have anticipated her arrival. He had no stomach for killing her. Me, it was a different story. Louis's sentimentality only went so far. I told Christy to pack up. I still had the .32. The Thompson was leaning against the wall, but there was no magazine in it. I couldn't believe what I was thinking. "We have to get out of here."

"Why? What's going on?"

"I'll tell you in the car." As I opened the door, a flash of light caught my eye, and then I saw a familiar color between a couple of trees along the long drive. It was Sexton and Lawrence's Buick. "Get back in!"

The house looked like a fort on a hill, but it wasn't designed like one. The sight lines were all wrong. You could get within ten feet of the house on three sides without being seen from a window. We had only one gun to defend three entrances. I tried not to think about how Sexton and Lawrence knew where we were. And how they showed up when Louis was gone. Then I remembered something that had caught my eye when Louis and I were rummaging through the house that first time. I raced to the closet in my bedroom and reached for a box on the shelf. Inside was the old western style .44 pistol. There were six bullets in the cylinder and about five more in the box. I gave Christy the .32.

"Do you think you can handle this?"

"I've never shot a gun. Why? What's going on?"

"Just aim and pull the trigger. It's ready to fire."

She had a puzzled look on her face as if she had arrived at her senior prom in her pajamas.

"Sexton and Lawrence are out there. I don't know how or

why but Louis sold us out." I could hardly believe my own
words, but they had to be true. "Stand here. If somebody
comes through that door, shoot. Don't ask questions."

"I don't know if I can."

"You have to!" I took the old Colt, praying that it was not
some museum piece that was going to blow up in my hand.

I hoped I could surprise them. Louis probably told them
what to expect in terms of firearms. I crouched near the front
window and saw a flash of green behind a tree to my left. That
meant the other one would be coming from the right. It was
too much trouble to get through to the back. They had me in a
vee anyway. I had to go on the offensive. I had a lot of faith in
Christy, but I didn't know if I could count on her to protect my
back.

I figured that they would probably move in concert so that
one would reach the side door at the same time the other
reached the front door. If I got one early enough, I might be
able to get the other as well. I watched for the green of the
coat to appear again. Fortunately, he was moving in a too-
predictable zigzag pattern for his own good. I trained my sight
on the bush where I calculated the man in green would soon
appear. It was the only way I might get him with a pistol at
this distance. I got a good sense of the rhythm of his movements and counted off to myself, as the green sometimes was
visible and sometimes hidden behind a tree. When he appeared right on cue, I knew I had him if the old Colt didn't let
me down. I counted and fired the moment the man in green
should have been behind a big bush. I fired again. I never saw
him, but I knew I hit him. I could almost feel the bullet enter
his flesh.

"Varian, Varian! Are you okay?"

"It's okay. Keep down. Watch the back. Don't worry."

"Sure thing, Tex."

There was no window that gave me a view of the woods on
the other side of the house. I couldn't risk opening the door. I
didn't think he was crazy enough to charge through the door
by himself. He knew I had a gun and knew how to use it. We
were in a standoff. I considered what he might do. A fire?
Maybe even a hand grenade? The one thing I couldn't antici-

pate was how the surviving member of the team would react to seeing his partner fall. I hadn't counted on loyalty or grief, but It worked in my favor. Now I could see him trying to reach his fallen comrade. It was always a surprise when you found your enemy was actually human.

I took advantage of his lack of discipline and raced out the door, hoping to catch him by surprise. I jumped off the porch and set myself up behind the car. Bullets hit the window, the railings, and the car, but now I had a line on him. He stood. It was Sexton. He had an automatic rifle. He kept firing as he screamed at me. I couldn't tell what he said except that it was full of pain and then he was dead. At least one of four bullets had hit him. I walked slowly toward the body, trying to screen myself behind the trees.

A strange warm breeze came up from the lake. As I got closer, I crouched down, listening for movement, for groans. When I reached the bushes that hid the man in green, I saw the two bodies. Lawrence's face looked like chopped sirloin. Sexton had a widening circle of blood in the middle of his chest. I heard a branch crack. I hoped it was Christy. It wasn't.

"I should have known you would be able to take them, but they wanted you bad. You killed their friends. You killed them all." Louis was holding his sleek black automatic. There was a look of genuine sadness in his eyes. "I should have known I would have to be the one to do it. There was no way to avoid it. They wouldn't make the deal without giving you to them. They don't like you very much."

He pointed the barrel at my arm. I dropped the Colt. There were no bullets left anyway. "So what happened? Were you in with them from the beginning?"

"Oh, no, my friend, I was with you. On your side. But when it all began to come together and I knew this wasn't about a girl's murder, I had a sudden change of heart."

"Was it money?"

"Don't insult me. There was money involved. A necessity, however, to make my case. They would never believe my real motives. But you might."

"Your real motives?"

"I never thought I would have the chance to avenge Liev's

death. You are a friend, Liev was much more. And the irony is that you were going to wind up helping Hall anyway."

"How?"

"You gave him his excuse for bringing a Nazi home—just rescuing an old teacher from the devastation of Europe."

"What about that girl in Pennsylvania?"

"There's nothing there. No way to tie Hall to it anyway. So de Paul falls, so what? So there is no way you get Hall. If you and I couldn't get Hall, I had to go after the FBI. Hall has a better chance of getting Hoover."

"We could get them both."

"No, you couldn't. They have it set up. Why did you bring Christy back with you? She's a remarkable woman. She was even right about Lara and Hall. Can you believe it? I want you to know her blood is on your hands. I tried to warn you. I did not want her here."

"I thought I was your friend. You would sell me out for what?"

"You are my friend. Brutus was a good friend of Caesar. But I had a better friend. Even if I didn't, Hoover is not only evil, he is powerful. No matter what, you were being canceled out anyway. They would see to that. My help didn't make much difference but it got me in."

"But how could you throw in with people like de Paul and Hall? They're Nazis. Look at what they're about. They killed Lara. They're worse than Nazis. You know what they would do to you the first chance they got."

"They can be controlled. They are a means to an end. They won't last very long anyway. They're not that smart. Look how they bought your diary story."

"You gave them the diary."

"They are busily trying to decode it as we speak. I added a few juicy entries."

"This isn't a joke."

"I know. I want you to know that there is nothing in my life I regret more than having to kill you."

"What are you talking about? They'll snuff you out the minute they have what they want from you."

"I don't think so. But the risk is worth it. There are moments when an individual can change the course of history. This is one of those moments for me. I can't resist the opportunity."

"They killed your dogs!"

"That's right. That's right. As soon as I found that I could entertain the possibility that I would not avenge them, I knew I could betray you. Ironic isn't it. You seem to suffer their loss more than I do."

"So what are you going to do? Shoot me and Christy? We can get Hall and de Paul. Sexton and Lawrence are dead. We can get them. We know too much."

"But knowledge alone isn't the key. It's the ability to use what we know that matters. You are powerless. You can't really use what you know. Would you call a hearing? Contact Edward R. Murrow? You don't even have the book anymore. Or the diary. If something is going to happen, it's going to be through Hall and, if that is the case, you have to die. They want you dead and that's it."

"Why?"

"Because they require it. That's all."

"Deals can change. Double crosses become triple crosses. New deals negotiated. 'Everything is in flux,' isn't that what you say? Let's flux this whole thing. We can do it."

"Don't tempt me. You've been a good student despite my jibes and a better friend. But there are no changes now. When you suckered de Paul, you made them both cautious and vindictive. There's nothing to be done. They have Abbott and we don't. That's the crucial factor."

"Who's this Abbott?" I was trying to string things out as long as I could, hoping that Louis would have a change of heart.

"As we suspected, he's the FBI agent who was in charge of the surveillance at Los Alamos. He knew Fuchs was handing information to Gold, but they wanted bigger fish. They had big plans."

"You never met with the FBI, did you?"

"No, not when I realized what Hall could do. I went drinking with our dead friends here. I didn't enjoy it. They are not very interesting. They didn't want me wandering off."

"Why the ruse?"

"It was a good story."

At that moment I could hear Christy slipping out from behind the car. I tried to keep Louis talking so he wouldn't notice. But he soon realized I was stalling. Then for the first time
he noticed my gun on the ground. It was not the .32 he expected to see.

"Where did you get that—"

Before he could finish the question, two bullets entered his
back and blood shot from his nose. His mouth was in the
shape of a question mark. A third bullet ripped through my
jacket and a fourth tore bark from the tree behind me.

Christy slumped to the ground as I examined Louis's body.
Her face had lost its color. She wouldn't look at me or the
body. Louis was dead. Simply, definitively, and I realized that
I never found out what his real name was. I really wanted to
know.

"Are you okay?"

"Yeah. How about you? I thought I had shot you."

"You did. I'm just a little luckier than Louis."

"Go ahead make a joke. You might be used to shooting
people. It's a first for me." The hand that held the gun was
shaking. The pistol was on the ground.

"Just remember he was going to kill us."

"Why did he do it?"

"He was a philosophy major. Who knows?"

"Let's get out of here."

We walked back to the house. About six feet apart. Each of
us trying to understand what had just happened. But not sharing what we discovered. What separated us now was a lot
more than words.

EPILOGUE

Christy and I headed back to Stamford in silence. The silence that divided us was of a different sort, dark and suffocating. It covered us like a shroud. What had separated us before, a misunderstanding between lovers, had now become something malignant. Killing has a way of doing that. That what had happened had changed things was not surprising. What was startling was how quickly and completely the dream had been reduced to ashes.

She must have wondered, too, how the excitement of her adventure had turned so dark. How in a few fatal moments she had become a killer. She had to wonder how it was that she had pulled the trigger. How she killed a man she liked in order to protect a man that she hardly knew, a man who had put her life at risk. This was an impossible thought even a day before. It had not turned out like the movies.

So here she was, sitting next to a man who had killed four other men in a week. How could that make sense to her? She had to wonder how many more I had killed. She had to think—did she think about Louis—a man who had looked into her eyes and charmed her? Or her dead husband?

How far she must have felt from that desk in the Biddle school. I couldn't know because there was no way to reach her. She just sat there in the car, rubbing her hands as if the gunpowder had infected her skin. When I tried to get her to talk, I realized that I had no words. If I told her that killing was no big thing to me, that it was killing Louis, as close to a best friend as I had, that bothered me, could she do anything else but hate me? What would it mean to her to say I had gone over and over those last seconds? I couldn't really convince myself that Louis would have killed me, finally, if it came down to pulling the trigger. He wouldn't have talked so much if he had made the final choice. Maybe he was looking for an out. I couldn't tell her that. Why didn't it make all the difference that she had saved my life?

She looked straight ahead, ignoring the countryside, not caring about the music on the radio as if the mere possibility that I might appear in her line of sight was unbearable. She seemed calm. But there was something unnatural about the way she sat there like a spring in a trap. Every so often, she would slowly release a small breath as if to get a weight off her body.

I knew the first thing she would do when we got to Stamford would be to head back to Pennsylvania. I was right. All I could say to her when it was time to say good-bye was that I would handle it with the authorities. It made me feel cheap to make such a promise. It was as if I had offered to pay for an abortion. I couldn't find anything else to say.

Standing in front of Bob's Sports on Atlantic Street, we looked at each other for the last time. There were still Christmas decorations all over the city. Jolly candy canes and festive wreaths on every lamppost. Cars drove by. Friends honked at what they must have seen as a budding romance. Others had no idea what was happening right in front of them. They didn't recognize that this was the end of a story.

The funny thing was that I felt closer to her than I had ever felt before. I *wanted* to hold her. I wanted to tell her things, all the things that she wanted to hear from me in the car that time so long ago, the day before yesterday. I couldn't even kiss her. Quietly, almost inaudibly, she whispered my name and stumbled over the words that were supposed to follow. I watched her turn the corner. I stayed there for a long time, wanting to see time go into reverse as easily as that blue Ford could have if she wanted it to.

❧❧❧

A few months later, I had a sudden change of heart. I woke up feeling like there were balloons in my chest. It was as if all my doubts had turned into a fog, which was rapidly burning away in the light of day. For the first time in a long time, I could see clearly, and what I saw was Christy. And how stupid I had been. I would be her partner, her husband, her auto mechanic, and her first baseman, whatever she wanted. I was so excited that I misdialed her number twice before I got through.

She answered as if I were a distant relative, who needed updating on the family news, but there was something in her voice. I wanted to believe it, anyway, that suggested that she regretted our not becoming partners, in some way.

She told me she was engaged to a man who owned a tree service. There was going to be an engagement party that weekend. He was from a big family. They wanted to make a fuss. His name was Bill. She had started working for him shortly after she got back from Connecticut. He had a seven-year-old daughter named Amanda. His wife had died of breast cancer when she was only 29 and when his daughter was only two. She told me that he was a good man, a strong man, who had raised a fine daughter. They were going to live in her house. She was getting Amanda's room ready. She would work for her husband after they were married. She had found her partner. She didn't invite me to the wedding.

She also told me that the Biddle School was in the process of being sold to the state to be used as a branch of the state university. She hadn't seen or talked to Ryckman since she had gotten back. She had meant to, but somehow she didn't know what to say to him. She thanked me for keeping the police away from her. She said for days and days she expected to see them come after her with handcuffs. Just before she hung up she said that she still often thought about me.

"But it seems so long ago, doesn't it?"

"Yes, it does," I lied.

And then I said that a day hadn't gone by when I didn't think of her. She made a noise that sound almost like a hiccough, but it wasn't and then the line was dead.

I had gone to the FBI right after Christy had left for Glenside. There were just too many bodies. It was embarrassing for all of us. There was no way they could ignore two more dead CDA agents and Louis. Even Hall couldn't construct that many fables. I didn't want to be caught by surprise. I wanted to tell the story anyway. They were willing to listen, but Louis was right. I had no real evidence on Hall. The story sounded weak even to me. They were willing to hear the three names that Lara had written on the sanitary napkin. They made some phone calls while I was waiting. Then they asked me about Donch and Gerhard.

A few days later, they called and told me they had checked out my story at the lake. They asked how I had killed Louis, Sexton, and Lawrence with two different guns. It wasn't hard to come up with a story. A week later, they had me come back again. They told me that everything was fine as long as I didn't tell anybody about the case. Otherwise, they had enough murder charges that they could occupy the rest of my life in court even if I didn't go to jail. To make their point, they unnecessarily reminded me that there was no statute of limitations on murder. I was there too long. I was beginning to tire of them. They looked exactly like Sexton, Lawrence, Donch, and Gerhard.

Nothing happened out there in the big world either. On either side just as Louis predicted. Hall continued to make speeches about the Red Menace, but he didn't worry so much about the state of our schools. There were no hearings on the Klaus Fuchs case. Neither Hall nor de Paul was arrested. Things went on as they had before. Hall and the FBI were as powerful as ever. And I still had to look over my shoulder. The worse thing about it all was that I felt like I was the one who had betrayed a friend. Nothing had changed—except everything.

A few times, I thought about going to Hall and telling him what I knew about de Paul and Marie Considine just to see his face. I even thought about finding some columnist who might be interested in Hall's physical condition. I didn't think the FBI would mind that. Once I even drove by Hall's estate in Greenwich. I planned how I would get close to the house. But I didn't do it. I thought about a lot of things that would get things even for Lara's death. Most of them very stupid. In the end, I didn't do anything. It came down to the fact that just thinking about Hall and de Paul reminded me of Lara, Louis, and Christy and that made me sad, not angry.

In May, Freddie Greenbaum came to see me. He looked a lot older. Or maybe I just hadn't paid attention to how he looked before. He sat down across from me in the old leather chair. I knew I had made a bad mistake not going to see him right away.

He lit a cigarette and watched the smoke for a few seconds. "How's it been?"

"Okay, you?"

"Okay, you still watchin' the fights?"

"The novelty's worn off."

"Know what you mean."

He told me that Manny and Sophie were getting a divorce. The loss of Lara had been too much for the marriage. First, they blamed themselves, and then they started to blame each other. Finally, they just wound up hating each other. Sophie was going to get the house and Manny had already moved to Fairfield where he sat around his apartment all day. He stopped going to the office. His practice was falling apart and he didn't seem to care. Freddie was worried that he might do something drastic. "It's not like him, you know."

"I know."

There was more that Freddie wanted to know. He hesitated to ask like a friend coming to collect the money owed him. "I guess nothing happened with the names you found that night."

"The names?"

"I guess they didn't lead to anything."

I decided that Freddie finally deserved the truth. I had thought about it many times. I knew he deserved to hear the story. But every time I was about to call him or see him, I would get cold feet. I just couldn't tell him that I knew who killed his niece, but there was nothing he could do about it. I didn't want to tell him that I knew too much about Lara, things I shouldn't know, that I still thought about her and wished I had her diary. But this time it was different. From what Freddie said, I was worried about Manny, too. I didn't want to be responsible for another death in the family.

As I told Freddie the story, I could see a change come over him. He sat up, nodding his head as I went over the details, sparing him only the most intimate. I could tell he was listening with all his being. He asked me questions, mostly about Lara—why she did what she did. I told him I thought she was the only real hero I had ever met. I went through as best I could all the plots and counter plots of the CDA and the FBI. He kept asking me if I was sure. And then we went over it again. I told him about Louis.

"How come it wasn't in the papers?" he asked almost plaintively.

"That's the way it is these days. You only know what the government wants you to know."

"That's not right. They know who killed my brother's daughter?"

"You won't find anybody who will admit it."

"That's not right."

Then he wanted to know why I hadn't told him the story before.

"I wanted it to come to something. I couldn't stand the thought that Hall and de Paul were going to get away with it. I keep thinking there is still some way. I haven't given up."

"But that's not for you to decide. That wasn't your place. I hired you to find out who killed Lara. What gave you the right to make such a decision, that you would decide what we could know? How long were you going to wait?"

I tried to explain again, but it sounded even weaker than before because I knew I was wrong. I had really forgotten about him. Almost from the beginning, it didn't have to do with the Greenbaums. And he knew it.

"You're not the police. You didn't need proof. If you told me that this guy killed my niece, I would have believed you straight out. Just a name. That's all I wanted was a name. And that would have been it. I didn't need or want a case for the prosecution. I thought you knew that this wasn't about law. It was about—" He stopped to take a breath. He was trying to keep the anger from overwhelming him. "—an eye for an eye."

He stopped again as if he expected me to make a speech about how revenge never works. I didn't say anything.

"You should have told me. I hired you. I thought you were my friend. You know that night? I told Manny you knew a lot more than you were letting on. I had a feeling that you were really on to it. But then we didn't hear anything, I thought I was wrong."

"What could you do except feel worse than you already do? Or do something that would ruin even more lives. Think of Annie."

"That's for me to decide. Not you. You have no right to mention her name. It wasn't your choice what to do with the information. It was mine. And Manny's. It was paid for."

He felt betrayed. And the anger came pouring out. It was what he came for. I didn't blame him. If he had to hit me, I would have let him. Instead, he wrote out a check for $1000 to make sure that I knew that it was over between us and that I knew exactly what he thought of me. I sent it to his daughter on her graduation, but that wouldn't change things. Freddie knew it was to make me feel better.

Right after talking to Freddie, I took the job in Mexico and was there until the middle of summer. When I got back, things had changed a lot. There were no more get-togethers for Monday or Wednesday Night Fights. As soon as everybody got televisions, and you could see that almost everybody had one, there was no reason to get together to watch it. No one even talked about it anymore. It was like having a telephone. Just before dark, when I looked out at the city all I could see were the tops of the houses against the darkening sky. On top of them were all these bare metal limbs like the trees on the burned out hills of San Pietro. In just a few months, watching television had gone from being a special social occasion to being a very private one.

I seemed to lose touch with more than the Greenbaums. I would see people on the street, we'd say "How's it going?" and move on. I bought a small boat with the money from Mexico. One day in the middle of July, while I was sitting in the middle of the Sound, pretending to fish for flatfish, I saw an item in the *Advocate.*

A close aide to Congressman Lindzey Hall had been shot in a freak hunting accident on the grounds of Hall's Greenwich estate. As Hall and his aides were preparing for a hunting party, a gun had accidentally fired and a bullet struck Henri

Krims in the neck, killing him instantly. Krims had been a close advisor to Hall on foreign policy. His council would be sorely missed according to the Congressman. Krims was not married and left no known relatives.

I knew it wasn't an accident. At least that's what I believed with all my heart. The only one out hunting that day was Freddie Greenbaum. Freddie must have gotten his Springfield out of the attic. The single shot to the throat was his signature. I wondered how long Freddie had stalked him. How far away he had been when he shot him? It had to have been one of his best shots. I never talked to him again so I couldn't ask.

One effect de Paul's death seemed to have was to bring Manny and Freddie closer together. I heard that Manny had moved back to Stamford and had recovered most of his practice. He was a good dentist, they said. He made you laugh without gas, they said. And he didn't charge an arm and a leg. He and Freddie played golf and often sailed on the Sound together. I once saw their boat heading out of Stamford Harbor, but I went off in the opposite direction. I also heard that Annie was going to Vassar and was doing well. Manny threw a big party for her at Yacht Haven. I wasn't invited.

I wouldn't have gone anyway. It would have reminded me of Lara's absence. By the next summer, my memories of her were already fading. I was angry that I had never heard her voice. Somehow, I felt I could have held on to her words longer if I knew what she sounded like. Without her actual voice, the words that I heard in my head began to sound more and more hollow, as if they were coming through a cheap microphone. There were some days that I thought she was the gutsiest, the most amazing girl I had ever run across. Then there were days when I thought she wasn't that much different from Louis. In any case, even now, just the mere reminder of her makes me sad. I wish I could remember her without remembering everything else. I wish there were some way I could tell the brothers how I felt, without making them want to kill me.

A few weeks after de Paul was killed, Hall announced that he had decided not to run for another term. The pressures of campaigning had taken their toll on his family. He and his wife had been unable to have children. He announced that they would adopt a Korean War orphan. The mood of the country had changed. McCarthy was now a big joke. The Army Hearings and the Senate had pretty much taken care of him. There has been a shift in the mood of the country. There wasn't as much to be gained from finding communists everywhere. Anyway, juvenile delinquents were the new threat to the nation's security.

Sometimes I wondered if Hall thought that it had been the FBI who had assassinated de Paul, a little nudge to make him consider retiring early. At least that's the way I liked to think it was. I wondered if I had told the story to Freddie differently, if Hall would have been in his sights Freddie's. It was fifty/fifty either way. And I hardly cared now. I was glad for Manny and Freddie. Small comfort but it seemed to have helped bring them together. I wondered if the two brothers would ever go after Hall himself. I kept my eyes on the papers, waiting for the news. It never came.

I thought, too, a lot about Louis. I missed him. There were times right after I got back from Mexico where I would be thinking about a case, listening to jazz, and find myself on the road to New Canaan without knowing where I was going until I saw the road that led to his house. I would turn back immediately. I didn't want to see his house. I didn't want to think of the times we had had there talking about jazz, listening to him talk about art and politics. I wanted to confront him one more time. I wanted to continue that conversation, our last, the one interrupted by bullets. In my mind, I always had the last word. He had been right about a lot of things, but if I had the chance I would have proved that on this last thing he had been utterly and stupefyingly wrong. Now that I couldn't win the argument, I couldn't forgive him either.

I still listened to jazz. It was hard to hear it without Louis's voice in the background commenting on the solos. I still loved it, but Miles Davis's trumpet seemed infinitely sadder than it ever had before.

About the Author

Jack DeWitt was born in Stamford, Connecticut and went to Catholic schools there for twelve years. After graduating from Fairfield Prep, he attended to Northeastern University in Boston where he received an AB in English, started a family, and began writing poetry. Later he studied with William Gaddis at the University of Connecticut, who encouraged DeWitt to write fiction. It has been a long road. Along the way, DeWitt finished a PhD in English at UConn, began teaching at Drexel, and then joined the faculty at what was to become the University of the Arts. There he served as department chair for a dozen years and held two different Deanships. During that time he published five books of poems.

Among his more recent works is a book of poems, *Almost Grown (2008)*, about growing up in Stamford. His 2003 study of hot rodding, *Cool Cars, High Art: The Rise of Kustom Kulture,* received a starred review in *Booklist*. It was also a *Street Rodder* Hall of Fame selection. DeWitt's work has been included in three anthologies. He writes an irregular column for *American Poetry Review*. "Cars and Culture" was identified as a notable essay in *Best American Essays 2010* edited by Robert Atwan and Christopher Hitchins. DeWitt retired from UArts in 2013 to devote his time to fiction. Recently divorced, he lives in Glenside, PA. His three grown children all live within driving distance and, except for the granddaughter who now lives with him, he doesn't see his grandchildren nearly enough.

Made in the USA
Middletown, DE
28 October 2015